SOUTHERN SINNER

A North Carolina Highlands Novel

JESSICA PETERSON

ALSO BY JESSICA PETERSON

THE SEX & BONDS SERIES

An outrageously sexy series of romcoms set in the high stakes world of Wall Street.

The Dealmaker (Sex & Bonds #1)

The Troublemaker (Sex & Bonds #2)

THE NORTH CAROLINA HIGHLANDS SERIES

Beards. Bonfires. Boning.

Southern Seducer (NC Highlands #1)

Southern Hotshot (NC Highlands #2)

Southern Sinner (NC Highlands #3)

Southern Playboy (NC Highlands #4)

Southern Bombshell (NC Highlands #5)

THE CHARLESTON HEAT SERIES

The Weather's Not the Only Thing Steamy Down South.

Southern Charmer (Charleston Heat #1)

Southern Player (Charleston Heat #2)

Southern Gentleman (Charleston Heat #3)

Southern Heartbreaker (Charleston Heat #4)

THE THORNE MONARCHS SERIES

Royal. Ridiculously Hot. Totally Off Limits...

Royal Ruin (Thorne Monarchs #1)

Royal Rebel (Thorne Monarchs #2)

Royal Rogue (Thorne Monarchs #3)

THE STUDY ABROAD SERIES

Studying Abroad Just Got a Whole Lot Sexier.

A Series of Sexy Interconnected Standalone Romances

Lessons in Love (Study Abroad #1)

Lessons in Gravity (Study Abroad #2)

Lessons in Letting Go (Study Abroad #3)

Lessons in Losing It (Study Abroad #4)

WHERE TO FIND JESSICA

- Join my Facebook reader group, The City Girls, for exclusive excerpts of upcoming books plus giveaways galore!
- Follow my not-so-glamorous life as a romance author on Instagram @JessicaPAuthor
- Follow me on Goodreads
- Follow me on Bookbub
- Like my Facebook Author Page

Published by Peterson Paperbacks, LLC

Cover Design: Najla Qamber of Najla Qamber Designs
Photographer: Wong Sim
Model: Charley Santos
Editor: Marion Archer
Copyeditor: Jenny Sims
Proofreader: Karen Lawson

www.jessicapeterson.com

Created with Vellum

PROLOGUE

Hank

April

I have to get the fuck out of here.

Yanking my sweater over my head, it's the first thought I have when I walk into my house after Sunday supper. I'm a little drunk and a lot worn out from playing nice.

From pretending that seeing Samuel and Emma so damn happy together doesn't make me feel like dying.

I grab a fifth of Appalachian Red whiskey from my liquor cabinet and take a pull straight from the bottle. It burns a trail of fire down my throat.

It does nothing to lessen the intense ache inside my chest.

Doesn't stop me from taking another swig before I set down the bottle and wipe my mouth with the back of my hand.

I glance around my pristine, silent kitchen. Not so much as a glass or napkin is out of place. Probably because I don't really live here.

Sure, I sleep in the bed every night and get ready in the

gleaming master bathroom every morning, but otherwise, I'm hustling around the resort.

Work has become my life. And it took falling in love with my brother's girlfriend to see how much I'm missing out on.

So fuck it. What do I have left to lose? I'm gonna stop putting my family first and give myself the top spot instead. I'll do what I want when I want to do it.

I want to travel.

I want to fuck around.

I want to meet people who've never heard of Blue Mountain.

Tomorrow, I'll get with my team and work out the details of my leave from guest relations. Then I'll get on the phone with my travel agent and book a private jet to—

Where?

As far away as I can get, I guess. Thailand? South Africa? Madrid?

All I know is my broken heart ain't gonna heal if I'm anywhere near this place.

I can't stop thinking about how Emma looked at Samuel across the dinner table tonight. She was lit up. Eyes glowing and full, like she was so happy she might cry. I heard them flirting, talking about all the ways they'll fuck tonight.

A slice of searing, urgent pain rips through my torso. I grab the bottle and drink, and then drink some more.

"Hey." I startle at the voice behind me. I turn to see my brother Rhett looking at me, his brow furrowed with concern. He gently takes the bottle from my hand and sets it down. Crossing his arms, he leans his back against the counter. "I'm sorry that happened, and I'm sorry you're hurting."

I nod, swallowing hard. "Me too."

He dips his head toward the whiskey. "Please tell me you aren't going to cope by drinking yourself into a shame spiral."

"I'm giving the shame spiral twenty-four hours, max. Then I'm hitting the road."

"Oh? Where ya going?"

I lift a shoulder, eyeing the bottle. "Not sure yet. Someplace where there's a bar on the beach and beautiful women."

"The best distractions in the world." Rhett nods. "Let's start in the Bahamas. Paradise Island."

"We?" I arch a brow. "Who said you're invited?"

Rhett grabs the bottle and takes a swig, smacking his lips. "I did. I have three months until training camp starts. Besides, someone needs to babysit you at that beach bar. You won't be able to pick up all those beautiful women if you're wasted."

I laugh, the tightness inside my breastbone loosening ever so slightly. "Stop. You just wanna be my wingman."

"Well, yeah." My younger brother grins. "If I happen to meet a lady or two while I'm making sure you don't give yourself rum poisoning . . . well, I won't hate it."

"Okay." I take the bottle from him and have another sip. "The Bahamas. Then where?"

"We'll go around the world, obviously. Hop from the Bahamas to Ibiza. Then Mykonos, and the Seychelles . . . Bangkok. Australia. Hawaii. Final stop—"

"Vegas," I say.

Rhett's grin deepens into a smile. "My adopted hometown. Perfect."

He plays for the pro football team that recently moved from California to Las Vegas. Rhett's got a definite wild streak, so the new location suited him just fine.

Me? I'm an old soul. While I had my fun in Sin City, I never really got why my teammates and college friends were so obsessed with it.

Maybe this trip will change that.

I hold up the whiskey. "Let's do it. Think you can leave tomorrow?"

"Hell yeah, I can."

I take one last pull of whiskey before handing the bottle back to Rhett. He drinks too, and for several beats, we stand there in silence.

I don't know what he's thinking about, but as usual, I'm thinking about Emma. How I don't want to go on this trip, and I don't want to leave Blue Mountain, because she's here. She's been the bright spot in my days. The reason I jump out of bed in the mornings more excited and invigorated than I've felt in years.

It happened really fucking fast, me falling for her.

I don't fall easily. Not like that. Not for someone who doesn't want me back.

But it happened, and now my head won't stop spinning, and I can't stop hurting. The embarrassment is real and so is the pain. This is horrible.

I never, ever want to feel this way again.

I want to forget.

"Make me a promise," I say.

"Shoot."

"Don't let me do anything really stupid."

"Like?"

I look Rhett in the eye. "Like fall in love again. That shit—Rhett, it hurts something fierce."

He frowns. "Hank," he says softly. "You can't punish yourself like that. Yeah, you obviously need to give your heart time to heal, but don't cut yourself off that way. You're a good guy, and you deserve to be happy."

The words he doesn't say hang in the air between us. *You deserve to be happy the way Samuel and Emma are happy together.*

I swallow again. Look down at my feet and shake my head. "Just—promise me, okay? That's all I ask."

I feel his eyes on me. A heartbeat passes. Then another.

"Okay," he says at last. "But that promise expires at the end of this trip, you hear? Then all bets are off."

I wave him away. "By then, we'll be in Vegas, and who falls in love there? I'll send over the flight details when I have them."

Running away like this is a gamble. What will happen to my job? And what about my relationship with Samuel? Will my absence really help all of us heal?

I have no idea. But leaving is a bet I'm willing to make.

Chapter One

HANK

January

"This seat taken?"

The brunette at the blackjack table glances up from her cards. Her warm brown eyes meet mine, and my pulse skips a beat.

She's gorgeous. She's got long, dark eyelashes, full lips, and tousled hair that falls past her shoulders.

And those luscious tits spilling out of her shirt? Curvy hips and thighs filling out a pair of gray-washed jeans?

Yeah, I'm really hoping this seat is free.

"All yours," she replies. Her gaze flicks down my body, lingering a beat too long on my arms and shoulders before she turns back to her cards.

My fingers curl into the ivory leather of the seat back. My lips twitch.

I fucking love Vegas.

I also love when girls don't recognize me. It makes the chase that much more fun.

"Let's split these aces," she tells the dealer.

I slide onto the chair and set my chips down on the table,

eyeing her left hand as she places a pair of green chips—hundreds—beside an identical pair below her cards.

No ring.

"Split aces?" I ask.

The brunette turns her head to look at me. "I always split aces and eights."

I settle my elbows on the edge of the table. I don't miss how her eyes move appreciatively over my bare forearms.

"Why is that?"

"Because the deck has more face cards than anything else, and face cards are—"

"Worth ten." I grin. "I'm only part newbie gambling jerkoff. I know enough to lose most of my money, not all of it."

She grins too, her gaze locking on mine. "Then you know we're trying to get our cards to add up to twenty-one in blackjack. So if you've got an ace, which counts as one or eleven, or an eight"—she taps the card with a dark-painted fingernail—"and odds are you're going to get a face card when you hit, then voila! You've got eighteen or blackjack, times two. Isn't that right, Helen?"

The dealer, a petite middle-aged woman, nods. "Absolutely, Miss Carter."

Miss Carter's eyes are lit up, and she's biting her bottom lip as she smiles.

She knows her shit, and she's proud of it.

"Okay." I nod at her cards. "Let's see if it works."

She taps the card again, glancing at Helen. "Hit me."

Helen slides a card from the dispenser and flips it on top of Miss Carter's first ace with a crisp *flick*.

Queen of spades.

Miss Carter flashes me a wide, blindingly white smile. "Told ya."

"All right, all right. Let's see if you can do it again."

Helen moves to the second ace, flipping over an eight of clubs. I wait with bated breath for Helen to deal herself a card. She draws a two, making twelve with her Jack, and then draws a ten.

Bust.

Miss Carter's arms fly up, and I immediately reach for a high five. No way is anyone else beating me to this girl. Not Helen, not the old dude on the other side of the table, and definitely not the younger dude next to him.

Miss Carter high-fives me, a solid smack that sends a zing down my arm. She turns that supermodel smile on me.

For a second, her hand lingers on mine, and a charge of electricity moves between us like lightning in a summer storm, unexpected and potent. Almost makes me jump.

Damn.

Today began like any other on what my brother Rhett calls my belated retirement bender: breakfast in my suite. A workout to sweat out my hangover. Lunch. A round of golf at the hotel's course while Rhett was at practice.

I always start cocktail hour with a turn on the casino floor, and I expected that to be the same too. Same plans to meet up with my buddies. Same High West rye whiskey, neat. Same dinner and dress and the best table at the best club, probably XS because it's right here in the hotel, followed by another table late night at Drai's. Sometimes we mix it up with sunset helicopter tours of the desert, concerts at Caesar's, or a fight at the MGM Grand.

Yep. We're fucking spoiled.

It hasn't been a bad gig. Being away from work has put some much-needed pep in my step. But after nine months of pure, I-don't-give-a-fuck partying, the whole thing has started to feel . . . routine, I guess? Each night bleeds into the next, and if you asked me where I was and who I was with a week or a month ago, I couldn't tell you, other than: pretty girls in hotel beds, great entertainment, late nights, good liquor.

But with Miss Carter's palm pressed against mine, something suddenly, thrillingly feels different.

She's different.

As evidenced by the way she wins hand after hand. Like the rest of the table, I watch in growing awe as the girl's stack of chips grows. I ask why she doubles down on an eleven ("all comes back to the odds of you getting a face card"). I figure out why she sets chips at the top *and* bottom of her cards—the top chips are her betting with the dealer, so when Miss Carter wins, which is often, so does Helen (you're always supposed to tip your dealer).

Miss Carter tips her very, very well. I take note and do the same.

Only when Helen is exchanging Miss Carter's chips do I realize how much money she has on the table. Holy shit, are *all* of those thousand-dollar chips?

Fuck, I'm gonna get hard watching her stack 'em. It's not the money that turns me on. It's the nimble, knowledgeable way her fingers work. The little smile of satisfaction on her lips. How she knows when to press and when to pull back.

She's not reckless, but she is definitely not afraid. She's generous too.

She's a fucking master. Makes me wonder if she'd be the same in bed.

How have I not seen her before? She must've arrived today with the rest of the weekend crowd.

"Thank you, Miss Carter," Helen says when she hands her the biggest tip yet.

Miss Carter puts her hands on the lip of the table and pushes her chair back. My pulse skips a beat.

She can't leave. Not yet.

"How many times do I have to ask you to call me Stevie?"

Miss Carter says. "I know we just met, but I've been at your table for an hour."

"Stevie?" I say. "As in Nicks?"

"My parents were big Fleetwood Mac fans." She lifts a shoulder. "It was the eighties. Although, to be fair, it doesn't suck being named after a musical goddess."

Fu-*uck*. Not only is this girl a killer queen at the blackjack table, but she knows her classic rock too?

"I'd argue Stevie is *the* music goddess. That voice," I say.

"Those lyrics."

"The tambourine."

"Right? In her hands, it becomes, like, this vessel of truth and a *serious* come-on."

I hold out my hand. "I'm Hank. And I just became your biggest fan."

"Ha! I'm flattered." She takes my hand and gives it a warm, firm shake. There's that electricity again. "I'll be here all weekend."

I give her my best grin, the one that makes the dimple in my left cheek pop. "I'm glad to hear it. Can I buy you a drink?"

"No." Stevie holds up her purse, packed so tightly with chips they're spilling out of the top. "But I'll buy you one."

"Deal."

We walk across the casino floor to the bar outside the Tower Suite elevators. It's just shy of eight, and the place is buzzing with slickly dressed people—mostly dudes—fueling up for a Friday night in Vegas.

A few stare at me. Guys tend to recognize me more often than not. Luckily, they leave us alone as we approach.

I take the opportunity to check out Stevie. She's thick, ass and tits for days, and my mouth goes dry watching said ass move in those jeans.

Luscious doesn't even begin to describe her. I wanna sink

my teeth into that ass. Grab those thighs while I look her in the eye and fuck her, hard.

"Hank!" Ben, the bartender, holds up his hand. "Get over here. You two, yes, excuse me, but those seats are reserved." He expertly shoos away a pair of bros in blazers, making room for Stevie and me.

I pull out the barstool for Stevie and try not to stare myself—fuck it, I stare—as she sits and runs a hand through her long hair, tossing it to the side and revealing an elegant neck. There's a dark freckle there, just underneath her ear, and a matching one on her cheek.

I sidle up to her right, resting my foot on the brass railing underneath the bar. Raw interest floods my body, gathering low in my core, and I want to get closer to her. But she hasn't given me permission—yet—so I keep a little distance between us.

"What can I get you guys?" Ben asks after we shake hands.

I gesture to Stevie. She narrows her eyes at the taps on the wall. Then she grins. "I'll take a Blackjack Babe Hefeweizen, please."

"Blackjack Babe?" I arch a brow at her. "Is that named after you?"

She grins, eyes lit up and all. "Yes."

"I'll have the same," I say to Ben.

Ben brings us our beers in frosty pint glasses. I tap mine against hers. "To splitting aces and eights."

"And doubling down on eleven." She points at me. "Don't forget that."

Stevie doesn't sip her beer. She drinks it, tipping her head back as she takes a long, slow pull that has ninety percent of the bar staring at *her* now.

Fuck the guy who set rushing and receiving records his first year in the pros and was voted Offensive Player of the Year twice.

This girl is the truly spectacular one.

She closes her eyes before she swallows, the lines of her throat working in smooth, sinuous motion.

Does she suck dick like that? I'm suddenly, viciously eager to know the answer to that question. I set my beer down with a *thud*, making Stevie swallow again and lick her lips.

"You okay?" she asks.

"You always drink beer that way? Like you're tasting wine or some shit?"

"I do." She turns her head to face me, moving in such a way that her hair swings over her other shoulder, tousled and perfect and smelling like some kinda girly shampoo. "I'm a brewer."

I blink. "That's fucking awesome."

"I know," she says, grinning, and I decide right then and there I'm not letting this girl out of my sight until she leaves for the airport. "You like it? The beer?"

"I do." I take another sip. It's clean, cold, crisp for a wheat beer. "I don't usually drink Hefeweizen, but this is good. Really good."

"I'm glad you think so, because it really is named after me. I made it."

"You made it?" I blink again. "As in, you really made this beer at your really awesome brewery?"

She laughs, angling her legs toward me as she crosses them. "How do you know Lady Luck's Brewhouse is awesome?"

My gaze rips down her body, rips back up. "Don't play coy with me, Miss Carter. One, that's the best name ever for a brewery. And two, I just saw you dominate that blackjack table. I imagine you dominate the brewing scene too." I hold up my glass. "This what brought you to Vegas? Your beer?"

"I lobbied for a solid two years to get Lady Luck's products into places like this." She tips her chin at the bar. "I finally made it happen last year—one of my biggest goals for my company is expanding our distribution, especially in states outside of Tennessee, where we're based."

"Nashville?"

"Yup."

"Love that town. I actually caught Greg Allman at the Ryman a few months back."

Her eyes go wide. "Stop it. I was there!"

"No shit." I smile, and her eyes flick to my dimple. "I like your taste in music."

Those eyes flash. "I like yours too. So, I always enjoy drinking my favorite beer in my favorite city, but I'm actually here for a different reason. Two reasons, really."

"Which are?"

"I just turned forty—"

"Happy Birthday!"

"Thank you. Forty feels pretty freaking great." She sips, then swallows. I want to scream. "I also finalized my divorce, thank God. My ex and I have been separated for nearly three years, so this is a big win."

The way she says it, how she lets out a breath that makes her shoulders fall back—relief and joy are written all over her. Because she's over *it*, whatever went down.

Whatever she felt for that guy and that relationship.

For a second, my mood dims. When am I gonna get to the other side?

When am I gonna get over the girl who wasn't meant for me so I can be with one who is? A girl my family loves, the way they love my brothers' partners?

But then nine months' worth of platitudes and pep talks flood my thoughts. *She wasn't meant for you. Meeting new people is the best way to move on. Time heals all wounds.*

So does hanging out with gorgeous girls who know their games of chance and their classic rock.

"You have a lot to celebrate then, Stevie. What are your plans for tonight?"

She nods, taking another pull of beer. "My girlfriends and I are doing dinner at Sinatra's—"

"Excellent choice."

"And then we're going dancing." She looks at me. "I want you to come."

I'm digging my phone out of my pocket before the sentence is out of her mouth. She sure as hell doesn't beat around the bush, which makes this whole exchange feel refreshingly easy. Fun.

"Put your number in my phone." I hold it out to her, and she takes it. "When my boys and I figure out where we're getting a table, I'll shoot you a text. Sound good?"

"Sounds great."

Our fingers brush as she hands back the phone. We look at each other for a heartbeat, the pull between us kicking my pulse up a notch.

"I got lucky running into you," I say.

She draws the toe of her shoe up my calf. "I think we'll both get lucky tonight. Should be fun. Although I don't want to waste your time . . ."

I'm picking up what she's laying down. As luck (heh) would have it, I'm looking for the same kind of fun she is.

"Honey, wasting time is exactly what I'm trying to do."

Chapter Two

STEVIE

The line for XS stretches down Encore's swanky shopping gallery. Girls in towering heels tug at the hems of teeny-tiny dresses; guys in dark jeans and blazers check their watches.

The echo of a bassline pumps through the marble floors.

A twist of excitement has me grabbing my friend Kate's hand as we bypass the line, heading straight for the club doors.

"We're here," I say. "We actually made it back to Vegas. And we're going dancing."

"God, when was the last time we danced?" my other friend, Lauren, shakes her head. "I've missed it."

Kate smiles, tucking her snakeskin clutch underneath her arm. "Imagine telling our thirty-something-year-old selves at my bachelorette that we'd be back in Vegas five years later celebrating a vasectomy, a divorce, and a big-ass birthday."

"And judging by the way everyone's looking," Lauren says, surveying the line, "we still got it."

"Forty is the new thirty," Kate says.

Lauren lets out a throaty laugh. "Forty is freedom."

"It's also peeing your pants when you sneeze."

"Not me," I say. "Thankfully, I've been spared that particular indignity."

"Lucky bitch," Kate mutters.

A blazer with black hair looks up from his phone and gives us a disgusted look.

I refrain from giving him the finger. I ignore him and keep going.

"Let's not forget Stevie is wearing a transparent dress." Lauren nods at my outfit. "That could have a lot to do with all this attention."

I pull back my shoulders, putting my generous bust on display. Another blazer we pass chokes on his cocktail.

"Damn," I hear him say, his gaze hot on my backside.

"It's Friday night," I say. "Rookies may dress to impress on Saturdays, but Vegas veterans know the first night in town is always the best. The whole world is down to—"

"Party," Kate says, returning my grin. "Hence the see-through dress."

It's a look, that's for damn sure. The dress itself would be modest—black, turtleneck, long sleeves, midi length—if it wasn't for the fact that it's made of transparent gauze. I *am* wearing a black bodysuit underneath it, almost like a strapless, silky one-piece bathing suit. I'm not a reality TV star; I'm not here to flaunt my nipples.

But I am here to have a good time. And this dress? With the black strappy stilettos, simple gold hoops, and high ponytail I've paired it with?

I feel like a million bucks in this getup. And when I feel good, I tend to have a really good time.

"Says the mother of three under four rocking a leather miniskirt," I tease.

"Mama doesn't get out much. When she does, welp." Kate sweeps her hair over her shoulder. "She makes it count."

"As one should," I reply with a firm nod. "I'm teasing. The skirt is hot."

Kate's grin becomes a smile. "I agree."

"So the guy we're supposed to meet up with—what's his name?" Lauren asks as we approach a bouncer with an earpiece and a clipboard.

I dig my phone out of my purse and scroll through my text messages, biting back a smile when I pull up my exchange with Hank. His texts are flirty without being pushy —*I hope you don't blow me off tonight, blackjack babe, cuz I still got a lot to learn from you*—and I can't remember the last time someone gave me a flutter of excitement like this.

"Hank Beauregard?" I say to the bouncer, ignoring Lauren's sharp intake of breath behind me. "We're guests at his table."

The bouncer's eyes skip down my body before he glances at the clipboard. Checking off our names, he unhooks the velvet rope guarding the line marked VIP and instructs us to follow him.

"This Hank guy," Lauren murmurs in my ear as the bassline gets louder, "is he, say, five ten, with the most beautiful biceps you've ever seen, hazel eyes, and short blond hair?"

I remember the way my heart skipped when Hank flashed me a smile the first time, revealing a dimple in one cheek as his eyes—more brown than green—swept over my body. He wasn't tall, maybe a few inches taller than I am, but the breadth of his athletically chiseled body, along with his cocky, easygoing sense of humor, gave him a big presence.

His thick-as-molasses accent sure as hell didn't hurt either.

"Yes, actually." I glance down at Lauren over my shoulder. Even in her heels, my petite Asian friend is a head shorter than I am. "Do you know him?"

"Yeah," Lauren scoffs. "Well, I don't *know* him know him, but I, like, know *of* him. A lot of people do."

I slow my steps for a second. "What does that mean?"

Lauren glances at Kate, who just shrugs, as clueless as I am.

"Hank Beauregard is only one of the best—and sexiest—running backs to ever play the game."

Kate's brow furrows. "What game?"

"You know how I feel about that sports ball stuff," I say.

Lauren rolls her eyes. "Y'all are hopeless. *Football*. This *football* guy is famous. And gorgeous. And rich as fuck."

I shrug, stepping over the threshold into the club. "All I care about is the gorgeous part."

It's true. I'm not the least bit interested in a relationship. But a hot hookup with a cute, funny, open-minded guy—not many men at the tables are willing to take gambling tips, much less from a woman—is exactly what I'm after.

I dreaded turning forty for a while, and it didn't help that my life fell apart there for a bit.

But now that I'm actually here, forty feels less like a liability and more like letting go. For the first time ever, I feel like I genuinely know what I want and who I am, and I'm not afraid of going after it anymore.

Walking through the club, I see the way a few people look at me. *The balls on her*, their eyes say, moving over my wide hips, thick ass, and the cellulite on my thighs.

Again, I'm tempted to give them the finger. And again I just move on, head held high.

Fuck 'em, I'm free. And I'm about to do some real dirty dancing with a real hot guy.

We follow the bouncer. And keep following him. He unclips another velvet rope and leads us up a small flight of stairs. We pass several tables, the ones whose bottle service goes for north of a couple thousand bucks.

We keep going.

The DJ booth is getting really, really close. That's where the best tables are located—the ones usually reserved for celebrities. Another velvet rope, another set of stairs, and we arrive on a dais-type thing. It's like breaking through the clouds. We have a bird's-eye view of the entire club, throngs of people below us losing themselves to the beat of Meghan Thee Stallion.

I smile, glancing at my girls. They're smiling too.

There's that flutter again.

"This is so cool!" Lauren shouts over the music.

We follow the bouncer all the way to the DJ booth. Kygo is supposed to come on later tonight—all the big clubs in Vegas host celebrity DJs on the weekends—so another DJ, a woman with bright pink hair and a face tattoo, is manning the raised booth. She's so close I could reach up and touch her arm.

We're led to a roped-off section that wraps around the DJ booth. It's lined with velvet couches, and my eyes catch on a large table at the far end set with an impressive bottle service. Grey Goose, Cuervo, and magnums of champagne chill in ice buckets, while waitresses in red corsets and fishnets pour drinks.

"This is it," the bouncer shouts, unclipping one last velvet rope. "Enjoy."

I step into the space, suddenly feeling a little awkward. There's a good-looking crowd up here—a few guys, lots of girls—but no Hank.

I take a few more steps, grateful for the extra height of my heels.

Then I see him, and my heart dips. Lips move into a wide smile.

He's sitting on one of the couches alone with a half-empty

glass in his hand. Girls surround him, but his head is turned away from them, like he's looking across the club.

Like he's looking for someone.

I grab Lauren's hand and head Hank's way.

Leaning down so he can hear me, I say, "This seat taken?"

He swivels his head. His eyes fall on my face, and they immediately light up. He smiles, dimple and all.

Ugh, that dimple. It's so damn cute.

Kate and Lauren are not immune to the cuteness either. They stare as Hank stands, his eyes roving up my legs, my dress, my boobs.

My heart begins to pound in earnest. Heat gathers between my legs.

Already. I'm already turned on, and the guy hasn't even touched me yet.

"Wow." He shakes his head. "Stevie, you look—wow. I'm kinda speechless right now." He glances over my shoulder at Kate and Lauren. "Y'all let her out looking like this?"

"Always," Lauren replies.

"Thank you. Sincerely." He holds out his hand to her. "I'm Hank."

I shamelessly check him out while he introduces himself to my friends and then introduces two of his guys to them too. He's not wearing anything particularly fancy—jeans, a light blue button-up, a watch—but because he's so handsome, and because he's in such great shape, he looks *good.* The jeans are fitted enough to show off his massive thighs. The sleeves of his shirt are rolled up, revealing the most delicious forearms on earth and a classic but probably insanely expensive watch on a brown leather strap.

His short hair is styled just the right side of hipster, and the square lines of his clean-shaven jaw gleam in the club's multicolored lights.

He looks like a Disney prince who's ready for some debauchery.

I am so, *so* here for it.

He holds out his hand to me and leans in so I can hear him. "I'll be honest, I'm not quite sure what to do here. Do we shake hands again? Hug it out?"

My pulse spikes. He smells like sex. Some kind of cologne that's clean and subtly woodsy.

I bite my bottom lip. "How about a high five?"

He holds up his hand and I step closer, our thighs brushing as our palms meet. The space between us thrums. He smiles, a blindingly handsome flash of straight, white teeth. My gaze lingers on his lips, the heat between my legs aching at the idea of kissing him.

At the idea of him kissing me *there*, where the heat continues to gather.

His fingers curl over mine, drawing my gaze back up to his eyes. I see desire in them, real and raw.

My stomach flips. His touch is tender, and my skin ignites.

"You're gorgeous," he says.

"You're hot as hell." I glance at the glass in his hand. "What are you drinking?"

He glances down too. "Vodka." Glancing back up, he lets his eyes linger a beat on my tits. "You."

I let my arm fall but twine my fingers through his so his arm falls with it. Our hands are clasped now, resting against our legs.

"Which has you buzzing more?"

He meets my eyes. "I'd say the girl in the see-through dress wins that contest real easy." He nods at the table behind me. "But the vodka is giving me the liquid courage to talk to said girl, so . . ."

I grab the glass from his hand and take a sip. Vodka soda.

Not delicious by any means, but it is well-balanced—sting from the liquor, bright bubbles from the soda, hint of sweet from the lime.

"Who said I wanted to talk?" I ask.

His lips twitch. He takes the glass back and sips, eyes never leaving mine. "What did you have in mind, blackjack babe?"

"See, I think that's such a cool name for a beer, but when you apply it to a person, it sounds kinda ridiculous, right?"

He laughs, and I do too, and the electricity between us thickens. "It's your beer, honey. You call it whatever you want."

Honey. Oh, I like that.

It's been years since I've felt this free—free to be happy. Years since life wasn't complicated.

Tonight is my night to finally let loose. And Mr. I-Wanna-Waste-Time-Football-Hottie is the perfect place to start.

"Are you giving me permission to do what I want, then?"

He holds out his drink, and I take it. Take a sip. "If you give me permission to do the same."

"Okay." I set the drink on the table. "I want to dance."

Right on cue, a Britney Spears remix comes on.

It's Britney, bitch.

I smile, and he smiles, and then he guides our clasped hands up to his chest. "Lucky for you, I'm a connoisseur of early 2000 TRL hits. PS, hashtag FreeBritney."

"You saying you know your way around Stevie Nicks *and* Britney Spears?" I curl my hand around the nape of his neck and play with his hair. His gaze darkens.

"Maybe not so much with your hands on me."

"Should I—"

"Don't you fucking dare." He grins and loops an enormous arm around my waist, pulling my body flush against his as he begins to move to the beat.

"Gimme more," he sings, hitting the notes perfectly. "Gimme *gimme* more."

"You really do know your Britney," I say as I wrap my arms around his neck.

His other hand is on my waist now, low enough to flirt with my ass but not quite there.

Not yet.

I curl my hips into his, and he curls back. An expert, unspoken push and pull that sets my body on fire.

Glancing over Hank's shoulder, I make sure my girls are okay. Lauren gives me a thumbs-up. Kate just stares and mouths, "*Fuck yes.*"

Britney talks dirty dancing, and I turn around, pressing my ass into the cradle of Hank's pelvis. He settles his arms on my shoulders, his firm chest flush against my back.

"Aw yeah!" he hollers when I bend over and put my hands on my knees, giving my hips a good shake. "Get it, girl."

His hands are on my waist. Mine are on his. His fingers wrap around mine, and he pulls our arms over our heads, swiveling his hips as he keeps up with my every move. He's athletic, and he's confident, and he sings along to nearly every song, from Kendrick Lamar to Madonna to Maroon 5 remixes.

We laugh.

We sweat.

By the time Kygo comes on, I'm buzzed out of my mind. Not on vodka, but on Hank.

This is fun. This is perfect.

This is exactly what I needed.

Chapter Three

HANK

Kygo ends his set with a banger of a Whitney Houston remix. The place goes nuts. Confetti cannons go off, arms are raised, and drinks fly everywhere.

Stevie's got one hand on my nape, fingers playing with my hair—fuck, I love when she does that—and the other on my waist.

My hands are on her ass, where they've been since she put them there a while ago.

The girl has ass for days and days.

The song ends, and Stevie leans back to look at me. Our eyes meet, and hers smile, and I know I'm this fucking close to popping the woody I've been fighting all night.

"A hand of blackjack?" she says. "And then . . . bed?"

A piece of confetti lands on the tip of her nose, and I grab it, thumb grazing her cheek. "Yes, ma'am."

Taking her hand, I head for the exit. Rhett cuts me a look, eyebrow raised. *You good?*

I nod. *I'm good.*

Stevie waves to her girls, and then a bouncer escorts us to the VIP exit just off the stage.

We spill onto the casino floor, the two of us blinking at the sudden onslaught of light and the chime of slot machines. I check my watch.

It's almost four, but the casino is packed. People crowd the tables, jockeying for a seat, and guys wait four deep for drinks at the nearby bar. The energy in the place is palpable.

I'm wide-awake. My ears are ringing, and so is my body.

Looking at Stevie for the five hundredth time tonight —*Jesus fuck*—I wonder if I've ever been more turned on in my life.

"One hand," I say. "Just one."

Stevie turns her head to glance at me, digging her teeth into her bottom lip. "But not just once in bed, surely?"

I let out a bark of laughter. "Naw, honey, I hope you didn't have plans to sleep tonight 'cause I sure as hell ain't gonna let you."

We manage to nab a seat at a five-hundred-dollar-minimum table. I start to pull out the chair for Stevie, but she presses her breasts against my chest and shakes her head. "You play."

"You're the expert."

"And you're the student. You only get better if you practice."

I smile. I cannot fucking wait to put my mouth on those tits.

I wanna put my mouth all over her. That is something I'd definitely like to practice.

"If you say so." I take the seat and grab a wad of cash from my wallet. Stevie stands behind me, hands curled over the back of my chair.

This dealer is a lot less fun than Helen was, so I'm glad we won't be staying long. I still play my hand with him the way Stevie taught me, setting a few chips closer to the center of the table so he can gamble with me.

"Fast learner," she says behind me, swiping a finger across my shoulder blade.

"Easy enough when you learn from the best."

My first card is an eight. Waiting for my second, I hold my breath.

Another eight.

I glance over my shoulder at Stevie. She's smiling, and I'm struck dumb the way I always am by this Julia Roberts thing that's wide and real and nothing short of beautiful.

Yeah, probably should be careful with this one. There's a reason I gave Rhett explicit instructions at the start of our trip not to let me fall for anyone. I've played the love-sick asshole before, and it's a sucky role.

Especially when you're lovesick for your brother's girl.

A girl who's now his fiancée. A month or so ago, Rhett gave me the news that Samuel and Emma had gotten engaged.

I wait for the way my chest clenches anytime I think about them and how badly I fucked up.

I wait some more.

Stevie's finger moves up my nape. My skin ignites.

Wow. Wow, the awful tightness actually isn't happening. Guilt is still there, don't get me wrong. It sits on my breastbone like a goddamn gorilla night and day. But longing, for Emma at least, doesn't rise to meet it.

Halle-fucking-*lujah*. The relief's been slow to come, but tonight—being with Stevie—it's hardly even a thought.

She's setting me on fire.

Reaching behind me, I give Stevie's thigh a quick grab. She responds by pressing her tits into my back.

Fuck careful. Where's the fun in that? I've been careful my whole damn life. While it's paid off in some respects, it didn't stop disaster from happening in others.

"You know what to do?" Stevie asks.

"Split 'em," I say to the dealer.

I split my cards and put more chips on the table. And whaddya know, the dealer busts, and I end up winning north of three grand.

"Hot damn!" I stand and give Stevie another high five. Our fingers twine like we've done it a hundred times. "You know your shit, honey."

"And now you know yours. Shall we celebrate in my suite?"

"I'm sure a high roller like you has a nice room. But mine is nicer."

"I did hear you might be famous."

"Might be?" I smirk. "How about this? Let *my* suite do the talking, and then you can decide if I'm famous or not."

"So cocky."

I lift a shoulder. "Well, yeah. How could I not be now that I know how to crush it at blackjack?"

Stevie's hand in mine, I flash my player card at the door to the Tower Suites. The sounds of the casino fade as we step into the private lobby, a gleaming, perfumed oasis for Encore's most exclusive guests.

Another couple is waiting in the elevator bank. But because lady luck is on my side tonight, two elevators arrive at the same time. The other couple takes one. Stevie and I take the other, turning around so we're facing the doors. I hit the button for 35. The doors glide shut with a hushed *whoosh*, and I join Stevie at the back of the elevator.

We're alone for the first time. For half a heartbeat, the silence between us swells.

I turn to face her and press her against the elevator wall with my body. I grab her wrists in one hand and pin her arms above her head. Her chest rises on a sharp inhale, and I imagine her nipples dragging up my chest.

My dick is in agony.

Her dark eyes are fire.

I lean in and press my lips to hers. Her hips roll forward to meet mine, and I open my mouth to groan, the kiss deepening when I lick my tongue over the seam of her lips. She opens her mouth too, letting me taste her.

She's breathing hard, and I am too.

I work my mouth over her jaw, and her head falls back, eyes catching on the far corner of the elevator.

"There's a camera," she pants.

I kiss the freckle on her neck. Her skin tastes clean. "Don't care."

The guy I was back home would care. As (former?) head of guest relations at Blue Mountain Farm, he'd care very much if people were making out in the resort's elevators.

Good thing I'm not that guy in Vegas. Hell, I don't know if I'll ever be that guy again.

Good thing Stevie makes it easy to live in the moment. This feeling—the one that keeps my mind from wandering—is the whole point of my retirement bender.

It's what I've been chasing from day one, when Rhett and I boarded a plane for the Bahamas back in April.

I kiss a trail down her neck, her chest, kissing the swell of her breasts through the fabric of her dress. She shudders when I lick her there, and I glance up to see her sucking in a breath, eyes fluttering shut for a moment before she opens them, determinedly meeting my gaze.

Huh. Almost like she's . . . I don't know, fighting the surrender.

Like she's playing it safe. Why?

Fuck that. I wanna drive this girl wild.

I kiss her one last time, a bruising caress that has her moaning into my mouth, before the elevator doors open on my floor.

"Come," I growl and grab her hand.

I try not to walk too fast. Stevie's wearing killer heels that can't be comfortable, especially after a night of dancing. But I'm impatient to disappear into the privacy of my suite. I gotta get her naked, now.

My hand shakes when I slide the key card into its slot. It takes me two tries, but the door finally swings open. I gesture for Stevie to enter first, and she stops three steps into the room.

"Oh, Hank," she breathes. "This is unbelievable."

The living and dining area of the suite is a two-story behemoth, ridiculously grand in true over-the-top Vegas style. It's decorated in shades of cream, brown, and white with pops of bright red. An enormous chandelier hangs overhead, and cushy furniture dots the space: velvet couches, marble tables, and a leather-clad bar.

But that shit isn't what catches Stevie's attention. Instead, she stares at the wall of floor-to-ceiling windows that gives us an incredible view of the Strip below. She walks over, touching her fingertips to the glass.

I sidle up behind her, slipping my arms around her waist while I press a kiss to her neck. Her body is warm and soft, and I love the feel of it against mine.

Our reflections are visible in the glass. Our gazes lock there, our bodies a shadow over the lights of the neighboring Wynn.

"Okay, you're famous," she says and reaches behind her to slide her fingers into the hair at my nape.

I begin to gather her dress in my fist, hiking it up her legs. "That gonna be a problem?"

"No." She looks to the side. "Actually, it works better."

"Because you wanna fuck an athlete?" I nudge her nose with mine.

Her brows snap together. "No."

"Hey, I'm not here to judge you."

"And I'm not here to chase . . . whatever you are. I'm just

making a very rude assumption that, because you're famous and hot, you like to play the field. Pun intended."

I've got her dress hiked up over her hips. I run my hand over the tops of her bare thighs, reaching for the place between her legs.

"That *is* a rude assumption."

"Is it true?"

"Maybe."

"Are you"—her breath falters when I cup her pussy through the second layer of her outfit, the bodysuit thing—"going to do rude things to me for making it? The assumption?"

"Yes." Even through the silky fabric, I can feel how hot and damp she is. My dick goes full mast. "I got three bedrooms in this place, plus a billiards room, and I'm gonna fuck you in all of 'em. But first, you gotta tell me how to get this thing off you."

She laughs, turning around to face me. Her eyes flash, playful and hot, and she grabs the hem of her dress and slowly pulls it over her head, mussing her ponytail in the process.

Eyes on mine, she holds up the dress between her pinched forefinger and thumb. She releases the pinch, fingers straightening as the dress drops to the floor beside her. She plants a hand on my chest and gives me a firm shove, sending me backward so I can take her in.

For several beats, I just stare. I wonder vaguely if I've experienced cardiac arrest and am now floating somewhere between heaven and hell.

The bodysuit has suddenly become the sexiest lingerie ever. Combined with the stilettos and her slightly swollen lips, it is a sight to be savored.

And when she starts walking toward me, swaying her hips and smirking?

I am definitely a dead man.

I'm also a giver. I grab her hand and lead her to the billiards room. My butler (yes, the suite comes with twenty-four-hour butler service) must've swung by while I was gone because the lights are on and the balls are racked up on the table, ready for a game.

Again, Stevie's gaze moves to the view outside the windows. Lights twinkle in every color and rhythm, and the outline of the mountainous desert beyond is just visible.

I shove the rack and pair of pool cues aside with my arm. They somersault over the lip of the table and land on the floor with a clatter. Stevie jumps, then smiles.

She plays right into my hand, resting her ass against the edge of the table with a come-hither look in her eyes. I settle my hands on the table on either side of her hips and lean in, drawing my nose up her throat.

"Hey, honey," I breathe, relieved to finally, *finally*, have her all to myself.

She takes my face in her hand. "Hey," she says and covers her mouth with mine.

The kiss is savage, deep, our lips and tongues moving in tandem. I lick my tongue into her mouth again, drawing her chin up as I sip her, then drink her in deep, long pulls that have her fisting my shirt in her hands.

I cup her breast, massaging it. Gently, cursing with the effort to be patient, I work the cup of her bodysuit down, propping her tit above it. I thumb her nipple, and she bites down on my lip.

We both look down at the same time, foreheads touching. We watch as I work the other breast free, both tits propped up for us to savor.

They're generous, soft, with large, dusky pink nipples.

I groan and duck my head, leaning in to take her right nipple in my mouth. I suck, lathing my tongue over the pebbled point, and she hisses.

Her head falls back. She digs a hand into my hair, panting, and rolls her hips.

She's begging.

"This too." I reach around to her back, searching for a clasp, a zipper. "How—"

She reaches behind her and finds my hand, leading it to the zipper at the top of the garment. "Like this," she says, and together, we guide the zipper down.

Getting on my knees, I help pull it over her hips and down her legs.

My gaze is level with her pussy. Her pubic hair is dark and lush.

It glistens with her arousal.

I look up at her. She's beautiful, naked save for her heels, and I resist the urge to reach into my pants and give myself a stroke. I'll come in five seconds flat if I so much as graze my dick, much less jack off.

I put my hands on her thighs and say, "Can I?"

"Can you what?" she pants, cheeks burning pink.

"Here." I touch my middle finger to the place just beneath her belly button and drag it down, sliding it between her legs. Parting her lips. She's swollen and soft and *perfect*. "Can I kiss you here?"

She hesitates, just for a second. Her eyes gleam with something I haven't seen before. Vulnerability?

Her fingers find my hair again. "You're famous, you're hot, and you're considerate?"

"Total package. I know. Now get on the table and spread your legs."

Stevie hikes her ass onto the table and gives me a gorgeous view of her pussy. She's so wet my fingers make a slick, crude sound as I circle them over her clit.

"Hank," she breathes, brows snapping together as she watches me.

I curl my hands around the backs of her knees and spread her wider. Stop to admire the dimples along the inside of her thighs. I lean in.

The first taste is rich. Warm. I go slowly, deeply, and Stevie moans, hips rolling again. I lick her slit front to back, then dip my tongue inside her, savoring her heat.

Christ, it's gonna feel good to be inside her.

I suck on her clit. Press my lips to it. Slip a finger inside her. Reach up and gather her nipple between my thumb and forefinger.

Her moans get louder. She pulls my hair. Pulls it harder, making my heart thump.

"What is it?" My eyes go wide. "Did I hurt you?"

She shakes her head, breathless. "No. I—bed. I'm close, but I don't—I want to make it last—"

"I got you." I stand, and she takes both hands I offer, rising to her feet. She sways a little; I hold her, steady her, and she kisses my jaw. "Let's go to bed."

Chapter Four

STEVIE

The bedroom is massive. A wall of windows provides yet another jaw-dropping view of the Strip. The king bed is neatly made in Encore's signature fluffy, buttery linens, and a mountain of pillows beckons. The doors to the bathroom are open, and from what I can see, it's an exquisite white marble palace.

But it's the acoustic guitar in the far corner that catches my eye. Sitting on the edge of the bed, I study it as I hurriedly take out my earrings and let down my hair. The guitar's darkened wood and slightly scuffed edges look out of place in the suite's immaculate, slickly modern space.

I don't want to be curious, but I am.

"You play?" I ask, tipping my chin toward the instrument.

"I do."

I glance at him from unbuckling my heels. At some point tonight, my feet were killing me. And at some point, I stopped being aware of any sensation other than the insistent throb between my legs.

I wait for Hank to elaborate. Instead, he kneels in front of me, knees cracking, and shoos away my hands. "Let me," he says and unbuckles the clasp at my left ankle.

My stomach flutters. A different kind of flutter. Deeper. More certain.

Rarer.

I do my best to ignore it. But the gentle way his fingers graze my skin—how he runs a hand up my calf, giving it a firm, reverent squeeze before moving to the other shoe—

"How the hell do you wear these all night?" He holds up the strappy stilettos. "These things look like damn weapons."

I grab the shoes and smile, grateful for the distraction. "They are weapons. Just not the kind you're thinking of."

"Weapons of seduction?"

"Or empowerment. I like the way they make me feel. Most of the time, anyway, until my feet really start to hurt."

"Poor feet." Hank picks up my foot and starts massaging it. He presses his thumb into my arch, just firm enough to feel glorious, and my eyes nearly roll back in my head.

Too intimate.

This is too mushy. He's being too nice.

I'm five seconds from coming. Time to get down to business.

Guiding my foot out of his grasp, I hook a finger in his shirt. "Where are your condoms?"

I can't tell if he looks relieved or disappointed at the question. Whatever the case, his expression smooths, eyes sharp with hunger.

"Bedside table." Placing his hands on his knees, he pushes up to standing and unbuttons his shirt while I grab a couple Trojans.

He rolls back his shoulders, tugging the shirt off. My mouth goes dry at the sight of Hank's bare chest and stomach and shoulders. Is he the hottest guy I've ever been with?

He *ripples* with strength. The muscles and veins in his

forearms bunch against his skin as he unzips his jeans and shucks off his black briefs.

His cock juts lewdly from between his sculpted hips. It's just the right combo of length and thickness, with a wide pink crown and a slit that glistens with precum. A thatch of dark blond hair, neatly trimmed, covers his balls.

My pussy clenches. Yeah, definitely the hottest guy I'll *ever* be with.

"You're beautiful," I manage.

"Thank you." He leans over me, planting his hands on the bed beside my legs, and kisses me. I taste myself on his lips. "Cool if I turn on some music?"

"Of course."

He puts on a Bruce Springsteen cover, John Mayer singing "I'm on Fire." It's moody and sexy and perfect.

"I like this. You have a hookup playlist, don't you?"

"Don't you?"

"Yes." I grin. "And this song is on it. Although I've got the AWOLNATION cover instead."

"That's a good one too."

Hank kills the lights, making the view outside the windows pop, and my pulse kicks up a notch. I toss back the covers and settle against the pillows.

As I watch him roll on a condom, anticipation thrums through me, heady and hot.

"I know you said you wanted to make it last," he says, climbing on top of me. "But you come first. Got it?"

This is the loveliest kind of danger I think I've ever experienced.

There are numbers I can call back home—numbers I do call, often—when my vibrator isn't cutting it. My regulars aren't bad guys; they're discreet, they're kind, and they always make me come.

One thing they didn't do? They *never* showed such sincere concern about my orgasm the first time we hooked up.

I shove the comparison from my thoughts. Maybe Hank likes to take care of his partners in bed. But I bet his consideration and his generosity don't extend much beyond that. Not in real life, anyway.

I've learned that sharing real life with real men results in whatever the opposite of bliss is, domestic or otherwise.

Good thing Vegas isn't real life. And Hank—the guy he's being tonight—he can't be real. He's a fantasy, a flash in the pan whose combination of hot and kind is so excellent it must be fictional.

I reach for Hank's dick, and he holds up his hips, allowing me to wrap my hand around his length. I give him a solid tug, thumb lingering over his slit. Or what I can feel of it, anyway, through the latex. I settle him at my entrance.

Hank's eyes are lit up with the reflection of the lights on the Strip, a smattering of tiny stars that give him an ardent, earnest look.

Talk to me, those eyes say. *Tell me everything*.

I close my eyes.

This is sex. I love sex. I've gotten pretty damn great at it over the years since my separation.

I am determined to enjoy this sex for what it is. Gloriously hot and epic in all the right ways.

He rocks his hips and slowly sinks inside me. This time, my eyes really do roll to the back of my head behind my closed lids.

"This all right, honey?"

I nod, swallowing, and grab his ass to push him all the way inside. "So good."

Our mouths meet in a hungry kiss, tongues tangling as I wrap my legs around his waist. He starts thrusting, gliding in and out of me with ease, and I revel in the feeling of fullness he gives me with each lingering swivel of his hips.

Our bellies are flush, and he's grazing my clit as he moves. Just enough to make me want more, but not to make me come.

The tease, the tension—it has me making sounds I don't recognize.

Hank cups the back of my knee and guides it to my chest. The feeling of fullness increases.

"Yeah." I bite his shoulder. "*Yes.*"

He's starting to sweat, his skin sticking to mine. I lick his skin, tasting the salt. He groans and spears me with a hard, deep thrust. *I like this.*

I roll onto my side, reaching for his cock when he slips out of me. He hikes my leg back toward my chest, but at an angle this time so that I'm spread wide. He gets on his knees and holds me by my calf and hip. He gently enters me again. I thrust my pelvis, welcoming him inside.

I like this too.

My heart is pounding, and now I'm sweating too. Turns out sex with an athlete is, well, athletic. My tits bounce on every thrust, and Hank watches them move, eyes hazy.

He's stronger than me, bigger, but he still lets me take the lead, gladly following me wherever I go.

I roll onto my stomach and prop myself on my elbows, raising my ass in the air. Wordlessly Hank settles behind me, thighs flush against mine as he enters me from behind in a modified doggy style position.

I like it. I like the sound his balls make when they slap against me with every thrust. I like the way Hank holds my hips, thumbs massaging the small of my back as I meet his movements.

He's moving a little slower now, our bodies rocking in a deeply satisfying rhythm. This angle makes me feel full, like

I'm being stretched, *pushed*, and I turn my head, close my eyes again, and open my mouth, flexing my jaw at the delicious overwhelm of it.

He reaches between my legs and thumbs my clit. Sensation spirals through me, tight and hot, and my legs start to shake.

His grip on me tightens, holding me up. Keeping me from shattering.

My heart swells, and I know I should slow my roll, I should pull away a little so he's not touching me everywhere, but I can't. I don't want to.

I like feeling adored and exquisitely cared for.

My pussy spasms and I surrender, teetering on the edge of the precipice.

"Honey, I gotta see your face when you come."

I nod, too scattered, too scalding hot, to resist the invitation.

I let Hank roll me onto my back. Then, to my surprise, he scoots back and settles his head between my legs.

Eyes locked on mine, he kisses my clit, tongue and lips and tenderness.

The bastard shoves me right off that precipice.

My orgasm rips through me. I arch my back, rising up to meet the spiraling sensation. I'm helpless against the onslaught. Helpless and boneless. I cry out Hank's name, reaching blindly for him.

He finds my hands—of course he does—and twines his fingers through mine. Covering my body with his. Kissing my neck, my jaw, my mouth.

Behind my closed lids, splashes of vibrant color explode. A rainbow kaleidoscope that makes me feel keenly, almost painfully alive.

He slips inside me when I'm still coming, wrapping my leg

around his waist. He grunts when I pulse around him, and his thrusts become fast, uneven.

"So good," he breathes into our kiss. "Honey, you feel like heaven."

The echoes of my orgasm still ripple through me when he finds his, clenching his teeth against a muffled *fuck*.

He lowers himself onto me, resting some of his weight on his forearms so I'm not crushed. Still, the solid weight of his body presses me into the mattress. The smell of his skin fills my head. Skin and sex.

We breathe hard, his head buried in my neck. When I'm able to move again I reach up and play with his hair. He grunts again, swiping his thumb over my side. "That feels like heaven too."

Thoughts are starting to swirl inside my head.

Dangerous thoughts.

This feels too good. Being with this guy feels too fucking good.

I need to think of something else, anything else, so I don't add fuel to the fire burning inside my body, my mind.

I open my eyes and look at the ceiling. Look at the lights outside the windows, trying to formulate a plan for tomorrow. Maybe the girls and I can check out Giada's restaurant. Do some shopping at the Bellagio, or even get massages—

"Penny for your thoughts."

I startle at the sex-roughed sound of Hank's voice. He's kissing my breast: slow, careful kisses, and the thoughts start to swirl again.

"Are you kidding?" I shoot back. "How am I supposed to think after *that*?"

Even I'm surprised by the speed of my recovery. Guess it's almost become a reflex, backing up when people get too close.

Much safer this way.

"Did I fuck your brains out?" he says, laughing, and I laugh too.

I gotta get out of here.

"And that's my cue to go," I say, giving his chest a gentle push.

"Didn't you say downstairs you wanted to do it more than once?"

"I changed my mind. I don't mean to be rude, but let's keep it fun, yeah? And morning breath and awkward conversation are not fun."

Searching my face, Hank presses up onto his hands, hovering over me. His biceps literally ripple on either side of my head. "Listen, Stevie. If you wanna leave, I'm not gonna stop you. But I'd really, really like you to stay for round two."

I lick my lips. "Sometimes, a second go isn't a good idea."

He looks genuinely mystified by this, his eyebrows drawn together and mouth in a frown. "Why the hell not?"

"Because I've got things to do," I say, trying to grin so my words come off as playful. I don't want to fake anything, but I also don't want to hurt the guy's feelings.

"Let me do you. Don't tell me you didn't enjoy it enough to want more."

I'm laughing again, and I don't want to be. "I did enjoy it. A lot."

"So stay." He ducks down to kiss the swell of my breast again. "I'll beg if I have to."

Why does he have to be so *warm* and *generous* and *lovely*? Why does his dick have to be so perfect?

Also, why does my favorite The Weeknd song have to be on his fucking playlist?

I glance out the windows.

Screw it. I came to Vegas to celebrate being officially, legally free from a controlling ex, and if having great sex with a hot guy in his massive suite isn't the definition of doing whatever the hell I want, well, I don't know what is.

Besides, it's just one night. You don't get in over your head in one night. Not when you're forty and free, and you know better.

"What does this begging entail, exactly?"

Hank smiles. "How about we move this to the shower? I'll lather you up. Touch every inch of your skin. Then I'll tell you to bend over and put your hands on the wall. There will be hot water everywhere. And steam, lots of steam. I'll sink my fingers inside you from behind, two of them. After you come, I'll dry you off and take you to bed and fuck you just how you ask me to. Deal?"

Oh, God. This guy is good.

"Deal," I say.

I let Hank take my hand and lead me to the bathroom.

Chapter Five

HANK

The next morning—or maybe it's afternoon, who knows—Stevie stirs. She lets out a soft, unguarded sigh, and my chest twists.

She's on her side, turned away from me. I wrap my body around hers, silently cursing when I find her skin cold to the touch. I put my arm around her middle and pull her to me, determined to warm her up.

Her naked body is soft.

My dick is not.

"Can I?" I murmur in her ear. "If you're sore—"

"Yes." Her hand finds my dick underneath the covers. "I mean no. No, I'm not too sore. Please."

I put on a condom, and we fuck slowly and quietly on our sides. I keep her wrapped in my warmth while I play with her nipples. Then I reach between her legs and play with her clit. She's soaking wet, and she comes with a breathless moan, pussy clenching around my cock. Milking me to my own orgasm, which rockets through my sleepy limbs like a jolt of caffeine.

Speaking of caffeine.

"Hot or cold?" I say, trailing my lips over the slope of her shoulder. She's still clinging to me, riding out the last of her orgasm, her fingers curled into my side like she's holding on for dear life. Same as she did last night.

Not gonna lie. I'm as drawn to her vulnerability as I am to her badass-ness. Maybe because I've forgotten what vulnerability looks like. It's been a while since someone opened up to me this way.

It's been a while since I opened up myself.

Stevie laughs, her grip loosening. "Hot or cold what?"

"How do you like your coffee?"

Stevie hesitates. "You know I'm only here to fuck an athlete, right?"

I laugh and nick her jaw with my teeth, making her breath catch. "Yeah. And how was that?"

"As good as I'd hoped it would be. But seriously." She rolls onto her back and turns her head on the pillow to face me. "I should go."

"My morning breath really that bad?" I brush her mussed hair out of her face.

She looks at me, lips twitching. "You don't have morning breath. You brushed your teeth. I can taste it."

"I did." I kiss her mouth. "Stay for coffee. All the restaurants downstairs are gonna be mobbed anyway. You'll wait in line forever at that Starbucks you're thinking about."

"How do you know I'm thinking about Starbucks?"

"Lucky guess. Stay. Please."

She's still looking at me with warmth written all over her features. She's still hesitating too, and I'm not quite sure what else to say. She wants fun and fun only. How do I prove to her that's all I want too? Fun, only the extended version that includes coffee and brunch and coming again on the couch in the living room?

"I fell for my brother's girlfriend," I blurt, "and I think I may still have feelings for her."

The words come out of my mouth too easily. Or maybe too . . . painlessly. The reality behind them is excruciating, yet they float between Stevie and me, weightless as a feather.

Her expression softens, and it hits me where the weightlessness comes from: Stevie doesn't judge me. Doesn't pity me either.

She just listens.

And yeah, maybe I'm also questioning if I should still feel this way about Emma. If I actually *do* feel this way. It's a thought that's been popping up lately.

"And you came here to get over those feelings."

"Something like that."

"So you've got it bad for someone else. And I'm determined not to get it bad—"

"Because of divorce and . . . stuff."

"Something like that." She grins, trailing her fingertips over my chest. "All right, all right, you've proved your point."

I'm hoping my blunt confession will inspire her to tell me more about this divorce. But she's quiet, the only sound between us the whisper of her fingers on my skin, and I know better than to push her when I agreed to fun, and fun only.

I imagine talking about divorce and stuff is definitely not fun.

"When do you leave?" I ask, tucking my hand behind my head.

"First thing tomorrow." She sighs, fingers going still. "Vegas is great for seventy-two hours, max. Then your body just starts to shut down on you."

"Try me. I've been here for three weeks."

She looks up at me, eyes wide. "How the hell is your liver still functioning?"

"There but for the grace of God go I." With my other hand, I reach under the covers and cup her breast. Thumb her nipple because I like the way her eyes flash, dark and hot when I do. "Hear me out. We have, what, eighteen hours, maybe less, to make this the most fun Vegas hookup we've ever had. Stay with me. Just for today. And for tonight too. You can teach me more blackjack strategies. We'll get dinner somewhere great. Then I'll go down on you until your flight leaves. Sound good?"

As I wait for her answer, my heart pounds. Not gonna lie. I really want her to stay. Like, *really* want that. I like how being with her clears my mind. She's this wild mix of class and crass, confidence and vulnerability, and I want to know more.

I want more, period.

Rhett and I have traveled a lot of miles since April. Even though he was in Vegas for preseason and then the season itself, I went to Madrid, Mykonos, Macau, and Melbourne before finally landing here in Sin City. Along the way, I met plenty of women willing to throw down. I've rarely been lonely. But in the quiet moments between flights and fuck buddies and hangovers from hell, I've missed what I left behind at Blue Mountain. Emma included, pathetically enough.

But Stevie's woken something inside me. Can't quite put my finger on it. She's so . . . alive. Real. She knows what she wants, and she goes after it.

I have a lot to learn from her, and I'm not just talking about blackjack strategy.

Something about her has shaken me from the guilt-ridden stupor I've been in, and I know enough about the world and how it works to realize a person with a touch like that is a rare fucking thing.

I also like having someone to do stuff with. Someone to

look after. Maybe I miss my family more than I'm willing to admit.

"I came here to spend time with my girls, you know."

"They get to go home with you tomorrow. I don't."

Stevie's lips twitch. "True."

"Why don't you text them? Let them know you're alive and *very* well, thanks to me. We can all hang out together if you want. Maybe some cocktails later and a game of chance or two?"

After a small eternity, Stevie smiles, and my heart works double for a different reason.

"I'll take an iced latte, please. Almond milk if they have it."

Stevie and I don't sleep a wink the next night.

Still, I buzz with the high of a weekend well spent as I ride the elevator down to the lobby with her Sunday morning. I've got her suitcase in my hand, and she's got an iced almond milk latte in hers. I slipped out earlier to grab our coffees while Stevie was in the shower. Thinking about someone else —someone besides Emma—makes me feel grounded. Helpful.

Good. It makes me feel good.

"Any idea when you'll head home?" she asks.

I shrug. "Not really. Thinking I may head up to Aspen. Or Whistler. I've never skied out west."

She rolls her eyes and smiles. "Is that where famous people winter?"

"Yes. Me and Mariah Carey and Kylie Jenner. It'll be a hoot."

Stevie's girls, Kate and Lauren, wave to us from the revolving door at the front of the lobby. Yesterday afternoon, the four of us had a great time playing blackjack here at the hotel before Stevie and I left to get dinner at The Country Club, probably my all-time favorite restaurant in Vegas. Stevie loved it too.

I give them hugs, glancing over Kate's head when a maroon Rolls Royce Phantom pulls up outside. The hotel has a few of them, reserving their plushest rides for high rollers and celebrities.

"Think y'all's car is here," I say, glancing at Stevie.

Stevie looks out the windows. Looks at me. "Stop."

"It's how famous people get to the airport." I tuck her hair behind her ear. "I called in a favor."

"I really wish you didn't."

"I'm really glad you did." Lauren nudges Kate. "C'mon, we'll hop in first."

They say their goodbyes and head outside, leaving Stevie and me alone. The swoosh of the revolving door fills the silence between us as a small army of bellhops helps the girls with their luggage by the Phantom.

I smile. So does Stevie.

"Best Vegas trip ever?" I ask.

She curls her hand around my nape and digs her fingers into my hair. "Yeah. It was great. Really, really great, Hank. Thank you."

"Have a safe flight. I'd tell you to keep in touch, but since you're only using me for my fame, I won't. Because this is just fun, and we left nothing on the table."

"Only because I was your blackjack coach. Otherwise, you would've left a lot of cash on the table."

"Fact." I search her eyes. "So . . . have a nice life, I guess?"

She laughs again, giving my hair a little tug. "It doesn't have to be like that. If you're ever in Nashville, give me a ring."

You do the same if you're ever in—

Where? Where the hell is home? I wonder vaguely how my old assistant, Gregory, is doing as interim head of guest relations at the farm. He took over after I left, as Beau didn't want to hire someone new.

"It's not a matter of *if* you'll come back," Beau had said. "But when."

"I might just have to make a pit stop in Music City, then," I say to Stevie. "And, you know, my family owns a little place near Asheville—we've got a restaurant, and I'd love to see Lady Luck on the menu. I make no guarantees, but should you find yourself in the area, give me a call and I can set up a tasting or something."

Stevie digs her teeth into her bottom lip. "That'd be awesome. Thank you for the offer."

I'm leaning in for one last kiss when there's a familiar slap on my shoulder. I whip around, annoyed, and see Rhett grinning at me like a goddamn Cheshire cat.

"What?"

"Aren't you going to introduce me to the girl who's kept you busy all weekend? Dude, you can respond to at least one text message. I thought you were dead."

Running a hand over my hair, I let out an aggrieved sigh. "Stevie, this is my brother. Rhett, this is Stevie. I was just wishing her safe travels when your rude ass interrupted us. What would Mama say?"

Rhett smiles and holds out his hand to Stevie. "Mama would say Stevie's a champ for putting up with your shitty attitude all weekend. Hi."

"Hello," Stevie replies with a smile. "And you know, Hank here was actually the champ. He killed it at the blackjack table."

"No shit." Rhett raises his eyebrows at me. "He's not much of a gambler these days. Not with his—"

"Wallet," I snap. "Can you go now? Stevie's got a flight to catch."

Rhett glances through the doors at the waiting Phantom. Glances at me, a strange gleam in his eyes. "Now who's being rude? Stevie, it was a pleasure to finally meet you. Don't be a stranger, you hear?"

"Nice to meet you too."

"*Go*," I say and glare at him until he does.

"Well." Stevie chuckles, flattening her palm on my chest. "Y'all seem to be close."

"My family." I shake my head. "I love 'em, but they are a huge pain in my ass."

"How many siblings do you have?"

"Too many."

I don't want to talk about my family anymore, so I bend my neck and press my lips to hers. I kiss her mouth deeply this time. She rises into the caress, rolling up on the balls of her feet.

A flare of heat ignites in my center. We've fucked fifteen thousand times, so much and so often my dick's a little raw, but I can't seem to sate the hunger I have for her.

Girl's got a story to tell. I like stories.

Or used to, anyway.

I'm equal parts relieved and bummed when Stevie breaks the kiss, adjusting the bag on her shoulder.

"You're a good guy, Hank."

The gorilla on my chest makes itself known, settling its weight on my breastbone. "I wouldn't be so sure about that."

"You are. They don't make them like that where I'm from." She gets a faraway look in her eyes as she toys with the collar of my shirt. After a beat, she draws a sharp breath through her nose and blinks hard. "Aces and eights. Don't forget."

"Never." I reach for the revolving door, but she stops me with a hand on my chest.

"Don't. You've already done too much."

"You gotta let me walk you out."

"I'm good, really. Bye, Hank."

I hold up my hand. "Bye, blackjack babe."

She pushes through the door, calling "See? Ridiculous!" over her shoulder.

I watch her climb into the car, tossing her hair. The Phantom pulls out of the drive, and I'm left with a throbbing hangover and a funny feeling in my gut.

I guess I just haven't felt something real in a long time. Hell, I've hardly felt much at all over the past nine months, other than horny or hungover.

And now there's this. A lightness.

I like it. I want more of it. I just don't know where to find it.

"Hey!" I turn around to see Rhett tilting his head at the door to the casino. A bellhop holds the door open for him. "You look like hell. Let's get some food in you."

Chapter Six

HANK

"Fuck *me*!"

I take my two hundredth tumble of the day. This time I lose not one but both of my skis, a pole, a glove, and the baggie of pre-rolled blunts I'd shoved in my coat pocket earlier.

Hey, weed is legal in Colorado. Thank God for that—it's the only thing that relieves the full-body ache I get from skiing all day.

To be fair, I wouldn't call what I'm doing "skiing." It's more like me splitting my time between falling on my ass, falling off the lift, and cursing loudly as I creep my way down Aspen mountain.

Yes, I grew up in the mountains back in North Carolina. But football was my life. I was so focused on it when I was young I didn't really do much else, sports-wise. When I played in college and the pros, I wasn't allowed to do stuff like skiing because of the risk of injury.

But being the thick-skulled asshole I am, I thought, *hey, I'm athletic. I'm no stranger to snow.* How hard can coasting down a hill on sticks be?

It turns out, it's way, way harder than James Bond makes it look.

"Mon dieu! What is this? Monsieur Beauregard, you are having a yard sale! Haha!" My instructor, a French dude named Clyde, glides to a crisp stop beside me. "Is it okay, your bodies?"

"My bodies is done with this lesson, I think." I reach for my pole with a grunt. "What's a yard sale?"

Clyde clips out of his skis and grabs mine, setting them side by side perpendicular to the slope. "It is a great joke, yes? The yard sale happens when the person goes *poof!* in the snow, and they lose all their things, even sometimes their dignity. Haha!"

"Hilarious." I nod at the blunts. "Hand me those?"

By the time I get to the bottom of the mountain half an hour later, I'm somehow soaked with sweat and frozen at the same time, with shins that scream and an acute need for a toke and a beer.

Look, I get that being in Aspen is the stuff of dreams. Growing up, I'd never imagined I'd step foot in a place like this, much less stay here in a five-star hotel on downtown's swankiest street. I'm one lucky bastard. But for whatever reason, I'm just not feeling the whole ski bum thing.

Heading for Ajax Tavern to meet up with Rhett—it's *the* place for après ski in Aspen—I wonder if they'll have any Lady Luck on tap. That Hefeweizen I had in Vegas a few weeks back was delicious.

I step inside the restaurant. I groan. It's packed with a mix of wind-burned skiers and pretty young things. The tables are crowded with fondue spreads and pricey craft cocktails, while buckets of champagne sweat at the service station toward the back.

Samuel would love this place. So would Emma.

My knee-jerk reaction is to shove those two from my

head. But lately, my thoughts about them are less guilt-ridden and murder-y, and more . . . neutral, I guess? Some thoughts, like this one, would be downright pleasant if it wasn't for the gut-punch of longing they gave me.

It's been almost ten months since I left Blue Mountain. I didn't miss the place—or the people—much at all at the beginning of this bender.

Now, though? Now I think I am starting to miss the farm. A lot. So much so that it's making me grumpy, as evidenced by today's lessons with Clyde.

The hostess leads me back outside to a slopeside table on the deck. There are heaters everywhere, and a gas fire flickers merrily from the center of the table itself.

As usual, Rhett is surrounded by a clutch of beautiful women. It's the same wherever we go: he's the life of the party, cracking jokes and flirting while everyone rips shots.

Something that's not the same? How I've had no interest in that shit since Vegas. A place like Ajax would've been right up my alley a couple weeks ago. But now? Now the "scene" just makes me feel tired, which sucks because Rhett's team didn't make the playoffs, and he's in full beast mode this week, partying harder than ever.

I tear off my hat and land heavily in the chair beside my brother. I'm gonna eat, and then I'm gonna hole up in my hotel room for the rest of the afternoon. Get stoned and maybe play some guitar.

Rhett's mouth twitches. "How's skiing?"

"Hate it. How's blacking out?"

"Love it." He leans forward to grab a fry from one of the girls' plates and looks at me. "We need to have a word. Mindy, you and your girls mind giving us a minute?"

Mindy gives Rhett a long, heated glance before rising, her girls following.

Rhett watches Mindy go, his eyes glued to her ass in her

tight pink ski pants. He rubs his hands together and lets out a low breath. "I like Aspen."

I grab a menu. "What'd you get?"

"But you—I don't think you're feeling it here."

"Honestly?" I toss the menu back onto the table. "I'm not. It's cold. My ass hurts. And I can't tell if Clyde is intentionally making me feel bad or if being rude is just a French person thing."

"Who's Clyde?"

I wave him away. "No one you want to know."

"Welp, hate to say it, but the news I got ain't gonna make you feel any better."

My stomach knots. "What's up?"

"I don't think there's an easy way to tell you this, so I'm just gonna spit it out." His expression softens. "It's Samuel. He wants to talk to you. He and Emma are ready to set a date, but they aren't gonna do it without your blessing. They're having an engagement party next month. We're all invited, obviously, but they really want you to be there so they can make sure you're okay before they, you know, commit to planning the wedding."

I screw up my face. "What? That's ridiculous. They should just do what they want."

Glancing over my shoulder, I make sure no one's too close, and there aren't any kids around. Then I dig a joint out of my pocket and light it with the table's gas fire. I take a hard pull, the smoke burning my lungs on the way in and my eyes on the way out.

I don't offer the joint to Rhett, and he doesn't ask for it.

"I'm serious, Hank." He grabs my wrist when I try to take another toke and looks me in the eye. "He needs to know *you're okay*. We all do. This bender you and I are on, it's been awesome, and clearly, I'm in no rush for it to end." He motions to the empty shot glasses in front of him. "But at some point, it has to. We gotta go home, and life—it has to go on."

Maybe it's the marijuana, or maybe it's the earnest look on Rhett's face, but it all hits me at once: how much I miss my mom, and how much I miss Milly's sass and baby Maisie's smiles and Bel and Beau's company, and good Lord how I'd love to show up to this week's Sunday supper and chow down on whatever deliciousness Samuel's whipping up.

One thing I don't miss, though? Work.

I didn't hate my job as head of guest relations. In fact, I fucking loved a lot of it: interacting with guests and working with an incredible team of smart, driven people. Strategizing and implementing a guest experience that rivals some of the greatest resorts in the world. Eating and drinking at the south's best restaurant under the guise of "research."

Sharing my family's brand of southern hospitality with the world.

But I dove headfirst into the job right after I retired from the pros. I don't know what I expected life would be like post-retirement, but I hadn't anticipated eighty-hour weeks and a nonexistent social life for the two-plus years I worked at Blue Mountain.

At first, I didn't mind working like a maniac because I was doing it for our family. For my own little family, the one I'd dreamed about having for as long as I could remember. I want the fuss and the excitement and the sense of purpose that comes with getting married and having babies. It's a big part of why I retired from football in the first place. I wanted to be present for my future wife and kids—healthy too—in a way my father wasn't.

But I didn't have time to think about starting a family, much less meet a woman who'd help me make that happen when I worked like I did. Guess I got a little resentful after a while. Coming home exhausted to an empty house got really fucking old.

I was doing the good thing, the right thing, by helping build the resort. But if I'm being honest, I wasn't happy. I felt lost.

I felt like I was drowning.

And then the whole Emma thing happened, and . . .

Yeah. Maybe I'm asking too much of the universe not to only want a relationship like Bel and Beau's, or Samuel and Emma's, but a relationship with someone they'll love and accept. Because at the end of the day, my family's opinion matters to me. *They* matter.

I glance down at the blunt in my hand. Smoke curls lazily from the lit end, a misshapen question mark that rises between my younger brother and me.

"Are you feeling any better about it?" Rhett lowers his voice. "Do you still think about Emma? I know in the beginning . . ."

"I did think about her. But now I don't." Rhett raises an eyebrow. "I mean it. Mostly. Especially in the past couple weeks, I haven't thought about Emma, or Samuel for that matter, much at all. Am I over her? Am I over what happened? I mean . . ." I lift a shoulder. "One thing I do know, I'm not gonna be the guy who holds back his brother from marrying the girl of his dreams. Even after all the shit that went down between us, Samuel is still family. I love him."

Rhett flinches. "Pretty words, Hank, and I wanna buy 'em. But you gotta convince Samuel, and to be honest, I don't think you're there yet."

"How the hell else can I prove to y'all that I'm okay? Show up with my own fiancée or some shit?"

"Ha." Rhett runs a hand over his stubble. "That would work. You finagle an engagement I don't know about? That chick from Vegas? I knew y'all were up to no good. If Elvis officiates the wedding, Mama'll kick your—"

"Don't talk smack about Stevie. Or Elvis."

"Kidding, kidding," Rhett says, holding his hands up in mock surrender. "I liked her, though. Stevie. Gorgeous girl."

An image of her supermodel smile flashes across my thoughts, followed in short order by the image of her standing naked in stilettos in my hotel suite.

I shift in my chair. "Stevie's a fucking knockout."

Repeating her name, I catch a wild idea in my head.

A ridiculous, problematic, highly moronic idea.

Dangerous too.

But talk about fun—we could have so much of it all over my house. In my car too, and maybe in the stables if we were feeling especially adventurous . . .

She'd be great with my family.

My excitement grows as the pieces continue to click into place. I wouldn't be violating her *just fun* rule. It'd be one weekend of incredible sex and fake dating, and then we could go our separate ways. I'd prove to Samuel that I've moved on from Emma. Stevie would get orgasms, as many iced almond milk lattes delivered directly to bed as she wants, and whatever else she asked for. That tasting we talked about, maybe?

I shake my head. This is way too fucking wild. I couldn't ask her. I shouldn't. The question could offend her. Besides, would she be able to fake that level of interest? Would she want to?

"Samuel, being the fancy as fuck person he is, is making a big deal out of this party," Rhett is saying. "Fireworks, live music, the whole nine yards. But the one thing he wants most is for you to be there."

I look down at my hands, excitement dimming. The idea of the party doesn't hurt. It's the idea that Samuel cares enough to consider my feelings, even after my betrayal, that kills me.

As if I didn't feel enough like a piece of shit.

My brother is good people. But me? I'm not so sure.

Exhibit A: this harebrained idea that won't leave me alone. What the fuck is wrong with me, thinking I can pull off a *Bridgerton*-esque Hastings and Daphne scam?

"What if I called him?" I ask. "Tried to convince him I'm all right that way?"

Rhett shrugs. "Wouldn't hurt to try. But I would have a plan B ready, just in case."

I tap my thumb on Samuel's name and bring the phone to my ear. I settle my forearms on the balcony railing and look out over the veil of snow that shrouds Aspen Mountain.

It's freezing out here, but my palms are clammy. My heart races.

He picks up on the first ring. "Hank. Hey."

I startle at the sound of his voice. We haven't talked since I wished him and Emma well and boarded a private jet for Nassau nine and a half months ago.

"Hey," I say, rocking back on my heels. "How've you been?"

"I've been all right. You?"

"Same."

A pause. I hate this. I hate talking to the brother I've always been close to like he's a stranger.

I glance down at my boots. "I hear you have some news. I haven't congratulated you on the engagement."

"Rhett told you?"

"Yeah. And I just wanted to say—I'm good with it. You

and Emma getting hitched. Y'all deserve to be happy together, and I'm . . . I'm ready to celebrate you guys."

I've rehearsed the words over and over, and it sounds like it.

"I appreciate you saying that, Hank. I do." Samuel lets out a breath. "But you don't sound good."

"I'm good."

"I thought we agreed not to lie anymore."

"I'm not—" I shake my head. "I want to do this for you, Samuel. I owe it to y'all after the way I acted. I'm not proud of it, but I am—I'm trying, brother. To do better."

Samuel's muffled voice comes through the receiver. He's speaking to someone in the room with him. Is he at home with Emma? Cooking, maybe, a night of Netflix and chill ahead?

That sounds so fucking nice.

"Sorry." I hear the quiet *click* of a door, and he lowers his voice. "I'm trying to do better too, Hank. We all are. But I gotta know you're really, truly okay with this. You have to prove it. I don't mean to be a pain in the ass, but I'm trying to protect us all, you know? I don't want anyone getting hurt again. You say you're ready to move on? Great. Show me by coming home and being *you* again."

"Being me?" I scoff. "I don't even know what that means."

"It means we want the old Hank back. The one we had before—"

"Right."

Before I kissed the woman he's going to marry.

I've wondered a million times what the hell I was thinking at that moment.

The thing is, I wasn't. It was one of the few times in my life where I knew I was making a huge mistake, but I did it anyway.

I remember the whole thing in excruciating detail, starting with my confession: *there's nothing sexier than a woman who knows what she's doing and what she wants. I'm falling in love with you, Emma.*

My stomach twists at the memory of her embarrassment, how she tried to let me down easy. An impossible task, considering she'd just confessed to falling in love with Samuel.

Why him? I'd demanded to know. *He was such a dick to you.*

I should've walked away then. Instead, I let Emma hug me, and when I saw Samuel approaching, I saw red.

Why not me? Nice guys really do finish last.

Shaking with rage, I'd leaned down and kissed her, knowing full well Samuel would see and it'd crush him.

Knowing it'd crush Emma too.

I couldn't have done a worse thing. I didn't ask for consent. Didn't think about anyone or anything other than my own hurt and shame.

"I'm sorry," I say and drag my thumb and forefinger over my eyes. "I know I keep saying that, but I mean it, Samuel. I've told Emma the same thing, many times."

"We're sorry too. We want you to be a part of the wedding. Come home. Let me see you. If you're not a strung-out, hungover asshole—"

"Hey. That's Rhett."

Samuel laughs. "If you're really okay, if you've really moved on . . . welp, we'll start planning the damn thing."

"I'm telling you, I'm fine."

"I'll believe it when I see it." Another pause. "Please, Hank. Mama's dyin' without you. Milly, she's always full of piss and vinegar, but she's been especially ornery since you left. Granted, I think that might have to do with Kingsley—"

"That fucking guy."

"No shit. But yeah, everyone's missing you something fierce. Not to mention the resort. It isn't the same without you, brother."

"Hogwash. I'm sure y'all are getting along just fine."

"You know that's not true. Come home."

I glance out at the mountain. Skiers and snowboarders are making their last runs of the day. I imagine Clyde is out there too, torturing some other poor shithead.

It hits me like a freight train, the certainty that I'm done here.

I'm done with my retirement bender.

Still, I'm not entirely sure if I have a place to land anymore. Can I go back to Blue Mountain and look my brother in the eye and tell him I'm okay?

Do I believe that? If I don't, how the hell do I get Samuel to? I'm not gonna hold up his wedding. I've done too much damage as it is. I thought I was fixing it by leaving North Carolina. But now I see that to fix it, to really make things right, I have to go back home.

Samuel and I say our goodbyes. After we hang up, I scroll through my contacts, slowing when I reach C.

Stevie Carter.

She's on the other side of a thumb tap. It's that simple. But I still hesitate, the pad of my thumb hovering over her number.

I'm not sure if I'll need to fake it—fake that I've moved on. I've felt so different lately about a lot of things.

Regardless, I need to convince Samuel I'm fine with him and Emma spending forever together.

Maybe I need to convince myself too. And hell, another weekend of hot sex sounds pretty sweet. So does having someone to take care of. Stevie kept my hands busy.

I like being busy.

So I hit her number and pray like hell she doesn't hate me for what I'm about to ask.

Chapter Seven

STEVIE

I look up from a roll of blueprints at the sound of my ringtone.

My brow furrows, and my heart skips when I see none other than Hank Beauregard's name lighting up the phone screen.

My first thought is *oh God, I hope he's not calling to tell me he gave me an STI.*

My second thought is *oh God, I hope he wants to have phone sex.*

I pick up the phone, glancing around the office. It's a little after five o'clock, and the place is still bustling. As proud as I am of the fact I oversee a team of ten (!) full-time employees, I kinda wish I had the place to myself right now.

I bite my lip. Even from how many thousands of miles away, Hank still has the power to turn me into a total lady perv. Good thing too. Since Vegas, I haven't been tempted to even call my regulars, much less see them. I was beginning to worry my sex drive had shriveled up and died.

"Hello?"

"If it isn't blackjack babe. Hi, Stevie."

My nipples pebble at the gravelly timbre of his voice. "Hi, Hank."

"I was calling to have a little cocktail hour with you over the phone. I've got my tallboy can of your namesake brew right here. You got a few minutes to spare?"

"For you?" I get up and move through my office door, heading to the taps that line the far wall of Lady Luck's workspace. Our brewhouse is downstairs, so I had keg lines run up another floor. It's a perk my employees and I very much enjoy. "Always."

Tucking my phone between my ear and shoulder, I pour myself a Blackjack Babe. "Where are you these days?"

"Aspen. It sucks. What about you?"

"Aspen sucks? That's a bummer." Ria, my assistant, looks up from her screen and catches my eye. She gives me a thumbs-up, eyebrows raised. *All set for the day?*

I tilt the phone away from my mouth. "All set—amazing work on this week's newsletter. Now get out of here and go celebrate your anniversary. Tell Nico I said hi!"

"Assistant?" Hank asks as I breeze back into my office, closing the door behind me.

"How'd you know?"

"I have one too. Or had. Maybe I still have him. I don't know."

"Should I ask what you mean by that?"

"Actually, I wanted to ask you a question. A bizarre, batshit crazy, probably immoral question."

"Ooooh, that sounds fun." I set my beer on my desk and roll up the sleeves of my chambray top. "Tell me more."

"First, you gotta tell me how you've been."

My stomach does a neat little backflip. This is why Hank made such an impression a couple of weeks back. Sure, he was sexy as hell. But he also gave a shit. He was *interested*. He got how important my company is to me and never once talked about my work or my passion for it condescendingly.

Unlike some men who used to be in my life.

"Pretty good, actually. I was just looking at plans for our new brewery. My finance team and I wooed a big investor last year, and we got the green light on the construction of our new space. Twenty-four-thousand square feet of brewhouse bliss. We break ground in three weeks."

"Holy shit, Stevie, that's awesome. Cheers to your success. I'm not at all surprised."

"Thanks. And cheers from afar." I sip my beer and remember the one I bought Hank at that bar on the casino floor. The beer tastes good now, but for some reason, I remember it tasting better then.

Probably because of the excellent company.

I've had a lot of beer in a lot of places over the years. And while I love the drink itself, I love how it brings people together even more. "The company you keep is just as important as the beer you drink" is Lady Luck Brewhouse's slogan for a reason.

"So, about this batshit question of yours," I say.

"Yep." I hear him gulp. "Sorry, just gathering the liquid courage to ask you. I'm warning you, it's a doozy."

"I'm a big girl. I can handle it."

"I hope you don't hate me."

"I don't think I could ever hate you. Not when you brought me coffee every morning."

For half a heartbeat, he hesitates. "It's a bit of a long story —hence the beer—but here's the gist of it: I want you to come up to my family's farm and pretend to be in love with me at my brother's engagement party. I have to convince him I don't have it bad for his fiancée anymore. He wants to marry her, but he won't start planning the wedding unless he knows I'm okay."

I nearly spit out my beer. What the actual hell?

"That is a doozy," I say. "I don't even know where to begin."

"Let's unpack the fake dating shit first. That's easiest."

"Okay." I take a long pull from my pint glass. "You really want to do that? With me? Like in *Bridgerton*?"

"You watch that show?" he asks, referencing the Netflix phenomenon based on a series of romance novels by Julia Quinn.

"*You* watch it?"

Our marketing intern, Paige, waves to me through the wall of glass that lines one side of my office. I wave back, making a mental note to look at the Facebook ad data she sent over earlier.

"Hey," he sniffs. "I happen to like costume drama. There are always tits involved. Lots and lots of tits."

I laugh. "And romance. And excellent writing."

"Well, yeah, that too. But the tits—man, they're the breast on television. I mean *best*. Best on television."

"Boobs on the brain?"

"Since I met you, yeah. Yours are kind of the best."

"Thank you. Anyone ever tell you that you have this half dorky, half dirty dad humor going on?"

"You're not the first."

I blow out a breath. "Wow. Okay. Not gonna lie, I'm intrigued, but I'm also . . . yeah, a little frightened. I know we're supposed to start with the *Bridgerton* stuff, but I have to know—what's the story between you and your brother? The one whose girlfriend you have feelings for. You told me a little bit about it in Vegas."

"It's my brother Samuel and his fiancée, Emma. What I didn't tell you was that I kissed her. In front of him. Knowing full well he was in love with her, and she was in love with him too."

My stomach drops. "Oh, Hank."

A pause. When he speaks, his voice is different. Rougher. "I wanted to hurt them, I guess. I was hurting too. It was a dark time for me."

There's a tug in my chest. I want to ask him about that time—what made it dark enough that someone so thoughtful and self-aware would do something so awful. Why he hurt, and if he's still hurting.

But one, that's none of my business. And two, I don't get personal.

So instead, I say, "I can't imagine. I'm sorry."

"No one is sorrier than I am." Another pause. "Anyway, it was stupid and wrong, and I was ashamed. Ashamed enough to leave Blue Mountain Farm to go on a bender."

"Wait, wait," I say, head throbbing as I try to keep up with all these bombshell revelations. "That little place you own in Asheville—it's Blue Mountain Farm?"

He clears his throat. "It is."

"Jesus Christ, Hank. That's not a 'little place.'"

"Well, it used to be. When I grew up there, it was the fuckin' sticks."

"It's not anymore."

"That, it is not," he says, a little sheepishly.

I fall back in my chair and stare at the ceiling. Not only is this guy famous, gorgeous, and generous; he also owns the South's premier five-star resort. That place has a cult following thanks to its luxurious accommodations, incredible food, and impeccable service.

Wow.

Just . . . *wow.*

Granted, I probably could've discovered this nugget of info if I'd googled Hank. I was tempted to look him up after our fling, but because I don't blur lines—not anymore—I decided to let what happened in Vegas stay in Vegas.

I kinda regret that now.

"I'm a big fan," I manage, blinking. "I've never been to Blue Mountain, but the resort is mentioned a lot in the hospitality scene. Y'all are the best of the best—I've had several friends stay at the farm, and they all rave about it."

"I'm the best of the best in bed too, right?"

I'm laughing again, even as my mind continues to spin. "I'd give you five stars there too, yeah."

"I need you to know what you're getting into," he says, his tone suddenly serious. "What the rest of my story is, I mean."

I should stop him right there. This is veering into dangerous territory. But before I can open my mouth, he plows ahead.

"I retired from the pros almost three years ago, and I never really got a break between playing ball and working at the resort. Needless to say, I got burned out, so after that shit went down with my brother and his girl, Rhett and I decided to jet off to the Caribbean. Officially we called it my 'retirement tour,' but it was also . . . yeah, it was a much-needed escape from a horrible situation. Granted, it was a situation I one hundred percent got myself into. It's not my family that was horrible, or my job—it was the whole love triangle thing with Samuel and Emma. I had to get out of there, away from the farm. Now, though, I'm ready to go back. I *have* to go back. That's where you come in, Daphne."

I blink again at the *Bridgerton* reference.

"If you want to hang up on me, I wouldn't blame you. It was a piece of shit thing to do, going after my brother's girl, and it's kind of a shitty thing I'm asking of you now too."

I shake my head. "I'm not going to hang up on you."

"Thanks."

"I'm sure you had your reasons for what you did. You were clearly very, very hurt if you had to leave your family for, what, how long?" I cringe as the question leaves my mouth.

The information it would require him to reveal is too personal. Too private.

"Nine months and seventeen days."

Yet I *still* can't help asking, "You know it down to the day, huh?"

"I'm tight with my family. Or I used to be, anyway. And I did have my reasons. Samuel—he's really great, but he and Emma, they weren't exactly honest with me when they, you know, fell in love. They had their reasons too, though."

A beat of silence. The hurt and the history that fills it from his side of the phone practically vibrates between us.

"So," I say, finally having the presence of mind to veer the conversation back to *Bridgerton*, "you need a fake girlfriend."

"Something like that. Yeah." Another pause. "You haven't hung up on me yet."

"I haven't."

"Daphne, dear," Hank says in a terrible British accent, "do I dare hope you're considering my scandalous proposal?"

Am I considering this?

Why wouldn't I? It'd be a weekend of great sex with a great guy at an incredible resort.

And yeah, now that I know the place Hank owns is Blue Mountain Farm, it could be an excellent opportunity to introduce Lady Luck to the powers that be there. He did offer to put together a tasting for me.

My heart thumps. It'd be a big fucking deal if Lady Luck got on Blue Mountain's menu. The farm's restaurant, The Barn Door, is a mecca for foodies across the south; it doesn't get much more prestigious than that.

"You're quite the devil, Hastings."

"You haven't the slightest idea, darling."

I shake my mouse, bringing my computer back to life. "These fake relationship situations—both parties get something out of it."

I hear the smile in his voice when he replies, "Of course."

"I want to set up that tasting you mentioned. I'll bring the beer, and you bring the suits."

He laughs. "We don't wear suits on Blue Mountain."

"The boots, then."

"That, I can do. The engagement party is on Saturday night. I'll try to schedule the tasting Friday night or earlier Saturday."

A big ass smile is working its way across my face as I pull up my calendar. "Works for me."

"By the way, I want to make something crystal clear." His tone is serious again. "This is not an exchange of sex for business favors. We don't have to have sex if you don't want to—I haven't brought it up for a reason. Hell, we don't even need to do this fake relationship thing. You're welcome to come up to the farm anytime to pitch Lady Luck. Seriously, just tell me to fuck off—"

"I'm going to stop you right there. You're right. This is absolutely not that kind of exchange. This is two *consenting* people helping each other out and possibly having a good time doing it. You hopefully make your family happy, and I hopefully land a spot on a new menu. If sex happens along the way? Great. And because we have really great sex together, I want to have a lot of it when I see you. Like, a lot. I've hit a bit of a dry patch, so . . ."

"Fuck," he says.

"What?"

"You just gave me a chubby."

My smile hurts. "I want a dozen orgasms. At least."

"Done. At least a dozen orgasms, courtesy of a famous football player."

"You're famous?"

"Oral in the shower," he continues crisply. "The best food and wine the South has to offer. The best accommodations on the farm. More oral and orgasms. Iced almond milk lattes every morning and whiskey by the fire every evening. Did I mention I'd be eating your pussy every chance I get?"

Heat, heady and delicious, settles between my legs and in my cheeks. I put a hand on my forehead and lower my head, lest my employees catch a glimpse of me all hot and bothered.

I love what a dirty talker Hank can be.

Not gonna lie. This whole fake relationship thing might turn out to be a lot of fun.

"How long would you need me? And when?"

"Party is February thirteenth. So, that weekend? Friday through Sunday?"

"Valentine's Day weekend, huh?"

"My brother and his fiancée are romantics. What can I say? Plus, it gives us a good explanation as to why we're getting together."

"Because we want to celebrate the day of love together."

"Exactly."

Lifting my head, I pull up my calendar and quickly scan what I've got going on. Luckily I keep my weekends open as a rule, so I'm free.

"That Monday is a holiday," I say. "Would you like me to stay then too?"

"We have an extra day to bone? I mean bond? Like the grossly in love couple we'll pretend to be? Uh, *yeah*, I'd like you to stay."

I tuck my phone between my ear and shoulder and enter the dates on my calendar. "Will we be just in love, or are we engaged, or did we have a shotgun wedding in Vegas . . .?"

"Meh. In plain old love sound good to you?"

"Not the real thing, no. But the *Bridgerton* version, sure. Besides, I have exactly zero interest in getting married again, pretend or otherwise."

"Should I ask what you mean by that?"

"Nope."

"All right." I hear him take a breath. "Is that a yes?"

I shake my head again, even though I've already blocked off the weekend. I do feel for Hank; unrequited love is not a fun place to be. I haven't asked him if he's over Emma, but does it really matter? My heart's been closed for business since Dan and I split, so I'm not worried about catching feelings other than arousal and appreciation for Hank. Now it's just a matter of getting my ducks in a row before the time away. Speaking of—I need to draft an email to Ria with details on everything I'll need for the tasting.

Really, I have nothing to lose here.

"I believe it is."

"Great. I'll get a jet lined up. And if you're cool sharing your address—totally cool if not too—I'll send a car to pick you up and take you to the airport."

"A jet?" I ask, pulse skipping.

"You're with me, so you fly private."

"I'm fine flying the normal, non-famous way."

"I'm not. Private jet. Got it?"

"Your snobbery is insufferable."

"Is this role play thing already turning you on? Because I've got a full-on woody now."

I shake my head and sigh. "You and your rakish ways. I'll see you in two weeks."

"Ten days, madam. It's only ten days."

Chapter Eight

STEVIE

"You'd better snap a pic and Instagram that shit. If your private jet isn't on your feed, did the flight even happen?"

Settling into my comfy seat, I accept a glass of champagne and a tray of artfully arranged fruit from the flight attendant. "Maybe I'll get a picture of my beers on board. Could be good for Lady Luck's feed?"

"Yes!" Kate gasps. "And the hashtag could be high roller! I love it."

"Hashtag FancyAF."

"Hashtag, I can't believe you're really doing this."

I pop a chocolate-covered strawberry into my mouth. "Hey. You promised not to judge."

"Girl, I'm not judging. I'm jealous as hell. You hear that?" There's a scream in the background. "My toddlers—yes, both of them—are teething. The baby is going through a sleep regression, and the dog has some horrible anal parasite thing that's just—well, I'll spare you the details. To top it all off, Jane is out of town all weekend at some genius surgeon conference. So while you're flying to a five-star resort to fuck a famous dude, I'll be here trying to keep my kids from swimming in the toilet. Yes, that's happened, and yes, there was shit involved. Literal shit."

"Domesticity is just as magical as they said it would be, isn't it?"

"Ugh."

"There's a reason marriage and me don't mix."

"I want a do-over. Actually, I just want to be you. Have hotel sex and sleep in for me, okay?"

I sip my champagne. "I will. Good luck."

"And hey—if something goes wrong, I can be in Asheville in two hours, three tops."

"Kate, the drive takes four."

"Not in my minivan, it doesn't."

"Just don't drive that minivan off a bridge, okay?"

"I have three children under the age of four. I make no promises. Have fun. And be safe. And be sure to keep me updated. I want details. I may be married, but I'm not dead."

I already read the itinerary for the weekend Hank sent over a few days ago. But I pull up the email on my phone anyway and read it again, sparks of anticipation darting up my spine as I scan the now-familiar schedule of events.

Friday 2/12: 4:47 PM flight arrives in Asheville. Airport pickup provided. 6:30 PM: Sunday Supper at Samuel's house (family will be in attendance)(and no, I did not fuck up the days . . . we usually have Sunday supper as a family every week, but because of the engagement party, we bumped it to Friday)

Saturday 2/13: 8 AM morning sex (if you're in the mood). 9 AM.: Coffee in bed. 12 PM: Lady Luck Brewhouse Tasting at Stag Pavilion with Beau, CEO of Blue Mountain Farm Incorporated; Samuel Beauregard, Director of the farm's Food Program; and Emma Crawford, Director of our Wine & Beverage Program. 7 PM: Samuel + Emma's engagement party in The Library, Main House.

Sunday 2/14: 8 AM morning sex (please be in the mood). 9 AM:

Coffee in bed 11 AM: Brunch with the family (maybe) Afternoon: Free. Ever been to the Biltmore?

Monday 2/15: 12:15 PM flight departs from Asheville.

Grinning, I tuck my phone into my bag and look out the window. It's what I end up doing for the rest of the forty-five-minute flight, my mind wandering. I'm excited. And tired, the way I always am on Friday evenings.

And turned on.

When my marriage fell apart, part of me wondered if my sex life was dead for good. I was still sensitive to the horribly sexist, completely ageist cultural messaging that women in their late thirties—especially curvy women—are pitiful, not sexy. A few well-intentioned but ignorant acquaintances even counseled me to stay with my ex. I could read between the lines; they didn't think I'd find someone better.

Someone who could make me happy and who could make me come to boot. Because clearly, that was too much to ask.

Lots of therapy and life experience later, I'm happy to report they were wrong. Not only have I had the best sex of my life over the past three years, my recent dry spell notwithstanding; sipping my champagne, I know I'm having the time of my life too.

Don't get me wrong, being single isn't all rainbows and unicorns. I've had to kiss many frogs and endure a lot of heinous dates with Bumble matches to get where I am now. I also had to endure the special hell of an extended separation. I was ready to sign the divorce papers a year in, but Dan made me wait for two more. It was awful. Also awful? The fact that I'm sure there will be more dates with more frogs in the future. I get lonely and frustrated sometimes. But it's no accident that my career and my orgasm count took off after my marriage ended.

I land in Asheville just as the sun is setting. The trees that cover the sweep of mountaintops are mostly bare, but the thin winter light coats everything in this pink-purple glow that takes my breath away. The sky here is huge, fading to dark blue at the edges.

It's epic and sexy, and it's perfect for the place Hank Beauregard calls home.

An Escalade with Blue Mountain Farm's insignia is waiting for me on the tarmac (flying private has even more perks than I thought). I'm whisked twenty minutes outside of town to the entrance of the resort. The driver is a cute young guy who fills me in on the things we pass.

My eyes are glued to the windows as we head through the main gate. Gas lamps flicker from stone pillars, licks of light against the growing darkness. We emerge from a copse of trees, and I almost gasp when the resort comes into view. Several buildings dot the hill ahead: an enormous blue barn, a stable, a giant cedar shake house with wide porches. We pass a creek and a large, neat garden. A few adorable stone cottages with cedar shake roofs.

The grounds are immaculate with neatly mowed expansive lawns. The towering trees are eerily beautiful in their bare winter state. A garden stretches as far as the eye can see to our right, bisected by straight lines of something leafy and green. Kale, maybe?

The car keeps going. Past the sign that says *Main House Stay Right*. Past a handful of riders on gleaming chestnut horses. More cottages and a large guesthouse with white shutters and an arbor covered in naked vines I imagine bloom into something beautiful and fragrant in the summer.

We finally turn onto a gravel drive marked *Private*.

More gas lamps.

More trees.

A house materializes from the darkness, and my heart stops. It's gorgeous, big without being obnoxious. Same stone, cedar shake, and white shutters I saw before, but different, somehow. More custom, perhaps, with sweeping rooflines and an almost Cape Cod vibe. Ivy creeps up the wall beside the massive front doors, and the windows glow warmly.

My hand shakes when I reach for my bag. I'm here, and I really am doing this.

I dig my phone out of the front pocket and quickly check my texts and calls. My door opens, and I startle at the sudden sound.

"Hey, honey," a voice says, and I turn to see Hank, his handsome face creased in a very convincing smile.

He's wearing a blue-and-white check button-up and jeans, and oh my God, did he get hotter since Vegas, or did he get hotter since Vegas?

"Hi," I breathe. "Hey."

Hank holds out his hand. I take it and climb out of the car, wobbling a little in my heels on the gravel. I didn't wear anything too aggressive—just some suede booties—but even so, I can't seem to find my balance.

Ever the excellent fake boyfriend, Hank puts a hand on my hip to steady me.

"How much did you drink on the flight?"

I grin, reveling in the way my entire body ignites at his touch. "Just a glass of bubbly. Although I definitely wanted more."

"I did send the good stuff."

"Are you always so thoughtful?"

His eyes—something about them changes. They get softer. "When my girl is involved? Absolutely."

I glance at the driver, who's busy unloading my suitcase from the trunk and bringing it inside the house. Hank and I have already come to the unspoken agreement that our *Bridgerton* ploy begins now. And damn, is he already good at it.

I won't be beat.

Putting a hand on Hank's chest, I tilt my head up for a kiss. "It's so good to see you, baby."

"Very good," he replies, curling an arm around my waist and pulling me against him. He's hard. He rolls his pelvis into mine. The heaviness between my legs flares to new life, the air around us crackling with electricity as Hank leans down and presses his lips to mine.

My toes curl inside my boots. The kiss is familiar and fiery, our mouths moving in expert tandem.

"Inside. Now," he growls. Then he holds out a hand to the driver, who's just emerging from the front door. "Christopher, thank you for your help tonight. You did an excellent job transporting some very precious cargo. I'll see you in the morning."

Christopher takes his hand and gives it a good shake, smiling at Hank's praise. "My pleasure, Mr. Beauregard."

"C'mon, just because I was gone for ten months doesn't mean we're strangers again. You can still call me Hank."

"Right. I wasn't sure if you were a guest, or my boss . . ."

Hank laughs, even though I see something unpleasant flicker across his face. "These days, who knows? Either way, let's stick with Hank. Mr. Beauregard is my oldest brother."

"Got it." Christopher ducks his head in my direction. "Good evening, Miss Carter. Hank."

"I can already tell the service at this place is insanely great," I say to Hank as we climb the front steps.

Hank opens the font door wider, allowing me to enter first. "Of course it is. I literally wrote the handbook on guest relations last year. We had a few bumps implementing it, but overall, I'm pretty damn proud of the staff."

The first thing I notice when I step inside the house is how immaculate it is. It's an open floor plan, with the entrance hall leading directly into a soaring living area. I can see a little of everything: the furniture, the art, the drapes, all of it done in pristine shades of white, gray, and slate blue.

It's beautiful. No doubt the cushy sofas and silk rugs cost a fortune. Same as the designer who probably selected them for Hank. And while the rooms are magazine-worthy, there's also something . . . a little sterile about them? A fire crackles in the fireplace in the center of the room, but the structure itself is unblemished, no fire-darkened stone or bed of ashes from previous fires; the hammered brass fireplace tools don't bear a single mark. The pillows on the sofa are perfectly placed and expertly fluffed, while the marble-topped coffee table gleams in the light of the fire, not a single scratch or speck of dust marring its surface.

It doesn't look like someone actually *lives* here. Then again, Hank has been gone for almost a year, so that makes sense.

Still, questions bloom inside my head. Has he always lived alone? Why have this big house for just one guy? Hank may be cocky, and he may like nice things. But he doesn't strike me as super flashy, the kind of man who'd have a big house just to have a big house.

There's a reason behind it. One I don't want to think too hard about, so I don't.

Hank shuts the front door, and I turn around to see heat in his eyes. The same heat I feel all over. A beat of silence throbs between us as we drink each other in.

"I'm baby?" he asks with a smirk, making his dimple pop. The backs of my knees tingle, a happy, sudden rush.

I drop my tote bag on the floor. "If I'm honey."

"You gonna share that honey with me?"

"Is that the gross euphemism I think it is?"

"Two minutes into the weekend, and already you got my mind in the gutter."

We lunge for each other at the same time, our bodies

colliding in a tangle of limbs and mouths and hunger. I'm grabbing his fly and unzipping his jeans. He's gliding one hand up my shirt and the other down my pants. His fingers slip inside my panties and find my slit. He glides them inside, a smooth, confident motion that ignites a fire inside my skin.

"*Fuck*." He breaks the kiss, leaning his forehead against mine as he pulls out his fingers and looks down at them. They glisten. "You're soaked."

"Been this way since I woke up."

"Why the hell didn't you tell me?"

I meet his eyes. "Could you do something about it in front of Christopher?"

"Watch yourself, honey, or I'll fuck that smart mouth of yours."

"Sounds lovely," I say with a grin.

Hank pulls down my pants and underwear and roughly spins me round. He gathers my ass cheek in his hand and gives it a hard, quick squeeze, making me yelp and yearn all at once.

"Bend over," he grinds out. "Hands on the table."

I do as he tells me, gripping the edge of the beautifully weathered antique console set against the wall. A foil packet rips. Hank curses again. Then his hands are on my ass, and he's spreading my cheeks, and I feel the pressure of his broad crown against my entrance.

Firming his grip on my body, he buries himself inside me with one hard, almost brutal thrust. I cry out. His hips hammer again and again, fingers curled into my ass, holding me in place.

I turn my head and watch our reflections in the window beside the door. Hank's jeans are pooled around his ankles. My shirt is hiked up my back, and my tits hang heavy and full, bouncing with every punishing thrust.

Hank reaches around and runs the pads of his first two

fingers over my clit. He uses that hand to hold me even tighter against him as he plays with me. I feel simultaneously trapped and safe, expertly handled and wildly at risk, like the train we're on is about to blow off the tracks and flatten us both.

I want to come, and I don't. I want to make this last forever.

The throbbing in my clit coils tighter, and it's my turn to curse, head falling back. My knees are jelly now, but Hank holds me up, hand firmly on my hip, fingers of the other hand still between my legs. The table bangs against the wall, but Hank doesn't seem to mind. I roll onto the balls of my feet to meet his thrusts, arching my back to swallow him deeper. To feel more of him.

Hank responds by reaching inside my shirt and cupping my breast, swiping his thumb over my nipple through the silky fabric of my bra. Sensation bolts from the pebbled tip straight to my clit.

"Come for me," he rasps. "I've been waiting for this all fucking week. C'mon, honey, give it to me. I wanna feel you lose your mind."

He folds his body over mine, and I turn my head to meet his eyes, and he captures my mouth in a searing kiss I didn't know I needed.

I come.

I clamp down on his dick and catch his bottom lip between my teeth. Waves of release pound through me, drawing the muscles along my sides and legs taut. I close my eyes, and there are those earth-shatteringly beautiful colors again, the same ones I saw in Hank's bed back in Vegas. They're so bright and real they burn my eyes.

My orgasm keeps rising up to meet me, Hank's body moving over mine as I try to catch my breath. I reach back and dig my fingernails into his thigh, holding on, and he fucks me harder.

God, I've needed this. The release. The feeling of being turned inside out, my head and heart emptied of anything but pure, obliterating sensation.

Hank is that good.

He comes with a roar. A literal roar that makes me jump. But before I can move an inch, Hank is curling his arms around me, his front glued to my back, surrounding me with his heat and his heartbeat. It drums a quick rhythm against my back, an echo of my own frenzied pulse.

He breathes heavy and deep, his nose buried in the nape of my neck. His breath is hot against my skin. He smells like that woodsy cologne that fits him just right.

We stay like that for a minute, then another, both of us heaving.

His warmth and his want are soaking through my clothes into my skin.

I shift, making our contact a little less intense, and glance at our reflection in the window again. I watch Hank turn his head and glance too.

We look like something out of a bad porno. Pants at our ankles, Hank still inside me. My hair falls over my face in a disheveled curtain. His mouth is open, and his chest rises and falls sharply, and we've definitely left some marks on the wall.

My shoulders shake, laughter rising through my chest. If I don't laugh, I might do something else. Something embarrassing and stupid.

After a beat, Hank lets out a bark of laughter too.

"What is *wrong* with us?" I manage.

Hank lets out a long, low breath and shakes his head. He reaches down and pulls out of me slowly, resting his latex-covered dick on the curve of my ass.

"I dunno. You turn me into a rabid animal, and I ain't mad at it."

I straighten, giving my legs a wiggle to make sure they still work. I'm about to reach for my pants, but Hank beats me to it, his knees cracking in a now-familiar way as he bends down and hikes my jeans up my legs, stopping to kiss my right thigh along the way.

I tear my gaze from him. I feel hollowed out and hungry. For food this time. A drink, too, would be nice.

"Post-coital cocktail?" Hank asks, reading my mind. He zips up his jeans. "I made a batch of whiskey sours if you like brown liquor. If not, I've got—"

"Whiskey's the only cocktail that feels right after *that* kind of sex."

His face creases in a bright, handsome smile. "Agreed."

Chapter Nine

HANK

"How can I help?"

I wave Stevie's question away, then raise my chin at one of the chairs by the fire.

"All good over here. Go sit. You just came a long way to help me out. The least I can do is pour you a drink."

Stevie blinks, a bewildered look on her face. What's taking her off guard? The whiskey? How we just fucked in my foyer because we can't keep our hands off each other for a single goddamn second?

To be fair, my hands aren't exactly steady either as I pour my homemade whiskey sours into heavy-bottomed crystal tumblers. I spill a little on the floor and scramble to remember where my housekeeper put the kitchen towels.

Christ, I hate feeling like I'm a stranger in my own damn house.

"Thanks," Stevie says when I hand her a glass and settle into the chair beside hers. I try not to stare as she sips. She's always beautiful. But in the flickering light of the fire, her eyes are liquid pools of black, and her hair is gilded with licks of copper. There's a pink mark by that freckle on her neck where I sucked on her skin. Not quite a hickey, but definitely visible.

She's fucking stunning.

Looking at her, I could almost forget the shitty reason I brought her here.

"What?" she asks, catching my gaze. She's grinning.

"You know what. You're gorgeous. I'm glad you came." I hold out my glass. "Thank you."

She taps her glass to mine. I notice her fingernails are painted white this time. "Thank you for this delicious cocktail. And for the private jet. *And* for the five-star accommodations." Her eyes flick to the room around us.

"No gratitude for the dick?"

She trails her tongue along her bottom lip. "Your dick just got the appreciation it deserves and then some."

"There's that smart mouth."

Her eyes dance. "Maybe I'll let you fuck it later."

My dick twitches. I'm ready to go again?

That's gotta be a record.

"Listen," I say, adjusting my fly. "As much as I wanna talk dirty with you right now, I think we should discuss the weekend before, uh, things get out of hand for the second time in ten minutes."

Her eyebrows pop up, and she scoots back in her chair, sitting a little taller. "Let's. Is it weird that I'm excited? Because I actually think this could be fun."

Phew. Her enthusiasm makes me feel slightly less like a douche for asking her to play this game.

"Honey, I'm gonna try my damndest to make it as fun as possible for you. We should have a story, right? Something we agree on?"

Stevie sips her cocktail and licks her lips, nodding. "Yes. But I think it's best if we stick as closely to the truth as possible. That way, we have fewer"—she winds her wrist as she tries to think of the right word—"inventions to keep track of. Plus, we can really engage with our story then. Let's just say our meet-cute went down exactly the way it did."

"At a blackjack table in Vegas, when you won me a grand by showing me how to split aces and eights."

"I *am* a solid teacher."

"Damn right, you are. So you showed me the ropes. I bought you a drink."

"I bought *you* a drink."

I remember how her purse was so stuffed with chips they were falling out of it. *No, you can't buy me a drink, but I'll buy you one.*

Goddamn, is she a pistol. And goddamn, do I like it.

"The second I tasted your beer, I knew I was in trouble. Then we had fun at a club, and *then* we—"

"Had coffee." Stevie smiles, her teeth gleaming in the firelight. "Lots and lots of mind-blowing coffee."

"I'm sure my family will buy that."

"Does Rhett know?" Stevie arches a brow. "About us pretending to date? Obviously, he was there in Vegas, and I know y'all traveled together afterward. Won't he know something's fishy?"

I shake my head. "The second his team's season ended, Rhett was balls deep in either a bottle or a blonde. He was often in both at the same time, and he's played that game ever since. I don't think he knows what day it is, much less who I'm seeing. But just in case, I told him I didn't say anything about you because I didn't want to jinx it. Our relationship. It was new and exciting, and I wanted to see how it panned out before I clued anyone in. He seemed to buy it."

"Good." Stevie nods, sipping. "So we've seen each other since Vegas."

"You came to visit me in Aspen before Rhett arrived."

"And you came to visit me in Nashville right after."

Sounds plausible enough. After I spoke to Samuel, Rhett returned to Vegas the next day while I hung out in Aspen for a few more days before flying back to North Carolina.

"We talk constantly." I hold up my phone. "We haven't known each other long, but our connection is special."

"Right. What have we bonded over?"

"Besides coffee? And your amazing ass?"

Stevie catches the tip of her tongue between her teeth, her eyes sparkling. "Thank you. I happen to like your ass too."

"Good. I work fucking hard on it."

"I say we also share a love for hospitality. Treating our people to a good time."

My heart twists. I ignore it. Just like I'm trying to ignore how nice it feels to have someone over at my house. Been an age since I've had company. "Yes. I also like how you know your shit. Blackjack, beer, business . . . you're really, really great at all of that, and it turns me on."

Her smile softens. "Really?"

"Yeah, really. Why? Guys don't usually think your prowess is incredibly, ridiculously sexy?"

She looks away. Looks down at her drink, which she lifts off her palm with her fingertips. "Not always, no."

Now there's a nudge in my chest. I want to know more. I want to know Stevie's real story. Is her ex one of those prickless, spineless assholes who's threatened by a powerful woman?

But she hasn't been forthcoming with that information, and it's not my place to pry.

Besides, the last thing I need is to get personal. Because once that happens, it's a slippery slope, and I'm not about to get in deep with yet another woman who doesn't want what I do.

Granted, I don't know what Stevie wants, exactly. But

she's made it pretty clear she's not interested in something serious. I'm not either—at the moment. Eventually, though, I would like to start that family of my own, if I can ever figure out how to do it.

"You're down to earth, but adventurous too," I say.

That makes her look back up. "And you're sweet. Thoughtful."

"Your favorite drink is beer. Obviously."

"And yours is . . ."

"Blackjack Babe Hefeweizen. But if that's not available, I like my whiskey." I hold up my glass.

"You like to play guitar. If you hauled that thing around the world with you, I imagine you must really like music. Do you write your own?"

"I used to, but not anymore. I'll still play for you, though."

"Of course you will. Because you're a sweet, thoughtful boyfriend."

"When did we fall in love?"

Stevie considers this for a minute, pushing out her already generous lips. God, I want 'em around my cock. Girl sucks dick like a champ.

If I don't stop fantasizing about fucking Stevie's every orifice, I'm gonna give myself a raging case of blue balls. Which cannot happen, considering I'm about to have dinner with my family for the first time since I fled the farm in disgrace.

"It wasn't love at first sight," Stevie says. "But it did happen fast. At this point in my life, I know what I want. Hank, you're it."

Glancing at what's left of my whiskey, I grin. If we're going with truths . . .

"I also happen to like older women."

She scoffs. "Wait, for real?"

"Since I met you, yeah." And maybe that's why Aspen fell

so flat. All the girls there were . . . girls. Not women. Not like this woman, who knows her mind and isn't afraid to speak it.

"How old are you?"

"Just turned thirty."

"Damn. I'm a cougar who robs cradles." She lifts her eyebrows as she sips. "I kinda dig it."

"Whatever, it's only ten years. But yeah, if the age difference turns you on, then I dig it too. So we fell in love in . . . Nashville. Music City. We danced all day at Honky Tonks, split some hot chicken at Hattie's, and as we were washing it down with an ice-cold beer at your brewery, I fell for you. Hard."

Stevie's nodding again, her face glowing with a wide smile. "I like it. I like it a lot. Think your family will buy it?"

"Let's hope so."

Stevie crosses her legs. "Tell me about them."

This time it's my stomach that twists. As much as I'm excited to see my family again, I'm dreading what is sure to be an awkward conversation with Samuel and Emma.

"My family's great. You're gonna love 'em, same as they'll love you. There's Mama, who likes to be called June. Beau's the oldest. Then there's his wife, Annabel, and their baby girl, Maisie. Samuel's next up. You know all about him and Emma. I'm Beauregard number three, and Rhett is number four. My sister Milly is the baby. You'll know which one she is right away—she's fuckin' intense. She's Blue Mountain's event planner, so she'll be kept busy this weekend."

"There's a lot of y'all," Stevie says, blinking.

"You have no idea," I groan. "I apologize in advance for how loud it gets. Everyone's gonna be all up in our business, asking completely inappropriate questions, and I apologize for that too."

"That's all right. We have a good story to tell."

I run a hand over my jaw. "You have siblings?"

"I do." She sips the last of her cocktail. "A younger brother. We're close, but he lives in Charlotte with his wife and kids, so I don't get to see him as often as I'd like."

"Don't tell me your parents named him, like, David Bowie or something."

"Bon Jovi, actually."

I widen my eyes. "Seriously?"

Stevie cackles. "God, you're easy to fuck with. Of course my parents didn't name my brother Bon Jovi. His name is Philip."

"Right. So a brother named Philip and parents . . ."

"Who live in Knoxville, where I'm originally from. My dad is a professor at the University of Tennessee's medical school, and my mom stayed home to raise us. Peter and Jeannie."

"Peter and Jeannie. Have I met them?"

She nods. "You did, when you came to visit me. I was hesitant at first, but my mom said I wouldn't shut up about you, and you really wanted to meet them, so . . .we had dinner at their house. They adored you."

"Wow, I really do move fast."

"I'm your teacher, remember? And I taught you to trust your gut and go after what you want."

"Gotcha." I set my empty glass on the side table between our chairs and put my hands on my thighs, arms akimbo. "Anything else?"

Stevie shakes the ice in her glass, draining the last drop of whiskey sour. I smile. She clearly enjoyed the cocktail, but I think I'm enjoying *her* enjoyment even more.

"Just so we're clear"—she sets the glass down next to mine —"you don't expect me to wait on you or anything, do you? As your girlfriend?"

I make a face. "What? No, absolutely not. Why? Is that what you think a girlfriend should do?"

"I used to." She checks her watch. This time, it takes some real self-control not to keep digging. I'm getting the feeling her experience with men has been downright awful. "What about Samuel and Emma?"

"What about them?"

"How can I help you there? I know you've gotta be anxious to see them again after what went down. You want me to break the ice? Talk to them first, maybe under the guise of introducing myself or something?"

Glancing at my empty glass, I briefly contemplate pouring myself another cocktail before deciding it's a bad idea. I have to be on point tonight. Not only because I'll be seeing Samuel for the first time in nearly a year, but also because Stevie's already being a top-notch fake girlfriend. I want to return the favor.

I like her idea. Having a little moral support when I approach Samuel and Emma definitely won't hurt.

"I'll approach them first," I say. "Samuel will appreciate that. I'm the one who fucked up the worst, so I'm the one who needs to extend the olive branch. Just—if you wouldn't mind being with me when that happens, I'd appreciate it."

Grinning, Stevie extends her arm and curls her fingers over mine. Hers are cold from holding the cocktail, but I still feel a zip of warmth from the contact. "I'm your ride or die all weekend long. Just say the word, and I'll come to your rescue."

"What's our word?"

She bites her lip. "Blackjack."

"All right," I reply.

And you know what? For the first time in a *long* time, I almost do feel all right.

Chapter Ten

STEVIE

Grabbing my hand, Hank leads me up the front steps of Samuel's mansion.

Hank wasn't lying when he said his family was loud. I can already hear the voices and music from inside the massive house.

He pauses at the front door, taking a deep breath as he rolls back his shoulders.

I give his hand a quick squeeze. He glances at me, our eyes locking in the light of the gas lamp above our heads, and a shiver runs through me. It's cold outside, yeah, but his eyes —they're soft. Sweet.

It's kinda cute, how nervous he is.

"You got this, Hastings."

"Only because you're here, Daphne," he replies and opens the door.

The rich smell of roasting meat hits me the second I step inside. Voices rise from a distant room, and I duck my head to glance around the nearby wall. I'm so curious about Hank's family. On the walk over here, Hank told me his family is kind of a big deal in the football world—his dad and all of his brothers played pro football.

What are they like? How did they shape Hank into the man he is today?

And what led to him kissing his brother's girlfriend?

Fingers curl into the collar of my puffer coat, brushing against my neck.

"Lemme take this for you," Hank says from behind me.

My pulse skips a beat. I unzip my puffer and let him peel it off me, shivering again when the warm air inside the house meets with my skin.

Hank furrows his brow. "You cold?"

"No." I shake my head, drawing a quick breath through my nose. "Thank you."

He puts a hand on the small of my back. The gesture is simple but foreign, and I resist the urge to arch away from his touch.

It's not real. Which means I'm allowed to enjoy it without worrying about getting in over my head. That's the beauty of drawing boundaries: you always know where you stand.

"Ready?" he asks.

I nod. "Ready."

"It's not too late to back out."

I perk up at the sound of approaching footsteps. "Hate to tell you, but I think it is."

Rhett emerges from the hallway, his slightly red face lit up with a smile. He holds up his arms in greeting. "Y'all made it! Stevie, it's great to see you again. I had no idea you two were actually a thing. In Vegas, I'd assumed—"

"You were out of your mind in Vegas," Hank cuts him off. "How much wine have you had tonight, brother?"

Rhett looks at me and rolls his eyes. "Is he always this fun with you?"

"Hi, Rhett," I say, laughing, and he pulls me into a hug. "How've you been?"

He pulls back and shoves his hands in his pockets. "Meh. The season didn't end the way I wanted it to. But at least it ended. Here, y'all come on in. Samuel's got his roast goin', and Emma's pouring some ridiculous wine."

He leads us down a hallway to the kitchen.

The first thing I notice is how enormous it is. No joke, it might be bigger than my entire house back home. I've got a little bungalow, just over a thousand square feet, so it's not hard to beat.

Even so, this kitchen is a showstopper by any standard. Two marble-topped islands dominate the space, along with a fancy-looking range on the far wall. Another wall is lined with stainless steel refrigeration and freezer units. A wine column with a glass door glows from within, highlighting several magnums of what is no doubt some costly stuff.

The second thing I notice is the towering guy standing at the range. He's got a pair of tongs in his hand and a kitchen towel tossed over his shoulder. He's chatting with the other towering guy beside him, who's pouring maple syrup into a steaming pot of what appears to be mashed sweet potatoes. A woman—has to be Emma—is shoving her nose into a wineglass, while another woman with a toddler in her lap sips wine from her perch on a barstool at the island. I glimpse two others setting the table in the nearby dining room, both blondes, the clatter of dishes and clink of flatware just barely audible over the hearty, strangely familiar laughter of the big guy with the tongs.

My heart does a happy little leap. There are a lot of stereotypes out there about people with accents like ours. But it's obvious Hank's family is evolved. More than mine ever was, at least. You'd never, *ever* see my dad hanging out in the kitchen, much less making a meal there. The same goes for the rest of the men in my family. On holidays and at family gatherings, they'd be sitting in front of the TV while the women, me included, chopped and stirred and scrubbed, stopping only to refresh the men's cocktails or calm a screaming child.

It's heartening to see that script flipped. Of course, this is a special occasion; who knows what the Beauregards' lives look like on a daily basis? But it's cool to see a woman sit down for a change. It's cool to see everyone in the family helping out. No one seems frazzled or resentful, the way my mom and aunts always did while waiting on their husbands.

The way I waited on mine too.

The guy with the tongs turns around. My stomach flips. He's much bigger than Hank, with lighter eyes and a bushy, dark beard, but they share the same square jaw, straight nose, and full lips. And that laugh I heard—they share that too.

I can tell by the way he looks right at Hank, brow creasing ever so slightly, that this must be Samuel.

I can also tell by the way Hank goes stiff beside me. Lacing my fingers through his, I lean into him, making our arms brush. A silent reminder that he's not alone. I'm not interested in being Hank's real girlfriend, but that doesn't mean I can't be a good friend to him.

Lucky for me, being a good friend looks a lot like being a good fake date.

This time he's the one who gives my hand a squeeze. A silent thank you.

"Hey, y'all," Hank says, even though he's still looking at his brother. "Hey, Samuel."

All chatter and noise come to a sudden standstill. I can practically hear everyone holding their breaths as Samuel wipes his hands on his towel and drops it on the counter, moving toward us. "Hank! You made it. Welcome home."

"It's good to see you, Samuel. Thanks for having us."

Hank untangles his fingers from mine and goes in to hug Samuel. Hank is still stiff, and Samuel is still frowning a little, so the hug is awkward. But they hold it for a long beat, Samuel closing his eyes as he pounds Hank's back once, twice.

I can't help but feel a twinge of sympathy for each of them. I glance at Emma, who's set down her wineglass and is looking at the guys with a tired expression. There's still some hurt here. The kind that will probably take more than a long weekend to fix. But I'm glad I came to help in my own small way. There's something about seeing Hank like this, surrounded and scared but still showing up—

Nope. Not going there.

Hank steps back, and I step up. We move to slide our arms around each others' waists at the same time, Hank circling his hand around my side. He slips his pinkie finger in the back pocket of my jeans. Grinning, I glide my hand up his back, the starched fabric of his shirt sighing as I settle my palm on the ridge of his shoulder blade.

I sense the kitchen letting out the proverbial breath it proverbially didn't know it was holding.

"Samuel, I'd like to introduce you to my girlfriend, Stevie. Stevie, this is Samuel. He's the director of Blue Mountain's food program and one hell of a cook—hence the insanely good smells coming from those ovens over there."

"It's great to finally meet you," I say, holding out my hand. "Thanks for having us. Your home is beautiful."

Samuel takes my hand in the paw of his own. "Stevie. Welcome. We're so glad to have you. Here, let me introduce you to my fiancée, Emma." He glances over his shoulder and gives Emma a nod. She smiles and walks over to us. "Look, Emma, Stevie's real."

I laugh. "What, did you think Hank made me up or something?"

"I'm lame, but not *that* lame," Hank says, cutting me a

glance. He grins. I resist the urge to wink. Who knew having a shared secret could be this much fun?

Emma shakes my hand, then holds up her arms when she gets to Hank. "I'm really, really glad you're back, Hank. We've missed you like crazy."

"I've missed you guys. I'm glad to be home."

A prick of something that feels suspiciously like jealousy stings as I watch Hank wrap his arms around Emma. She's beautiful, a petite woman with an athletic build and dirty blond hair.

Whatever, I'm probably just biased. I'm on Hank's side, even though I don't know all the nitty-gritty details, and I'm feeling protective of him.

Interestingly, this hug isn't at all awkward. It's warm and appropriately timed, and when they release each other, I notice Hank blinks as he steps back, a pair of creases appearing between his eyebrows.

His mouth, though—that almost curves into a disbelieving smile.

"You all right?" I murmur when Emma turns back around to pour us some wine.

Hank gives my ass a playful pinch. "Yeah. I think I—"

"If it isn't my long lost brother." One of the blondes, the younger one, saunters in from the dining room. "Where have you been, and why the hell did you keep us waiting so long?"

"Milly!" Hank really smiles this time, tugging her into a tight hug. "Goddamn, I've missed you. And I made y'all wait to torture you, clearly. Or make y'all love me again. Like Daddy used to say, absence makes the heart grow fonder."

Milly pushes her brother back, arms locked on his shoulders. "Or it pisses everybody off. At least you had the decency to come back with this lovely lady. Stevie, I'm glad you're here, and I'm really glad you're not a stranger Hank met on the internet."

"Hey," Emma says from behind us. "Nothing wrong with strangers you meet on the internet."

Milly rolls her eyes, even as she grins. "Y'alls' story about being secret internet sex partners is not appropriate conversation for Sunday supper."

"Emma and Samuel were secret internet sex partners?" I ask, too stunned—too curious—to be polite and keep my mouth shut.

"Yup," Samuel replies proudly. "Like a much less wholesome Meg Ryan and Tom Hanks."

Milly lets out a bark of laughter. "Tom Hanks? You wish." She turns to me, her smile tightening as she extends a hand. "I'm Milly."

"Stevie," I say. "Lovely to meet you."

She studies my face with eyes that aren't exactly kind. My heart skips a beat. Glancing at Hank, I wonder if he's sensed it too—the fact that she seems to be suspicious.

But then Hank is slipping an arm around my waist and introducing me to his mom, June, and then to his oldest brother, Beau, and Beau's wife, Annabel.

"And my *goodness*, is this Miss Maisie?" Hank holds out his arms to the toddler. She smiles shyly at him. "Y'all, she's gotten so big! And look at all those teeth!"

It takes a second for her to warm up to him. Bel tells us the baby started getting leery around strangers when she turned one, but after a few minutes, Maisie finally allows her uncle to hold her.

"She's absolutely beautiful," I say, glancing at Beau. "How old is she?"

"Fifteen months," Hank answers, lifting her above his head when she lets him pick her up. "Baby girl is a Scorpio, just like me."

"Two troublemakers," June says with a smile, eyes meeting mine. "They keep you on your toes, don't they?"

"They do," I reply. "In the best possible way."

Hank airplanes Maisie around the kitchen, sound effects and everything, biceps rippling against the sleeves of his shirt. She smiles, giggling, the sound infectiously cute. Hank coos between telling her how much he's missed her and how bad he feels about not being at her birthday party.

I expect him to hand her back to Beau or Annabel. But instead he rests Maisie on his hip and quizzes her on her words. *Mama. Dada. More.* He tries to get her to say Hank, but she just buries her head in his chest and shakes her head. He kisses her chubby cheek, making a loud smacking noise, and Maisie giggles again.

Lord above, they're sweet together.

I don't know Hank all that well. But I have a pair of eyes, so I do know this: he wants what Annabel and Beau have. Hank has family man written all over him. I didn't see it until now, but the pieces are clicking together. The dad jokes. The big empty house, just waiting to be filled with babies.

It's not that I don't want a family or kids. But I realized early on in my marriage families require a huge amount of work—work that fell disproportionately to me.

I was the one always emptying the dishwasher and remembering to take the dog to the vet and having an answer to the dreaded six o'clock *what's for dinner* question. I was already drowning in my responsibilities as a wife; how much worse would it get if I became a mother?

Don't get me wrong, I admire family, and recognize its value. Some people, like Kate and Jane, and my brother and his wife, are able to find happiness being wives and husbands and mommies and daddies, and kudos to them for making it work.

I couldn't. And I know with bone-deep certainty I don't ever want to attempt it again.

Why, then, does my heart do this weird twisting thing

when I see Hank with his siblings? His mother? His niece? It's bewildering, maybe because it is so different from the way my family interacts. My parents definitely aren't tender with each other the way Annabel and Beau are. And while there's some tension here tonight, it doesn't hold a candle to the boiling resentment that seems to permeate my mom and dad's house back in Knoxville.

Samuel claps his hands. "Dinner's ready!" he shouts.

Hank helps Beau get Maisie set up in her high chair. It's quite the process, and involves a pink rubber bib, two sippy cups (one milk, one water), and a plastic spork that Maisie immediately chucks to the floor with glee.

"Hey," Hank says, coming to my side to put that hand on my back again. "Why don't you go inside and grab a seat? I'll make you a plate. Oh! And give you a wine refill too. Emma, you have more of that Zin, right?"

Emma smiles warmly at us. "I've got a bottle already decanted with your name on it. Stevie, go sit. I'll bring a fresh glass to you."

"Are y'all sure?" I eye the small army of people now gathered between the stove and sink, prepping and carving and rinsing. "I haven't lifted a finger since I arrived. Here, let me help."

Samuel looks up from the tenderloin. He points the carving fork at me. "Absolutely not. Hank's brought someone home with him for the first time in years, and we all gotta be on our best behavior in the hopes you'll stay. I haven't seen him smile this much since—"

"Fuckin' forever," Rhett finishes.

Beau, dangling a spoonful of sweet potato in front of Maisie, shoots eye daggers at Rhett. "I swear to God, Rhett, I'll s-t-a-b you if she repeats that word."

Rhett has the grace to look sheepish. "Sorry. I'm the d-u-m-b-a-s-s who forgot there was a baby here."

"You and your heathen bachelor ways." Shaking her head, June gives a big bowl of kale salad one last toss. "Have a glass of water, son. Trust me when I say you need it."

Milly knocks back her wine, then reaches for a tray of cornbread. "Honestly, it'll be a miracle if Stevie stays through this d-a-m-n dinner."

"You know Maisie's going to show up to preschool spelling all these words for the other kids, right?" Annabel says with a smile.

"F-u-c-k," Beau mutters.

I laugh. And then I go take my seat at not-Sunday supper.

Chapter Eleven

HANK

Holy shit, I'm not in love with Emma anymore.

Glancing at her across the table, the certainty of it settles in my center like a warm, solid weight.

Makes me almost feel giddy.

Stevie did say to trust my gut. And my gut is telling me I'm finally a free man.

I waited for desire to hit me when I saw Emma for the first time in nearly a year.

I waited for it to hit me when I took her in my arms, the scent of her perfume filling my head.

But it never came.

I felt nothing.

Wait, that's not true. I felt a tiny ache somewhere behind my heart. It's longing, that much I know, but it's not longing for Emma. Not anymore.

On the heels of that ache came relief so sweet it left me feeling kinda dizzy. Stevie had looked at me weird, like I was about to pass out or something. Even though I was fine, it was nice to know she was there, her grip firm on my back. Cool to have someone check in on me like that.

I grab my fork in one hand and Stevie's thigh with the other. She's luscious here, soft, and I give her a long, hard squeeze. Her fork pauses midair, a rare piece of meat speared on the tines. She gives me a small smile, dark eyes flashing, and makes a little show out of gliding the fork in her mouth, then gliding it back out.

"I see that." I move my hand up her leg so that my pinkie is resting against the seam of her jeans. Right where I want her.

"You're supposed to," she murmurs. "You're gonna get me in trouble with your family, touching me like that."

A voice in my head says I'm the one in trouble, but it's easy to ignore when Stevie starts playing footsie with me underneath the table.

I wanna kiss her, lean in for a quick one, but I don't. I tell myself it's because I don't want to lay it on too thick. We don't want to be pawing each other like lovesick teenagers. But I'm having a real hard time keeping my hands and mouth off this girl.

I don't know what happened between *oh shit, I have it bad for my brother's girlfriend* and *I'm free.* The tension between Samuel and me is definitely still alive, but I wonder if meeting Stevie has anything to do with how much better I'm feeling now.

Over the course of my bender, I could sense it—the pining and the hurt slowly fading, visiting me less the more time that passed. I had plenty of distractions, and I indulged in them constantly, losing myself in the moment so I didn't compulsively revisit the past and the girl who was always in my head but never by my side.

I'd go a whole hour and then a whole afternoon without thinking about Emma or Samuel. Then I'd go a whole night. A day. Never a week, but close enough.

But then Stevie shows up, and I don't think about Emma

much at all. Come to think of it, since Vegas, I didn't think about Emma until that day Rhett told me Samuel wanted to speak to me.

I'd panicked then. Lost my shit worrying about him and her and how it would be to see them again after all this time. Maybe that's why I'm only just realizing where my head's at and how I truly feel.

Where *is* my head at?

Watching Stevie clean her plate, I can honestly say I have no thought other than to show my fake girlfriend a real good time. And why not? Why can't I be over Emma? I fell for her quickly, and nothing ever happened between us. Well, except for the kiss, and that was just—yeah, a terrible thing I did. There are all those old wives' tales about how the time it takes you to get over someone is directly related to the time you were together.

Emma and I were never together.

And I still took the better part of a year to lick my wounds. What if they're healed?

What if I really have moved on?

That would mean I'm free to do anything. With anyone. Fake. Real. Whatever. I don't want to fall in love again. I have enough sense to know I need to pump the brakes a bit here. But the relief is real, and I want to celebrate it.

I just have to convince my brother I really am over Emma. Which shouldn't be hard, considering it's the truth.

Stevie's running her boot up the back of my calf while chatting with Beau about how he's been learning to cook from Samuel. She's engaged. Relaxed. Her lips are stained a deep shade of plum thanks to the wine.

I'm just buzzed enough to think having her shake her ass in front of my family is a good idea. Because I'm gripped by the sudden, fierce need to enjoy my freedom to the fullest.

I wanna see if Stevie really does know her Fleetwood Mac.

"So y'all," I say, setting down my fork and wiping my mouth on one of Milly's fancy monogrammed napkins. "Would you be up for a little impromptu musical accompaniment to dessert?"

"Yes!" Annabel says.

Milly holds up her wineglass. "Yessir. Will you be taking requests?"

"Nope." I turn my head to look at Stevie. "But if I play, I'm gonna need someone on the tambourine."

Stevie's eyes light up. "You actually have a tambourine?"

"What kind of Stevie Nicks fan would I be if I didn't?" I stand and take Stevie's plate. "You okay if I do some dishes real quick, then run back to my place to grab what we need? Shouldn't take more than five minutes, tops."

Stevie looks at me, forehead crinkling for half a heartbeat before it's smoothed by a smile. "Of course. Thanks for checking, baby."

Her smile—it's not totally fake, but it's not totally real, either. Feels a little forced, almost.

That bothers me.

I have a right to my feelings. We all do. But I have absolutely no right to wonder why being looked after trips her up so much. I promised her this weekend was an extension of our fling, so while faking a relationship is totally kosher, digging into real pain and unhappy pasts is not.

I lean down and press a kiss to her mouth. "I'll always check in with you, honey."

I grab her plate and mine and head for the kitchen. Milly follows me, and that's when I notice her eyes are a little red.

"Hey." I nudge her with my elbow. "You all right?"

She turns on the faucet and keeps her gaze trained on our dirty plates as she gives them a rinse. "I'll be okay."

"What happened?"

She finally spears me with a glare. "Can you not take a hint? I don't want to talk about it. It's nothing, anyway."

"Then why were you crying?"

"I don't cry. I kick ass."

Chuckling, I elbow her aside, relieving her of dish duty. "Everybody cries, Milly."

For a second, her lips purse and her chin crinkles, like she's holding in a sob. Blinking, she swallows and looks away. "Love's a bitch. That's all."

"Who hurt you?" My hands go still. "And where can I find him?"

She makes an annoyed sound in the back of her throat and rolls her eyes, elbowing me aside to take over again. "This is why I don't tell y'all shit. It's nothing. End of conversation."

She's using the same tone Mama does when she means business. I want to know more, but I also want to play some music with Stevie.

So I let it go and run home and back. Literally. As I bolt through Samuel's front door again, guitar and tambourine in hand, heart drumming hard inside my chest, another truth hits me: I like having someone to hustle back to.

Someone to hustle for.

I make sure Stevie gets the homemade vanilla bean ice cream and caramel apple pie Samuel prepared for dessert before we head to the great room. Beau's stoking the fire, two chairs already pulled up in front of it for us. My family trickles in with bowls of ice cream in their hands and smiles on their faces.

I know I'm not the only reason they're having a good time. But Milly and I chatted often while I was gone, and she always mentioned how Sunday suppers were "quiet" since I'd left.

The Beauregards do not do quiet. They're certainly not quiet tonight. It makes me feel good, knowing they're glad

I'm back. Or at the very least, able to relax when I'm around. Glancing at Stevie, I realize it also makes me feel a little bad. My family is happy to see me, but they're also happy *for* me. They're celebrating the fact that I found someone. What's gonna happen when Stevie leaves on Monday afternoon and never comes back?

I shove the thought from my head. I'll cross that bridge when I get there.

Stevie picks up the tambourine and gives it a little shake. "Any pointers?"

"You're the Stevie in this relationship." I duck underneath my guitar strap. "You tell me."

She watches me tune the guitar, eyes lingering on my hands a beat too long. "I'm just buzzed enough to think I could be good at this."

"You're gonna be the best. Here, let's sit."

Stevie glances over her shoulder before sitting in the chair to my left. "What are we playing first?"

My knee brushes hers as I sit beside her, adjusting the guitar so it sits in my lap just right. "Someone's bedtime is coming up." Glancing at Maisie, I give her a wink. "So I think we'll start with this one. Ready?"

Stevie meets my eyes. She's wearing this cute smile that's a little shy and a lot eager, her eyes glimmering with a challenge. *Let's show them how obsessed we are.*

I nod. *Done.*

I give her *a one, a two, a one, two, three, four*, and then I burst into a rousing rendition of "Wheels on The Bus."

Stevie laughs at the same moment Maisie literally screams with delight. I try to remember all the verses Bel would sing to Maisie when she was really little.

It turns out, I don't remember much.

To my surprise—*why am I surprised?*—Stevie fills in the gaps for me, guiding me through one verse after another. All the while, she uses the tambourine to do the hand motions—wheels turning, doors opening and shut—and Maisie follows her, padding right up to us to get in on the action.

I watch Maisie watching Stevie. Damn, that little turkey is cute. Egged on by Stevie's encouragement, she follows her motions, clapping her little hands and stomping her little socked feet.

I watch Stevie. She's an uninhibited, enthusiastic participant, eyes going wide at just the right moments, her smile growing just like Maisie's. She keeps the beat with the tambourine, and gives it an extra shake every now and then to make Maisie laugh.

My heart wrenches.

This.

This right here. I don't know what it is, exactly, but something about Stevie and Maisie and "Wheels on the Bus" feels . . . right.

I can't get enough of it.

The song ends, and we get a big round of applause, Stevie handing Maisie the tambourine and letting out a holler when the little girl shakes the thing for all it's worth.

Maisie screams again. Only this time, it's because she drops the tambourine on one of those little feet.

"Oooh, sweetie, I bet that hurt!" Stevie bends down to rub Maisie's foot. "I'm so sorry."

Beau lifts the baby into his arms. "And that's our cue. Time to go night-night." Annabel starts to get up, but Beau waves her away, hiking the baby onto his hip. "You stay and relax. I'll put her to bed."

"I was hoping you'd say that," she replies, kissing him before settling back into her spot on the sofa. "It's been way too long since I heard Hank play."

Beau turns back to us. Leaning down, he presses a kiss to Stevie's cheek. "We really are glad you're here, Stevie. If this crew doesn't scare you off between now and then, I'll see you in the morning, all right?"

"Hard to get scared off by y'all's insanely wonderful hospitality. Thank you, Beau." She puts a hand on his arm. "And thanks for being such a good brother to Hank. He talks a lot about you guys, and I know he's missed you like crazy. I see why."

Stevie looks at me. I look at Beau. His expression softens, blue eyes glistening with genuine joy, and goddamn if I don't have to rein in the impulse to—

To what? Hold my hand up to Stevie for a high five? Throw her over my shoulder and take her home and not let her leave until she promises to come back next weekend, and the weekend after that?

Because what she said just then was sincere. And sincere doesn't square with what we're trying to do here.

Or maybe it does. Just because we're pretending to be in love doesn't mean Stevie is blind to what's going down between my siblings and me. I *have* talked to her about my family. I *have* missed them. She's stating the truth. Just so happens to be playing a part while doing it.

There's a rub there, I can feel it. I just don't know how to phrase it yet. Or why it makes something catch in my chest.

I glance at Rhett. *Don't let me fall again.*

Thank God I know better now than to dive headfirst into something that's not real.

But sex? I can dive headfirst into that real easy, especially if Stevie's involved.

The room is focused on giving Maisie good night kisses and hugs, so I take the opportunity to ask Stevie a few questions, leaning in to murmur in her ear.

"One, how the hell did you know all those verses to 'Wheels on the Bus'? And two, where did you learn to be such an incredible pretend girlfriend?"

Stevie catches her bottom lip between her teeth, giving me that supermodel smolder that drives me fucking crazy.

"One, that song just so happens to be my nephew's favorite. Last time I was at my brother's, we listened to it nonstop. And two, did you really not think I would kill it as your fake love interest?" She leans back and pins me with a look. "I only make smart bets, Hastings. And when I do, I go all in."

I smirk. "Poetry."

"Shut up," she says, giving my shoulder a flirty nudge. "Where did you learn to sing like that? You've got some serious Sam Hunt vibes going on."

"You sayin' I sing real sexy-like?"

"I'm sayin' there's a good chance you're gonna get laid tonight, yeah."

I catch Samuel's gaze from across the room. He's watching us, me and Stevie, eyes narrowed. Not like he's pissed. More like he's squinting, the kind of squint you make when you're about to smile.

He's buying it.

"All right, y'all, time for adult swim." Taking a swig from the wineglass at my feet, I look up at Stevie. Someone's lowered the overhead lights, and she looks lovely in the dimness. Soft. "Show me what you got, girl."

She holds up the tambourine and gives it a saucy shake. "Bring it."

It's a ballsy choice, playing "Leather and Lace." It's not a deep track, exactly, but it's not one of Stevie Nicks's flashier hits.

It's also a really sexy song.

But in the vein of Stevie Carter, I go all in. I play the opening chords, the strings singing as I move my fingertips over them, gaze on Stevie's face all the while.

She's not smiling but her eyes are, just like Samuel's, and

when she takes a long, slow sip of her own wine before raising the tambourine again, my heart nearly beats its way out of my chest.

I sing the first verse—Stevie Nicks's part—and my Stevie starts out by tapping the tambourine against her knee. Steady. Quiet.

I sing, and she smiles, those dark eyes flicking to my mouth one time too often. Jesus Christ. I'm glad my guitar's in my lap 'cause otherwise—yeah.

When I get to Don Henley's verse, I figure I'll keep singing. But immediately Stevie pipes up, nailing the lyrics perfectly.

And you know what? She's got a real pretty voice.

Or maybe it's her confidence that's pretty. Or the way she knows every single fucking word to one of the best fucking songs ever written.

All I know is I stop singing and somehow manage to keep playing while I stare at her, shaking her head just like Don would, shaking the tambourine just like our favorite rock goddess. She closes her eyes and lets it rip, really getting into it. Feeling the music exactly how I like to. A little drama, some southern-inspired twang, a lot of emotion.

She ain't afraid of any of it.

Milly hollers somewhere in the background, and Rhett lets out a half-assed hog whistle followed by a half-assed apology, blaming "a little too much wine" for his dry lips.

"There she is!" Emma says.

Mama raises her arms and wiggles her hips. "Good*ness*, girl, you got it."

I feel a swell of affection for my family at that moment.

There's swelling of an entirely different variety between my legs for Stevie.

She gets to the chorus and opens her eyes, meeting mine. She smiles, nods, and I join her, the two of us singing about lovers and mountains and leather and lace. Our voices don't sound amazing together, but they don't sound awful, either, and after a few lines we find our groove, eyes locked as we do our best to harmonize.

It's not half bad.

It's a ton of fucking fun. Laughter rises along the sides of my torso, gathering in my belly as I sing the next verse solo and Stevie ducks her lips, spreading her arms before bringing them back together to bang the tambourine against the heel of her hand. It's like she's working a stadium crowd, urging them to clap with us. And because my family is my family—drunk and willing—they really do clap.

Everyone claps. Samuel. Emma. Mama. Bel is smiling so big at Stevie and me her face is about to split open. Milly jumps to her feet and starts dancing, pulling Rhett off the sofa to dance with her. Then Stevie is getting to her feet too. She's shaking the tambourine above her head, shaking her hips, getting low in that slow, confident way of hers, ass carving the kind of clean turns Clyde tried to teach me on the slopes in Aspen.

When our joint chorus comes up, Stevie turns to me and shimmies her tits in my face as she sings. I can't help it. I laugh, stumbling on the lyrics, my dick throbbing. I lean up and kiss the freckle on her neck.

Heat, real and raw, flashes across her eyes, and that ache inside my chest suddenly isn't so tiny anymore.

"Aw yeah!" Rhett yells.

"*Y'all*," Milly says with a smile. "Get a room, would you?"

Bel gets up to dance too. "Please don't, because this. Is. *Amazing*."

Because we've got the room dancing, and because the song is too fucking perfect for the circumstances, I dive right into "Sorry" by Justin Bieber.

Judging by the way Stevie bites her bottom lip, she very much approves.

Now the entire room is dancing, all of us singing about being sorry at the top of our lungs. Spinning Emma underneath his raised arm, Samuel catches my gaze. He grins.

Something inside me breaks free, and I close my eyes and lose myself in the music.

Lose myself in the knowledge that I am forgiven. For tonight, at least.

I open my eyes and Stevie's ass is in my face. She's bent at the waist, and she glances at me over her shoulder as she pops her hips. Desire surges through my core, gathering in a painfully sweet throb at the tip of my dick.

I take my hand off my guitar for half a heartbeat to give her ass a squeeze. But then Milly is pulling Stevie over to dance with her, and Rhett takes the tambourine so Milly and Stevie can make a bridge out of their arms for Mama to dance through. Samuel takes Stevie for a spin too. She moves effortlessly in his arms, the two of them giggling when she goes up on her tiptoes and tries to get him to spin underneath her arm.

Stevie doesn't miss a single lyric all the while. Girl knows her blackjack, her classic rock, her toddler *and* Bieber hits.

And now she knows my family.

The ache in my chest won't let me be. Neither will my half-hard dick. Wasn't I just promising myself I wasn't gonna repeat past mistakes?

But this—Stevie, tonight, the current between us—it feels so, so different from anything I've experienced before.

I'm just sober enough to realize if I'm not careful, I'm gonna catch real feelings for my fake girlfriend.

And I'm just drunk enough to wonder if that wouldn't be an entirely bad thing.

Chapter Twelve

STEVIE

I draw up short at the threshold of Hank's enormous master bathroom.

All my lotions and potions are neatly laid out on one of the vanities beside a stack of pristine white towels. The door to the closet is open, and I see my clothes have been hung up, my shoes marching in a straight line directly beneath them.

A fluffy robe, embroidered with Blue Mountain's insignia, hangs from a hook beside the vanity.

I turn when Hank presses a kiss to my nape, right where it slopes into my shoulder. "What's this?"

"I had the butler unpack your things," he replies, mouth still on my skin. "We do it for all our guests at Blue Mountain."

I stare at my vanity. Stare at our reflection in the mirror above it.

My stomach dips. Hank is kissing my neck, tongue like velvet as he turns his handsome head to get a better angle. The muscles in his chest and shoulders strain against his shirt; the sharp line of his jaw gleams in the low light of the bathroom.

He is so beautiful it hurts.

His front is plastered to my back. His erection presses against my ass, not lewd or overly eager but very much there.

I'm a smidge taller than he is in my heels, but he's got so much bulk and brawn he still dwarfs me.

Still makes me feel deliciously, dangerously feminine. Just like he did when he watched me dance and sing and play the tambourine back at Samuel's house, eyes hazy and hot. That was *fun*.

"Let me guess." I reach behind me to run my fingers through his hair. "It was your idea. To unpack for everyone."

He meets my eyes in the mirror. "Why do I get the feeling that bothers you?"

I shake my head, sucking in a breath when he slips a hand inside my shirt. I watch it move up, up. He cups my breast, kneading it over my bra, running the pads of his first two fingers over my nipple.

In his hands, my body becomes a live wire. Sensation rips through me, making my clit pulse, and I close my eyes.

"It doesn't bother me," I pant. "I think it's great, the way you take care of your people. It's just . . ." *Giving me this funny feeling in my chest that's scaring me*. "It's not something I've seen a lot of. In guys, I mean. That kind of thoughtfulness."

Hank spins me around to face him. Hands curled possessively into my sides. "Because we're just having fun, I'm not gonna ask for your story. And I definitely won't ask why that kinda thing freaks you out so much."

A jolt of anger—fear—arrows through the arousal spreading in my center.

"It doesn't freak me out," I say defensively. Total lie.

"I call bullshit."

He's digging. He's concerned, and I don't want to believe that means he cares because that would make this funny feeling bigger.

I run my tongue along my bottom lip. His eyes flick to my mouth, just like I knew they would.

And just like I knew they would, they get hazy again.

I lower myself onto my knees, one leg at a time. Never breaking eye contact.

Hooking a finger into the waist of his jeans, I begin to unbutton them. "Don't make me call bullshit on your promise to fuck my mouth."

I unzip his fly and his stomach caves, nostrils flaring as he looks down at me.

"I see what you're doing." His voice is hoarse. "You think you can change the subject by distracting me—"

"Can't I?" I tug his jeans and briefs over the curve of his ass. His cock bounces in my face, the slit at the head already leaking. I take him in my hand, curling my fingers around his silken length. He's hot and hugely hard, his girth pulsing in my palm. I give him a slow, *slow* tug, smiling when his expression contracts. "What's wrong with distracting you? Do you not like the way it feels?"

He grabs my hand, stilling my motion. He looks at me, really looks, and a muscle in his jaw ticks. "I can't imagine you like the way it feels—not letting anyone in."

There's that anger again. The sore spot.

My heart feels heavy and tight, like I'm in the middle of a workout.

His hand is warm and dry around mine.

"You don't know me," I say.

He cups my chin in his other hand. "That's just the thing, honey. I want to."

I blink, hard, trying my very best to ignore the way that makes my pulse flutter.

Goddamn it, we were having so much fun. This was *fun*, but all of a sudden it's getting feel-y, it's verging on serious, and I've got my dukes up.

"I can't go there," I say softly, flattening my hand on the plane of his stomach. "Please don't ask that of me. I understand you wanting it, wanting to know someone that way. But that someone isn't me, all right? I'll give you everything I can offer, Hank, believe me. Just not that."

He searches my eyes. "What kind of crime do you think you committed?"

The crime of failure.

The question and my silent answer hang between us for a long beat before I manage to paste on a smile. "Why do you ask questions you know I'm not going to answer?"

I can't read his expression. He's horny, yeah. But something's changed. He's looking at me differently. Not in a bad way. Just with more intensity, I guess. More naked interest that's sexual but soft too.

I will myself to look away. Settling my gaze on his cock, I lean in and lick the tip. Lap up his cum, his taste savory in my mouth. He sucks a breath through his teeth and juts his hips, pressing the crown of his penis against my lips.

Resisting the urge to look at him, I open my mouth and roll my lips around my teeth. I take him inside me bit by bit, rolling my tongue along his length. He groans. Groans again when I wrap my hand around him and jerk him off, pulling my head back. Then I move my head forward, taking his dick all the way to the back of my throat on a hard swallow.

"Oh, honey, yes." He gathers my hair in his hand and fists it. "Just like that. Go a little deeper. Uh-huh."

Hank pulls my hair, guiding himself even deeper. I gag and my eyes water, but when he tries to pull back I catch him by the ass and hold him there.

"Honey, you're gonna choke," he says, but he still sinks inside my mouth, cursing when he hits my soft palate. I swallow and pump my hand.

I bob my head and he pulls my hair again, this time to set

the rhythm. He moves his hips too, fucking my mouth slowly at first, then faster and faster.

The fist in my hair, the cock in my mouth, the pace—what he's doing is crude.

At the same time, I feel his eyes on me. He's trailing a thumb down my cheek, his touch reverent and gentle. He wipes saliva from the corner of my mouth.

I crack open an eye and see him watching me. Brow furrowed. Jaw hard but eyes soft and full.

I squeeze my eyes shut. Of course he looks at me that way. All guys do when you're sucking their dick.

He pulls out. I lick his head. Run my tongue along the side of his length. He goes back in. His hips are rolling wildly now. I can tell he's close. I pump faster with one hand and reach for his balls with the other, giving them a lingering caress.

"I wanna come on you," Hank growls. "Let me."

My clit screams and I nod, ducking my head at the same moment he pulls out of me.

"Get on the bed." Hank gestures toward the bedroom before whipping a towel off the ring beside his sink. "On your back—lie on your back."

I lie on my stomach. I don't like how raw his words sounded.

Or maybe I like it too much, and I know if I look him in the eyes when he comes I'm not going to be able to stay in control.

"What the fuck, Stevie?" he spits out when he comes into the room. "I said *on your back*."

I glance at him over my shoulder. Cross my ankles and bend my knees so my heels nearly touch my butt. "No."

"Stevie." He gives himself a rough stroke. "So help me God—"

"*No.*"

The challenge hangs between us. I grab the hem of my shirt and pull it up, revealing my bare back. "Take it or leave it."

"Fine," he growls. "But you watch. Understood?"

I smirk. "Yes, sir."

Watching Hank touch himself might be one of the most erotic experiences of my life. He's a wall of solid muscle, his entire body tensed as he works himself over with hard, fast strokes, hips circling, lips parted. He moves closer to me. Closer. His thighs meet with the edge of the bed.

His gaze is glued to my back, my ass. I'm glad. It feels safe this way.

I feel safe, having that distance between us.

But I still have to tease him. Urge him on. Give him a piece of me.

"Imagine your dick's still in my mouth. I'm savoring you, loving how hard you are. How your skin feels like silk on my tongue. Let go, Hank. Come how you want to—all over me."

"*Fuck*," he shouts. The sinews in his neck pop and he sucks in a breath, fist jerking back and forth. Then he grabs my shirt and hikes it up higher, resting his weight on one hand beside me as he holds his body half a foot above mine.

With the other he guides hot ropes of cum all over my skin. The breath catches in my throat like it's my release too, and my pussy throbs, heavy, hard beats that have me squirming.

Hank comes and comes. Semen lands in my hair. He flexes his hips, slowly guiding himself in and out of his fist.

He's finally empty, and our gazes lock.

Now it's my heart that's beating hard. Because he's got this look in his eyes. It's primal and possessive, and *oh God,* it's delicious.

My grip slips, and I look away. Focus on the patterned weave of the duvet cover. "I'm glad you came first for once."

"Let's not make a habit of it." I hear the linens sigh as he straightens. His fingers curl into the waistband of my jeans. "You on birth control?"

My stomach dips. Can't help it—I look at him, too curious for my own good. "Yes."

"Good." My jeans are stretchy enough that he can pull them down without having to unbutton or unzip the fly. He gives them and my underwear several good tugs until they're bunched at my ankles.

My pussy smarts at the sudden rush of air.

"Why?"

He unzips my booties and takes them off. Then he guides my pants and undies over my feet, dropping them on the floor. "I'm clean. I'll send you the report. I wanna use this"—he stands, swipes his first two fingers in the cum on my back—"on this." He nods at my pussy.

My stomach dips again, harder this time. Using his semen as lube is wrong. Not because it's dirty—I have no problem with that—but because it's intimate.

It's exchanging bodily fluids the way people do in actual relationships.

It's trusting each other in a way people in fake relationships don't.

It's also really, really hot.

"I don't need lube," I reply, spreading my thighs. "Clearly."

Hank steps between my legs. "That's not what this is about. Please, honey. Lemme give you what I want."

I don't want his possessiveness, his urgency, his *lewdness*, to turn me on. But it does. The muscles in my legs quake. My clit is in agony, begging to be touched.

Need coils so tight between my legs I think I'm going to die.

"Okay," I say, against my better judgment. Not because I don't trust Hank.

But because I don't trust myself.

I don't have time to second-guess my decision, because his fingers are parting my slit. Opening me to his caress. He coats me in his cum, a slick, front to back motion from behind that's wildly sexy. The tip of his tongue is pressed to the corner of his mouth, like he's concentrating.

Like he wants to get this just right.

Oh, Lord, does he. His thumb finds my clit, spreading his semen all over me, warm and sticky. Circling. Slow. Firm.

I can't.

I close my eyes and hold on to the duvet for dear life. He presses his thumb against my clit, making my hips buck up into the air.

He takes that as an invitation.

That thumb moves up. Stopping just beneath my asshole.

"Let me?"

Ugh, of course Hank Beauregard is not afraid of ass play.

This guy is dangerous.

"Yes," I breathe, nodding. Hiking my hips up a little higher.

His exploration is gentle. Curious. He gathers more cum on his thumb, a quick swipe up the furrow of my spine, and then he presses the pad of that finger against my entrance. He circles it.

Circles his middle finger against my clit at the same time.

That's it.

That's all it takes for me to come so hard it hurts.

I thrust my slit against his hand, crying out into the duvet as I'm fucking *flattened* by pounding sensation. The sweetness is unbearable, and I find myself thinking—feeling—things I shouldn't.

I want him close.

Being the dangerous human being he is, Hank reads my mind and flips me over onto my back. I can only whimper, and I don't resist when he covers my body with his and kisses my mouth, guiding my hands up to his sides so I can hold on. I curl my fingers into his flesh and just . . . take my time, and my pleasure.

No one has ever been so forward with me in bed.

No one has ever encouraged me to take with such reckless abandon.

The best part? Hank asks *nothing* in return. I feel a familiar rise begin inside me, one that says I owe him something for this, that I'm getting away with something I shouldn't be.

It's an echo of the demands and expectations that took down my marriage.

Give more.

Take less.

I'm shaking by the time my orgasm recedes. Hank stops kissing me just long enough to make me open my eyes. And there he is. Nose brushing mine as he looks down at me, his cock soft against the inside of my leg.

We're both breathing hard, our eyes locked because . . .

We can't look away.

Who the hell is this guy, and how did I let him sneak past my defenses?

He's a thief, and if I'm not careful, he'll steal something I'm not willing to part with.

I'm about to tell him to look away, let me up, when he says, "Hot shower sound good? You're cold."

That's not it, I want to say. *That's not why I can't get a grip right now.*

I gently push him off me, blinking. "Yeah. Sure. Just let me use the bathroom real quick."

I don't want him to help me to my feet but he does. I pad to the toilet. I feel soaked in every sense of the word.

Nothing about what just happened was careful.

I am not being as careful as I should be.

I put my hand on the doorjamb. Take a breath. Hank's cum has started to dry on my back, making the skin there feel tight.

"You okay?"

Glancing over my shoulder, I see Hank standing a couple of feet behind me in the bathroom.

He's buck naked and beautiful.

"That—what just happened there—it felt different," I manage, too tired—too *something*—to keep my defenses up. "And yeah, I'll admit to that freaking me out a little."

His forehead creases. "You're freaked out?"

"No." I give my head a vigorous shake. "Yes. Maybe. I don't know. That felt too good to freak out over, you know? Or maybe I'm freaking out because it felt so good."

Hank scratches his head. "Well, that's a first."

"Where'd you learn to make someone come like that?"

"Same way you learned to play tambourine. Or blackjack." He smirks, one corner of his mouth kicking up. "If you got it, you got it."

I roll my eyes, even as my torso lights up at his unique combination of cocky and cute. I look at his chest, at the smattering of hair in the center growing back from a recent shave.

"Tonight I realized something," he continues, smirk fading.

"That your family is awesome and you should've come back sooner?"

"You only think that because they're not your family. No, I realized I'm definitely not in love with Emma anymore."

This time it's my heart that dips. I need to pee already—last thing I need is to get a UTI on the first night of what will probably be the sexiest weekend of my life—but I can't seem to make myself move.

This is how you get in over your head.

"That was fast," I say, holding the jamb in a death grip.

"When you know, you know."

"Lots of dad-isms happening in this conversation."

"I knew I didn't have it bad for her anymore. I didn't think about her like I used to. But yeah, the certainty of knowing I'm really and truly done there is surprisingly . . . certain?"

There's a flutter in my chest, and I laugh. "That's awesome news. It'll make convincing Samuel that much easier."

"I thought he bought it tonight, don't you?"

"Hank, it's a real pleasure being your pretend girlfriend, and I think it showed—how much fun we had together."

He gets this look in his eyes. Not hazy, exactly. But sweet. "Some of it felt pretty damn real to me."

"Of course some of it's real," I say quickly. "We're friends, aren't we? And friends are good to each other. That, I'm not faking."

"Friends. Yeah. I like that," he says.

Although it sounds like he doesn't like it very much at all. Or maybe that's just me.

Chapter Thirteen

HANK

Stevie isn't the least bit nervous as she puts the finishing touches on her tasting table the next afternoon.

Dressed in tall black boots and an elegant wrap coat, she drops menus at each place setting, stopping to adjust a glass's position or switch a place card. She's got this light in her eyes, and a pep in her step, that makes her glow.

Could also have something to do with the pair of orgasms I gave her this morning. One before coffee, slow and snuggly in bed. And one after. Hot and fast on the floor of my formal living room.

I'm determined to fuck Stevie in every room in my house before she leaves on Monday.

She said we were friends last night. That should've made me happy. Wasn't I just bitching about how lonely I was? But her brushing off my comment about how real our connection is beginning to feel by saying it's *friendship* bummed me out. Maybe because that's what makes this whole thing refreshingly different—the authenticity of it. Ironic, yeah. But the intensity of our connection is night and day compared to the connection I thought I had with Emma. I'm starting to see how I made a mountain out of a molehill there. I wanted to hit it off with her so, so badly. Hell, I wanted to hit it off with *anyone*. I was desperate in a way I shouldn't have been, and maybe that's why I tried to force a round peg into a square hole.

This—me and Stevie—it doesn't feel like that. At all. It's easy and fun and fiery.

Still, I made some promises last night, and I'm gonna stick to 'em.

For now.

Folding the last of Lady Luck Brewhouse's butter-soft sweatshirts—in true Stevie style, she brought only beautifully branded, high-quality merchandise—I catch her with a hand on her hip.

"What else can I do?"

Pausing, she scans the table of shirts and stickers and koozies and rewards me with the kind of smile that makes the skin around her eyes crinkle. Pressing a quick kiss to my lips, she says, "Nothing. Thank you so much for your help. And for inviting me to do a tasting up here in the first place. Everything looks insanely great, probably because this might be the most beautiful place on Earth."

We're in the Stag Pavilion. It's Blue Mountain Resort's indoor-outdoor event venue. Essentially an open-air cabin, it's got soaring ceilings, a massive fireplace, and room for a seated dinner for a hundred.

Today, though, we're doing an intimate tasting for five: Stevie and me, of course, plus Samuel and Emma, the farm's food and wine directors, respectively, and Beau. Milly had a large farm table placed in front of the fireplace, and Milly being Milly, she took the liberty of decorating it with bouquets of white hydrangea and gerbera daisies. I see she's thrown in some tablecloths and heirloom silverware too.

There are candles in mercury glass votives and gleaming china, also in shades of white and green.

It all matches Lady Luck's merchandise perfectly.

I smile. Milly was polite enough to Stevie last night, and I think she likes her. But I know Milly did all this for me, even though it's technically Stevie's tasting. It's Milly's love language, her way of showing she cares.

I appreciate the gesture more than she knows.

"Pretty day," I say.

Stevie stops to look outside, curling her hands around her low back. "Pretty view."

A panorama of the Great Smoky Mountains stretches out before us. It's a radiant winter day, the sky crisp, the air cold. Mountains undulating in waves as far as the eye can see. The trees are bare, giving the landscape a bluish-purple tint.

Stevie turns her head and watches a staff member disappear down the steps that lead to the smoking patio. Then she looks at me, eyes serious.

"You had to have missed it while you were gone," she says, voice low. "The mountains. Your family. Everything."

I slip my hands into my pockets. Think about my answer for a minute. I could go with the old line, the one I gave everybody about how I loved the farm but needed a change of scenery. That I was in Maui or Madrid to recharge my batteries so I could return to Blue Mountain refreshed and ready to give my all.

It's not a total lie. But it's not the whole truth either.

Looking at Stevie looking at me, the idea of giving her that answer suddenly makes me feel tired. Bored, even. Like I'm finally fed up with my own bullshit.

"I think I missed how things used to be," I say. "My family was never perfect. But growing up here, I was happy. I felt safe. But then my dad got sick . . ."

She returns my gaze steadily. I don't think either of us

expected me to give this answer to that question. But undeterred, Stevie waits for me to continue.

"He committed suicide." I want to look down at my shoes but I don't. "He played football too, and turns out he had a real bad case of CTE. Degenerative brain disease. Kinda shattered the little bubble we lived in up here, you know?"

Stevie's expression softens. She slips her arm between mine and my torso and curls it upward from behind, trapping my shoulder in a hug.

She holds me like that. Doesn't say a word. No empty platitudes. No awkward offers of sympathy. She just looks and listens and lets me know she's there.

"Anyway, we lost Daddy—that was years ago. I was sixteen at the time. We didn't fully understand back then how early CTE could start, so I threw myself into football. I had to stay busy, you know? I played in high school. College. Well, for a few years, anyway. Then the pros. When I finally retired, I threw myself into the resort. I was busy then. I knew I wasn't happy, but I was helping my family, so I just . . . worked. Then Emma walks onto the farm, and I see her with Samuel—" I shake my head and look at my feet. "It hit me how lonely I was. I came home to set down roots. Get married and shit. But that wasn't happening."

She looks at me for a beat with this weird expression on her face. "You want the whole shebang, huh?"

"Shebang?"

"Wedding. White picket fence. Babies and maybe a dog too."

"I'd love to have a dog, yeah."

Her face falls. But then she blinks, drawing a quick breath through her nose, and gives my shoulder a squeeze. "Takes a lot of energy, always running and moving and doing. So much effort to stay busy so you never have to stop and face the thing you don't want to talk about."

My gut contracts at the same time something in my chest swings open.

We shouldn't. I shouldn't. This is super personal territory we're crossing into. I want to keep going, but Stevie doesn't.

"Yup," I say like an idiot. "Christ, I'm getting in the weeds here, aren't I? I don't mean to ruin the mood right before your tasting. We can talk about this later. Or not. But for now, how about we crack open a beer? Wake the palate or whatever."

Stevie searches my face. She waits a beat. Then another. I can see the conflict working itself out behind her eyes.

I can feel myself hoping she'll open up, whatever she's debating she'll share.

To my surprise, she does.

"Fake girlfriends don't talk about these things with their fake boyfriends. But because you're sharing your tale of woe, Hastings, I'll share a little bit of mine. For years I ran myself ragged trying to stay busy so I didn't have to face certain things."

"Like?"

Stevie blows out a breath. "Like my shitty self-esteem. How I felt that I was unlovable in some essential way, so I believed I had to earn affection and respect. Work for it. Lord, did I work. I tried so hard to be everyone's perfect everything. The perfect daughter. Perfect wife. Thing is, the harder I worked, the unhappier I got. I became resentful. And angry."

"Sounds rough," I say, heart skipping. "So what did you do? How did you fix it?"

She shakes her head. "Wish I had the answer for you. That's something only you can figure out—how you're gonna fill that hole inside you, and what you want to fill it with."

Stevie's deflecting. But damn.

I never thought about it like that. I knew my father wasn't

the only thing I lost when Daddy died. But I hadn't considered how that hole wouldn't just heal on its own—it wouldn't close up and scar over with time, the way my incision did after the ankle surgery I had freshman year.

I need more than time.

I don't need to make a joke about filling Stevie's holes.

Looking at her, I wonder if I need—

"Look at y'all, being all cozy and cute," Samuel says, striding into the pavilion. He's got Emma on his arm and a grin on his face. "Hope we're not interrupting?"

I put on a smile and grab Stevie's hand, twining our fingers. "Not at all."

"Hi, guys," Stevie says. "Thanks again for last night. Emma, the wine was insane, and that cornbread? Samuel, I'll be dreaming about it for months."

Emma and Samuel exchange a glance. A grin too. They've mentioned cornbread before—think it's some kind of pervy inside joke they share. Before it would annoy the hell out of me when they'd do this, exchange a private joke in a public place.

Now? Not so much. Maybe because I have Stevie to turn to and say, "I'll be dreaming about that tambourine. Specifically you playing it, shaking your—"

Stevie presses a finger to my lips. "Don't make me use that tambourine on you."

"You mean you wanna—"

"Yes. Specifically, I want to use it on your—"

"Very fine ass, Daphne?"

"Ew, y'all," Beau says, appearing at my elbow. "Who the hell is Daphne?"

Stevie's eyes flash. Real? Fake? "We should start the tasting, no?"

"Right." I clear my throat. Turn to my brothers. "So. Hey. Stevie set up this amazing spread. I'm just her right hand man today, but I want y'all to know that this tasting isn't some bullshit exercise in nepotism. I didn't offer her this chance because she's my girlfriend. I offered it because she's kick-ass and so is her beer, and I genuinely believe in the awesomeness of her product. Lady Luck is special, just like its CEO. I'll turn it over to her."

Stevie rewards me with a smile—I'd bet my bottom dollar it's real—and, curling an arm around my waist, nods at the table. "Y'all take a seat. First beer up is our Peanut Butter Porter. I know, I know, it sounds bizarre, but trust me when I say it's *good*."

"Starting strong," Emma says, folding her napkin on her lap. "I like it."

Stevie cracks open a tallboy can and begins to pour us each a generous taste in a miniature stout glass. "I typically like to move from darker, heavier beers to lighter ones. That way you're not trying to cram a heavy porter into an already full stomach."

She pours herself a smaller taste and holds up her glass. "The company you keep is just as important as the beer you drink. Cheers, y'all. Thank you for having me, and thanks for the opportunity to introduce you to the great love of my life —beer."

Everyone laughs at that. It's a great line, and she delivers it breezily. If I didn't know Stevie any better, I'd think it was a joke too.

"Going back to the Peanut Butter," Stevie says as we bring the beer to our lips. "Subjectively speaking, it seems random, and even a little off-putting. Who wants peanut butter with their beer? I thought a lot about doing our porter the way I'd seen it done before. You know, hints of coffee, or chocolate, or maybe coconut if we were feeling extra adventurous. But none of that spoke to me, and over the years I've learned to trust my instincts."

It's cold and flavorful, exactly the right beer for exactly the right moment—the time before a meal when you're hungry and thirsty, and have room for something indulgent. I take another sip, wanting to experience the complexity of flavor again. The porter taste is there. Bitter. Bright. And then there's just the tiniest hint of peanut butter, sweet and rich. Even a little salty.

Totally satisfying.

"Goddamn," Emma says, licking her lips. She takes another sip. "The peanut butter is there, but it's not overpowering. Just that hint of sweet to balance the bitterness."

"The balance is perfection," Samuel adds. "That is *really* good. I'm not a porter guy, but I'd definitely order this. I love peanut butter."

Stevie sips her beer. Her tongue darts out to grab a slick of foam on her upper lip. "So do I. The flavor is different, but." She shrugs. "I like different."

"Different is what we're all about up here on the farm." Samuel drains his glass. "We like to stand out. Service, accommodations. Food and wine. And this beer? It stands out. Well done."

Beau exchanges a glance with Samuel. "Very well done."

We taste an IPA next, Hop Girl Summer, that's out of this world. Not too hoppy, not in your face, just solid, clean flavors. Stevie follows it up with a blackberry sour that's just the right combination of sweet and savory.

"Tell us about Lady Luck," I say, smacking my lips. "Why beer? Why now? It's obvious your beer is beautifully, painstakingly crafted. Why pour—pun not intended—your heart and soul into making it?"

Samuel grins. "You know the answer to that."

"Of course I do. But y'all don't, so listen up. Stevie's got a good story to tell."

She presses her teeth into her bottom lip. "Thanks for that."

"I mean it."

"I focus on what I like to drink," Stevie says, turning to my family. "Which just so happens to be what my girlfriends like, and what their girlfriends like. We draw a predominantly female crowd at the brewery, which I love."

"Very cool," Samuel says.

Stevie's eyes sparkle. Pulling out the chair at the head of the table, she sits. "My parents were always beer drinkers, so naturally I stole a few beers here and there throughout high school."

I cock a brow. "A few?"

"Meh, maybe a few more than a few. I remember thinking the taste was gross, but clearly we weren't drinking it for that. Over time, though, I found myself actually liking the stuff." Stevie grabs a nearby can and refills her glass. "I liked how unpretentious beer was. How it worked for any occasion. I also liked the craft involved. For some reason, making something like, say, wine"—Stevie nods at Emma—"seemed like an impossible dream. But crafting your own beer? That I could see myself doing. How cool would it be, making art that people could drink every day?"

"So you love the artistry involved," I say. "Beer is your blank canvas. A creative pursuit that jazzes you unlike anything else."

"Yeah." Stevie crinkles her forehead. "That's a line from an interview I did with a blog back in Nashville."

I glance across the table at my brothers. Beau's got this proud look in his eyes, and Samuel's eyes are narrowed in that just-about-to-smile way again.

What a fucking relief. But I feel a tug of something else too. Something new and not exactly pleasant. Guilt?

"Your butt isn't the only thing I admire, Stevie. Your

passion and your incredible business sense are equally arousing."

Beau scoffs. "Christ almighty, how many times you gonna make me say 'ew' today, brother?"

"A lot," I say, gaze locked on Stevie's.

She blinks, hard, and looks away.

Her cheeks are pink.

She's biting back a smile.

How you gonna fill that hole, Hank?

"Craft breweries were just beginning to pop up back then," she continues, flattening her palm on the tasting menu and gliding it forward. "But I was still intimidated by the whole thing. Actually taking the leap, learning the craft. Learning how to run a business. So I played it safe for a while —I worked for other brewers, other business owners—and learned as much as I could I homebrewed a lot during that time, experimenting with recipes. I did countless hours of cellar work. It took me a while to finally get the courage to strike out on my own. Actually"—her eyes flick to meet mine —"my life had to fall apart before I finally said 'fuck it, it's now or never.'"

I nod, finishing the last sip of my blond ale. "You had nothing left to lose."

"I had nothing left to lose," she repeats.

As she looks and I look, feeling swells between us. A charged pull that seeps into my skin and electrifies it.

She blinks again. Looks away. "I had to hit rock bottom. I lost my job, my marriage, and my house, one right after the other."

"The low point." Emma runs her fingers down the sides of her glass. "Been there. It is not pleasant."

"No shit," I say. "I've said it before and I'll said it again, I'm sorry, Stevie."

I actually haven't said that before. But for the sake of our ruse, I go with it.

Stevie shakes her head. "Darkest time of my life. But hey, I wouldn't be where I am if it hadn't happened. Losing it all taught me lessons I needed to learn. It showed me how resilient I am, and how important persistence is."

"Cheers to that." Beau holds up his glass and sends a pointed look my way. "I think we can all relate to the power of second chances."

My body is buzzing now. It's the beer. But it's also my brothers. It's this stunner of a girl sitting at my family's table and baring herself in a way that speaks to the stuff between my blood and bones.

I touch her knee underneath the table. By the way her eyes go wide, I can tell she knows.

She knows this touch has nothing to do with made-up love stories.

My brothers and Emma can't see what I'm doing. Which means I'm doing it for me. Us. Stevie and me. It's an admission. A breach of contract.

A way of assuaging this awful tug in my gut.

Her lips part and for half a heartbeat I think she's going to silently admit something too.

And she does, by shifting her body so my hand falls from her leg.

My heart falls too, and I find myself struggling to keep my expression from doing the same.

Chapter Fourteen

STEVIE

Closing my eyes, I take in a lungful of air.

It's cold, and it makes my chest burn. The clean, Christmas-y scent of pine fills my head as my feet crunch on the dead needles that litter the trail.

After Emma and Samuel shook my hand and informed me they'd be placing a "sizable order in the very near future," I should've stayed at Stag Pavilion to celebrate.

I should've taken Beau up on his offer of coffee at The Barn Door Restaurant at the very least.

But I felt short of breath—like the organs inside my torso were too big to fit in there anymore, squeezing my airways—and so I excused myself, claiming I had a call with a distributor, and hightailed it out of there. I changed into some leggings and sneakers, and now here I am, alone on one of Blue Mountain Farm's hiking trails. I had to get out, I guess. Get away from Hank and his house and his intensity.

My pulse pounds as I remember the vulnerable look in his eyes when he told me about his dad.

It pounds harder at the memory of his enthusiastic, uninhibited support during the tasting.

Pounds hardest when I think about how uninhibited that made me. I want to cringe. Did I really have to go into so much detail about my personal life? It was completely unnecessary, but I did it anyway, instigated by the warmth of Hank and his people.

They are really, really great people.

I stop beside an enormous pine and put my hand on the trunk, trying to catch my breath. I'm in good shape—best shape of my life, actually—so it's not that.

This is something different.

Something that is truly scaring the shit out of me. An ache I can't shake. Hank wants to set down roots. I want to grow wings. We're after totally different things, which means it should be easy to keep my distance.

Only, it's not. I don't understand it. So I do what I always do when I can't tell which way is up.

"Kate," I breathe into the phone when she picks up. "Hey."

"Don't tell me you're calling from bed. Because it sounds like you and that loverboy just went to pound town—"

"No. I mean, yes, we did that this morning, but right now I'm on a hike. Alone." I glance at the flat trail in front of me. "A very steep, strenuous hike."

"Uh-oh," Kate says.

Pressing my palm into the tree's scaly park, I drop my head. "Yeah. Kate, I think I'm in trouble."

"Tell me everything. No, wait, give me a second so I can lock myself in the bathroom. Teddy!" She's yelling. "Teddy, if that's dog food, I swear to God—here, y'all watch some *Cocomelon*. Yes, Hannah, I'll put on the frog song. Just give me a minute . . . hey, get your finger out of your sister's nose. Did someone poop? I think I smell poop." A few seconds later I hear a door close. Kate lets out a breath. "There. Sorry, my life is a nightmare and the only place I can be alone is on the toilet. Talk to me, honey."

My heart dips. *Honey*. Am I going to think of Hank's sexy, rumbly voice every time I hear that word now?

"He's so great," I begin. "Unexpectedly great."

"Like, dick-wise? Personality-wise? Obscene wealth-wise?"

"All of the above."

"Oh, jeez, you really are in trouble. But, like, the good kind of trouble."

"No. Not good at all. You know how I feel about this stuff, Kate." I dig my toe into the dirt. "I came up here to have fun."

"And now you're having great sex with a great guy at an incredible resort, which is making you catch a feeling or two."

"Did I mention he's wild for my beer and incredibly supportive of my career? He thinks what I do is the coolest thing."

I hear the smile in her voice when she replies. "What a jerk."

"He helps. Really, truly helps with stuff. Cooking. Coffee. Kids. He does it all *without being asked*."

"Listen, Stevie, if you don't want him, I'll take him. Even though he is one hundred percent still a jerk."

"I know, right? It's the rudest thing ever, being so fucking excellent. He's throwing me for a loop."

"And that's a bad thing because . . .?"

"*Because*." I scoff. "Boo-hoo for me. Look, I get it. I'm not complaining. I'm just—"

"Scared."

The word makes my gut contract. "Yes."

"Why don't you put all that therapy to use and try to work through that fear?"

"To do what? End up with this guy?"

"Not necessarily, no. You work through it so you can enjoy

whatever it is you've got with this football god of yours. I know you don't want to end up with anyone—"

"I don't. Not in the slightest. That kind of setup is a prison."

"Hey," Kate shoots back. "I have that setup."

I lift my head and close my eyes. "Shit. I'm sorry. I don't mean to imply—what you and Jane have, it's different, you know? I mean that in a good way. But after what I went through, it's not what I want for myself."

"That's fair. But that begs the question, what do you want?"

I open my eyes and glance up at the sky. The sun has started to sink; it's late afternoon, which means I need to head back to Hank's soon to get ready for tonight's party.

I put my hand over my belly to calm the sudden flutter there. Excitement? Nerves? The thought of being all lovey-dovey with Hank tonight seems both wonderful and terrifying.

A part of me wonders if I should leave. But another part . . .

"I want to stay," I say quietly. "I like how I feel when I'm with him."

"See? He's already worlds better than Dan."

"Kate, I was with Dan for a decade. I've been with Hank for all of, what, one and a half weekends? Of course I'm going to like how Hank makes me feel. Wanting to be with him is easy, because I don't have to pick up after him or ask him to take out the trash six hundred times. This isn't real life."

"Exactly. So, really, there's nothing to be afraid of, is there? Y'all are living in fantasy land. Maybe that's why you're getting all these feels. Who wouldn't be bowled over by the weekend you're having? Hot dude. Hotter sex. Being taken care of by the five-star staff of a five-star resort. Lady, that's heaven, and when you leave, the crash will be hard enough. Don't make it any harder by letting fear hold you back. You're not gonna fall in love with this guy, okay? If anything, it's a temporary infatuation of the teenage variety that'll fade after a week or two."

"Yeah," I say, even though I'm not sure I buy it. "Yeah, you're right. What we're doing, it's just a sexy little weekend where I play a part, and he plays my body the way he plays his guitar. He fucking knows *how*."

"Oh, shit, he plays the guitar?"

I close my eyes again. "Yup."

"He does sound lethal, I'll give you that."

My pulse pounds. "It's just a sexy little weekend."

"Right."

"I don't want to take care of another man. Which is why weekends like this are perfect—because the man takes care of me, and we all go home happy."

"Like I said, heaven. Now stop psyching yourself out and go, I don't know, engage in some ass play in your billionaire's wine cellar. Fuck in his sauna. Suck his enormous dick in his heated pool. He has a heated pool, right?"

I smile. "Honestly, I wouldn't know. We've been kinda confined to his house."

"Welp, it's a long weekend, which means you have forty-eight hours to fuck in forty-eight different ways. If you need reconstructive vaginal surgery, Jane knows a guy."

"Jane is that guy," I say, and I mean it. Kate's wife is a partner at one of the best plastic surgery practices in Nashville.

"She's sexy, right?"

"The sexiest."

"Cool." She sighs. "You good?"

I'm not sure if I'm good. But I do feel the tiniest bit better. Maybe I just needed the reminder that Blue Mountain

Farm isn't the real world, and if it's not real, then I can't be in any real danger.

"I'll be okay. Thanks for the pep talk."

"Anytime. And Stevie?"

"Yeah?"

"I just want you to know not all guys are like Dan. And not all marriages end up like your parents'. Jane and I are an incredibly imperfect testament to that idea."

My brows snap together at the mention of Mom and Dad. As much as I want to believe Kate's comment is out of left field, I know better, and so does she.

"There's these studies," I say, walking. "Studies done on older married couples. I'm grossly paraphrasing here, but when the wife dies, the husband's happiness goes down the drain. But when the husband dies, the wife's happiness goes through the roof."

"Ha. I believe it."

"Makes sense, right? All her life, she's had to take care of him, and the kids, and the dog and the house and everything else. But when he goes, she's free. I bet my mom would be happier without my dad, as fucked up as it is to say that. It's a total relief not to wait on someone day and night."

"My question is this: why did you feel like you had to wait on Dan that way?"

I scoff. "Because that's all I saw growing up. I'd internalized the bullshit idea that, as women, we owe the world for the space we take up. And I thought that doing everything for everyone was a normal part of that. I swore I wouldn't end up like my mom, but I guess toxic gender roles die hard."

"They do die, though, Stevie."

Looking at the sun, I squint. "They do. But I think it's harder—almost impossible—for them to die in a marriage. There's a reason Oprah never married Stedman."

"So do what Oprah does, and do whatever the hell you

want. There are no rules. You don't have to marry Hank, and you definitely don't have to wait on him. See? Nothing to worry about."

She's right.

I tell myself she's right.

The heaviness in my chest lifts. Allowing the flutter in my belly to spread all over.

Chapter Fifteen

STEVIE

Hank is working out when I get home, so I touch base with Ria about the tasting and Blue Mountain's potential order. Then I jump in the shower.

I'm curling my hair at the sink when Hank walks into the bathroom. My mouth goes dry. He's wearing shorts, sneakers, and a University of South Carolina tee with the sleeves cut off. His skin glistens with sweat, and his shirt is plastered to his broad chest and torso, revealing mountains of thick, bulging muscle.

His biceps are huge. Veins snake down his forearms, shiny with sweat.

I don't realize I'm staring until I smell burning hair.

"Shit!" I unwind a curl from the iron, releasing a puff of smoke.

One side of his mouth kicking up, Hank yanks his shirt over his head. "How was your hike?"

Rivulets of sweat work their way down his barreled chest. His nipples are tiny pink points on a broad expanse of skin and hair.

"Go-*od*," I yelp when he gives my ass a quick swat. I'm

wearing a robe, but I feel the contact as if I were naked. The zing goes right to my clit, and my breath catches. "Your workout?"

"Good." He toes off his sneakers and socks and pulls down his shorts.

He's hugely, unashamedly erect, and he's walking around the bathroom—opening a drawer, grabbing a condom—like it's no big deal. Steadily, like he's in no rush.

There's something sweet about it. So sweet, knowing we'll be together tonight at a fabulous party, and together after that in his bed. And together tomorrow and part of Monday too.

We're simultaneously running out of time and swimming in it.

"Question for you," he says.

"Go for it."

"You killed it at the tasting. You've got your beers in bars across the country. You own your own business. Clearly you've got a lot on your plate. But you're also . . . relaxed?" I laugh, and he holds up his hands. "I hope you don't take that the wrong way—I mean it as a compliment. I'm just wondering how the hell you kill it at work but also stay sane. I mean, you were able to take some time off to come here, right?"

Something lovely unfurls inside my chest. I laugh, if only to help me brush it aside.

"I was, yes. And do you mean how do I balance work and life? Because I do have a life."

"That's obvious. And yeah, I guess that is what I'm asking. Because when I was working, I thought I had one. But seeing you . . . I didn't have much of a life at all."

I lift a shoulder, like I didn't fail at that same thing for years. "Takes a lot of practice. Lots of trial and error. Don't forget, I'm a whole decade older than you, so . . ."

He grins. "So you've not only got more life experience, you've got fewer fucks to give."

"Exactly."

Exactly.

I look down and pick at my terrycloth robe. "I had to work around the clock when I started Lady Luck. Years of fifteen-hour days, no weekends, no vacations. But even when we were up and running, and I didn't need to work that way because I had the resources to hire help, I still did the fifteen-hour days. And I got so run down I finally went to my therapist and was like, 'please help me, I can't keep doing this, but I don't know how to change.' She got me to question why I worked like a maniac. Who won? Because it sure as hell wasn't me."

"Yeah." He runs a hand through his short hair, still wet with sweat. "That feeling of being run down. I know it well."

"That how you felt working guest relations?"

"Absolutely, yeah. But I guess I thought that was normal? I spent seven years playing pro ball. The kind of intensity that requires, the all-out dedication—I don't know how to live any other way. It's balls to the wall or nothing."

I glance up at his crotch. "Speaking of balls."

Hank cups his balls in a quick, lewd gesture that's insanely hot. "I got 'em, honey."

My pussy clenches. He wants to fuck, that much is obvious, but he's also looking at me with serious eyes. Like he's listening to what I say. Soaking it up because it matters.

Because I matter.

"I got smart," I say. "I hired help. Starting with my assistant, who took a lot off my plate. I forced myself to keep regular hours—nine to five, Monday through Friday—and made a point to plan stuff outside of work. Weekly tennis with my girlfriends. Blocks of reading time. Travel. It's absolutely a privilege to live and work the way I do. And I don't think I'll ever have 'balance' mastered—it's constantly a work in progress. But I can say with absolute certainty I'm fuller and more content than I've ever been. Having boundaries and being easier on myself has actually made me a better worker too."

His eyes—they're gleaming with admiration now.

Desire. The sexual kind, yes, but another kind too.

"You have a life," he says. "A real, grown-up life."

"You digging at my age now?"

He smirks again. "Never. You know I think forty is sexy."

"Good thing."

"Speaking of sex." He holds up a gold foil packet between his first and second fingers. "Do I need to use this?"

As promised, he emailed me his clean bill of health early this morning.

I emailed him mine right after.

I give my head a little shake, and he tosses the condom onto his vanity.

Then he makes for me. I have the presence of mind to move my hot curling iron to the far side of my countertop, unplugging it for good measure.

"I always use condoms," I say when he spins me around and lifts me onto the vanity, parting my legs and brushing the robe aside.

His eyes flick to meet mine. "No panties?"

"Not tonight, no."

He steps between my legs and lines himself up at my entrance. I feel pressure. I smell sweat. Salt and earth, and it's so weirdly hot I want to scream.

"I always use condoms too," he says, and shoves inside me with a grunt. "But you—I wanna fuck you raw, honey."

The pinprick in my chest is overwhelmed by the tide of arousal that floods my body.

He does fuck me, raw and hard and quick. No kissing. We

lock eyes and go for it. The kind of gritty sex that has me grabbing for the towel ring and Hank biting the corner of his mouth. It feels so good this way. Nothing separating us. We pant, possessed, shit spilling off the vanity as our movements become more crazed. The soap dish. Hair clips. The vial of moisturizer I'd been using, which lands on the marble floor with a *crack*.

Neither of us stops or says a word.

He reaches between my legs to roll his thumb over my clit. A surge of feeling moves through me, the beginning of the day's third orgasm. I close my eyes and lean back, overwhelmed.

But Hank curls an arm around my waist and tugs me roughly to him, pistoning his hips so he's buried to the root after every thrust.

There's that flutter again. But I'm in too deep to stop now, so I bury my head in Hank's shoulder and pray like hell Kate was right.

"Just so you know." Hank grunts. Presses his thumb to my clit. "I haven't been with anyone since you. Since Vegas."

I sink my teeth into his shoulder. *Don't go there*. Because I haven't been with anyone either.

But then I come, and I forget why that should scare me.

"Tell me now," he growls.

"Tell you what?"

"Tell me I can't come inside you, or it's gonna be too late in two fucking seconds."

Don't don't don't.

I want him to, but I shouldn't. Not because I'm worried about getting pregnant. I have an IUD.

I'm worried what it would mean.

How it would make me feel.

I don't give Hank my answer in time. He suddenly jerks out of me, covering himself with his hand. Teeth gritted, he closes his eyes and comes in his hand, clutching my thigh in the other.

His grip hurts, and I like it.

I like how he's considerate, thoughtful, even in the throes of what appears to be the kind of orgasm that just rocked me to my core. And then he seals it—seals *me*—with a gentle kiss to my forehead.

Hank cleans us up. Then he bends down and grabs the moisturizer, examining it before placing it back on the counter. "Looks okay. If you need another, let me know and I'll get one delivered. You okay to get down? I should grab a shower so we're not late."

I shake my head and gingerly lower myself to the ground. "I'm okay."

But my hands shake as I finish curling my hair.

When Hank gets out of the shower, I can only stare as he towels himself off. He lifts his arms to dry his hair, wet strands falling in his face.

He puts on an Ed Sheeran playlist—"this dude is one hell of a musician"—and makes quick work of getting dressed.

It's warm inside the bathroom. It smells like Hank's cologne and sex. The light glints off the mirrors, coating everything in a cozy glow.

We don't talk about what Hank said.

When he's fully dressed in a sharp suit and chrome Rolex, he disappears from the bathroom. I take the opportunity to finish getting ready. I put on on the sexiest bra I own. Finding bras that fit my generous bust well, don't cost a fortune, and are kinda-sorta cute is a constant battle for me. This one is as close to a triple threat as it gets: black satin, with a frill of lace that lines the cups. I hike up my Spanx next, followed by my most favorite dress I've ever bought. It's bold but classic, a bright orange Victoria Beckham sheath that's skintight and sexy as hell. There's an open panel on the stomach, allowing just the right amount of skin to show through (the opening is well above my belly button, so my Spanx don't show through).

I slip on a few gold bangles and a pair of matching stud earrings. Simple but pretty.

I'm stepping into my heels, nude stiletto sandals, when Hank comes back into the bathroom. He's carrying glasses of white wine in his enormous hands, the bowls deliciously frosted over.

He sees me and stops short. Stares. Lips parted, this soft, almost pained look in his eyes.

The romance of the moment works its way up my sides. It feels like the whispering touch of curious fingertips, making me want to smile and giggle and hide all at once.

"You okay?" I ask, a little breathless.

He holds out a wineglass and blinks, hard. "You look like a million bucks, Stevie."

"Thanks." I take the wine and sip. "I still need to put on makeup."

"No, you don't."

I grin. "You're cute."

"You're beautiful." He takes my chin in his hand and presses a hard, wet kiss to my mouth. He smells good enough to eat. "How are you feeling?"

"Sore."

"Shit, did I—"

"No. You did everything exactly right." *So. Fucking. Right.* "What about you?"

His lips twitch. "I'm good. Real good, honey."

"Hey," I say, tilting my head toward the vanity. "I'm gonna finish up. I'll be ready to go in fifteen, all right?"

"Sure."

I set my wineglass down and grab my makeup bag. Looking up, I see Hank take a seat on the edge of the tub. He crosses his ankle over his knee and grips that ankle in his hand.

I love his hands. They're strong and sure, and they feel fantastic on my body.

Smiling, I uncap my foundation. "You watching me get ready?"

"Yes."

Ed Sheeran is still playing. I apply my makeup, and Hank watches. I feel just the tiniest bit self-conscious. It's delicious self-consciousness, if such a thing exists. It makes me aware of everything good happening right now: the healthy beat of my pulse, the excitement in my blood. The certainty that, at this moment at least, I'm wanted and well taken care of.

No work to be done. No one to please. No rush.

The silence between us is companionable. Maybe because we said everything we couldn't say aloud while we fucked right here on the counter.

I lean over the sink to apply a swipe of eyeliner. Hank's eyes move to my ass. He grins, a small, private thing.

Yeah.

Tonight's gonna be a good night.

We arrive right on time.

Hank helps me out of my coat as I take in the room. It's technically called Blue Mountain Farm's "library," but really it's a large section of the main house with soaring ceilings, big, sophisticated furniture, and a huge fireplace. The lights are low, and tall taper candles are everywhere. A small army of servers offers hors d'oeuvres to guests, while bartenders are busy shaking up cocktails at the gleaming wooden bar on the far wall.

A guy with a guitar croons in a corner, and a good-looking

crowd mills around the space. Two sets of French doors lead out onto a wide terrace, set up with heaters, bistro tables, and another bar.

"The library at Biltmore inspired this room," Hank says into my ear. "I can't believe you've never been."

The Biltmore is the old Vanderbilt estate here in Asheville. It's billed as America's largest private home, and apparently, much of its gilded-age glamor is still intact for tourists like me to gawk at.

I can't resist. I give in to the pull of his presence and turn my head, our noses brushing. The desire to be close to him is acute. "I hear it's amazing."

"Let's go tomorrow, then."

"Don't you have to buy tickets, like, months in advance?"

Hank grins. "I know a guy."

"Of course you do." I look across the room. "Hey, there's Milly. I want to thank her again for her help with today's tasting."

He puts his hand on the small of my back and follows me. I realize that I'd completely forgotten about the evening's fake relationship component up until this moment.

Right now, I don't need to pretend.

"Hi, Stevie," she says.

She does not return my smile.

"Hey, Milly. You look gorgeous." She's wearing a raspberry-pink gown with puff sleeves and a slim Gucci belt. She's topped it off with oversized statement earrings, a swipe of dark lipstick, and hair in old-Hollywood glam waves. "Lady, you could be on the cover of *Vogue*."

"Thanks." Her eyes flick over my dress. "You too."

"I appreciate that. Working at a brewery—"

"Owning a brewery," Hank corrects.

"Right. Owning a brewery means I spend most days in

jeans. But any chance I get to doll myself up like this, I go all out."

"I will *never* forget that dress you wore in Vegas." Hank's hand moves to my ass.

I turn my head to smile at him. In these heels, we're exactly the same height, our eyes level. "That's a fun one."

"It was fun to take off."

"I'm gonna stop y'all there." Milly loops her arm through mine. "Hank, I'm stealing your girlfriend for a bit. Think you can survive fifteen minutes without her?"

"Honestly?" Hank looks at me. Hazel eyes full and serious. "I don't know."

My heart skips a beat, the threads of *real* and *fake* tangling inside my head. The sexual desire he feels for me is real.

But this look—this is another kind of desire, the kind we promised we'd only fake.

Only Hank doesn't appear to be faking it.

If he is, he's a really, really good actor.

Scariest of all, the longing spreading inside my chest feels real too. When was the last time someone looked at me this way?

"Too bad. We'll be back in fifteen." Milly nods across the room at Beau. "I think he wanted to talk to you anyway."

She whisks me into the crowd, tilting her head close to mine.

"So," she says.

"So."

"You and Hank seem to be hot and heavy."

Laughing, I reply, "Our connection was pretty immediate and pretty intense, yeah."

"But y'all haven't known each other long."

A feeling of unease moves up my spine. "A couple of months. Seems quick, I know, but we really did hit it off from day one. I'm not one to mess around—not at this point in my life—and neither is Hank. It's one of the things I appreciate most about him."

I cringe inwardly. That last bit is true. But telling Milly Beauregard I'm not messing around when that's exactly what I'm doing feels . . . not great, in a way I wasn't expecting.

I wonder where the hell this surge of conscientiousness came from. I willingly signed up to do the pretend relationship thing, didn't I? Knowing full well it would entail telling one gigantic lie and lots of smaller ones too. The ruse was supposed to be fun.

It doesn't feel fun at the moment.

I only wish Hank's family wasn't so damn great. None of them would pull a stunt like this. Does that make me a scumbag?

Milly slows her stride, stopping in front of the French doors. A waiter opens one, closes it; I shiver at the sudden gust of cold air.

"Look," she says, turning to face me. "I don't mean to be an asshole, but I love my brother, and I think I speak for my family when I say I don't want him to get hurt. He dove in headfirst with Emma, and now I see him kinda-sorta doing the same with you. The way he looks at you . . . I mean, you know, obviously. He's smitten. So you understand why I'm a little concerned. We all are."

My heart thumps. I grab a glass of water from the nearby sideboard and take a gulp. I want to thank her for her honesty. Milly's not a bullshitter, and I've learned to appreciate that over the years.

But I'm not being honest, and bringing up her honesty while lying to her face seems like the most bullshitty move of all.

"I get it," I say. "And that's a totally fair concern to have. Hank is a great guy, Milly—really, really great—and I'd never hurt him, not intentionally. He told me what went down with

Samuel and Emma, obviously. He also told me he learned a lot from it. I think"—another gulp of water—"I think he has a better idea of what he wants now."

Milly nods, sipping her champagne. "And you, Stevie? Do you know what you want?"

"Yes," I say. And I wait for the certainty of that truth to steel my spine, the way it always does.

I wait some more. Milly looks at me expectantly.

"I want Hank to be happy." I pick my words carefully. "I mean that, Milly."

"Right. We all want that. But what do *you* want? Like, what's your dream scenario here? Forever? A family? Because I know my brother, and I know that's what he's dreaming about."

Glancing down at my water, I fervently wish it was whiskey.

"Milly, Christ, are you torturin' sweet Stevie here? I told you to take it easy."

I look up to see Rhett and almost pass out with gratitude.

"She's not torturing me," I say.

Milly smiles. "Yes, I am. Sorry. I just get a little protective when it comes to family."

"Protective?" Rhett looks at his sister sideways. "I'd go with meaner 'n a snake. But sure, you can call it protective if you want." He puts an arm around my shoulders and presses a kiss to the top of my head. "How you doin', girl?"

"Great," I say. Because I am doing great. I'm having a great time.

But also, part of me is feeling *not* so amazing.

Fuck me, how did things get so complicated in the past half hour?

"Good. Here, lemme introduce you—" Rhett goes still beside me.

I look up. Look at the girl *he's* looking at.

"Shit," he mutters.

"What?" Milly turns and looks. Turns back to us and nonchalantly sips her champagne. "Huh. I didn't know Samuel invited Amelia."

"Who's Amelia?" I ask, trying to decipher Rhett's expression.

He shakes his head. "An old friend."

"It's the girl he almost knocked up in high school," Milly says.

I furrow my brow. "Isn't knocking someone up an either/or scenario? How do you 'almost' do it?"

"It was just a scare," Rhett says. "Everyone has scares when they're young and dumb."

"I never did," Milly says.

"Me neither."

Rhett shakes his head again and sighs. "Can we at least agree that your first one'll forever fuck with your head? I'm gonna go say hello. Y'all behave, all right?"

"First what?" I murmur to Milly after Rhett's gone.

"First love. Rhett had it bad for Amelia all through high school. Asheville was a small town back then—still is in many ways—and their relationship was like a real-life version of *Varsity Blues*."

"That movie is so bad but *so* good."

"Right? That *Dawson's Creek* dude was insanely hot in football pads." She looks at me. "Be good to Hank, all right? He's been through hell. I only want to see him happy. If you think you can help him get there, great. If not . . . don't waste his time."

I remember what Hank said the night we met. *Wasting time is exactly what I'm trying to do*. He meant that then.

I think he's starting to change his mind on that point now.

"Yeah," I say. "He deserves a happy ending. Definitely."

Luckily, Annabel comes to the rescue, giving me a quick hug before the three of us head to the bar. Then she and Milly guide me through the room, stopping to introduce me to cousins, aunts, college buddies, and people from town.

I should focus on charming Hank's family, but instead, I find myself sneaking glances around the room, looking for him.

He's working the crowd, shaking hands and slapping backs, a genuine smile on his lips. Joy looks good on him. So does that fucking suit.

I'm not the only one bowled over by his handsome charm. The women he talks to laugh a little too loudly. One touches his arm. A few more stare while sipping their cocktails.

I don't blame them. His charisma is magnetic.

I *feel* it, an ache in my center that won't let me be. It's a total Taylor Swift "gold rush" moment, and it's equal parts thrilling and . . . painful.

Thrilling: this guy—the one who's hot and sweet and, yes, famous—is wild for me. Physically speaking, anyway. He's crazy for what we do naked. I get to go home with him tonight.

Painful: this guy's going to have a million options to choose from when I leave. A million women who aren't too damaged or too jaded to do the white picket fence thing with him.

A million women who don't lie to his family about their intentions.

Chapter Sixteen

HANK

"You think she's okay with Milly?"

Taking a pull from his water glass, Beau glances across the room. A growing circus of curious relatives surrounds Stevie.

Looks like she's handling it like a champ. I knew she'd hit it off with my family.

I didn't anticipate, however, that tug of guilt I keep feeling—because it's definitely guilt—as I pull one over on them. I'm trying to do the right thing here by making Samuel and Emma happy. I just had no idea things would get so twisted up.

I didn't anticipate this weird feeling that I may want what Stevie and I have to be real.

Giving the ice in my glass a shake, I make a note that those two lines would make a good, if cheesy, lyric.

My muse burned out around the same time I did. This is the first time I've felt a spark of inspiration in years.

"Meh. You know Milly," I reply. "What's going on with her, by the way? Something's up."

Beau shrugs. "Hell if I know. If I had to guess, I'd say it has something to do with Nate Kingsley. I haven't heard dick from him since he asked me if he could date Milly, but I get the feeling they've been hanging out."

Nate Kingsley is a local whiskey distiller I've known forever. Our families had a little Capulet and Montague thing going on back in the day, and until recently, there was still some bad blood there. While I don't love the idea of Milly dating a Kingsley, I do want her to be happy. And if Nate is brave enough to take on that job, well, more power to him.

I tip back my glass. "I'd say good for her if she didn't look so down."

"I've asked her about it, but she keeps saying she's fine."

"She told me that love is a bitch."

Beau lifts his eyebrows. "Wouldn't Milly always say that? She isn't exactly a softie."

"True."

We watch her and Stevie together for another beat while we finish our cocktails.

"I'm just praying Uncle Larry doesn't share that story about his blushing bride," Beau says, nodding at our uncle, who's now chatting up Stevie.

"How she was a virgin on their wedding night?"

"Who tells people that shit?"

"Uncle Larry."

"You're right." I swallow a big slug of whiskey, wincing at the burn. "I should go rescue her."

"Wait." Beau puts a hand on my arm. "I know you've only been back a few days. But I wanted to let you know we're ready for you to return to work when you are. *If* you are. I'm open to talk about it anytime. You know that, right? The offer stands for you to head up guest relations again, same as it did nine months ago. We didn't hire anyone new because we wanted to keep the position open for when you came back."

"You knew I'd come home?"

Beau lifts a shoulder. "Had a hunch."

I hesitate. Sip my whiskey. "How's Gregory been doing?"

Gregory, the interim head of guest relations, is a hard worker, very detail oriented, but he's young and doesn't have the kind of experience someone in his role typically would. I knew he'd need a lot of hand-holding.

I probably should've checked in on our guest relations team while I was on my bender. But I needed a break, a real one, and I knew if I sat down to answer a single email, I'd get sucked right back in.

"He's done well, all things considered. It was a huge stroke of luck that you'd already implemented a lot of your strategies for the team, so really Gregory's been in a kind of holding pattern since you left. I've helped out, and so has Emma. Samuel too. We haven't gotten any complaints."

I let out a silent sigh of relief. I hated the idea of leaving everyone in the lurch, but I had no choice. It's good to know shit didn't hit the fan while I took the time I needed.

"Have you given coming back to work with us any thought? Like, at all?" Beau presses.

"I have. Of course I have, Beau. Blue Mountain is in my blood."

"So?"

I let out a breath. "I did enjoy a lot of what the job entailed. I'd consider returning. But it can't be like before, Beau. I can't work the way I did."

"Okay." He dips his head in a nod. "What do we need to change?"

"I'd need more help for starters." I train my gaze on Stevie. She catches me looking and smiles. "Another assistant. And I wouldn't want to work weekends."

Beau winces. "Weekends are our bread and butter. As head of guest relations . . ."

"Right. Welp, that's something we could talk about. But

five days a week, max. Obviously I'd be happy to work more for special events and stuff." I shrug. "Guess I just want to get my priorities in the right order. Because as much as I love the resort, it can't be everything, you know?"

"Dude." Beau puts a hand on my shoulder. "I had no idea you felt that way."

"You had a few issues of your own to figure out. And I wasn't exactly forthcoming about my feelings. Truth be told, I'm not sure I knew how burned out I was until . . ."

I don't finish the sentence. I don't have to.

Beau gives my shoulder a squeeze. "I did have shit to figure out. But as Blue Mountain's CEO—and more than that, as your brother—I should've been paying attention. I'm sorry."

"I'm sorry too."

"And I know what you mean when you say work can't be everything." He looks at Annabel, who's chatting with Mama by the fireplace. "Life is better when you've got people to come home to."

It is. I've had Stevie in my house for all of twenty-four hours, and I already don't dread going home the way I used to.

A hand grips my windpipe and squeezes. It's *really* gonna suck when she leaves.

"Stevie's great," Beau says, lowering his voice. "I'm happy for you, Hank."

Squeeze gets firmer. Pulse gets faster. "Thanks. I should probably—"

"Go get your girl. I don't need to tell you not to fuck it up, right?"

I force a laugh. "You're my big brother. Whether or not I need it, you'll always tell me what you think."

"Only 'cause I love you."

Turning toward the bar, I'm torn between getting a brown

liquor refill or slamming a glass of water. I'm getting heady, and the brown stuff helps with that. But I also don't wanna get shit-faced. I've only got two more days and nights with Stevie. I'd be a bonehead to waste time blacking out or being hungover.

Water it is.

"You all right there, sailor?" Stevie asks, eyes flicking to my water glass, when I finally do rescue her from the Beauregard circus.

"Just stayin' hydrated for you. I got some late night plans for us."

Her gaze softens, and so does everything inside my chest. "You're a good guy, you know that?"

Somewhere deep down, I do know that. But after everything that's gone down over the past year, it's still nice to hear.

Another lyric.

Damn I'm on fire. I just might have to get out the guitar tonight.

"What were you and my sister talking about?" I ask.

Stevie looks at me for half a beat.

"Milly's just looking out for you. It's sweet, how y'all care so much about each other." Stevie lowers her voice. "You do have an exit plan, right? A way to, well, explain why I'll leave on Monday and never come back?"

My chest twists. I brush the sensation aside and focus on the problem at hand.

The problem being I don't have a plan. Guess I just sorta assumed it'd work itself out. Stevie would leave. I'd start work again. Time would pass, and when my family would ask about her, I'd give them a line or two about us growing apart or some shit.

"I'll figure it out."

"Okay. Because it's important that you have a plan. I think

your family is getting invested in there being an actual, real-life us, and if we don't—"

"Stevie!" Mama appears at her elbow. "You're a sight for sore eyes. Sweetheart, you look fabulous."

Pasting on a smile, Stevie bends down to give Mama a hug. "Thank you, June. You don't look too bad yourself. That monotone pantsuit! How very Michelle Obama of you."

Mama preens. "I'd be lying if I didn't say that was what I was going for. Your compliment is the best I've gotten all night. Thank you."

"Didn't I hear someone complimenting you on how great your perfect children turned out?" I cock a brow. "That's not the best compliment?"

"Nope," Mama replies. "I'm proud of my children, but I'm prouder of this get up."

"As you should be," Stevie says. She laughs and Mama smiles and a happy mess of feelings blooms inside my center.

The thought appears clear as day inside my head: this whole *thing* is a happy mess. At least it is tonight. Tomorrow too. When Stevie leaves, it'll probably be a plain old mess that needs cleaning up.

But for now, I'm enjoying it.

"Y'all are only perfect because your parents are." Stevie glides an arm around my waist. "But truly, June, you raised this boy right." Stevie's eyes catch on mine. "He's thoughtful. Generous. Empathetic and considerate in a way not many guys are. Not the ones I know, anyway."

Mama holds a hand to her chest. "Perhaps I spoke too soon. *That* is the best compliment. Thank you, Stevie. I raised my kids to make good decisions. And part of that idea was teaching them to be good people who'd eventually make good partners." She looks intently at Stevie. "Like attracts like."

Stevie swallows, gaze straying to her feet.

"Stevie is a great partner," I say, and I mean it.

She looks up at me. "So are you," she replies. And from the naked, scared look on her face, I know she means that too. She blinks, the fear dissolving. "That's what makes him so dangerous."

"Not my fame or fortune or good looks?"

"Son, you best get that ego in check," Mama says, holding up a finger at me. "Now if y'all will excuse me, I'm being summoned. Looks like Rhett's gotten into the proverbial punch again. Perfect children my behind, *what* is that boy's problem lately . . ."

A beat of awkward silence settles between Stevie and me as we watch Mama disappear into the crush.

"What about you?" I finally ask. "Talk to me, sailor."

Stevie turns her head. "You really are dangerous, Hank."

I wanna find out what she really means by that.

Later. When we're in bed and she's soft with sex and sleep. Right now, I need to keep things light and fun. It's getting too easy to forget what we're here for.

"Is it my dick?" I ask. "I know it's the biggest and best looking you've seen, but you don't gotta be scared."

She laughs and gives my arm a playful shove. "That's one thing I'm definitely not scared of. I mean, I put it in my mouth not once, not twice, but—"

"Y'all talking about genitalia?" Samuel walks up to us with a bourbon in his hand and Emma on his arm.

Stevie turns her high-wattage smile on me. Bites her lip, cheeks going pink.

"Aw, yeah, y'all are definitely talking about genitalia." Samuel sips his drink. "So what's the verdict, Stevie? You enjoying those robust Beauregard—"

"Genes," Emma finishes, sending Samuel a sassy warning glance. "Also, who uses the word genitalia?"

"Who do you think you are?" I ask. "A doctor? A perv who

uses words that sound like scary skin conditions to describe people's privates?"

Samuel wags his brows. "I'm a doctor of love, yeah."

"That sounds fun," Stevie says.

"It's not," Emma replies, but she's got her hand on Samuel's chest and she's smiling. "I'll still keep him, though."

She's tipsy. Samuel is too. I can tell by the way he leans down to peck Emma on the lips. It's something I don't think he'd do in front of me if he were stone-cold sober. Despite the time that's passed, we're all still tiptoeing around a perceived freshness of wounds.

I'm so tired of being careful. I'm sure Samuel is too.

Again, I don't feel jealous. I don't feel hurt or wronged or sad or angry.

Again, I do feel that echo. That longing. Not for Emma, but for something.

Turning to Stevie, I amend that idea: it's a longing for some*one*.

With Emma, maybe I just wanted a warm body. Someone to start the life I'd always been dreaming of with. I'd been waiting for her to show up for so damn long, and I was tired of being patient.

Now I want someone like Stevie. As much as the waiting sucked, if it means I get moments like this one, it was all worth it. My heart's finally beating again.

Goddamn, I'm gonna write a whole song by the end of the night.

Maybe Stevie can help me polish it up.

Later. When I get to *take her home*. Second to last night I'll be able to do that. And then, I'll put my nonexistent exit plan into action.

"I am absolutely enjoying the Beauregard genes," Stevie says, smiling at me. "The Good Lord did see fit to endow y'all with big . . . hearts."

"And heads," Emma says.

"And genitalia," Samuel adds.

"All right, Doctor Pervy, that's enough bourbon for you." I grab Samuel's glass.

"Fair." Samuel shrugs, tucking his free hand around Emma's hip. "I don't think I've heard y'all's story. The real story—you know, what makes you guys nuts for each other."

Stevie looks at me. I look back.

"It all began with aces and eights," she says.

I nod, pulse skipping a beat as the memory hits me head-on. Her tits in that tee shirt. Helen the dealer. Tambourines and the scent of Stevie's shampoo floating over the stale-cigarette smell of the casino.

Magic.

"And then it progressed to Stevie introducing me to my favorite beer," I say.

"You flatter me," Stevie teases.

"I don't. Y'all tasted Lady Luck's beer." I nod at Samuel and Emma. "Is it not the best?"

Emma smiles. "It's the best I've tasted in ages, Stevie."

"It's a big deal when Miss Master Sommelier over here says that," Samuel adds. "Her tongue is a thing of wonder."

"Paging Doctor Pervy," Stevie says, and bursts into laughter. The silly, infectious kind, and suddenly we're all laughing, just lubed up enough on liquor not to give a shit.

People stare. I spill Samuel's drink all over my hand and shoes.

Spill it right onto Stevie's sexy as fuck dress. A stain spreads just to the side and underneath her left breast.

"Shit! Shit, honey." I immediately grab a handful of napkins from a passing waiter. I dab the spot, pressing the napkins against the fabric. "I'm sorry."

Stevie lifts her arm and bends her back, arching into my touch. "Don't be, baby."

Baby. Did the word sound huskier than it usually does when she says it? Or am I imagining things?

Handing Samuel back his drink, I wrap my free hand around her other side, just underneath her right breast. I firm my grip and she arches some more, melting into my touch as I continue to dab.

"I don't think you're getting it," Stevie murmurs.

"How about I grab some club soda—"

Stevie nudges me with her hip. "How about you use your mouth?"

I look up to see her lips twitching.

"It is good bourbon," Samuel says. "Hate for it to go to waste. I'll give you a hundred bucks if you do it."

"I'll bet a hundred bucks you won't," Stevie says, challenge in her eyes.

I level my gaze with hers. "Won't that make more of a mess?"

"Yup." She catches her tongue between her teeth. "That's kind of the point. Well, that, and proving to your friends and family we're not too proud to be caught wearing compromised garments in compromising positions."

This.

Fucking.

Girl.

"You got that hundred on you, honey?"

Stevie taps the top of her breast. "Right here in my bra. If you do a good job, I'll let you use your mouth to get that too."

"Damn." Samuel holds out his knuckles to Stevie. "I like you."

Emma smiles, eyes dancing. "Just when I thought our engagement party was feeling a little too stiff."

Samuel chuckles. "Speaking of stiff—"

"Don't," Emma and I say together.

I duck down and put my mouth on Stevie's body. Her

perfume fills my head; the sugar-spice taste of the bourbon hits my tongue. Stevie's torso expands on a breathy laugh.

I watch her nipples harden to points, deliciously blurred by the material of her dress.

I laugh too, my dick twitching in my pants.

"What the hell is this?" I hear Beau murmur.

"It's lust," Rhett replies.

"It's love," Mama says.

Chapter Seventeen

HANK

We stumble into my house at half past twelve.

Rhett was determined to keep the party going, and he invited a handful of late night revelers back to his place for, and I quote, "bongs, bourbon, and ball."

Stevie and I declined, but used it as an excuse to slip away from the party ourselves.

Wheels are really coming off for my brother. I'll have a chat with him on Monday about getting his shit together—even for him, this kind of partying is extreme.

I'll find out what's going on later. Right now, I got plans for my girl and me.

I help Stevie out of her coat, and she bends down to unbuckle her shoes, letting out a hiss of pleasure when she flattens her bare feet on the floor.

"Honey." I frown at the red indents that crisscross her skin. "Why didn't you say your shoes hurt? We coulda left earlier. I would've happily run back here to get—"

"Seriously."

"Seriously what?"

Stevie glances around the foyer. "We're not at the party anymore. You don't need to pretend to be my boyfriend."

An ice pick of hurt lodges itself in my center. Why this? Why now? I've been acting the same way all damn weekend.

"I'm not pretending. I'm just being a decent human being. That so rare in your world you think it's fake?"

Her expression falls. She shakes her head. "No. I'm sorry. Tonight was great. Too great. I'm confused."

"So am I. There such a thing as too great?"

She shoots me an incredulous look, hair falling over her shoulders in thick, sexy waves. "I think so, yeah. I really did have the best time. Well, aside from the whole Milly interrogating me thing."

"Sorry about that." I shake my head. "Although if someone was going to pull a Jack Byrnes, I'm not surprised it was her."

"I definitely had a Gaylord Focker moment there."

"Don't tell me nipples were involved."

Stevie laughs, and the realization of just how easy and enjoyable it is to just *be* around her hits me.

Our connection really is worlds different from any I've had before.

We're making messes left and right, and we'll probably leave a trail of destruction behind us in the end. But again, one hundred percent fucking worth it.

"No nipples. I saved those for you and your spilled bourbon. She did threaten to kill me, though."

My eyes bulge. "She didn't."

Stevie's laugh morphs into a cackle. "No, of course your sister didn't threaten to kill me. Jesus, Pamela Martha Focker, please don't stop being so easy to fuck with, because I'm having fun doing it."

This this this.

Whatever this is, I want more of it. I want it every Saturday night. Weeknights too.

"Let's make a real mess," I blurt. "Right here. Right now."

Stevie's eyebrows shoot up. "Mess up your house? For real?"

"Why so surprised?"

"Hank, your place is immaculate. It's so perfect it belongs in a magazine."

"Exactly. Feels like it too—like it's a movie set or something. Like no one actually lives here." I hold out my hand. "Let's put our mark on it, shall we?"

Stevie turns her head and looks at me from the corner of her eye. "So you're saying you don't want an insanely beautiful, perfectly put together home?"

"It's a beautiful house, Stevie, don't get me wrong. And it's not like I want to destroy it or turn it into a frat house or anything. I just want . . ." I think on it a minute. "Real. And real people don't live this way, in a house with zero character and zero memories."

Her gaze moves to the far wall, where a dark smudge mars the paint above the console table.

The one Stevie held on to while I fucked her from behind two seconds after she arrived.

How hot did she look in her jeans and boots? I remember with perfect clarity the feel of her pussy clenching around me. Us looking at our reflection in the window and laughing our asses off at how ridiculous we were.

Was that really only last night? Feels like a year ago. An hour ago. How is time simultaneously slipping through my fingers and standing still? Stevie fits in here so well it feels like she's been at Blue Mountain forever.

Yet that mark right there is a testament to how new she is.

How new *we* are. And how we promised our connection was based solely on Stevie Nicks and sex.

It's a promise I never intended to break. But here I am.

Breaking shit. Rules. Boundaries. Sheetrock.

Let's not forget she's got a huge career to go back to, a business based hundreds of miles from here. These feelings I'm catching don't have a future.

Should they, though?

"Well. Not zero memories," I say. "Thanks to you."

"You want more than memories," Stevie replies quietly, looking back at me.

"So what if I do?" It's a bold move, saying that aloud. But I've already lied so much tonight, it's time to share some truth. A half-assed bid to even the karmic scales.

And yeah, maybe I want to see how she'll react. Are her thoughts on our arrangement shifting too? She said she was confused. While I wouldn't say I'm *not* confused—because I am—I already sense that feeling passing.

It's becoming clearer by the second that I genuinely dig this girl.

"One night," Stevie says at last, taking my hand. "One night to make all the memories you want. And then it's back to fake dating, okay?"

My heart leaps and my cock stiffens. "Really?"

"Really."

I don't want to jump five steps ahead. That's what happened with Emma, and it got me in trouble. But I can't help thinking if Stevie gives me one night, who's to say she won't give me another, and another?

Leading her to the bar just off my kitchen, I say, "I hope you weren't planning on sleeping."

A flame ignites in Stevie's eyes, turning them to liquid pools of black. "I'm learning sleep is a moot point when we're together. Also, this bar is ridiculous. Hank, it's bigger than my kitchen."

"It's my favorite room in the house," I reply. "Only one I had any personal input on. The rest I just kinda left to my designer and the architect. But this room, I had a good idea of how I wanted it to look and feel."

It's done up in floor-to-ceiling cabinets painted a deep Oxblood red. A gleaming wooden bar I salvaged from an old Irish pub takes center stage, complete with brass foot railings and a Guinness tap. A series of shelves on the far wall is illuminated from behind, making the rows of liquor bottles glow in the low light.

I reach for a bottle of Appalachian Red. It's one of the world's best whiskeys, and also one of the most expensive.

Stevie, being the beverage goddess she is, knows this.

"Not that bottle," she says, grabbing my wrist.

I crack off the top with a twist of my fingers. "It's the whiskey your body deserves. Now turn around."

I unzip her dress. Not all the way, just to the point where the zipper meets with her bra clasp. I part the sides of her dress. I tuck her hair over her shoulder so it's out of the way.

I tilt the bottle and pour a single trail of whiskey down the length of her spine. It drips onto her dress and the fancy silk carpet that cost more than a car.

Her breath catches and her back straightens.

"Cold?"

"Wet."

I lick my tongue over the trail, pouring more. "Tastes hot. Wet and hot. Exactly how I want you."

Yanking her zipper all the way down, I tell her to pull the top down, and she does. I slip the straps of her bra over her shoulders one at a time, coating them with whiskey. She's dripping with it now, skin slick and slightly sticky.

I pour the whiskey down her chest, soaking her bra.

Walking around her, I pull the cups of her bra down, revealing her nipples. More whiskey. I lick it off one nipple, making Stevie gasp, and then move to the other.

Curling my fingers into her dress—it's bunched at her waist—I say, "I don't want to tear this."

"I don't care," she pants, and digs her fingers into my hair. "Maybe I wanna make a mess too."

"I'll buy you a new one. A new dress."

"I'll buy myself a new dress." She gives my hair a tug. I nibble her breast. "Don't fucking stop. Please. Your tongue —on me—"

I bite down on her nipple and she pitches forward, thighs clenching.

Like a man possessed, I yank down her dress. The fabric rips, making staccato sounds that seem to tear apart the air. Stevie gasps.

My dick throbs when her dress hits the floor.

"What are these?" I ask in wonder, running my hand down the pantyhose-type thing she's wearing.

Stevie laughs. "They're Spanx."

"They're sexy."

"Are they?"

"They are when they're on you."

Stevie looks at me. "They do have a slit in the crotch."

I use my hand to guide her legs apart. Slide that hand up the inside of her thigh. "Oh really? And what am I gonna find there?"

"Wet and hot. Just how you like it."

Dropping to my knees, I dribble whiskey across Stevie's stomach and lick and drink my way to her pussy. She moves her legs a little wider and I press my tongue into her slit.

I curse. She convulses.

"Jesus fuck." I yank her Spanx down too. "Fuck, Stevie, I need all of you. Bare. To me. *Gimme.*"

I sound like a malfunctioning *Westworld* robot, but I could give a shit.

She shimmies out of her Spanx and I roughly spin her around and use the flat of my hand on her back to press her forward, bending her at the waist.

Her ass is in my face. Asshole and pussy right there for me to do with as I please.

My buzz is getting a little too intense. So I pour a little more whiskey on her ass and toss the bottle aside. Let it bleed out on the carpet, two thousand bucks' worth of liquor.

I won't miss it.

But I will miss Stevie.

I trail licks and tiny bites along her left ass cheek. I take my time and taste her, reveling in her yelps. In the way her hips begin to roll, splaying the inner folds of her pussy wide.

I finger her there while I work my mouth down and down some more. Slipping another finger inside her, I lick her asshole at the same time.

She *screams*.

Literally screams, the kind that sounds like some kind of murder just went down, and if I wasn't sure before, I know now that Stevie really likes ass play.

She comes, clamping down on my fingers, and I bite her ass cheek. Hard.

Then I get to my feet and shove her against the wall. I kiss her neck, her jaw, and thrust my hard-on against her stomach. She gets the memo. Her hands move to my zipper, but she has trouble pulling it down.

Is she as riled up as I am?

I grab her hands. They're shaking.

She's shaking.

I pull back to look her in the eye. "You okay?"

"Stop asking me that. Stop being so great."

"I won't."

"I'm drowning," she pants. "In you."

I tighten my grip on her hands. "Tell me you're okay."

"I'm okay."

"Here, lemme help you." I unzip my pants and guide my dick free. Can't help it—I give myself a hard squeeze, and my hips jerk, my body burning to fuck.

Stevie looks down and watches me pump my hand again. She claws at my chest, fingernails digging into my skin through my shirt.

A surge of something that's deeper and scarier than lust rips through me. I crush my mouth to hers and spin her around, walking her backward until her legs meet the bar.

My beautiful, expensive, perfectly arranged bar.

I lift Stevie onto the countertop. Bottles skid and clatter as I push her ass farther onto the bar. A handle of something falls to the floor and shatters. I step on it, glass crackling beneath the soles of my shoes.

The piney scent of juniper blossoms between Stevie and me.

"Gin," Stevie murmurs against my mouth. "Smells good."

Smiling, I reach for a bottle of vodka and swipe it off the counter onto the floor. It shatters, and Stevie jumps.

"And that one?" I line myself up at her entrance and grip her thigh, guiding her leg around my waist.

Stevie wrinkles her nose, rolling her pelvis ever so slightly so that my cock head slips inside her. "Rubbing alcohol. Vodka."

I wanna fuck, but I also wanna make this last. Keeping my eyes trained on Stevie's face, I sink inside her slowly, watching as her mouth falls open and her eyes go hazy. She's tight and perfect, and I fill her with everything I've got.

I love the feel of her raw.

She's ruining me for anyone else.

Once I'm sunk to the hilt, I guide myself back out and go back in. Stevie blinks, her breath hitching.

"Sore," I manage. "I'll go slow."

Stevie wraps a hand around the back of my head, fingertips trailing across my scalp. Goose bumps break out on my arms. "Since when do you read me like a book?"

She uses that hand for leverage, tilting back so she can rock her body porn-star style. Her tits bounce as we find our rhythm, nipples hard and high as she arches her back. All the while, her eyes are locked on mine. Sweet and soft, like she wants to slowly milk my cock, like she knows that's what I want too.

With her other hand, she grabs a shelf behind her.

"Break it," I say. "Take the fucking thing down. Lemme help."

"But the work," she pants. "The work it takes to make liquor like this, and the craft—"

"Indulge me. Just a bottle or five."

Together, we manage to pry the damn thing off the wall. I pull so that it tilts away from Stevie, the bottles it held rolling off to the side. One hits the floor with a heavy *thunk* but doesn't break. Another rolls to the sink, the cap popping off. Liquid pools everywhere.

My balls tighten. Sensation spirals in my core, the muscles in my legs tightening. It's all I can do not to pump into her like a maniac, but that would hurt, and tonight, I'm not in the business of that kind of sex.

I lean down and take a nipple in my mouth. Her skin is stickier than before and still tastes of whiskey.

She smiles, digging her teeth into her bottom lip. "Making messes with you is fun."

"I'm gonna make a mess of you yet, honey," I say. Catching her mouth with mine, I sip a long, slow kiss. It's lips and tongues, with just the barest hint of wine on hers. I fall into the wide-open space behind my closed eyelids. A little dizzy from the booze. Dizzier still from how good this feels. Her fingers are in my hair, and my heart is in my mouth, and I give it to her.

I let her have it.

Sparks of urgent need—release, I gotta let go—ignite at the base of my spine.

I break the kiss and pull out of her. Taking my dick in my hand, I meet her eyes and give myself one last stroke.

Cum spills from my head onto my hand. Onto her legs, her stomach. The countertop and my beautiful oxblood cabinets.

All the while, she looks at me, and I look at her. The expression on her face—brow furrowed, lips open, eyes suddenly clear and sad and pretty as fuck—makes me think she's feeling this too.

That deeper-than-lust emotion.

I'm emptied out, teeth gritted.

And still, we look at each other. Drinking each other in. Gulping the moment in deep gasps and sputtering breaths.

She's covered in me.

"Hank."

It's a whisper.

It's also a confession. Or maybe I just want it to be.

"Hank, look at—" Her eyes finally stray from mine, moving around the room. My gaze follows her.

The bar is a fucking disaster. There's broken glass everywhere. Bottles on the floor, whiskey on Stevie's skin, semen on the wall.

It smells like a dive bar and looks like a fight scene.

For the first time ever, it feels like *home*.

"It's a story now." I kiss Stevie's neck. "This house needs stories. Let's go write another one in the bedroom."

Stevie pulls back. Her gaze darts to my hand. Eyes go

wide as she gently reaches for my index finger. "Hank, you're bleeding."

"Shit, I am." It's not bad, a slice from the broken glass, but it is bleeding a good bit.

"Here, I'll get you cleaned up. Bandages and antibiotic ointment in the bathroom?"

"Nurse Nicks. I like it."

"My friend's wife is a surgeon. She taught me a few tricks. You're in good hands." She smiles. "I hope."

Chapter Eighteen

STEVIE

I don't notice the bruise until I'm in the bathroom early the next morning.

After I use the toilet, I wash my hands. Notice the overturned canister of Q-tips on the vanity. The rumpled towels on the floor and the mounds of bubbles still in the bathtub.

Smiling, I turn around and look at my backside in the mirror.

There, right in the middle of my left-butt cheek, is a bright purple bruise.

It's shaped in a rough crescent. Some parts more red than purple.

A bite mark.

My smile fades. My throat swells, and my pussy floods with heat at the same time.

I'm drowning in you. It wasn't just a line. I am drowning in Hank, and now I'm in over my head.

Panicking, I try on the lines Kate gave me. *It's just a weekend. Teenage infatuation. Who wouldn't be bowled over?* Eighteen hours ago, those lines fit. They felt right-sized for the situation I was in.

This morning, they feel laughably inadequate.

What is it about making messes with Hank that speaks to me?

The real question: how the fuck could I be falling for someone this quickly? It's never happened before, and I never would've agreed to come to Blue Mountain if I knew it was even a remote possibility.

There were hints of it in Vegas—how intense my connection was with Hank. But I chalked it up to the excitement of a hot hookup in my favorite city. People do ridiculous shit there. Having a ridiculously amazing time is a logical result of that.

The end.

Only, it wasn't the end. And now the control I've so carefully cultivated is disintegrating. I need to shore it back up. I need to do something to put some space between Hank and me.

Time to say *blackjack*. Only I don't need Hank to rescue me. I need to rescue myself from him.

Meeting my eyes in the mirror, I square my shoulders. I'm tired as shit; we've barely slept a wink. Maybe I'll take the almond milk latte Hank's already ordered from the main house and camp out in a guest room, pleading exhaustion or, I don't know, a need to answer some emails. I do have some notes to send about getting more Lady Luck swag up here for the Blue Mountain staff. And our contractor for the new brewery is due to give me a finalized schedule any day now, and once that comes in, I'll have a flurry of instructions to send.

Whatever the case, I need some breathing room, and taking an hour or three for myself can't hurt.

I wash my face, brush my teeth, then I wrap myself in a robe and march back into the bedroom, fully prepared to do the smart thing.

The right thing.

But then I take in the scene before me and draw up short, bare feet catching on the carpet.

A fire crackles in the fireplace (yes, there's a fireplace in the bedroom), and the savory-sweet smell of burning wood is just starting to fill the room. Hank is in sweatpants, sitting on the floor in front of the fire.

A guitar rests in his lap, and he's tucked a sharpened yellow No. 2 pencil behind his ear.

Early morning sunlight shines through the windows, lining the thick slopes of his bare shoulders and arms in a golden halo. He's smiling, eyes bright.

The glow inside my chest is written all over him, and for a second, I can't breathe.

Oh shit, oh shit, oh shit.

"I'm a lot horny and a little hungover. Perfect mood to write some music." Hank pats the carpet beside him. "Come, sit. I have a feeling you'll be good at this."

"Hank."

"What?"

I glance at the windows. "I gave you one night. That's it. One night—"

"To make memories. I know. And this morning, we'll be making music. Not the same thing."

"I'd argue it is."

He reaches behind him and produces a styrofoam tray holding our coffees. "Don't make me threaten to take away your latte. Didn't you say it was the best you've had? Ever?"

Goddamn it, I did. Because it's true—everything I've had at Blue Mountain Farm has been the best, from the coffee to the food to the people. The music and the wood-burning fires . . .

The sex.

The absolutely phenomenal, mind-blowing sex.

I'm sore enough to merit an Advil or two. But I guess my body left behind any sense of self-preservation in Nashville because I'm sitting on the floor beside Hank and crossing my legs, curling my hands around my iced latte while the left side of my body tingles from the growing heat of the fire.

I notice an open notebook on the mantel. Its pages are blank music sheets.

"You really write your own music?" I ask, drinking my coffee and wanting to die because it's so fucking delicious.

"I used to. When I played pro, it was my way of winding down. Blocking out all the noise, you know? But I haven't written much at all in the past few years. Inspiration's been in short supply." He looks at me over the plastic lid of his cup. "Then yesterday, the bug bit me. So let's write."

He sets down his coffee and puts his hands on his guitar. The sinews and muscles in his thick forearms ripple as he strums. He plays a few chords each of songs I recognize. Fleetwood Mac. Beyoncé. The Beatles.

He stops suddenly, forehead creased with thoughtful lines. Then he starts again, this time plucking out a tune I don't recognize.

"*I don't know if wanting you makes me a saint or a sinner*," he begins.

Goose bumps break out along my arms and legs. His singing voice is lovely, deep and just a little twangy.

I feel myself sinking into the moment. I should *get up* already and get to those emails. But Hank's presence pins me to this spot.

Hank stops singing but keeps playing.

"Your turn," he says, nodding at me. "Gimme a line."

"How do I—"

"Just something honest." He strums. "Whatever comes to mind."

My heart leaps to my throat. I blink, the words spilling

out of my mouth. "*Whatever the case, there won't be a clear winner.*"

Hank's nod deepens. "*My wandering eye's suddenly fixed on you.*"

"*I just—*" I think for a second, waiting for the beat. "*I just don't know if I can see this through.*"

"Yes! That's perfect. Hang on, lemme write this down." Hank grabs the pencil from behind his ear and scribbles some notes—literal music notes—on the blank page. He jots down the lyrics underneath them.

"*You're heaven and earth,*" he continues. "*I wanna make it work.*"

I blink at the sudden heat in my eyes. "*You're the stars and the moon. You make me wanna twerk.*"

Hank bursts out laughing, and Lord, if the sound doesn't make my heart leap again. As dangerous as this little music-making game is, it's also really fun. Saying the truth aloud, even through the lens of song lyrics, makes me feel free.

"Just kidding," I say. "How about *you're the stars and moon. You bring up old hurt.*"

"*Dig up old hurt.*" He scratches out a word and writes another. "Great. Okay. What about a chorus about making a mess? Being messy? Like *honey, I'm a mess, I'm a mess for you.*"

"*Honey, we're a mess, but it's the sweetest kind of blue.*"

"*We're* a mess?"

"Yes."

A pause.

"And the blue. Is that blue as in—"

"The ache. You know the one you feel here." I move my hand in a circle over my torso. "You feel it all, the excitement and the fear and the want, and it's like this sweet, awful torture. Basically how you feel when you watch *Bridgerton*."

"Ah. Got it. So *honey I'm a mess, I'm a mess for you. Honey, we're a mess, but it's the sweetest kind of blue. Skip the lies and tell me your truth 'cause, honey, I like makin' messes with you.*"

The ache intensifies. Sipping my coffee, I bring my bottom and top teeth together with a quiet, bony *tap*. "That's good, Hank. Really fucking good."

He grins, looking handsome as hell. "I know you're really into beer, but have you ever considered a career in songwriting? You live in the right place for it."

"I do live in Music City."

What I'm really saying: *I live three hundred miles from everything you are and everyone you love.*

"On to the second verse. *It all began as a joke, a bet,*" he continues.

I think on that for a minute, the heat from the fire burning through my robe. "*Didn't know it'd be my biggest gamble yet.*"

"Yes! Yes, that's it." He writes the words down. The tip of the pencil breaks, and he curses. I notice there's another on the mantel, so I grab it and hand it to him, our fingers brushing.

"*Now my luck's run out, time to show my cards,*" I say.

"*I wasn't expecting it would be so hard.*" Hank pauses when I giggle. "Pun not intended."

"But most certainly appreciated."

"Okay," he continues. "*I'm ready, I'm willing, I'm hoping for the best. I adore who you are*—"

"*And what you're about.*"

He's scribbling frantically now. "That's awesome. So we'll insert another chorus there. And then—"

I bite my lip, mood dimming. "*Happy endings aren't for sinners like me.*"

"*Unless that's something you can make me see.*"

"*You deserve the world. That's what I want for you. But we're playing a game that could end in tragedy.*"

His pencil goes still.

"Tragedy, huh?" he says, looking up from his notebook.

My heart thumps. "The hardest falls happen from the greatest heights."

"You read that on a mug?"

I manage a smile. "A key chain, actually."

"Please," he says quietly. "Talk to me. I know I said I wouldn't push you, but . . ."

"But you are."

"Because I give a shit." He stares at me. "That's what this whole thing is about, Stevie. You're making me give a shit."

Oh, God, *back up.* I need to back it up, but a voice in my head says it's too late. "You gave a shit before."

"Not about the right things. I gave a shit about money, stats, and other people. That served me for a while. Made me rich, I guess. But like you said—who's winning? *Not me*."

I give him a flirty shove because I don't know what else to do. "Fuck you, Hank. Being the kind of rich you are is a big deal."

"Of course it's a big deal. I recognize that, trust me. Before Daddy made it in the pros, we were poor as all get-out. Even after he started playing, we didn't roll in the dough. Players back then didn't make anything remotely close to what we do now. No one appreciates how life-changing that first big paycheck is more than I do."

I nod, throat swelling all over again. Hank's had every opportunity to become a douche and take advantage of people like me.

Instead, he's maintained a sense of honor. Integrity. He's had a few slips along the way, sure. He's not perfect, and he knows that, but he still tries really fucking hard to do the right thing.

What if he really is different?

The one-in-a-million guy who'd be a real partner and not

some insecure, lazy man-baby?

But even if that were true, it doesn't change who *I* am, or what a long-term commitment entails. It also doesn't change the fact that I became Susie Homemaker Simmering With Rage (yes, she deserves capitalization) when I gave forever a try.

But for the first time, I'm wishing I were different. Because I think Hank and I could actually be happy together if I weren't jaded.

There's that heat behind my eyes again. I stand abruptly, my insides mush.

"I need a breather," I say. "I'm gonna go . . . take a nap. Or something."

Hank reaches for me, but I dodge his hand, pulling my robe over my legs. Like that will protect me from Hank or the things he makes me feel.

"C'mon, Stevie, don't shut me out."

Anger shoots up my sides. I welcome it. It's so much easier and clearer than all the other things I feel right now.

"I'm not trying to be a dick. But this—whatever's happening here"—I gesture between us—"it's not real. This is a *fake* relationship. We're pretending to have it bad for each other. And you know full well that's all I was willing to do. Pretend. If you want more—"

"No fucking way."

My stomach plummets at the familiar voice by the bedroom door. I turn and see Rhett standing there with his arms crossed and brows pulled together in confusion.

"No fucking *way* y'all are faking it," he continues. "Really?"

I look at Hank. He looks back. His expression is crestfallen. He's scared, yeah.

But I know he's also crushed. Rhett didn't do that. I did.

And that crushes me too.

Chapter Nineteen

HANK

"What the hell are you doing here?" I snap at my brother, jumping to my feet.

I carefully lean my guitar against the fireplace and head for Stevie. I don't wanna touch her, not when she made it perfectly clear she doesn't want me to. But I do want to protect her. So I do my best to stand half a step in front of her, my body blocking hers from view.

Rhett shrugs. He's got bags under his bloodshot eyes and stubble that's a day too scruffy. "We were up early. Amelia had brunch with some friends—"

"Wait, wait, wait. Amelia spent the night at your place?"

"It's not what you think." He has the grace to look sheepish. "Nothing happened."

"I call bullshit."

"I swear it, Hank. Trust me when I say she's not interested. Honestly, I think she kinda hates me, which . . . whatever, I get it. Besides, she said she's got a boyfriend. I didn't lay a finger on her." He holds up his hands. "Cross my heart and hope to die."

I rake a hand over the top of my head. "Christ, the last

thing we need is some guy coming up here and threatening to shoot you 'cause you slept with his girl."

"I didn't sleep with her," Rhett says forcefully. "Besides, it wouldn't be the first time a dude threatened my life."

I wave him away. "I don't wanna know, so I'm not gonna ask. Rhett, *leave*. We'll talk about this later, all right?"

"Nah, I think I'd like to talk about it now." Rhett leans his shoulder against the jamb. His eyes move to Stevie, who's peeking over my shoulder. "I had a feeling something was up with y'all. I know my memory ain't exactly the best, but I definitely woulda remembered y'all catching up after Vegas."

I'm fisting my hair in my hand now. "Why the fuck doesn't anyone knock on this farm? You can't just barge in here—"

"You're one to talk. You were barging in left and right at Samuel's house when he and Emma—"

"Don't," I say sharply.

An awkward silence fills the room as I stare Rhett down. Stevie's breath quickens, audible inhales and exhales that tickle the nape of my neck.

"That's why you're doing this," Rhett finally says. "To prove to Samuel you're over Emma. That's fucked up."

"I know. But I wasn't gonna keep Samuel from his happy ending. I know how bad he and Emma want to tie the knot. The idea . . ." I look away. "It came from a good place."

I feel a hand on my shoulder. Stevie stands beside me. I feel a surge of gratitude. Of comfort too. I know whatever she's about to say will be the right thing.

"I can attest to that," she begins. "I knew Hank loved his family. But being here at Blue Mountain Farm, I've witnessed firsthand just how much he cares about y'all, and how much the happiness of his family means to him. He'll do anything for you guys."

Rhett cocks a brow. "He cares so much that he'll lie to us?

Hurt us, even?" He turns to me. "You tell her how you lied up and down to everyone before, right?"

I look at Stevie. She looks back, her forehead crinkled but her eyes kind. As usual, she's not judging me. She's just listening.

"I lied. You know that," I say to Stevie. "But you don't know what I lied about. I lied about having feelings for Emma. I asked Samuel point-blank if he wanted her, and he lied and said no. He asked me the same question, and I lied and said no too. We lied to each other over and over again. It was stupid, but I guess I was afraid of being humiliated."

"Were you afraid she'd reject you?" Stevie asks.

I nod. "Yes. That, and I didn't want to make her uncomfortable. She was our employee, you know? I also didn't want to step on Samuel's toes. I think I knew he had a thing for her, and it drove me crazy he wouldn't tell me about it. We used to tell each other everything. I missed how close we used to be."

"You were hurt," Stevie says.

"I was, yeah."

"You're gonna hurt a lot of people all over again with this fake dating crap," Rhett says. "You know Mama's gonna be heartbroken. And Milly? Lord, she's gonna kick your ass from here to Timbuktu. Because here's the thing, brother, we don't want to hurt you. We want you to be happy. And I don't know if y'all are really good actors or what, but we see how happy you are with Stevie. Beau and Mama and I were talking about it last night at the party—how we haven't seen you this lit up in ages."

Stevie goes stiff. My face burns.

"You smile more. You actually laugh. You look like you're having fun. Maybe pretending to be in a relationship is fun." He shrugs again. "Or maybe y'all really do light each other up. Ever thought about that?"

"This—" Stevie sucks in a breath. "It's an arrangement, that's all. A weekend thing. Fling. Whatever." But the way she says the words on her exhale is like a balloon deflating.

"Are you?" Rhett asks me. "Over Emma?"

"Yes," I say.

"That was quick."

"Well, quick to respond to you now, but not quick to get over her. Let's not forget I was away for a solid ten months—it took that long. But now I can honestly say I've moved on because it's true."

"So if you're over Emma." Rhett looks at Stevie. "And you're single, and you guys have a great time together, why not make it real? That'd tie this whole thing up in a neat little bow."

Why not?

"Because," Stevie says. We wait for her to continue. She's blinking hard.

My heart falls, and I wonder if I've ever felt more like an asshole in my life. I want to take her hand, touch her, let her know I'm the one who keeps fucking up. That she's not to blame for doing her job and doing it extremely well.

She's doing exactly what I asked her to. I just had no idea how hungry I was for something real until I got a taste of what that actually felt like.

"Were you ever gonna tell us?" Rhett asks me. My brother may be going through a fuckboy phase right now, but he's smart and self-aware enough to know when not to push Stevie.

Unlike me, apparently.

I run a hand over my face. *We're playing a game that could end in tragedy*.

"Eventually, yeah. When the dust settled, and Emma and Samuel were riding off into the sunset."

"You want me to go?" Stevie's voice is thin. "I should go—"

"No," Rhett says.

"Don't," I say.

Despite how upset she is, Stevie laughs. "Okay, then."

"He's the dipshit." Rhett lifts his chin in my direction. "Not you, Stevie. You, we adore. Stay. As a matter of fact, stay forever."

"Rhett," I warn.

"Hear me out.If y'all are faking it, then why are you writing music together in front of a fire on a Sunday morning?" His eyes move to the fireplace. "That doesn't look fake to me."

Stevie looks at me. I look back.

Neither of us has an answer. Or maybe we both do, but we're afraid to say it out loud. Her, for . . . reasons. Me, because I'm trying not to break *every* promise I've made.

Lie to *everyone* I know.

"Also, why is your house such a mess?" Rhett continues. "Looks like a pack of banshees had an orgy in your bed. How the hell did that pillow end up on the fan?" He glances up at the fan that hangs a good eight feet above the bed. A king-sized pillow teeters on the edge of a blade, feathers spilling out of its seam. "And why are the sheets wet? Actually, don't answer that."

I bite back a smile. Stevie and I may or may not have brought another bottle of whiskey into bed.

But Stevie isn't smiling.

In fact, her face crumples, and my heart keeps falling. And for the first time in a long time, I feel helpless.

I fucking hate feeling helpless. Last time . . . was when Samuel caught me kissing Emma? The time before that, when Daddy died?

I am coming out of my skin.

"Guys, I'm sorry," she says, pressing her fingers to her mouth. "I'm so sorry."

I watch her scurry out of the room, hair poking out of her messy ponytail.

I give my brother a death stare.

His face falls. "Hank—"

"*You* go. You've made enough of a mess as it is." Heading for the door, I stab a finger into his chest. "Don't you fucking dare tell anyone, all right? Let me figure this out. So help me God, if you end up hurting Stevie—"

"I wouldn't. I promise. I'm sorry, brother, but I know how much the lies hurt everyone last time. I don't want it to happen again. That's all." His eyes are wide. "I'm looking out for you."

"Yeah, well, you're doing a half-assed job of it. Just like you half-ass everything else."

The look of hurt on his face makes my stomach contract. That was uncalled for. But Rhett's fucking up an already fucked-up situation, and I can only handle one shitstorm at a time.

Stevie comes first.

"We'll talk later," I growl, and then I dart after Stevie.

Rounding the corner, I see one of the doors to the back patio close shut. A heartbeat later, I feel a gust of cold air.

Grabbing the throw blanket off the back of a nearby chair, I head outside.

The sting of the cold hits me head-on. My skin tightens, and the soles of my bare feet burn against the bluestone pavers.

Stevie's leaning against the banister, arms crossed tightly as her breath billows in a cloud around her. It's early enough that the morning is still pale. Pale pink sky, grass pale with frost. Mountains in the distance pale blue and purple.

It's beautiful this time of day. I've seen plenty of sunrises lately—one of the benefits of partying until seven AM—but nothing quite compares to catching the sun come up over the Blue Ridge Mountains.

I've missed my family, and I've missed the farm. I know my bones belong here. But I can't stay if things aren't different this time around.

Looking at Stevie, I'm not sure they will be.

I hold up the blanket. "Can I?"

Stevie looks over her shoulder. The breath leaves my lungs. Tears silently spill out of her big brown eyes.

"You want a family," she says, sniffing.

I freeze. That wasn't what I was expecting.

Draping the blanket over Stevie's shoulders, I stand beside her, the cold air making my lungs and heart feel tight. I shiver.

"Here," she says, taking the blanket off and wrapping it around my shoulders. She does it methodically, carefully, tears still coming as she brings the ends of the blanket together in the center of my chest, holding them tightly in her hand.

"What does my wanting a family have to do with anything?"

Stevie looks at me. "I want fun. I want freedom. Maybe this is me jumping the gun, but I feel like this thing between us is getting complicated, and I . . ." She searches my eyes. "I don't want anyone getting hurt."

"I think it's a little late for that."

She sniffles again, looking down at her hand on my chest. "Guess I have nothing to lose then." Taking a breath, she pulls back her shoulders. "My ex and I were together for ten years, married for five—we were separated for three of those years, though. Going into our relationship, I wasn't super young—I was twenty-nine—but I was more immature than I realized. Immature and idealistic. I believed he and I were equals. It turns out that wasn't the case at all."

"I don't understand," I say, furrowing my brow. My heart's started to pound, like it knows the KO punch is coming.

"It's difficult to explain." She rolls her tongue between her lips, thinking. "It's like marriage came with all these expectations I wasn't anticipating. Suddenly, there was all this pressure to do wifely things—obligations, I guess, like making meals and keeping a clean house. Being the perfectionist I am, I dove right in, determined to be the best wife ever."

I wrinkle my nose. "Sounds fucked up. Although you'd be great at anything you did, Stevie."

She looks at me for a long minute. "You know what's wonderful about you, Hank? I think you mean that."

"I do."

She looks away. "It started slowly. I cooked. I cleaned. Then I started doing all our laundry. Because I did the laundry, I organized the closets. Since I organized the closets, I organized the garage, and our calendar, and our meal planning too."

"Did your ex not help at all?"

"Not really. He'd walk the dog every so often, but I always had to ask him to do it twelve times before he actually grabbed the leash and did it."

I nod. "I see where the resentment comes in."

"Don't get me started." She rolls her eyes. "After a year or so, I did everything. It was just easier that way. I got tired of nagging him to get off his ass and help out. Mind you, while all this was happening, I was still working full time. My ex made more money than me, though, so the fucked-up math I did in my head made sense. He brought home the bacon, and I cooked it. Even though I'd imagined my partner and I would both bring home the bacon, and we'd cook it together. But obviously, that's not how it worked out."

"Okay," I say slowly, trying my best to grasp the ideas she's throwing my way. "So if I understand this right, even though you came into marriage thinking things would be equal, it turned out they weren't because your husband was lazy as fuck. But also because you felt pressure to always have his pipe and slippers ready when he walked through the door."

"*Yes.*" Stevie closes her eyes in relief.

"Where'd that pressure come from?"

She waves her hand in the air. "Society. TV. My parents. They very much embraced traditional roles—Dad had the big job, and Mom stayed home to take care of the kids. Which isn't a bad thing. There are ways that can be equal too, so everyone has a shot at being happy. But my parents aren't happy. My mom worked really, really hard to be a good wife and good mother, and while she is the best mom ever, I think she never felt appreciated or valued. And then she just . . . abandoned herself at some point. Now she's pissed about it, understandably."

"I get that." My mom had months of the year where she was essentially a single parent, raising all five of us on her own while Daddy played in the pros. But even when he was away, he always praised her. When he was home, he loved up on her constantly. We knew she was pretty spectacular in his eyes, and as a result, she was spectacular in our eyes too.

Sounds like Stevie's mom didn't have that kind of support.

"I promised myself I wouldn't be like her. Yet I still fell into that familiar pattern of putting everyone else first, especially after I got married. I was *good*. I was a *helper*. I made myself as small as possible so my husband could take up all the space he wanted. I was doing the good wife thing right."

"But you were miserable."

She nods, the sinews of her throat working as she swallows. "Overwhelmed too. Constantly burned out. It didn't help that my professional wins made Dan insecure. I tried to fix that. Tried to make that smaller. My career ended up suffering, and so did my friendships. He was controlling in many ways—I mean, the guy refused to sign the divorce papers for *years*. It took three years of separation to finally get him to do it. He said he 'wanted to take care of me,' that he wanted to make sure I was safe, but really, he just wanted me to set my life aside for him. When we were together, I felt like I was nothing. No one. Like I didn't matter. I was so, so lonely, Hank, I can't even begin to tell you."

I curl my hand around hers. "Holy shit. You weren't joking when you said things really fell apart."

"It was a disaster. But I didn't get it. Here I was, doing what I was told good women do, but I was unhappy and so was he. At thirty-six, I always thought I'd know who I was and what I wanted, but I was lost. Our sex life was nonexistent at that point. He wanted kids, but I knew from talking to my girlfriends that adding a baby to the mix would just . . . yeah, I knew I'd drown. We tried therapy, but nothing changed. So I left."

"I'm really sorry, Stevie."

She swallows again, looking up at me. "I'm sorry I had to go through a divorce to learn what I know now. I never meant to hurt anyone. But I learned I want nothing to do with the demands that come with commitment. I just—" She glances out over the mountains. "Marriage turns me into this, like, fembot Stepford wife version of myself. A Stepford wife who's simmering with rage and resentment because she has to take care of a man who never, ever meets her halfway." She squeezes my hand.

The punch lands with devastating force. I see.

I see what her *because* means.

"This is going to sound like a piece of white male privilege garbage," I begin.

Stevie scoffs, catching a tear in the crook of her first finger. "Try me."

"But I'd never thought about marriage that way. Not as a happy ending, but as a cage."

It's her turn to nod. "I know that's not the case for everyone. Some of my friends have genuinely great marriages. Others . . . don't."

"Right." I press my lips together. "And that's not a gamble you're willing to make."

Her watery eyes meet mine. They're puffy and tired.

"Can I play devil's advocate for a sec?" I ask.

"Go for it."

"What if I said I was different from your ex?" I manage a tight smile. "I think I've proven I clean up after myself."

She searches my face. "What if I said I believe you're different, but I might not be if we were to . . . you know, get serious? I've changed, sure. I've done a lot of work on myself, but old habits die hard. The demands put on women to be everyone's perfect everything still exist. I'm not going back there, Hank. I'm not risking what I've built. My life is full, and I don't feel like I'm missing anything. I'm sorry."

I'm gripped, hard, by the need to take care of her. Not so I can make her stay and convince her that I'm not her ex, that I'm not a lazy piece of shit, that I'm not stuck on marriage so much as sharing a beautiful life with someone I love.

I want to take care of her because it's the right thing to do.

"Being single is great." I talk slowly again, choosing my words with care. "Did you not see me in Vegas? I've had the time of my fucking life. But it can be hard too. Just like I imagine being married can be hard."

"It's definitely a give and take."

"There's this loneliness that comes with freedom. I get not wanting to take care of someone else. But cutting that out means someone else isn't taking care of you."

"I do miss that. But not as much as I'd miss doing whatever the fuck I want."

I dip my head. "That's valid. But how about you let me? Take care of you, I mean, for the rest of the weekend. At this point, it's barely more than twenty-four hours anyway. You can say it's pretend, or you can say it's real. Whatever the case, I'm enjoying it."

I got nothing to prove here, other than not all men are pieces of shit. And yeah, maybe I wanna show her what I saw in my parents growing up, and what I see now in Bel and Beau, and Samuel and Emma. A healthy, happy relationship, where respect is mutual and so is admiration and support.

"Hank," she says, "isn't that just gonna blur the lines even more?"

"Probably. But I can handle it." I tuck her hair behind her ear and lower my voice. "I'm not ready for you to leave yet. We've still got lots of rooms to make lots of messes in. And we're somehow supposed to squeeze in a trip to the Biltmore too."

Stevie's eyes light up, and pain arrows through my chest.

I *can* handle this, right?

I hate the idea that today's my last full day with Stevie. Tomorrow morning, we won't be able to sip our coffee while writing songs; Stevie will be busy packing up, and I'll be busy trying not to care.

If I've only got twenty-four hours left with Stevie, I'm gonna make the most of them. And there's this voice inside me—this tiny, stupidly optimistic voice—that tells me twenty-four hours is all I'll need. To do what, I don't know. Showing her what a healthy relationship looks like is only part of it, but it feels important to claim those hours anyway and make them count.

"I do want to see the Biltmore."

"And I want to get the fuck back inside. But Stevie?"

"Yeah?"

"You said we were friends."

She smiles, skin around her eyes crinkling. "We are."

"Friends don't treat each other the way your ex treated you."

She looks away. "That's a sweet thought."

The lyric comes to me as I'm opening the door for Stevie and following her inside.

Sinner or saint, now I know which one I ain't.

But goddamn, I'd hoped being on the saintly end of the spectrum would make me feel better. I've been a sinner for so long—that kiss with Emma feels like a decade ago—that I figured anything would be preferable to living under a cloud of guilt.

This arrow in my chest, though? It feels just as bad.

In fact, it feels worse.

Chapter Twenty

STEVIE

"You think we can trust Rhett not to say anything?" I ask.

Hank and I are waiting at the stoplight just outside the Biltmore's entrance. There's a pretty stone gatehouse ahead decked out in white Christmas lights; beyond that, a forest of towering trees obscures the view.

Hank adjusts his hand on the top of the steering wheel. "Rhett's a good kid. But he hasn't been himself lately, so . . . yeah. Let's hope for the best—"

"But prepare for the worst." I glance up at the ceiling of the car. It's covered in hundreds of tiny pinpricks of light, a sky of artificial stars. "Right."

Hank's got a garage full of cars, but the black on black Rolls Royce Wraith was his first pick for today's outing. It's just the right combination of classy and badass, and judging by the way Hank drives it—patiently, proudly, with one hand on the wheel and the other on my thigh—he knows that.

He ducks his head just as the light turns green. He accelerates through the intersection, and I can't help but stare. He is so fucking sexy. Freshly showered and shaved, his jawline gleams, and hazel eyes are bright, despite our almost complete lack of sleep over the past couple of nights. He's wearing a puffer vest over a sweater and dark jeans, and the woodsy scent of his cologne fills the car.

Longing blossoms in my center. I tear my gaze away from him and look out the window.

"What should our plan be if Rhett doesn't keep our secret?"

Hank squeezes my thigh. "How about we cross that bridge when we get there? I don't wanna think about it, to be honest."

I don't wanna waste time because we've got so little of it.

Watching the trees thicken around us, I wonder for the thousandth time if I'm doing the right thing or if I'm needlessly torturing everyone.

And for the thousandth time, I decide sticking to my guns is the right call. Because that's how the resentment starts—with small forfeits and denials and accommodations and questions. Are my expectations too high? Why ask for more when I should be thankful for what I've got?

But most of all: who do I think I am, turning down a guy like Hank Beauregard?

Not that he's offering marriage or anything. But I can tell he's starting to see the possibility of something deeper—something long-term—between us.

Am I seeing it too? The confidence he has in me is the sexiest thing ever. *You'd be great at anything you did, Stevie.* That's something I noticed in him from the start, his genuine belief in me and what I've accomplished. I bet having a cheerleader like that in my corner every day would be pretty damn lovely.

I shove the idea from my head.

Slowly, the landscape around us starts to take a more formalized shape. The road is narrow, a single lane of blacktop, and we wind our way through copses of moss-covered trees and clearings filled with lush gardens. A drop to our left reveals a bubbling stream that glints in the early afternoon sunlight. Stone walls, darkened with age, line the road.

This place has the feeling of history.

I decide to gently push my existential angst aside for the rest of the day. This is a special place. A special moment. Maybe I'm feeling a little muddled on what I do and don't deserve. But I know both of us deserve to enjoy this not-so-little field trip.

"I wonder what life was like when the Vanderbilts lived here," I say, straining to look around when we suddenly break out into an area of cleared rolling hills. A visitor's center stands court on a slope to our left; Hank keeps driving, stopping only to hold out his phone for a quick scan at another gatehouse. "Can you imagine owning all this? Oh wait, you *do* own a gigantic and insanely luxurious farm."

Hank grins. "Our little farm is a drop in the bucket compared to Biltmore." He gestures outside the window. Cows graze in neatly kept fields; a sign at a fork in the road directs visitors to Biltmore House, a hotel, a winery. "This is Queen of England shit."

I keep waiting for the house itself to come into view, but no dice so far. Just more hills and forest for another mile or two. Signs for parking lots appear, along with guys in bright orange vests directing visitors to certain lots. But Hank drives right past them, flashing a piece of paper.

"What's that?"

"Ticket for valet."

I roll my eyes, biting back a smile. "Only the best for Hank Beauregard."

He swings his head to look at me, the light catching his eyes and making them look almost green. They're flirty, playful, and I grin, relaxing into my heated seat.

Just when I think I'm drowning again, Hank lightens the mood.

"Only the best for you, blackjack babe. I'm just trying to maintain your high-roller lifestyle."

"I'm not the one driving a hundred-thousand-dollar car."

"It's closer to four hundred," he says, flashing me a smile, "but I get your point."

The amount of money these Beauregards have—it's starting to feel closer to that Queen of England shit than Hank and his siblings let on.

It's a different world. Even if I hadn't sworn off men and monogamy, I'm not entirely certain I could make a relationship with Hank work. His family isn't pretentious, but people with that kind of wealth exist on a different plane. They live by different rules and run in different circles.

That kind of wealth also means Hank is heavily invested in Asheville. Financially. Personally. Professionally too.

My life, though, is in Tennessee, and will be for the foreseeable future with the new brewery going up.

Approaching a towering gate, a charge of excitement has me sitting up in my seat. The gate is thrown open to a wide drive, and we pass through it, Hank hanging a quick right.

The house comes into sudden, startling view, and the breath leaves my lungs.

It's like something out of a fairy tale. An enormous lawn stretches out in front of us, punctuated by a circular pond. At the end of the long, U-shaped drive is the biggest, most beautiful castle-like home I've ever seen. It's awe-inspiring: turrets, towers, total decadence.

"What do you think?" Hank says.

"I think this has the Duke of Hastings written all over it."

"I aim to please, Daphne. By the way, when are you going to start calling me Simon?"

I throw a saucy look his way. "Don't you think we have enough nicknames for each other? It's getting weird."

"I think it's cute."

"Of course you do." I duck my head to get a better look as we approach the house's front entrance. It's truly enormous—a mall-sized, gilded-age beauty that's take-your-breath-away spectacular. The gray stone façade is a beautiful counterpoint to the dark roof, tinted green-blue with age. Dozens of chimneys dot the roofline while metal spires soar into the winter sky.

We pull right up to the entrance. Hank gets out of the car, and I can't tell if it's the famous football player or the ridiculous car that flusters the attendant more.

Whatever the case, Hank is opening my door before I've even unbuckled my seat belt.

"C'mon, Daph." He holds out his hand. "Let me give you a tour of my ancestral home I secretly despise for mysterious reasons."

"A damaged duke with a dark secret? Don't mind if I do."

I don't realize I've slipped my hand into Hank's until I'm on my feet in the sunshine.

I don't realize I'm warning him about his untied shoelace until the words are out of my mouth.

He grins, squinting against the sun. "Thanks."

"You're welcome," I say, bewildered.

Since when did looking out for him and him looking out for me become so second nature we don't even realize we're doing it?

It's sweet.

And scary. Because even though I promised myself I'd never be responsible for a man's well-being ever again, here I am, being responsible. Taking care of someone.

But.

A voice in my head wants to argue the point, but I don't

let it. I shove my hands in my pockets and wait for Hank to tie his shoe. A middle-aged woman appears at my elbow, smiling warmly as she shakes our hands and introduces herself as our private liaison.

I cut Hank a glance. He just shrugs, this adorably mischievous smile on his lips, and the flutter in my torso becomes a full-on rush.

The liaison leads us right past the line stretching out the front door. We're greeted by another woman in Biltmore's soaring entrance hall, and she begins our private "upstairs/downstairs" tour, inspired by *Downton Abbey*.

It's amazing. We see the rooms where the one percent of the one percent lived—library, indoor pool, solarium—and then we see the rooms inhabited by the people who worked for them. The laundry, where a small army of Black women would come in from the village every day to do the backbreaking work that was laundry before washing machines and dryers. A simple dining room.

My favorite part, though, is the massive kitchen in the house's basement. It has high ceilings and windows that overlook the rear gardens. A huge trestle table dominates the center of the space, and copper pots shimmer from the rack above it.

"Can you imagine what it must've been like to make food for upward of thirty guests, plus an enormous staff, several times a day?" our guide asks. "Back then, meals for the likes of the Vanderbilts were elaborate, multi-course affairs. Cook and his staff were kept exceptionally busy."

Hank slips his hand inside my jacket, his fingers giving the small of my back a quick scratch. "Speaking of meals. Since Sunday supper happened on Friday, tonight is all ours."

My breath catches as my skin comes alive. Our guide politely pretends to be engrossed in a cabinet of salt cellars.

I not-so-politely slip my hand in Hank's back pocket. "Tell me what you're thinking."

"I was thinking about your beer, actually. What if we make something that goes well with Hop Girl Summer? Some Sunday night comfort food. Chili, maybe? Samuel's got a recipe we can borrow."

The fact he's thought about incorporating my beer into a meal we'll make together has me weak in the knees.

Validation is sexy as hell.

"Love it. Hop Girl would make some great chili. What do I need to do to help?"

"Honey, you said you wanted to cook the bacon together, so that's what we're gonna do. We'll stop at the grocery store on the way back. Sound good?"

"Sounds great."

I try very hard to focus on the night ahead instead of the next morning for the rest of our tour. Because thinking about tomorrow bums me out. It shouldn't. I should be excited to get back to Nashville. So many great things are happening at work, and I've got a tennis lesson lined up with my favorite pro and my favorite girls on Thursday evening. I really do love my life there.

But I like spending time with Hank too. And in good conscience, I can't spend more with him after this weekend.

This is it.

Our last night together.

I wasn't expecting it to be so bittersweet.

Making our way up the servants' stairs back to Biltmore's first floor, I giggle when Hank gives my ass a pinch. He insisted on going behind me "in case you take a spill."

"I hope you don't mind me saying this," our guide says before leaving us at the exit, "but y'all are really, really cute together. It's so heartening to see guests like you enjoying yourselves at Biltmore. It's what George and Edith, our original owners, would've wanted."

Hank reaches for my hand at the same time I reach for his.

Tomorrow's gonna hurt.

Chapter Twenty-One

HANK

Samuel's chili calls for five pounds of meat, two days of prep, and a special kind of red chili flake Chef Katie has to order months in advance from another continent.

"Yeah," I say, scrolling through the recipe on my phone. "We should probably think about plan B. How about some beer cheese soup?"

"Followed by some beer-braised meat?"

I grab Stevie's hand and settle it on my crotch. "Wanna braise my meat?"

"God, that's terrible," she says, but she still laughs, the sound going breathy when she curls her fingers around the chubby in my pants. "Hm. Not as *tender* as I thought."

"Are things *heating up*?" I somehow manage to put down my phone and start the car.

"*Boiling over*, as a matter of fact."

She tugs down my zipper, and my dick jumps. "I think my dad humor is rubbing off on you, blackjack babe."

"You asking me to rub one out for you?" Stevie's hand glides inside the slit of my briefs. Her thumb glides up the slit on my head, and my hand tightens on the wheel. "Or you want me to taste you?"

"Taste," I say hoarsely, thanking God and Rolls Royce that the tint on these windows is so dark. "Since we're on the food theme."

Stevie leans over the center console. She flips her hair over her shoulder and shoots me a hot look.

Taking my head in her mouth, she keeps her eyes locked on mine as she bobs down, then bobs back up.

My other head falls back on the headrest. Need coils between my legs.

She sucks, taking me deeper, and I slam the heel of my hand on the wheel. "Fuck. *Fuck*, honey, you're good at this."

We're good at this, and I want you to stay.

"I know," she says, pressing the flat of her tongue against my tip.

I come in her mouth just as we're pulling into the grocery store parking lot. She swallows, and after I put the car in park, I take her face in my hand and kiss her hard.

"As much as I wanna return the favor right here, right now, I also don't want to get arrested. The second we're back home, I'm playing with that pussy."

Stevie catches her bottom lip between her teeth. Facing me, she leans her back against the passenger side window.

A beat of clean, intense desire blooms between us as I look at her, and she looks at me, heat blasting from the vents, the shockwaves slowly subsiding between my legs. Sunlight catches on her hair, making it look bright red. Her lips are a little swollen.

She's fucking spectacular. And I want her to be mine.

Mine to keep.

To worship.

I know what I'd say right now if she didn't have a *because*.

Let's make this real. Exclusive. Dating. Serious. Whatever the fuck you want to call it, I'm in. This isn't everyday shit between us, so let's figure out how to make it work.

I probably should've been more guarded. I needed to fall for another unavailable chick like I need a hole in my head. I get it. But this time, there are no lies. Well, not between Stevie and me, at least. This feels right and real in a way nothing else ever has.

The irony is killing me.

Same as this feeling in my chest. Want with sharp edges that keep catching on my ribs every time I think about Stevie leaving.

I know in my gut she won't be back. She's a good human being. She'd never toy with me like that. She'd never believe me when I'd tell her I'm cool with casual, that I won't catch any more feelings if we see each other again.

She's the kind of woman who doesn't have time for that shit.

It's a part of the reason I fucking adore her.

"Need you to get out of the car, Stevie. Right. *Now*."

She bites her lip. "Or what?"

"Or I'm gonna commit an act of public indecency. Get your ass out of the car."

She wiggles said ass as she does as I tell her. I follow her, grabbing her hand as we walk through the parking lot.

We take our time grocery shopping. It turns out, it's actually fun when you have a punch-drunk partner.

"You don't happen to have brown sugar at home, do you?" she asks, one hand on the side of the buggy as I push it down the baking aisle.

"Ha," I reply. "Good one." We both know I only have some half-and-half and year-old ketchup in my fridge.

"Mind grabbing the short ribs while I go get sugar, then?"

"I'll get the short ribs and the grits. Cheese too, 'cause grits without cheese are like you without a tambourine." I nod at a nearby aisle when she cuts me a disbelieving look. "Mama and I would shop here together back in the day. I know my way around."

Stevie's shoulder rises on a sharp inhale. "Of course you do."

"Oh! And what do you think about a salad? Get some more veggies in because I'm famous, and I gotta look good?"

Back at home, I unload and unpack the groceries while Stevie pours us a beer. I eat her out on the floor of my dining room. She comes with a cry, and after we make out for a while, I teach her how to light a fire. She picks out a Sam Hunt playlist.

"I got the leeks and the carrots," I say, grabbing a knife from the wooden block beside the stove.

Stevie lifts the short ribs, wrapped in brown butcher paper, off the counter. "I'll prep these bad boys. Salt, pepper, and some garlic powder sound good?"

"Fuck yes."

Sam Hunt croons about sinning with his lady. I get a little buzz from my first IPA of the evening. Stevie moves her hips in time to the beat: small, almost mindless circles as she sears the ribs in the biggest cast iron pot I could find.

"Why are you mouthing the words?" I wipe my knife on a towel. "Sing 'em, honey."

She points her tongs at me. "You're the one with the voice."

"Yours ain't so bad either. Sing."

Another song comes on—oh, Lord, it's the sexy one about speakers and making out in pickup trucks—and Stevie doesn't miss a beat.

I can't help it. I sing with her. Thinking about how I wanna have her in the back of my truck tonight. And tomorrow night. And the night after that.

Stay.

The song ends, and she changes the playlist. Duets, from what I can tell. I burst out laughing when "Islands In the Stream" comes on. She's got the Dolly parts, and I do Kenny Rogers. It's cheesy and perfect, and when "I'm Real" comes on next, I about die as Stevie attempts the J.Lo verses.

I, of course, nail Ja Rule.

"God, that smells good," I say, leaning over to glance at the pot. Stevie's taking the short ribs out one by one and setting them on a plate to rest.

"Wanna hit me with that garlic?" she asks.

I sidle up behind her and kiss her neck, pressing my groin into her ass. She shivers, grinning. She's soft and happy, warm too, and I can't help but wonder if we'd grope each other while making a delicious meal every night if we were together.

Sounds pretty fucking nice to me.

"You got it." Turning back to my cutting board, I gather the minced garlic on the edge of my knife and use my thumb to slide it into the pot. "Shit, that smells even better."

"Right? Delish. Time for the cover."

I lift said cover off the counter and drop it on the pot. Stevie slips on a pair of oven mitts and grabs the handles of the pot. I leap to open the oven door.

"Wow." She slides the pot into the oven with a grunt. "This thing is pristine. When was the last time you used it?"

I actually have to think about this. "Uh. Never?"

Standing, she shoots me a disbelieving look. "Really?"

I think some more. "Actually, yeah. Anytime I cook, I do it with my mom, or I'm over at Samuel's house helping with Sunday supper." I shrug. "It's always just been me here. And cooking for one isn't exactly exciting."

"Not when you can have food delivered from one of the best restaurants in the South."

Crossing my arms, I say, "Exactly. Although I do enjoy it.

This—cooking. Sharing a homemade meal with someone. It feels nice, right?"

Stevie looks down at the oven mitts. She's quiet for a second.

I hold up my hands. "I'm sorry. It's just easy to get carried away with you."

Shaking her head, she lifts her head and puts the oven mitts on the counter. "Should we get started on the soup? I've made it a few times before, and it doesn't take too long."

She's right. Between the two of us, whipping it together doesn't take long at all. I take sink duty, washing pots and knives and cutting boards as she discards them.

We turn on Netflix while we wait for the short ribs to cook, snuggling on my couch. As the sun sets in the windows behind us, she plays with my hair while I massage her legs and feet.

I light candles on my kitchen table, where we stuff ourselves silly as we sip our beers. The food is delicious, the smell of it filling the room.

My kitchen looks like a bomb went off inside it.

"What?" Stevie asks when she catches me looking around.

Smiling, I shake my head. "Nothing. Just thinking about how my house feels fucking *homey*. For the first time ever, I think."

"You know how much clean up *homey* requires?"

"I'm not afraid."

We finish our plates. Go back for seconds. The short ribs are amazingly tender, the meat falling off the bones.

We cuddle on the couch again, both of us dozing off for a few hours. I wake up to see that Stevie's still tucked into my side, eyes thoughtful as they search my face.

"Hey." My voice is rough with sleep.

She dips a finger inside the waistband of my sweats. "Hi."

"Whatcha thinking?"

She bites her lip. "I need something."

"It's yours."

"Let's get it all out of our system. Leave nothing on the table. I don't know how much energy I've got left, but there's still something we haven't done. In bed, I mean."

My dick perks up as the realization dawns.

"I think I know what you're talking about."

"You definitely know what I'm talking about." Her eyes are hazy. "Let's go to bed."

Chapter Twenty-Two

STEVIE

Hank lights a fire in the bedroom and turns down the lights. Shadows flicker across the ceiling; the fire crackles and pops, filling the room with a scent I can only describe as Blue Mountain loveliness.

The romance of it makes my heart skip a beat.

I'm aware of every inch of my skin, every sensation as I strip down to nothing: the feel of my hair falling across my bare back, the sudden shock of the chilly air.

The swell of heat between my legs.

I pull up the covers from where they're rumpled at the foot of the bed—Hank called housekeeping earlier and told them not to come—and crawl inside them.

Hank's disappeared into the bathroom. He comes back out carrying a plastic bottle and a towel. A couple of foil packets too.

"I'mma fuck you more than once," he explains, sauntering over to the bed. "Better safe than sorry."

Not only is he thoughtful, but he's careful and kind.

He's also shirtless, and an obvious erection tents his

sweats. His skin glimmers in the light of the fire, shadows highlighting the hard curves of his pectoral muscles.

My pussy dies a thousand sweet deaths just looking at him.

For the first time, I wonder how the hell I'm going to leave tomorrow. Because I'm going to miss this. Miss *him*. The way he walks and how at home he is in his body and the naked admiration in his eyes when they fall on me.

For the first time, I ask myself if we could continue this—our relationship, whatever that is at the moment—after the weekend ends. My life isn't in Asheville, but my heart could be. Which begs the question: could Hank and I actually make long distance work, and merge our lives somehow?

Does leaving tomorrow have to be goodbye forever?

I wish I knew. Am I being smart? Or am I letting fear win? What's safe and what's scary, and which one is the right path to follow here?

He shucks off his sweatpants and climbs into bed, his dick hanging heavy and unashamed between his legs.

He's that hard for me. The woman who's either too smart or too scarred to attempt an actual relationship with him.

For some reason, that makes me feel like crying.

I don't. Instead, I let him cover me with his body. He kisses me, opening my mouth slowly with his lips, his tongue. A full-body tingle moves through me, warmth rippling all the way to my toes. He kisses me like we've got all the time in the world. Slowly, deeply, drinking me in with patient, searing gulps.

My legs part, and my knees find his hips. The tip of his cock presses against the inside of my thigh. My pussy's begging for him.

My entire being is begging for this man.

You'd think after a weekend of nonstop sex, I'd be sated by now. My soreness hasn't gone away, and I'm so tired I know I'll probably pass out the second I get home tomorrow afternoon and sleep all the way to the next morning.

I can do that because *I have no one else to take care of.* I'm free to take time and rest when I need it.

Freedom aside, I'm not sated. I'm hungrier than ever for Hank. Maybe because when I wake up Tuesday morning, I know he won't be there, offering me the most perfect iced almond milk latte (he seems to be able to find the best ones on the planet) and an orgasm to start the day.

He bends his arms, lowering himself onto me. My nipples brush his chest, and my eyes roll to the back of my head at the feel of all this skin on skin. I glide my hands onto his shoulders, curling my fingers into the hard muscle and rippling sinew I find there. He's hot to the touch, and when he ducks his head to kiss my neck, bite my nipple, I close my eyes against the sudden burn I feel there.

"I need you," I breathe. "I want you. Inside. Now."

Wordlessly, he reaches between us and dips two fingers inside my slit. He swipes them forward, hitting my clit, and I nearly bite off my tongue. My hips buck. I open my eyes to watch him coat himself with those two fingers, the head of his cock glistening. His arousal? Mine? Both?

Using those same two fingers, he parts my lips and puts himself inside me. A feeling of fullness envelops me as he sinks all the way in with a single thrust.

My pussy flutters. The heaviness in my core is almost too much to bear.

He kisses my temple and thrusts inside me once, twice.

"Condom."

"Okay," he replies. I want to scream when he pulls out of me. He grabs a packet and tears it open with his teeth. Settling on his haunches, he tries to roll it on, but his hands are shaking too hard.

My heart twists. The burn in my eyes intensifies.

I sit up and roll it on for him.

"Sorry," he says with this shy little smirk. "Guess I'm a little too wild for you."

"No such thing."

I lube him up. Then he takes the bottle from me. "How do you wanna do this? What's the most comfortable for you?"

"Usually," I say, rolling over, "it's easiest to start on my belly with my hips up. The angle helps a lot."

He puts his hands on my hips and helps me angle them up so I'm on my knees and elbows. His touch is gentle, and I'm glad I have my forehead buried in the pillow so I don't have to make eye contact.

He uses his knee to spread my legs a little wider. And then . . .

Nothing.

A beat passes. Then another.

Turning my head, I ask, "You okay?"

He's staring at me. At my ass. My pussy. His eyes are dark and unreadable.

Expression feral, nostrils flaring and mouth tight.

He squeezes a dollop of lube onto his fingertips. Circles those fingertips against his thumb, warming up the lube.

"You." He takes my ass cheek in his hand and pulls it to the side. "Are." He arcs his thumb over my rim. Gently, touch barely there, but my nipples still tighten to painful, hard points. "*Beautiful.*"

I curl my hands into the sheets. Anticipation coiling inside my skin, making my pussy pulse.

If the idea of leaving Hank doesn't break me, this orgasm will.

But I'm too far gone to care. I want more. I need more. I want this man's hands all over me.

"Your thumb," I murmur. "Press it. There."

Ever the obedient student, he does as I tell him and

presses the pad of his thumb against my asshole. The pressure is exquisite, and I find myself pressing back up against him, seeking more. Needing more.

"Inside is okay," I say.

He switches it up, replacing his thumb with his middle finger. "I like it when you talk to me. When you tell me what you need. Because I like giving it to you. I like knowing what's going on inside your head."

He says the words as he pushes the tip of his finger inside me. The combination of the two—what every human wants to hear, what every human wants to feel—almost makes me come on the spot.

My legs tremble. My heart goes apeshit inside my chest.

"Baby," I say. "More."

His other hand moves up my side, thumb trailing a ribbon of sensation up my spine. He cups my breast and plucks at my nipple as he slowly pushes his finger inside me.

This isn't my first rodeo. But I'm still shocked by the pain that mingles with my rising pleasure. Hank's got thick fingers, and the pressure is intense.

It's forbidden, exciting, and it's exactly what I'm after.

Wildly, I wonder if I want to cross every orifice off the list this weekend because maybe then—when we've done everything there is to do—I'll finally have had my fill of Hank. Maybe if there's nothing new or exciting left to try, I'll get bored, the way I usually do with men.

But as I stretch around him, pain lessening, pleasure rising, my body tells me this is just the beginning.

It's too late to turn back now. My body is pulled taut as a bowstring. I'm on the edge of the precipice, and I want Hank to push me over the edge.

I want him to push me hard.

"So good," I pant, reaching around to grab his dick. "This. I'm ready. Please."

He keeps his finger inside me for another heartbeat. Then he slowly pulls it out. I hear him crack open the cap of the lube again.

"You're tight," he explains, voice rough. "More can't hurt."

He lines himself up at my asshole. The pressure of his crown alone has my eyes burning for a different reason. I like the pain, though. Maybe because I deserve it.

How fucked up is that? Wanting this excellent man to hurt me? I thought the punishment phase of my life was over. I'm done punishing myself for not being perfect. For the jiggle on my belly and the flab on my arms.

I thought I was done punishing myself for taking up space in the body I have.

Why, then, this guilt?

He pushes inside me with a grunt. He's right. I am tight; we're both struggling against my body's resistance.

"Talk to me." He massages my breast. "How do you feel?"

"I'm okay. You?"

"You feel like heaven, honey."

I turn my head, telling myself it's the last time I'll look at him until after we both come. "No, how do *you* feel?"

He's wearing this contracted expression, like he's in pain too. The kind of pain I'm in, that I like.

"I'm gonna miss you," he whispers as shadows flicker across his face. "So damn much."

I don't know what to say to that. I reach for his hand on my breast, twining our fingers and giving his a squeeze.

You're not alone.

He plays with my clit, stroking it with gentle fingertips. He sinks inside me inch by inch, the pressure enormous and enormously exciting. When his balls meet my backside, he pauses, both of us adjusting to the sensation of tightness.

My chest, too, is tight. Like there's a fist gripping my windpipe and squeezing, making it difficult to breathe.

I wasn't empty before. But now I'm full, just the right kind of full, and even though it's lovely, it makes me feel sad too.

Remember relationships are a trap. Remember you can't be trusted. Remember how lovely freedom is.

I guide his hand to my clit. I'm *this close*, and after holding off all night, I'm ready to let go.

"You can start to move," I say. "I'm good."

His fingers, still slippery with lube, stroke my pussy from front to back while he starts to thrust. Tiny thrusts at first, his breath coming in hot spurts as he rocks into me.

Hunger spirals through my core. He fingers me, fucks me, and my clit is so sensitive and so ready to explode it almost hurts.

But it's when he curls his body around mine—chest to my back, mouth on my nape, warmth everywhere—that I'm finally pushed off the edge.

I moan his name, my orgasm ripping through me with the force of a hurricane. *Pound, pound, pound.* The pounding doesn't stop. In my chest, my ears, and between my legs. Hank curses but manages to keep his rhythm, curling an arm around my waist to hold me tighter against him.

I'd forgotten how much I like being held.

I'd forgotten what it's like being cared for.

I'd forgotten how amazing it is to be so desired and that my needs *matter*.

He comes a couple of heartbeats later, sinking his teeth into my shoulder. It'll leave another bite mark.

We really are making messes left and right this weekend.

We lie on our sides and he pulls me into the curve of his body, touching me everywhere. The front of his thighs, furred with hair, meet with the back of mine; his fingers trace lazy circles across my hip.

Eventually, I go to clean myself up in the bathroom.

"Come here," he murmurs when I climb back into bed, and he pulls us onto our sides again. He pulls the covers up so we're cocooned in blankets because even though we just fucked like animals, it's chilly in the room, and I'm shivering.

Again, he tucks me against his body.

"You all right?" He nibbles at my ear. "I'm trying to get you warm."

"I think we blew past 'all right' a while ago, but thanks for asking."

We lie like that for a while, letting the fire die out while we catch our breaths.

I'm warm and cozy, and I'm surrounded by this man—his smell, his skin—in a way I haven't let myself be surrounded in a long time.

I'm so scared, which is ridiculous because *I'm not staying*. There's nothing to be scared of.

I'm still startled by the words that spill out of my mouth.

"What if this is just you rushing into something that's not right again?"

His mouth goes still on my neck. "What does that mean?"

"You wanting me this way—you wanting more—what if it's just another Emma situation? That wasn't right for you. Maybe this isn't either. Both happened *really* fast, wouldn't you say?"

He hesitates. "Well, yeah. But . . ." He lets out a breath that tickles the hair on the back of my neck. "I know it's hard to get because a lot has happened between you and me in a short amount of time. But this—you and me—it feels different."

"What, you didn't fake a relationship with Emma?" I say with a smile.

I can tell by the sound of his voice that he isn't smiling. "Is it so bad, what we did? We still had a good time. My family had a good time. And I'm pretty sure Samuel and

Emma are full steam ahead on the wedding now. Everyone's happy."

I can't help it when I look at him again, turning my head on the pillow. "What about us? Are you happy?"

"I'm not sure how to answer that, Daph."

For the first time, I wince at the nickname.

Chapter Twenty-Three

STEVIE

I'm having a hard time faking it this morning.

Hank's family appeared at the doorstep at eight AM sharp, bearing coffee and bags of breakfast wraps still hot from The Barn Door's kitchen.

"We wanted to see you off, Stevie," Annabel explains.

"Slash shamelessly ply you with coffee and food so you'll visit us again soon," Samuel adds, wrapping me in a bear hug.

We gather in the kitchen. Samuel and Emma, Beau and Annabel and little Maisie too. June and Milly and Rhett.

There are so many of them it's hard to get a word in edgewise. Not a bad thing in my current state. I'd much rather watch their interactions while trying my level best to muster an appetite than risk saying something dumb—or dangerous—myself.

"Dude, what the hell happened to your house?" Beau asks, tearing into a wrap as he glances at the mess . . . everywhere.

Hank sips his coffee, flinching when he finds it too hot. "Long story."

"Aw, yeah, y'all boned all over the place, didn't you?" Rhett asks.

June rolls her eyes. "Please, everyone, it's not even nine o'clock yet. Don't make me get the spoon."

"I'll send housekeeping to come clean it up," Beau says.

"Don't," Hank replies a little too quickly. "I got it."

Beau nods appreciatively. "I'm proud of you, brother. Mostly because you brought Stevie to Blue Mountain. If you can't tell, Stevie, we're a little obsessed with you."

"A little?" Annabel grins at me, the skin around her eyes crinkling warmly. "Try a lot. Hank, you done good."

He clears his throat. "I was the luckiest son of a bitch in the casino that night, no doubt about it."

I manage a queasy smile, and a lump forms in my throat. "I'm, um, the lucky one because I got to meet all of you."

"You say that like this is a one-time thing." Milly furrows her brow. "You're coming back, right?"

"Of course." The words pop out of my mouth too easily. "How could I not? You've been nothing but wonderful to me. I appreciate your kindness."

"And I appreciate your beer," Samuel replies. "You know, we've kicked around the idea of opening up a brewery on the resort. Maybe you could allow us to pick your brain on the business? We'll pay you for your time, of course."

I will the ground to crack open and swallow me whole. I feel Hank's gaze on me, but I can't look at him. I'm worried the truth will burst out, or I'll burst into tears.

The reality of the situation dawns on me: this pretend lovers thing will go down as one of my biggest regrets. It was a dumb fucking idea, and I should've never agreed to it. How could I not think about all the people we'd hurt? How could I not have realized I'd leave Hank to deal with the fallout on his own?

I close my eyes for a moment, telling myself that Hank and I had good intentions. He wants to see his brother happy. I want to see my business grow. I truly believed that what we were doing would be harmless at best, silly at worst.

I had no idea it would go down like this.

I had no idea I could catch such intense feelings for someone and their family in such a short span of time.

"No doubt it'll be awesome," I say. And because talking business always makes me feel better: "While we're on the subject, I spoke to my graphic designer, who handles all of Lady Luck's swag. Your extra goodies are on their way."

Only talking about my brewery makes me feel worse. Go figure. The whole fucking world is upside down right now.

"Thank you kindly," Beau says.

A beat of silence settles on the room as everyone—well, except Hank and I—chows down on their breakfasts. A cell phone rings and is promptly silenced. Rhett hands his mama a napkin when she spills some chutney on her lap. Maisie nearly bites Beau's fingers off as he feeds her chunks of scrambled egg and sweet potato.

"We've got news," Samuel says at last, cutting a glance at Emma.

Milly's brows shoot up, and she pauses mid-bite. "Y'all set a date!"

"Jesus Christ, Milly, do you have to ruin every surprise?" Samuel shoots back. But he's smiling. This big, stupid, goofy thing that makes my stomach clench.

I want that kind of smile for Hank. I want him to have that news.

I look at him. He's looking at Samuel. Hank's eyes are happy. But that muscle in his jaw jumps as though he's clenching his teeth.

It has nothing to do with the date. I believe Hank when he says he's over Emma, and I know he's genuinely happy for them.

No. I think it's got to do with the bittersweetness of the

moment. Hank did and didn't get what he wanted. Win: Samuel and Emma getting married. Lose: Hank *not* getting married.

He didn't even get the girl.

I don't think that's what he set out wanting. He didn't deceive me. When he called a couple of weeks ago—*was that really only a couple of weeks ago?*—he wanted a fake relationship, and he wanted to fuck.

But somewhere along the way, he began to want more.

Maybe that's where I went wrong, not pulling the plug earlier. Because I knew what was happening even though Hank assured me everything was okay.

Then again, what was I supposed to do? Bolt and leave Hank hanging? We were in too deep by then. And now we've inadvertently created a clusterfuck.

"June twenty-ninth," Emma says. "Hope everyone can make it."

Milly drops her wrap and grabs a napkin, tapping on her phone to bring the screen to life. "Wow. Okay. Doesn't give us a ton of time—"

"Milly, sweetheart, how about we congratulate the couple first?" June says, nudging her daughter with her elbow.

"Didn't we congratulate these two all weekend?" Phone in one hand, Milly waves June away with the other. "Congrats. Now let's talk bands."

Beau laughs, and Annabel goes to hug Emma.

I watch, feeling increasingly nauseous, as Hank extends his hand to Samuel. As they hug and pound each other's backs. As Hank hugs Emma, murmuring something in her ear that makes her smile widen.

Then Emma hugs *me*. "Thank you," she whispers. "For taking such great care of Hank. We've been worried about him. I'm glad he's found someone who's as amazing as he is."

The lump in my throat swells, making my whole head ache.

"Babies will be welcome," Samuel says, nodding at Maisie.

Emma looks at me. "So are significant others. Obviously."

"I'm assuming the best wine in the world will be served?" Beau asks.

Samuel wraps an arm around Emma's waist. "Only the best for my stuck-up sommelier."

"Hey." She elbows him. "You're the one with five cars, forty watches, and an *Iron Man*-themed wine cellar. If anyone deserves to be called a snob, it's you."

"I have fifty-seven watches, thank you very much." Samuel sniffs. "And I'm only a snob because you've rubbed off on me."

"Please, for the love of God, do not make any rubbing jokes," Beau warns.

I look at Hank. Hank looks at me.

Too late.

Because he can read me like a book, he grabs my hand underneath the island. We're sitting on a pair of stools together, our uneaten wraps on the pristine Herend china in front of us. His grip is warm and reassuring, and it makes me feel the tiniest bit better.

"So," June says, wiping her hands on a napkin, "when will we be seeing you again, Stevie?"

Hank scoffs. "Mama, I love you dearly, but that's a loaded—"

"It's a good question," Milly says, eyes on me. She crosses her arms. "Look at the two of you with your sad puppy dog eyes. Why so glum after a great weekend?"

Beau rolls his eyes. "Honestly, Milly, that's none of your beeswax."

"But it does make sense why they'd be bummed," Samuel says. "No one likes leaving."

"I know just how awful leaving can be." Annabel gives Beau a meaningful look. "Remember that?"

Beau runs a hand through his hair. "Do I remember the biggest fuckup of my life? Letting you walk away? Yeah, I'd say so."

"Language, son," June says.

Oh God, I'm going to puke. Not because Annabel and Beau are so cute together it's almost gross. But because I'm imagining Hank thinking to himself, *hey, I'm not going to make that mistake.*

He's not going to let me walk away.

"We'll see how things shake out," Hank answers for me. "Y'all are forgetting Stevie's kind of a big deal back in Nashville. CEO of a company. She can't just up and leave whenever she wants."

"Good thing you're unemployed at the moment," Rhett shoots back. "Why don't you go back to Nashville with her?"

I look up to see the two of them exchange a heated glare. My face burns, and my pulse kicks up a notch.

Saliva floods my mouth, and I clutch my napkin with my free hand, ready to bring it to my mouth in case I really do vomit.

"*Because.*" That muscle in Hank's jaw jumps again. "I just told you, dipshit. Stevie leads a team of ten. She's busy as fuck, and she doesn't need me underfoot all week long."

June glances around the kitchen. "Where the heck is that spoon?"

Beau claps a hand onto Hank's shoulder. "I've also chatted with Hank here about coming back on board at the resort. If y'all can behave for two seconds, maybe I'd be able to convince him to start this week."

My shoulders, stiff and achy, loosen.

If what Beau is saying is true, that's great news. I'd like to think I've had a hand in that decision—Hank was picking my brain about creating a more balanced life if he did go back to work at Blue Mountain again. It makes me feel less terrible, knowing I left Hank better off in one respect.

"Really?" Milly says, face lighting up.

Emma claps her hands. "I really, really hope you're coming back, Hank. Everyone's missed you."

"Even you?" Hank nods at Samuel. His tone is playful, teasing.

But Samuel is serious when he answers. "Damn right, I've missed you. With Rhett gone, and you gone, and Beau busy being all cute and shit with Bel, I don't have anyone letting themselves into my house without asking anymore." He shrugs. "Guess I liked your trespassing more than I let on."

"Aw," Bel says. "That's sweet."

Hank scratches his head. "Is it?"

His cheeks are pink.

My phone buzzes in my back pocket, making me jump. I grab it, and I don't think I've ever been so grateful to see my assistant's name pop up on the screen.

The perfect excuse to quietly slip away. I know it makes me an asshole to leave Blue Mountain without properly saying goodbye to everyone, but I don't think I can do it.

Then again, does it make me an asshole? Maybe me not saying goodbye will leave a bad taste in the Beauregards' mouths, so they'll be that much less heartbroken when I don't come back to Blue Mountain.

"I have to take this," I say.

But I try to make my escape a beat too late. Samuel pulls me into a hug and presses a scruffy kiss to my cheek. "You come back to the farm soon, you hear?"

I nod, the lump in my throat making it impossible to reply.

"Guys, quit it," Hank says. "CEO of her own company, remember?"

At that moment, I almost wish Hank would stop being such a great guy.

Everyone hugs me. Well, except Maisie, who's apparently having a serious case of stranger danger this morning. She shies away from me, emphatically shaking her head, and I can't help but laugh as tears prick my eyes.

"She'll get used to you," Annabel says. "The more often you come, the easier this'll get."

"And then you're gonna wish you never came at all 'cause once you're in Maisie's circle of trust, you are *in*."

"Exhibit A." June points at Maisie, who's clinging to her, head tucked into her shoulder. "She doesn't want me to put her down. Like, ever."

Hank's people—they're wonderful. If I were to do the whole in-law thing again—which I'm not—I'd want to do it with them.

Giving Rhett one last hug, I scurry to the bedroom and close the door. I need to call Ria back. First, though, I let the buildup of emotion finally break free.

Through a blurry film of tears, I take in the rumpled sheets on the bed, the ashes in the fireplace, and the guitar leaning upright beside it. The clothes on the floor, lube and condoms on his nightstand, and empty coffee cups on mine.

It's a delicious, ridiculous mess. But Hank and I want different things, and not even the exhilaration of the past three days can change that.

Chapter Twenty-Four

HANK

I drive Stevie to the airport, ostensibly because my siblings would think it was weird if I didn't.

The real reason? I'm still in denial that Stevie's leaving.

I take the Rolls because she seems to like it. But she's quiet on the drive, and there's this low hum of tension between us that's new.

I hate it.

I hate everything about this. I wanted to make metaphorical messes. But I ended up making a real mess out of something I never should've, er, messed with.

Why does this keep happening? Honestly, fuck me for life.

I can't tell if I'm angry or sad or horny as I take the familiar route. I just feel hollowed out.

And the fact that Stevie isn't talking to me . . .

"I'm sorry if that whole breakfast thing upset you," I say when I can't take it anymore.

She doesn't look away from her window. But I see her eyes blinking frantically, and my chest tightens.

"I feel like an asshole," she says. Her voice is thick.

Letting out a breath, I reply, "I can relate. I'm sorry, honey."

She looks down at her lap. "I'm sorry too. Your family is great."

"They can be, yeah."

"But they're going to crucify you when they find out."

"They're not gonna find out."

"Yeah, they are." She finally looks at me. Her eyes are glassy. "Y'all made that mistake in the past—not paying attention—so now they'll be paying more attention than ever. And what's happened—like your sister said, it's written all over your face."

"What's written on my face?"

Stevie tilts her head, looking at me from underneath her lashes. "Everything," she replies softly. "You hide nothing, Hank. It's one of my favorite things about you."

"I don't hide anything because I used to hide everything, and it got me in trouble." I smile tightly. "Guess trouble finds me no matter what choice I make. About my family—I've got it handled."

We approach the airport. Stevie's flying private, so we've got time. I pull into the cell phone lot and put the car in park. The throaty purr of the engine fills the silence between us.

My heart is pounding.

She reaches across the center console and puts her hand on my thigh. "You're a great guy, Hank."

This is where you and I end.

I'm becoming an expert at deciphering what she's really saying.

I thumb a tear off her cheek. "If you mean that, why are you crying?"

"I'm not crying," she says, sniffing, and we both laugh.

Her skin is warm and smooth against the pad of my thumb. "It's okay to cry, Stevie."

"I know." She nods. "I just feel—God, I feel silly. I don't want to create a scene."

I manage a smile even though I feel like dying. "But you're so good at it. We've made so many scenes. All of them excellent. In fact, I thought about writing to Shonda Rhimes and telling her just how good we are at *Bridgerton* shit. Maybe she'll write us into the show or something. I hear there's going to be more seasons."

"Cheeseball." But she leans in and kisses me.

I lick my tongue into her mouth. "Did you know dad humor turned you on before you met me?"

"I did not."

She sucks on my bottom lip, and I let her take what she needs. Only when the kiss becomes messy and my dick gets hard do I gently push her away, resting my forehead on hers.

We sit like that for several heartbeats, breath coming in hot pants.

It's now or never.

The last time I put myself out there with Emma, I got unceremoniously shot down. I should be more scared because chances are I'm about to be shot down again.

But you can't win if you don't have cards on the table. I've already lost more than I bargained for to this woman. Why not add my pride to the pile?

I can't ask her to stay. She's got her own life in Nashville, a business too, one she fought hard for after that prick of an ex pushed her to give it all up.

I'll be damned if I do the same. And what would she be giving it up for? I haven't decided what I'm going to do about my future at the Farm.

Still, I can't help but wonder if there's some way we could make a long-distance relationship work.

"I have to ask because there's nothing else I can do at this point." I suck in a breath through my nose. "Would you consider making this more than a weekend thing? I'm not gonna beg, but I know I'm gonna regret letting you go if I don't ask you about working an *us* into our lives somehow. You're a confident, accomplished, sexy as fuck woman, honey, and I don't want to say goodbye to you today."

She blinks, eyelashes fluttering against my own. "You're persistent, I'll give you that."

"I know what I want, and I want you."

"But deep down." She closes her eyes. "What do you really want? In five, ten years, where do you see yourself? Who are you with? What are you doing? What does your life look like?"

I don't answer. I don't need to.

That could all change. I'm tempted to say it. I could change. My dreams could change. I'm still young, and I've still got shit to learn.

But this is where my self-preservation kicks in. It's right to be honest, but it ain't right to beg. And a mean little voice inside my head wonders why I should have to compromise when Stevie won't. Especially on big, life-changing stuff like commitment.

We've got different dreams. But the stuff we're made of—that doesn't feel so different.

I don't know what to do. Except attempt to swallow the fact that this really is a tragedy. Right place, wrong time type shit.

Falling back in my seat, I nod. "You're right. I understand."

She pauses. "This is awful."

"I know." The silence becomes excruciating, so I put the car in drive. "Ready?"

"Yes."

I head to the terminal and park curbside. When I pop the trunk, Stevie and I push open our doors at the same time as though neither of us can get out of the car fast enough.

It feels all wrong.

This whole thing feels wrong. Even though we're doing what's right.

I lift her suitcase out of the trunk and set it on the sidewalk, popping up the handle with a neat *click*. Our hands brush when she takes it from me, hiking her tote bag over her shoulder.

We stand there, her on the sidewalk, me on the other side of the curb. We're the same height like this, our gazes level.

"It was a pleasure, Hank," she says. "The whole weekend. Thank you again for having me."

"Thank you for coming." We've said these words before. They sound hollow and stupid. Is this how our final scene is going to go down? Poorly written? Terribly acted?

I look at her. She looks at me, offering a watery smile, and goddamn, am I ever gonna get over how pretty this girl is?

"I wasn't prepared for you," she whispers at last and holds up her arms for a hug.

Something inside my chest cracks. I grab her and hold her and bury my face in her neck. "I was just thinking the same thing."

"I hate that this is the last time—"

Last time touching, last time talking, last time living this beautiful lie.

"Me too. But we'll be all right, okay? Let's think about the fun stuff."

She nods. "Okay."

"Listen." I pull back to look her in the eye. "If you ever need to talk, you know you can—"

"I don't think that's a good idea," she says, shaking her head. "As much as it's going to suck, I think a clean break"—

she chops her hand through the air, the edge of her palm meeting the flat plane of the other—"is the way to go. If we keep talking, we're just going to fuck each other up more."

I swallow. "If that's how you feel."

"That's how I feel. I'm sorry."

"I am too." Looking down, I toe at an invisible pebble. "I'm so sorry, honey."

I look back up. Her tits rise on a sharp inhale.

"Goodbye, Hastings."

"Bye, Daph."

I watch her push through the revolving door. She's inside. She's safe.

I put the car in drive and head home.

The house rings with silence.

Closing the door behind me, I take in the disaster that is my home. Can I even call it that anymore? A home? I thought that's what I was doing with Stevie—turning a series of boxes into rooms, rooms that held stories and memories and marks of a life. A life that was lived, not endured. Not held up as some kind of trophy.

I turned this house into a home.

Now, though, it just looks and feels like a sad, disgusting pigsty. Like a roving pack of dumbass college kids had their way with it. I half expect to find one of them passed out on my couch, a cigarette tucked behind his ear and an overturned Solo cup of jungle juice on the floor beside him.

The son my mama raised doesn't feel right about leaving the mess. But it also doesn't feel right to clean it up yet.

I'm also really fucking tired.

I toe off my shoes at the foot of my bed and fall face-first onto the mattress. Jeans and all.

Just my luck, I land on the pillow Stevie used, and it smells like her—girly shampoo and toothpaste.

For several beats, I can't breathe.

My phone vibrates in my pocket. I know without looking that it's Beau, and he's calling under the guise of checking in when really he wants me back in the office. Not because he wants me to work but because he knows it'll be good for me. As Daddy used to say, idle hands are the devil's workshop.

Tomorrow. I'll start tomorrow. Even though the thought of going back doesn't exactly fill me with excitement at the moment.

But hey, things will be different this time around. Stevie was only here for three days and nights, but I learned a shit-ton from her, mostly the difference between what I thought success looked like and what it actually means to me.

What kind of life do I have, though, outside my job? This weekend I had Stevie. I had her to cook for, to bring coffee to, to laugh with and write music with and fuck to the point of pain.

Now I have the gym and . . .?

An invisible weight settles on my back and presses me into the mattress. My legs ache, and so does my dick.

I understand it now: I wasn't so much in love with Emma as I was with the life I'd always dreamed about having.

A life I'm starting to think will never actually happen because the woman I could imagine it with is currently putting hundreds of miles between us. Literally and figuratively.

Fuck.

Chapter Twenty-Five

STEVIE

"You okay, Stevie?"

Swallowing hard, I glance up from my laptop screen to see Ria looking at me, pen poised over her notebook, her brow furrowed.

"Do I look that bad?"

"You look . . . tired."

I let out a mirthless laugh, the knot in my gut tightening. "Didn't we all just read a book about the importance of radical honesty?"

"I was the second member of Lady Luck's book club. Of course I read that one, along with everyone else in this office." Ria hesitates. "Okay. Yeah, you're looking rough today."

"Really rough," Alan, my social media guru, adds as he pushes his glasses up the bridge of his nose.

Shooting him a glare, I say, "I said radical honesty. Not asshat honesty."

"Sorry." He lifts a shoulder. "It's the truth."

"Want me to pour you a beer?" Paige, our intern, offers.

"You're sweet," I say. "It's also eight o'clock in the morning. Do I really look that bad?"

"Yes," all three reply in unison.

Ria peers at me. "Everything go all right this weekend? You sounded like you were on cloud nine when you called me Saturday after the tasting."

"Maya said Blue Mountain placed a huge order," Alan says. "I feel like we should be celebrating."

"But instead, you look like you got punched in the face," Paige says.

Alan gasps. "Did you get punched in the face?"

My eyes burn, and I close them. "No, I didn't. Of course I didn't. I—" *Fell for my fake boyfriend and now I miss him so much I haven't eaten or slept since I left him yesterday, and now I'm about to burst into tears in a meeting.*

This isn't like me. I'm a professional, goddamn it. I cried in meetings in my twenties. A decade-plus of practice later, I now save my tears for the bathroom stall farthest from the door or for my car, thank you very much.

But here I am, struggling not to burst into tears at my first meeting on my first day back.

See? Men fuck everything up.

The knot in my stomach won't go away. It's telling me something, but maybe it's not something I want to hear right now. I felt this way when my marriage hit the skids too. I just needed time. And therapy. And lots of hand-holding from my girlfriends.

Although the idea of calling Kate and Lauren feels . . . not great, either. Probably because they'll also tell me something I don't want to hear.

I put a hand on my chest. I feel short of breath.

I feel trapped. Like I'm being stonewalled in every direction, caught in a box that's suddenly too small to stand up or move around in.

"Okay," Ria says slowly. "Why don't we all take five and regroup after a cup of coffee?"

"Let's," I manage, my stomach turning over at the thought of said coffee.

You know it's bad when the idea of God's second most delicious creation (after beer, of course) turns you off.

Ria closes the door behind Alan and Paige.

"Hey," she says kindly. "I can clear your schedule if you need the day off."

I wave her away, trying valiantly to blink back tears before they spill over. "Too much going on. Don't want to miss our meeting with Jeremiah. He's supposed to have samples of those finishes and fabrics we talked about last time, and I'm so excited to see them."

If I keep telling myself that, I will actually feel excited, right? Because I *was* excited about meeting with our top-tier interior designer and his team to finalize the design for the new space before.

Before I met Hank.

Before I went to Blue Mountain.

Before I wrote a song with a famous football player and danced and laughed and drank with his lovely, foul-mouthed family.

I miss him, and I want nothing more right now than to dial his number and hear his voice.

But I can't, and it's killing me.

"I'm sure Jeremiah can reschedule," Ria says, swiping her thumb across her phone screen. "You don't need me to tell you mental health days are both necessary and restorative, right?"

I shake my head, blinking against a fresh press of tears at my assistant's kindness. "Since when are twenty-year-olds so wise?"

"I wish I was twenty."

"Do you really?"

Ria laughs. "No, actually, not at all. Twenty was fun, but . . . yeah, twenty-eight is better." She holds up her phone. "I can shoot Jeremiah an email."

I shake my head again, typing nonsense into a blank email on my laptop. "I just need a minute. Is it still raining? I'm going to walk over to Latte Larry's."

"Yep." Ria glances out the windows at my back. "Still raining."

Of course the weather would reflect my not-awesome mood. I'm starting to think Hank's fame, hotness, and helpfulness actually point to him being a god. An honest to goodness divine being with biceps of glory and the power to destroy a perfectly good Tuesday morning.

"I brought my coat," I say, reaching behind me. "I think."

The past twelve hours are a blur. I remember boarding the plane in Asheville. Remember getting home and ordering a pizza I didn't eat.

After that? Just lots of tossing and turning in bed with my phone in my hand in case Hank texted or called.

He didn't. At the airport in Nashville, I let him know I landed safe and sound, and I thanked him for the ride. *Thanks again for everything*, he'd texted back. That's the last I've heard from him.

"This doesn't have anything to do with the order?" Ria asks. "The one Blue Mountain put in?"

"Nah, the order's still good."

"We've had people change their minds before."

I swallow for the thousandth time. "The Beauregards are old-fashioned like that—they keep their word."

I'm not sure how I know this, exactly. I've been around Hank and his family for all of three days. But somehow, I know it. The sky-is-blue and grits-are-good kind of knowing.

"Go take your walk. We'll be ready for you when you come back."

"Thanks, Ria. I'm sorry about all this." I circle my hand in front of my face.

She puts her hand on the door handle. "Don't be. I'm sorry you're feeling so shitty."

"I'll be better for our meeting, I promise."

"Of course you will." She turns to the door and pushes the handle down, only to turn back to me. "Can I say something?"

"Yes."

"I'm proud of you."

My eyebrows snap together. "Seriously? For what? Crying at work? Even Paige, the intern, knows what a faux pas that is."

"I mean this as a compliment, but I'm proud of you for staying vulnerable. I think there's this myth around leadership that you have to be this hard-assed, man-eating, shit-kicking dominatrix to make it. And you can definitely be a hard-ass, Stevie, don't get me wrong. But you're willing to put yourself out there, which means you're willing to get hurt. You're brave, and that's something I admire very much about you."

If only she knew how wrong she is on that point.

Wiping my eyes with the flat of my fingers, I manage a tight smile. Then I shrug into my jacket—by some miracle, I did remember it, along with an umbrella—and head out in the rain.

The walk clears my head. So does a latte. I've always liked Larry's coffee, but now that I've experienced Blue Mountain's special brand of caffeinated magic, his espresso leaves something to be desired.

Has Hank legitimately ruined me for life? First, it's coffee. What if it's sex? Carbs? Air travel? Everything I experienced with him was top-notch.

Everything I experienced showed he valued me.

Respected me.

My hands shake on my way back to the office, latte in one, umbrella in the other. I'm getting worried that this is not just a case of day-after bumming.

But I don't have the luxury of wallowing in whatever this feeling is, so I do as my therapist told me and give myself a gentle pep talk.

I tell myself that it's the lack of sleep making this feeling in my belly worse. It's the comedown from a really great weekend. It doesn't mean I'm in love with this guy. Anyone would feel this way after a stay at Blue Mountain Farm; it's a five-star vacation.

It always sucks coming home from vacation.

Tomorrow will be better. I just need to be kind to myself in the meantime—go slowly, eat real healthy food, and rest. All I need to do right now is put one foot in front of the other, and that's enough.

My pep talk actually does make me feel better. Then my phone rings and my stomach somersaults, and I'm right back to square one, thinking about Hank, if it's him, what he'll say. What I'll say, despite the fact I know, rationally, I've already said it all.

Why, then, this urgent need to talk welling up inside me?

Why this urgent desire that it's him?

My hand shakes so badly as I try to dig my phone out of my jacket pocket that I drop it on the ground.

"Shit," I breathe, bending down to pick it up.

I turn it over, discovering not only is the screen cracked,

but it's my mom. Disappointment settles heavily in my center.

Again.

Interior design is one of my passions. I'm not very good at it —hence why we hired Jeremiah's firm to help us out with Lady Luck's new space—but I still get a kick out of sorting through fabric samples and ogling floor finishes.

"Jeremiah." Taking in the spread of fabric, hardware, and tile samples on the table in front of us, I let out a low whistle. "You've done good. Real good."

The designer, a ridiculously handsome thirtysomething guy with a Gatsby-meets-Robert Redford vibe, crosses his arms and smiles.

"I'm thrilled you like it. We really amped up the pretty elements with this round." He points at a square of pale gray leather and another of turquoise wool. "You'll still get that casual feel, but with a slick, feminine edge."

My project manager, Janice, meets my eyes and smiles. "I hope you're ready for this, Stevie. What we're doing here is really different, but I think it's going to get a great response."

A pulse of longing moves through me as I remember how Samuel talked about doing things differently at Blue Mountain Farm. *We like to stand out. Service, accommodations. Food and wine. And your beer? It stands out.*

"I do too," Jeremiah says. "This brewery is going to be top-notch quality all around—the beer, the interiors. And these bathrooms?" He holds up a zellige tile that gleams like mother-of-pearl. "They're going to be bananas."

Despite the dumpster fire that is today, I manage a smile. My pulse leaps with genuine excitement.

My team and I are knocking it out of the park. I'm so proud I could burst.

But on an off-beat, my pulse randomly crashes instead of leaps. My stomach clenches, and I feel sick all over again.

Stop. I can't keep letting myself get down like this. This meeting, and all the goodness that will come of it, is yet another sign from the universe that I'm making the right call by insisting on a clean break with Hank.

Even if we didn't want completely different things—even if I was open to his white picket fence dreams—how would we ever make a relationship work? Neither of us can "work from anywhere"; neither of us can quit and find something else. We love what we do. We love the people we work with. I'd never ask Hank to quit Blue Mountain to come live with me. Same as he'd never ask me to give up Lady Luck.

Taking a deep breath, I roll my shoulders back and reach for a sample of the custom glassware we're having made by a company down in Charleston.

"I'm ready to double down," I say. "Sounds like y'all are too."

Chapter Twenty-Six

HANK

I can't have the girl.

But I can have the kind of life she told me about. I'll give it the old college try anyway. Because right now, work is the only thing that might get me back on my feet. Once I'm up and running, I'll feel better.

When the fuck am I gonna feel better?

My eyes burn with exhaustion as I step into Blue Mountain's offices in a wing of the main house. I'm immediately greeted by the familiar smells of burning wood and whiskey. Milly passes by, stopping to give me a quick hug even though she's on the phone. Christopher holds out his hand and says what everyone else does—that they've missed me and they're glad I'm back.

For a heartbeat, the heaviness in my chest lifts.

I'm glad I'm back too. I've missed this place. The bustle, the people, the food, the cocktails, and the heady buzz the resort seems to generate all on its own.

I'm lucky to have this place and this job to come back to. A lot of my former teammates don't have a place to land. Many are married and settled, but they have no idea what to do about their future in terms of purpose or employment.

I've got both right here in front of me. With Stevie's ideas about balance in my pocket, I feel more confident than ever I'm gonna like heading up guest relations.

This part of my life will (hopefully) click into place. I just wish I could shake the sense that something is missing. That I'm very much back to where I started before I left Blue Mountain.

Fell for a chick I can't have? Check.

Empty house? Check.

Family treating me like a grenade about to go off?

Actually, I won't put a check next to that one. When I walk into Beau's office, he doesn't look at me with sympathy, or judgment, or even annoyance.

He looks relieved. Excited, even.

I feel like the world's biggest shithead. He only thinks I'm okay because I lied to him about having a girlfriend and having my life together.

What kind of person lies to his family over and over?

Not a happy one, I know that much.

My face burns with shame.

Beau's standing behind the desk. He's wearing his usual puffer vest and backward hat, hair curling out around his ears. He flips through a sheaf of papers, smiling at me. "Still hungover?"

"Guess so." I run a hand over my jaw. I showered and shaved not half an hour ago, but I still feel grubby. "Still on West Coast time, I think."

He sets down the papers. "I think you miss your girl."

My chest twists. I clear my throat and glance out the windows behind my brother. "Of course I miss Stevie. I hate that—" Jesus fuck, I hate so much about our situation. But I go with: "I hate that we don't live closer."

"Long distance is a beast. But y'all can do it. You're obsessed enough with each other."

I shove my hands in my pockets. "Maybe."

"Maybe?" He cocks a brow. "I don't like that answer."

"Yeah. Yeah, I don't either, but it is what it is."

"What does that mean?"

It means I wasn't going to start planting the seeds of my fake breakup with Stevie until later, maybe a week or two down the road, but pretending is starting to feel really, really awful.

I just want to rip the Band-Aid off and be done with it. But that would be suspicious—my family, Milly especially, is smarter than that—so I guess I'm stuck in this hellish in-between for a bit.

Fun times.

"Means I'm tired and hungover, and I really wish I woke up next to Stevie this morning." The words come out roughly, which is ironic because it might be the only bit of truth I share about my feelings today.

Beau's expression softens. "That blows. I'm sorry, brother. You'd think I'd be more sensitive about this shit, considering Bel and I pretty much had a long-distance relationship for, oh, a decade or so."

I grin, relief flooding my gut at the change in subject. "You were a fucking idiot."

"Yup. Which is why I'm not gonna let you make the same mistake." He claps his hands and rubs them together. "Staying busy helped me, so I'm thinking it'll help you too. Shall we begin negotiations?"

"Fuck yeah, we shall."

Beau hits a button on his phone and asks his assistant to send Gregory in. A minute or two later, my former assistant walks through the door and offers me a smile.

"Good to see you, man," I say, giving his hand a firm

shake. "Thanks for holding down the fort while I was gone. I really appreciate it."

"Happy to help. Although I gotta say I'm real glad you're back. This job is no joke."

"I hear you. That's what I wanted to talk about, actually. I've been thinking a lot about it, and I've decided it's really a two-person job. If you're down, I'd like to chat about you and me tackling it together."

Gregory smiles. "I like the sound of that."

I grab the chair in front of me and sit, followed in short order by Gregory. Beau sits too, grabbing his clipboard and a pen.

He motions to me. "Floor is yours, brother."

"Gregory, feel free to jump in whenever. I only speak for myself, but I'm open to hearing your demands too," I say.

Gregory's smile grows. "You do own the resort, so I'd say that's fair. I'm also pretty flexible at this point, so why don't you start, and we can go from there?"

"Great. For starters, I want to work five days a week, max. I'm at my best when I have dedicated time off. It doesn't have to be weekends, but I would like two consecutive days off. On the days I'm here, I walk through the door at nine, and I walk back out at five."

Beau's scribbling furiously. "Got it. What about this? Monday and Tuesday off, Wednesday through Sunday on? Fridays and Sundays are our obviously busiest days with the most check-ins and check-outs, so that way, you're here for the rush, but you get a nice break immediately afterward."

"Can you work Mondays and Tuesdays?" I ask Gregory.

He nods. "Absolutely."

"Great. That's done."

"What else?" Beau asks.

"We increase my staff. I want another doorman, plus

another assistant." I glance at Gregory. "You haven't been officially promoted yet, right?"

"Not yet."

"Great. Let's go ahead and promote Gregory to VP. I think having another layer of management there will help tremendously, especially as he's had a lot of hands-on experience."

Gregory beams. "Thank you, Hank."

"Thank you for stepping up to the plate when I needed you. It's the least I can do."

Beau nods. "Okay. I think we can swing that."

"I also want to bring back the bonfires," I say.

"The bonfires?" Beau grins, scribbling again. "You wanna whip out 'Wheels on the Bus' again?"

"Sure do." I lean back in my chair. "But really, I miss playing and performing. It makes me happy. I want to start hosting the bonfires again so I have an excuse to eat s'mores and sing."

Beau ducks his lips. "Fine by me. We've had a lot of returning guests ask about the bonfires, actually. It just didn't feel right having them without you."

There's a warm nudge against my breastbone. "I am quite the attraction."

"Shut up. How's this bonfire thing going to work with your nine to five?" Beau flips his hat off and runs a hand through his hair. "If memory serves, we ran it from, what, six to nine on Friday nights?"

I nod. "I thought about that. I considered coming in later on Friday mornings—"

"On check-in day?" Beau makes a face as he puts his hat back on.

I hold up a hand. "I got you. I considered it but realized it wouldn't work for exactly that reason. What if I worked longer Fridays in exchange for an afternoon off? Say, Wednesday afternoons, if Gregory can cover for me?"

"I can do that," Gregory says.

"Fine by me too," Beau adds, "as long as no one misses a beat."

"I won't because I'll have another assistant, remember?"

"How could I forget? I'm the one paying his salary."

I grin. "So generous."

"What else?"

Sucking in a breath, I think of how to ask for the last item on my list. Probably best to just come out with it. "Would Maisie be interested in taking music classes?"

Beau's eyebrows shoot up. "She's taken them before, yeah. Why?"

"I noticed how much she loved our music the other night. I thought—I dunno, maybe on my Wednesday afternoons I could play some tunes with her. For her. We could play together, and I could teach her how to play the guitar and . . . stuff."

"Hank, she's one."

"Well, yeah, okay, maybe teaching her to play guitar is a little ambitious. But I still think it could be fun. I'll hang out with her and, like, sing or whatever."

Beau's grinning at me. So is Gregory.

"What?" I ask, face starting to feel warm again.

"Just promise me Stevie'll wait till Maisie's eighteen to teach her how to twerk, all right?"

I manage to laugh even as a knife lodges itself in the center of my chest. Beau's thinking long term about Stevie. Which reminds me that I've thought long term about her too. How fun would it be to have music lessons with her and Maisie? She was so good with the baby.

She was so good with everyone.

But just because Stevie's good with kids doesn't mean she should have one of her own.

Just because she's great with my family doesn't mean she should be a part of it.

Goddamn, though, she'd fit in just right.

Everything about her felt just right.

"I promise," I say and slip my phone out of my pocket to check it. A dozen texts, a few missed calls, lots of emails. None of them from Stevie.

I can't get it through my thick skull that she isn't going to contact me ever again. We had a great time, and now we're done.

Except it feels unfinished. Or maybe I'm just imagining this break feels more like an intermission than an ending.

Beau, Gregory, and I chat for another hour—Gregory's requests, our budgets, the expansion, upcoming events at the resort, the new computer system and the IT team that came with it—before I head to my own office a few doors down. I'm draping my jacket over the back of my chair when Samuel walks in.

He looks happy and well-rested in an emerald green suit and fur-lined loafers—even after all these years, I still don't get why he tries to be football's answer to Macklemore—and for a split second, I hate him.

Why does he get the happy ending?

He holds out his hand, his smile fading. "You all right?"

"Sorry." I take his hand and give it a firm shake. "Guess I'm just missing Stevie. How're you? Looks like you're still on cloud nine."

Samuel keeps his hand clasped around mine. "When are you gonna ask her to move in? Because you should ask her to move in."

"Thanks for the advice I didn't ask for and don't need," I say wryly. "Kind of you."

"You look like you just lost a championship game on a bad call. Clearly, you do need some advice. Put a ring on it. Boo her up. Whatever the fuck the kids are calling it these days, you should make Stevie yours. You know it, I know it. She knows it. Why you even let her leave—"

"I told you, she has a life and a business to run. I can't keep her from that."

He finally drops my hand. "Y'all haven't talked about it? Your endgame?"

I want to crawl under my desk and hide there forever.

Instead, I run a hand over my face and look away. "Look, we're working on it, all right? I've got a lot to do today."

"I know." Samuel peers at me. "I just wanna make sure you're okay. You wouldn't lie to me about being okay after everything that happened last year, right?"

Scratch hiding under the desk. I want to get sucked down straight to hell, where I probably belong.

"I'm sad. And tired. And excited to be back. That's the truth. Now can we move on?"

Samuel looks at me for another minute before he unbuttons his blazer and takes a seat in a chair in front of my desk, crossing his ankle over his knee. "I'm trusting you," he says. "One last thing about Stevie—Emma and I were seriously impressed by her beer. We plan on stocking Lady Luck well into the future."

I sit, shooting my cuffs. I gotta cut off mentions of Stevie at some point, or I'm gonna die.

"So, Friday night bonfires. I want to bring them back. Let's talk about the food and beverage component."

Chapter Twenty-Seven

STEVIE

I wait to feel better.

The week is a busy one, filled with exciting but labor-intensive things. I'm able to lose myself in work for a few hours at a time, running meetings, recipe development. I love my job—that hasn't changed.

I play tennis.

I try to read.

I drink beer, and I make good food, and I listen to Brené Brown podcasts.

I do everything I can that usually makes me feel better. But every day, I wake up and feel worse.

By the time Saturday rolls around, I'm in tears before I even open my eyes. Here I am, nearly a week in, and I miss Hank so much I can't get out of bed.

Reaching for my phone, I do what I've done every morning since I left Blue Mountain. I check to see if Hank's called or texted or emailed.

Nada.

So I pull up his name and start typing out a text of my own.

I know I said I wanted a clean break, but I can't stop thinking about you. I'm so sorry. I miss you like crazy. I would give my left arm to be having coffee with you right now. Wait, I take that back. I guess I need two arms to play the tambourine. But I'd gladly offer a leg? Have you told your family yet about us? Do they think we broke up? I want to see you so badly, baby.

I can't shake the feeling I've messed up so, so badly.

I hover my thumb over the arrow button. I chicken out at the last minute, but this is definitely the closest I've come to actually pressing send.

Putting a hand over my eyes, I let myself cry.

I don't know what to do here. On the one hand, I know I've already hurt Hank, and I'd be hurting him again by reaching out. Nothing's changed; I still want freedom, and he still wants family. I still own and run Lady Luck, and he's still young, young enough to start fresh. What would sending a text like that accomplish? It'd only upset us both.

On the other hand, I'm trying to be truthful, and the truth is I'm hurting without him. Chances are he's hurting without me too. That look he gave me when he dropped me off at the airport—

I suck in a trembling breath. Tears are leaking everywhere, down my temples and cheeks, soaking my pillow.

That's it.

I can't take this anymore. Time to call in the cavalry.

Kate picks up on the first ring.

"Finally," she says. "I've been trying to get a hold of you all week! Where the hell have you been, and what are you not telling me?"

I scoff. "Good morning to you too."

"Aw, honey, you don't sound good."

A pause as the ache in my throat swells. "I can't eat, and I can't sleep, and I'm at a loss, Kate. I miss him." I take a shaky breath. "Can you talk? I know weekends are tough for you to get out."

"Please. Every day is tough for me to get out. But by some miracle, Jane is home today, and she's not on call. I'll be over in twenty." A wail sounds in the background. "Make that ten. I'm leaving now. Like, right now. PS I'm in my pajamas, so don't judge."

"Apparently I look like I got punched in the face, so. Yeah. No judgment here."

Kate does indeed show up in her pajamas, bearing gifts of coffee and bagels. Lauren shows up not long after with a box of tissues tucked under one arm and a handle of vodka tucked under the other.

"Why eat all those carbs"—she nods at the bagels—"if they don't have something to soak up?"

I nibble on my toasted cinnamon raisin bagel, heavy on the butter, while Kate gulps her coffee and Lauren stirs up a pitcher of Bloody Marys.

"Thank you guys for coming over," I say. "I'm sorry to call you at the crack ass of dawn on a Saturday."

Setting a Bloody Mary in front of me, Lauren waves away my words. "I lost the ability to sleep in when I hit thirty-five. Plus, Justin was snoring so bad this morning, I was happy to escape."

"Same." Kate plucks the celery stalk from her drink and bites down on it with a satisfying *crunch*. "It turns out toddlers love Saturdays so much they wake up at five."

I wince. "Ouch."

"Yup." She lifts a shoulder. "But kids that age are so freaking happy in the mornings. It's sweet. And exhausting. But mostly sweet. I do enjoy that time, even if I feel like I've lived a whole day by eight AM."

The normalcy of our conversation, along with the bed-mussed company of my friends, is an enormous comfort. My face is puffy and sore, but overall, things feel less dire than they did an hour ago.

"I'm sorry I haven't been in touch this week," I say, wiping my hands on a napkin. "I hoped I could get over this whole thing on my own. But clearly, that hasn't happened."

Kate sips her coffee. "What did happen?"

"In a nutshell?" I take a breath. My throat starts to ache again. "I fell for Hank. Really, we fell for each other."

Lauren blinks. "Okay. Wow."

"I know it sounds crazy. But our connection—"

"Was instant," Kate says. "I could tell. I saw it when we were in Vegas."

"You saw what?"

Lauren sets down her cocktail. "I'll be honest, I haven't seen you smile and laugh that way with anyone. Ever."

"Including Dan," Kate adds.

Rolling my tongue between my lips, I say, "Well, yeah, hard not to smile and laugh when you're having this sexy little weekend with a super hot guy."

"It was more than that." Kate shakes her head. "It was a sexy weekend, sure. I think y'all had this special understanding of each other. You saw him, and he saw you, and he adored you."

"And worshipped you." Lauren smiles. "Hank loved that you were such a badass at the tables. You loved how thoughtful he was. Plus those biceps . . ."

I wince again. "Please, *please* don't remind me of his biceps. Kate, didn't you tell me that I wasn't at risk of falling in love with Hank? You told me it was teenage fever. Now you're saying you knew we had it bad back in Vegas?"

She lifts her hands and shrugs. "You needed to be talked off the ledge. I didn't want you making a mistake by cutting short the incredible weekend you and Hank were having. I did what had to be done."

"As a good friend should," Lauren says.

"But you falling for him is still a problem," Kate continues, "because he's young and idealistic, and he wants to get married and have a family."

I nod. "It's not his age that's the problem. He's actually very mature. And thoughtful, like you said. It's the fact that we want completely different things."

Lauren reaches over and wraps her hand around mine. "I know you don't want to get married again. Trust me, I get it."

"We all do," Kate says.

"But what I don't get is why you're cutting yourself off from having any relationship at all. Especially with such a stand-up guy."

"Because." I sniff. "It will end badly. I know Hank is different than Dan. Probably one of the many reasons I'm so damn attracted to him. But what if I'm not different? It takes two to tango—my marriage ended because of failures on both our parts. What if my perfectionism rears its ugly head again? I am very, very bad at giving myself grace."

"Were," Kate corrects. "You *were* very bad at giving yourself grace."

It's my turn to shrug. "Maybe. Maybe not. Either way, I'm not willing to risk it." I bring my free hand down on the table. "Goddamn it. I was happy. So happy before I met Hank. I almost hate him for turning my world inside out, you know?"

Lauren gives my hand a squeeze. "Don't hate him."

"I could never actually hate Hank."

"Because of the biceps," she teases.

"And the dancing," Kate says.

"And that dimple," Lauren adds.

I shake my head, and my face crumples.

"Oh, honey, we didn't mean—"

"It's okay," I breathe. "You guys are missing the best stuff anyway."

"Like his dick?"

"Ooooh, or his butt? I bet he's got the best, most biteable butt ever."

If only they knew about the marks he left from biting *me*. "His butt's pretty great, yeah. But I was thinking more along the lines of his generosity and how he takes care of the people he loves."

"Aw," Lauren says.

"So, here's the thing," Kate says softly. "You say you're not different. But I say you are. I say you've changed completely since you left Dan."

"Yeah?" Another sniffle. "How so?"

She hands me a napkin, which I use to blot my eyes. "In lots of ways. You make yourself a priority. You've always known what you wanted. But now you actually say what you want. You ask for what you need to get it. And you let yourself have it, whatever it may be—success, or rest, or, hey, some vodka at nine in the morning. At the end of the day, I think you've stopped hating yourself. You love *you* too much to ever let expectations run roughshod over your life again. Men too—you know better than to put yourself last when you're with one."

My breath catches as the stuff inside my chest stops working for a minute. I imagine my organs floating through my torso, suspended in quiet disbelief.

What Kate's saying feels right. Thrillingly, frighteningly *right*.

I do ask for what I want. Especially when I'm with Hank. Thinking back on it, I wasn't afraid to take up space from the very beginning:

I want you to come dancing.

Blackjack, then bed.

Cold. Iced almond milk latte, please.

I want a place on the farm's menu.

Don't fucking stop. Keep your tongue there. Yessss.

There's something we haven't tried. I want to do it with you.

The best part is that he reciprocated my effort. He was up front about what he wanted too.

"Talk to us," Kate says gently. "I can see those wheels turning."

I shake my head, stunned. "I'm just thinking about how I felt with Hank. I'm unafraid to just be myself, you know? I remember trying so hard to be a good girl with Dan, whatever being good means. Small, I guess? Quiet? Easygoing? With Hank, though, I'm just me. I'm loud. I'm lewd. Like, downright dirty. I don't let the fear of inconveniencing him stop me from putting my desires out there, which makes everything messy." I blink, the realization bowling me over. "But he likes the mess. My God. *He likes the mess.*"

Lauren lifts an eyebrow. "I feel like there's a good story behind that sentence."

"I won't go into details," I reply, the weight on my chest dissolving bit by bit with every heartbeat. "But yeah, it involved a bar, broken bottles, and bodily fluids."

Kate's eyes sparkle. "Hot."

"You sure you don't wanna tell us more?" Lauren says.

I laugh, feeling light-headed. "Sorry, ladies, but what happens on Blue Mountain stays on Blue Mountain."

"Fair enough." Lauren squeezes my hand again. "But I'm glad you're seeing what we see. I know you've worked really, really hard to figure yourself out over the past few years."

"Watching your transformation has been an absolute joy," Kate says.

I let her words sink in. Of course I know I've changed since leaving Dan. But I hadn't realized I've finally, *finally* done what I set out to do in my thirties.

I really have stopped hating myself.

Because someone who doesn't hate herself isn't dependent

on other people's approval. She doesn't need to grind herself to dust or lose weight to earn her place, just like she doesn't have to set herself on fire to keep everyone else warm.

My value isn't in service to others.

It's in service to myself. My wholeness. My contentment. My well-being.

"But what if I slip backward?" I ask. "There's no guarantee I won't go back to who I was."

Kate looks at me, expression smooth with certainty. "That's not going to happen. Sure, being tender with yourself is a life-long practice. I don't think anyone ever perfects it. But the important thing is you've learned not only how to love yourself but also why it's important. That kind of wisdom never leaves you."

"No one gets guarantees in life," Lauren says. "Not when it comes to love, or money, or the years we'll get. We're all gambling, every second of every day. But Stevie, you of all people know why it's important to show up at the table anyway."

I grin. "Because chances are, I'll win?"

Lauren grins too. "And if you lose, you'll learn from it. It's all good in the end. The only mistake you can make is not showing up. So show up for this man who's crazy about you."

I take another breath. Everything inside me feels sore, but the soreness suddenly feels less like a death sentence and more like an accomplishment. Like I've just finished my first marathon or something. It was grueling and awful and so much fucking work.

But I did it.

I'm at the finish line. The only problem?

Now I see there's a whole other race to be run ahead of me. *Would you consider making this more than a weekend thing? I'm not gonna beg, but I know I'm gonna regret letting you go if I don't ask you about working an* us *into our lives somehow.*

"He asked if there was a way for us to do long distance," I say. "A way to combine our lives."

Lauren lifts her eyebrows. "So he didn't ask you to give up yours? Give up Lady Luck?"

I shake my head. "The opposite, actually."

Kate considers my answer. "See? He gets that a relationship isn't a one-sided compromise. It's a two-way street, one that doesn't have to end in marriage. What's wrong with pulling, say, a Kurt and Goldie situation? They've been together for, like, fifty years, and they never got married."

"Okay," I say, nodding. "Yeah, I'd definitely be open to something like that. I love the idea of making our own way with our own rules. But y'all are forgetting that Hank is traditional. I can't ask him to give up the things he's always dreamed about."

Lauren lets my hand go to grab her Bloody Mary. "Yes, you can. Worst-case scenario, he says no, that he can't compromise on that stuff. But he may surprise you. I think he wants what you want—to be together. Maybe it looks a little different from what he'd always pictured, but that doesn't mean he won't consider it. You just have to ask. And asking is something you've gotten really, really good at."

"Ask," Kate says.

I scoff. "You guys make it sound so simple."

"Because it is."

"But what about the long-distance thing?" I run my hands down the front of my pajama pants. They're starting to get clammy. "How do I address that?"

Kate laughs. "I love you, friend, but I can only help you fix one problem at a time. Go see your man. Figure out what his boundaries are. *Then* we can talk about distance. Or, really, y'all will, because I have a feeling Hank is going to be open to whatever you ask for."

"You really think that?"

She dips her head. "I do. You know why I think that? Without having met the guy? Because now that you like yourself, you wouldn't ever fall for someone who isn't open to compromise. You'd only be attracted to a relationship that's real and healthy and nuanced. Even if that relationship was fake for a hot minute."

"Christ," I groan, rolling my eyes. "Then there's that—the fact that we lied to his family's face. No clue how we'll clean that one up."

Kate meets my gaze. "It'll probably be a mess. But hey, as long as you're honest this time around, maybe there's nothing wrong with that."

"I think he wants kids," I say.

"I think you might too, if you're with the right person," Kate says. "Remember how you told me you'd consider kids if Dan helped more? From what you told me about the way the Beauregards operated during that Sunday dinner thing y'all did, *and* the ovary-destroying way Hank loved up on his niece, it sounds like he'd know how to work together with someone, Stevie. He knows what being an equal partner means."

"He does."

He really, really does.

"I am forty, though," I say. "That could be a challenge in terms of fertility."

"It could be, yes," Lauren replies. "But if y'all really want kids, you'll figure it out. You're very lucky to have the resources to consider things like adoption or surrogacy."

"Very lucky," I agree.

I'm gripped by a strong, smooth kind of excitement. I'm not sure about kids, and I'm not sure about the distance.

But I am sure I'll allow myself to have what I want.

Chapter Twenty-Eight

HANK

It's a rainy, dreary Sunday, the kind of weather that matches my mood.

I go through the motions at the Main House: shake hands, load trunks, hold umbrellas. This was part of the job I always enjoyed. My interactions with the guests after they've experienced an excellent stay I've helped engineer are satisfying in a bone-deep way.

Today, though, they just make me feel tired. Worn out.

During a lull in the action, I slip into my office and close the door behind me, leaning against it. I take my phone out of my pocket, and the familiar disappointment rolls over me like a boulder when I don't see Stevie Carter's name anywhere on the screen.

Is she even thinking about me?

I know deep down she can't be feeling great, either. She didn't come out of this thing unscathed. She's just trying to do the right thing by keeping her distance.

I close my eyes and let my head fall back on the door.

Hope is only prolonging the torture. It's time to give up the ghost.

Glancing down at my phone again, I pull up Stevie's contact.

My heart thumps as I hover my thumb over the "Delete Contact" bar.

I hit it, sucking a breath through my teeth. Rage, ugly and hard, surges through my center. And then—

Then I kinda go numb.

More motions: phone in pocket. Door open. Front desk.

Maybe the numbness means I've moved to the next stage of grief. Thank fucking God.

I don't want to move on to someone else. Not yet, anyway. I just want to stop feeling like shit. Clean up this mess I've made in the hopes the guilt will fade.

By six, things calm down considerably. As worn out as I am, the quiet is kind of a bummer because I'm due at Samuel's in half an hour for my family's weekly Sunday supper, and I do not want to go. I was hoping to use work as an excuse to get out of the damn thing altogether.

It looks like that isn't going to happen. Maybe I won't show anyway.

"What are you still doing here?" Beau asks, appearing at my elbow. He checks his watch. "Thought you were done at five."

I keep my eyes glued on the computer screen in front of me. "Maybe I'm taking the idea of balance a step further and figuring out what schedule works best for me. Right now, that means working longer hours today and maybe fewer later this week."

Beau nods. "I like it. Want a ride to Samuel's? I was going to grab Maisie and Bel and head over."

"I'm good, thanks. See you there."

"I will see you there, right?"

I finally cut him a look. "Yeah."

"I'm not convinced. C'mon, it'll help you feel better. We

could Zoom with Stevie? Set up Maisie's iPad at her place at the table?"

Because Stevie's got a place at my family's table.

I look back down at the screen. "Stevie works weekends too," I lie. "But I like the idea."

"Maybe next time. Or maybe she'll actually be here for next week's supper. When did you say she's coming up again?"

"Probably not for a while. She's breaking ground on the new brewery, remember? So she's busy."

"Too busy to see you?"

I blow out a breath. I'm hanging on by a thread here.

"Dude, can't you leave well enough alone?"

From the corner of my eye, I see Beau hold up his hands. "I'm sorry. I don't mean to be a pest. I only liked seeing you with her is all."

I don't reply.

"See you at Samuel's. Oh! And bring your guitar—Maisie's been requesting your version of 'Wheels on the Bus' all damn week."

I skip supper and take the long way home, meaning I drive down the mountain and loop around Asheville. My wipers go as the rain pelts my windshield.

Listening to XXXTentacion croon about messes and fuckups and fears, I lose myself in the quiet motion of my truck. I drove my F350 to work today because of the shitty weather and because my Rolls reminds me of Stevie.

I try, and fail, not to think about how nice it'd be to fuck her by the fire tonight. I'd feed her, and we'd write another song. Then we'd go to bed, and I'd hold her all night long.

The hole in the center of my chest pulses. I've tried writing this week. And while I feel so fucking full it hurts, nothing comes out. With my guitar in my lap, I stare at blank pages, wondering how the words flowed so easily with Stevie.

I'm one sad sack.

It's mostly dark when I drive back up the mountain. I can just make out the lights of the main house through the mist that's settled over everything.

Pulling into my driveway a few minutes later, I don't see the figure sitting on my front stoop until my headlights swoosh over it as I make the turn into the garage.

My body clenches, pulse roaring. I hit the brakes, making the truck jerk to a stop. The figure is in shadow again. Whoever it is, they're standing now, hood up against the rain.

My first thought: Stevie.

My second: so much for giving up the ghost.

The truck's wipers groan now that the windshield is dry, sheltered under the garage's awning. I don't bother turning them off. Heart hammering, I shove open the door, gravel crunching under my boots as I stalk toward the front door.

"Hello?" I call, blinking against the rain. "Can I help you?"

"Hank! Hank, it's me."

My heart explodes, and my blood rushes cold at the familiar voice. She's hit the gravel too, footsteps uneven as she darts for me, a tote bag slung over one shoulder.

It can't be. This can't fucking be real.

For half a heartbeat, I stare into the darkness, wondering if I really am imagining this.

Stevie. Here. Now.

"Roots and wings," she pants, and suddenly she's in front of me, her beautiful face streaked with mascara.

Feeling, intense and raw, wells up inside me, and I grab her and pull her into a fierce hug. Immediately her body melts into mine, shoulders shaking as she sobs against my shoulder.

My heart cracks open. Somehow her hood's worked its way back, and now I'm stroking her hair, damp with rain.

"Roots and wings?"

"You said you wanted to set down roots. And I want to grow wings." She turns her head to look up at me. "I thought you could only have one or the other. But now I know there's a way to have both. Together."

I close my eyes. Emotion whipsaws through me as I hold her tighter, pressing her into my chest. "Okay. Okay. I love that, yes."

She smells like girl and feels like heaven, and I'm gripped by a fierce sense of gratitude.

Stevie's really here. It takes a lot of balls for her to come back. I know it wasn't a decision she made lightly. Stevie being Stevie, she's got a plan, and I know from what she's saying that plan has something to do with us being together. For real.

As for me? I'm not going to make the same mistake twice. I won't let her go until we figure out how to make that plan work.

Rivulets of rain work their way down my temples and into the collar of my sweater. Somewhere it registers that the water is ice cold, but I'm too busy falling head over heels in love with this woman to notice.

She's here.

"I've missed you," I breathe into the hollow underneath her jaw, lips brushing the freckle there.

She tightens her arms around my neck. "Hank, I've been a mess."

"I have too."

She pulls back, hands sliding to my forearms. The headlights catch on her eyelashes. "Can we talk? I'd like the chance to explain myself."

I search her eyes. "On one condition."

"Yeah?"

Tucking wet clumps of hair out of her eyes, I say, "We walk through that door together, and whatever happens next is real. No more pretending. No more fake relationship shit. Just you and me and the truth, all right?"

She bites her lip, eyes welling. "That's exactly what I wanted to hear."

"Good," I murmur, slipping my arm around her waist and hustling her to the garage door. I tell her to go inside while I park the car, but she waits for me. She's shivering when we push inside my mudroom. Stripping off her jacket, I realize I'm shivering too. My hands shake so badly I can barely get the zipper down.

Her teeth chatter. I feel her breath on my skin.

My blood warms at her nearness. I look up, our noses nearly brushing, and she's got that look in her eyes—soft heat.

My dick perks up. I haven't fucked this girl in almost a week, and I'm suddenly, ferociously in need.

I can't help it when I go in for a kiss. My mouth is already partly open when I capture hers. She moans, stumbling back, and I catch her, pulling her roughly against me.

The familiar sweetness of her taste makes me wanna burn down the world for keeping us apart.

I slip my tongue into her mouth, the two of us sucking in breaths as we cling to each other, her body rising into my caress.

"Wait." She plants a hand on my chest and gives me a gentle push. I look down and see her white fingernail polish is chipped. My heart twists. "Hank, wait."

It takes every ounce of strength to pull back. "This not okay?"

"It's fine. And I want to. So badly I can't even . . ." Blowing out a breath, she shakes her head, focusing her gaze on the hand she's got on me. "But we're going to get carried away. I need a clear mind to have this conversation, okay? I can't have you sweeping me off my feet first thing because then my brain—and my willpower—will be mush."

I duck my head, trying my best to nod. "I get it. Let's talk. But first, lemme light a fire and get you some dry clothes."

"I brought clothes."

"Nuh-huh. You're in my house. I wanna see you in my shit."

She tugs her bottom lip between her teeth. "Sure."

In my closet, I grab us sweaters and sweats. I get her dressed first, wanting to scream when I see she's going commando underneath her wet yoga pants.

Her pubic hair glistens. Arousal? Rain?

"Oh, yeah," Stevie says when she catches me looking. "Apparently, my body doesn't want food. It wants you."

Her pussy lips part when she raises her leg to step into my sweats, and I glimpse her pink center. The head of my dick jams against my zipper.

"You touch yourself? While you were gone?"

She lifts her shirt over her head. "Thought of you the whole time."

I shove my jeans and briefs down to my ankles. This time she's the one staring at me.

My cock, really. "See, I haven't. My way of torturing myself, I guess. Punishing myself. Which means I'm raging, honey."

"I can see that." She swallows. Closing her eyes, she pulls my cashmere sweater over her head. She flips her hair out of the collar, giving it a good shake.

It's wild and wet, and it smells like her shampoo.

I get dressed quickly. Taking her face in my hands, I

thumb away the streaks of mascara and look her in the eyes. "Talk first. Then I'm gonna feed you. Then we get naked."

She swallows again. "So decisive tonight."

"You're giving me the second chance I didn't think I'd get." I press a kiss, soft this time, to her lips. "I'm not gonna fuck it up. C'mon, let's get you in front of a fire."

Chapter Twenty-Nine

STEVIE

The fire blazes, and I defrost quickly in Hank's sweater and the blanket he wrapped around me when I sat on the bedroom floor.

Ever the thoughtful host, he hands me a tumbler of whiskey as he takes a seat beside me.

His guitar is where we left it a week ago.

I hold up my glass. "Thank you for hearing me out."

"Did you really think I wouldn't?" Hazel eyes locked on mine, he taps my glass. "Stevie, you gotta know I'm crazy about you."

The whiskey burns a delicious trail of heat down my throat. "I'm crazy about you too. Which is why I had to come back. I probably should've called—"

"Calling's for cowards. Showing up at my front door is a gamble, sure. But I love that about you—how unafraid you are to go all in."

I drink, watching the light of the fire catch on Hank's smooth skin. His eyes look more green than brown tonight, the way they sometimes do.

My stomach and pussy clench in unison. He's unbelievably handsome.

He also gets me. *I love that about you—how unafraid you are to go all in*. He appreciates me too.

Lord above, I am definitely in deep with this man.

Only now, that idea doesn't scare me. Well, I guess it still does, the way falling in love with someone will always be scary, but my reaction to that fear is different. I'm excited now. Hopeful.

I'm no longer waiting for the other shoe to drop.

Egged on by this newfound optimism, I dive right in.

"I want you," I say. "Long story short."

Hank sips his whiskey and swallows, running a hand over his mouth. He looks up and lets out a breath before looking back down at me.

His eyes are wet now. And happy.

"That's my line," he says at last, lips twitching.

"I'm borrowing it. Look." I set my glass on the fireplace, then grab his hand, twining our fingers. My body, already lit up, positively sings at the contact. "I realized something when I went home. Remember how we talked about you being totally different from my ex, but how I was worried I would be the same if I were to ever be in another relationship? I was so afraid of turning into the person I was with him."

Hank nods. "Right. The Stepford wife simmering with rage."

"Exactly. But now I've realized I'm different too. I've changed since then, and I'm never going back to Stepford wife Stevie."

He trails his fingertips up the sides of my fingers, eyes serious as my words sink in.

"I love this idea," he says at last. "And I one hundred percent agree. I could never imagine you being that person, much less turning into her for a second time. But I have to ask—what's changed? Just a week ago, you were pretty damn convinced a relationship with me wasn't worth the risk."

I lift a shoulder. "Another long story short, but it hit me just how much I like myself now. I didn't back then. I was afraid to ask for what I wanted. I was afraid of being a pain in the ass, of having boundaries and coming off as lazy or ungrateful. Before I would think, *wait, who the hell do I think I am to ask for fulfillment? Fairness?* Now, though, I skip the toxic thought process and just . . . go after what I want, so I can be who I am."

Hank curls his fingers over the back of my palm. Electricity blooms inside my skin, and I wonder if I'll ever get over how lovely his big, broad hands feel on my body.

"I love who you are," he says softly.

Heat presses against the backs of my eyes. "I love you, Hank. I'm so fucking in love with you."

"Oh, honey." He leans in and kisses me, slowly, gently, and for several beats, I'm overtaken by the sensation of falling through space. "Honey, I love you."

I'm dizzy when he pulls back, thumbing away tears that fall out of my eyes left and right.

"I'm sorry for putting you through hell." I sniff. "But I had to be sure, you know? I wanted to be sure I could really do this commitment thing before I came back."

His eyes dart back and forth between mine. "So you'll consider it? A relationship?"

"A real relationship. Yes. And I'm not just talking about one that isn't fake. I'm talking *real*—you want the picket fence? We can talk about it. A family? We can talk about that too. I make no guarantees, but I'm open to ideas in a way I wasn't before."

"Wow." He blinks. "Wow, Stevie, that's one hell of a one-eighty."

I laugh. "Don't get ahead of yourself. One thing I'm still not interested in is marriage. The whole exchanging vows and stuff. We still have a lot of talking to do, and a lot to figure out, but I'm willing to give it a try. Let's make it up as we go along. Do happily ever after our way, not the way the world tells us we should."

Hank grins. "I like this. I like it a lot."

"But what about what you want?" I grab my whiskey and sip, steeling myself. "That kind of relationship means you're going to have to compromise on some pretty big things. A wedding, for one thing. A wedding ring for another."

"Are you shitting me? Yeah, I guess I've always thought I'd end up married, but really, what does a ring matter when you're with the one? At the end of the day, that's all I want, Stevie—I just want to be with you. You're the one. You make me happy. You turn me on. You let me be who I am, only a better version of it."

I smile, butterflies taking flight inside my torso. "A version who actually knows how to play blackjack?"

"Exactly." His expression is serious. "I'm pretty sure I'll be happy with you whether or not we wear rings or have a picket fence. Let's just *be together*. In the end, that's all that matters."

I don't know what to say to that. Light blooms all over my body, the poignant sensation clearing all thoughts from my head except *I'm his and he's mine.*

We're the one for each other. That's stars-aligning type stuff, and it is lovely.

For so long, I'd only considered the pitfalls of love. How it would rob me of opportunity and freedom and contentment.

I'd forgotten love also comes with this—the opportunity to see and be seen in return. The freedom to be who I am. The contentment that comes with companionship and compromise.

Because I'm his equal, and he's mine. I know that in my

bones. I'm not going to be the second-class citizen I was in my marriage. He doesn't see me that way, and now neither do I.

It's refreshing.

Our relationship will never be perfect. Love's a double-edged sword, but if Hank's taught me anything, love can always be done differently. It can be done right.

I'm excited to try that on with him.

"Okay," I manage. "Okay. Yeah."

He looks at me. I look back.

"What?" I'm smiling so hard my face feels like it's about to split open.

"My fake girlfriend just became my real girlfriend. I'm pretty fucking stoked about that."

"Ever thought you'd end up writing songs about me when you sat down at that blackjack table?"

Hank nudges his knee against mine. "You wrote that song about me too."

"Co-conspirators *and* co-writers." I nudge him back. "We make quite the team."

We keep looking at each other, my sweater absorbing the heat of the fire.

I want to live in this moment forever. But we can't.

Before I can fully surrender, fully relax into the reality of our new situation, I need to talk through a few things.

I take another fortifying gulp of whiskey. "So, the logistics. We don't need to get into the nitty-gritty tonight. But you and I 'just' being together won't be easy. It'll require a fuck-ton of legwork. How are we going to iron out the whole Nashville-Asheville thing? Neither of us can just up and move."

Hank lets out a breath and thinks for a beat, then another. "Wish I had an answer for you right off the bat, but I don't. Why don't we do this—let's come up with a preliminary plan. We'll start by splitting our time between your place and mine? Set up a schedule? Something we can pencil in and modify as we go. Work's been a little bit of a nightmare this week—I'm still figuring out what balance means—but because nothing's set in stone yet, I've got lots of flexibility."

"So you went back! Good for you. Starting something new is always tough. I hope it gets better."

Finishing his whiskey, he nods. "I hope so too. I like the work, especially now that I've promoted my old assistant, Gregory, to be my right-hand man. And it's nice being around my family again. With Emma and Bel on board, we're taking Blue Mountain to the next level, and it's exciting to be part of that. I just don't wanna drown in it. I want to have my life at the farm and my life here." He circles his hand between us. "Behind closed doors."

"I want that too," I say softly. "And I'm down with your plan. I do worry we'll never feel settled, going back and forth. And it will be hard not to keep score."

"I'm aware," he says, and I wonder if there's anything sexier than a man who really is as acutely aware as Hank. "But let's be real, I have the means to make travel between here and there super convenient. And no, you will not be flying commercial ever again."

"You do love to brag about your jet."

"Honey, I'm famous. Let me flaunt it."

His cockiness is turning me on. It's becoming more and more difficult to focus.

"But really," I say. "How lucky are we that we have access to all these incredible conveniences?"

"We're blessed, that's for damn sure. I joke around a lot, but you gotta know I don't take privileges like private jets for granted."

I nod, grinning. "I know. As I said, it won't be easy. But we have comforts at our fingertips that a lot of people don't."

"I live to keep you comfortable," he says, kissing the tip of my nose.

"What about long-term, though?" I manage. "I know you want to put down roots here."

He shrugs. "I won't lie, I'd always thought I'd end up close to family. But Nashville's not far. It's still in the South. Still got good food and hot women."

"So you'd be willing to consider a move there?"

"I would. If you'd be open-minded about moving here one day too. One or both of us could commute. And hey, who's not to say that changes every few years? Again, let's make it up as we go."

Here it is. The surrender.

I've got more whiskey in my glass, but I want to be fully present at this moment. I want to experience the fear and the excitement. I want to remember the moment I accept the fact that I don't know what happens next, and that's okay.

There is no safety net.

I'm putting myself in the hands of the universe, and I have to trust I'll be taken care of. Privileged psychobabble? Maybe. But what choice do I have? I'm in love. I want to be with this man. I can't torture us anymore with what-ifs.

Either I trust and I stay, or I doubt and I go.

I squeeze his hand. "I would consider a move here someday, yeah."

His face lights up, and so does the stuff inside my chest.

"Thank you," he says, bringing our joined hands to his lips. He brushes them against my knuckles. "I know you're scared. I am too. But we can do this. I'll work my ass off to make you happy, honey. You have my word on that."

The butterflies tickle my sides.

"I promise to try my best to make you happy too."

He grins, dimple popping. "Now that we have that settled,

I'm taking you to bed. I have a feeling make-up sex with you ain't gonna suck."

My pussy clenches. I want make-up sex, so badly.

But there's still one thing we have to cover.

"What about your family?" I ask, swallowing what's left of my drink before setting the tumbler on the edge of the fireplace.

Hank's grin fades. "What about them?"

"We have to come clean. About the fake dating stuff."

"Do we?"

He's joking, but I still say, "Yep."

"I know." Looking away, he runs a hand over his head with a sigh. "I've felt like shit about it all week. But let's . . . can you give me some time? Lemme think about how I wanna do it."

"We can both think about how *we'll* do it."

He lifts a brow. "You don't have to. It was my idea."

"But I had a starring role."

He hesitates, searching my eyes. And after a few beats, he says, "Thank you."

My pulse skips a beat. "But you don't think they'll respond well?"

"Honestly?" He runs a hand over his head again. "Yeah, Samuel won't like hearing what I have to say. Beau'll call me out for sure. And Milly? Christ, I don't even wanna think about what she'll do."

I make a face. He's right.

"Short-term, it's gonna suck," I say. "Long-term, it's definitely the right call."

He nods. "I know," he says, looking at me. "Let's think about that tomorrow. Tonight . . ."

"Make-up sex." I grin. "Right."

"Lemme throw together a playlist real quick." He leaps to

his feet and darts to the bed, grabbing his phone from where he threw it when we entered the bedroom. "Gimme a sec."

After he's done, I let him pull me to my feet and undress me, slowly, his mouth on my neck, my breasts. My belly.

I surrender. I'm scared as hell but going in anyway, because for the first time, I know I'm not going in alone.

Chapter Thirty

HANK

I hit a button on my phone, and "I'll Make Love To You" by Boyz II Men spills out of the speakers in the ceiling.

Stevie, lying naked on my bed, bursts out laughing.

"For real." I reach behind me and grab my sweatshirt by the collar, yanking it over my head. "I wanna make love to you."

Her eyes go hazy as they rove over my bare chest.

Even hazier when I shuck off my sweats. Her gaze lands on my dick, and it throbs, swelling to the point of pain.

"You've already done that," she replies.

"Not officially." I step out of the sweats and climb onto the bed, the mattress dipping beneath my weight. I climb over her, my cock meeting with her belly as I plant my hands on either side of her head and lean in for a kiss.

Her lips and legs open to me, and I hike her leg over my forearm, then hike it higher still so it's draped over my shoulder.

I inhale the scent of her skin and close my eyes against the dizziness that hits me head-on.

I'm still in shock that she showed up on my doorstep. She

did it in true Stevie style: unannounced, at just the right time, in just the right way.

It was right because she meant it.

"We've done everything," I murmur into her neck. "Everything but this."

I notch myself at her entrance and slip inside her. No condom. No fuss. My dizziness increases at the tight, soft feel of her. How does she feel even better than before?

Maybe because I was holding back then. Maybe I did have a shred of self-preservation left, and I was trying to pump the brakes any way I could.

I can finally lose myself in her fully, and I do.

I kiss her mouth, and I move over her in deep, patient thrusts. Her body arches up to meet mine, and I sip the breathless sounds she makes as I run a hand up her side, gathering her breast in my hand. I swivel my hips. I move my hand to her pussy, and I play with her clit. She tightens around me, and the need for release coils in my core.

I break the kiss to catch my breath. Opening my eyes, I see her watching me. Her expression is soft, her mouth parted.

We watch each other rise to meet completion. Her body is soft and sweet beneath mine, tits bouncing as my hips increase their speed, seeking relief.

I tangle our fingers and bring her arm over her head, using it to gain leverage as I rock into her. Her body is laid out and stretched taut.

Beautiful.

So fucking beautiful. I worship every inch of her I can with eyes and hands and mouth, savoring her.

Boyz II Men turns off. I started the playlist kinda cheesy, but deep cuts come next.

Fiona Apple. David Grey. Alicia Keys.

She reaches down to play with her nipple, but I nose her

fingers away, taking it in my mouth and giving it a slow, hard suck.

At the same time, I press my thumb to her clit, and Stevie cries out, her pussy spasming.

She grabs my chest and tucks her head into my neck, sinking her teeth into my throat as she rides out her orgasm. I feel needed. Capable.

Strong. Not because I made her come, but because she feels safe with me at her most vulnerable.

Everything inside me turns to mush. At the same time, my dick's so hard I wanna scream. My hips jerk.

I'm about to pull out when she grabs my ass in her hands and urges me deeper inside her.

"Stay," she whispers.

Heart bursting, I do as I'm told. I thrust one last time, and then I come, emptying myself inside her.

This time, I bury my head in her neck. This time, I cling to her, every pulse of my orgasm a riot of sensation I can't handle on my own.

I clench my teeth and let the moment rip me apart. I'm a goner.

The riot subsides, a feeling like lightning rising in its place.

Lightning and exhaustion. It makes no sense, but here we are. Maybe now that Stevie's back in my bed, I'll finally be able to get some fucking sleep.

I raise my head and rest my brow against hers. She's still breathing hard, skin sticky with sweat.

She's finally warm.

"So," I say, flipping open my laptop the next morning.

"So." Stevie sips her coffee, glancing at me over her own

laptop. She grins, and laugh lines appear at the edges of her eyes.

Eyes that aren't ringed with purple anymore. She got the sleep she needed last night too.

"When do you have to get back?"

"I can stay through Tuesday. I've got a site visit first thing Wednesday at the new brewery—we break ground that day. Think you can come back with me?"

I enter my password and pull up my calendar. Growl when I see I've got meetings set up with The Barn Door team that day, plus a tasting for the new spring menu Thursday.

"That doesn't sound good," Stevie says.

I grab my coffee off the kitchen table and take a gulp. "Why you gotta make things so damn hard?"

"Hard?" Her eyes flick to my crotch. "Thought we took care of that this morning."

The image of coming in Stevie's mouth flashes across my thoughts, causing my dick to twitch.

"Don't," I warn, still growly. "For the love of God, I'm never gonna be able to leave this house if we don't stop with the innuendo. At least before nine AM."

She laughs, a throaty, full sound, and I'm struck by how gorgeous she looks right now. She's sitting across the table with her back to the windows. She's wearing a Blue Mountain robe, bare feet propped up on the edge of the table.

No makeup, and no fucks given.

She's a CEO at work on a Monday. Glowing from great morning sex and an inbox that'll keep her busy with work she loves.

I know I'm still glowing too.

This is my life now.

Yeah, the long-distance juggle is going to be a nightmare, at least in the beginning. But if I can figure out how to come back from kissing my brother's fiancée (to be fair, she was just his girlfriend then), I can figure this out. Being able to wake up next to Stevie makes it all worth the effort.

"Wednesday's no good for me, unfortunately."

Stevie nods. "I get it. Not easy being spontaneous when you own a resort."

"Almost as *hard* to do when you own a brewery."

"I thought you said no innuendo?"

I grab my dick through my sweats and give it a lewd little tug. "Can we put that rule into effect next week? I only have another twenty-four hours with you. Not that I'm counting."

It's her lush mouth. Her perfect pussy. Her willingness to try new things.

All of that turns me on. But right now, what turns me on most is how she gets it. She understands what a job like mine entails. She understands how much it means to me, and she gets the importance of doing it right.

Yep. Totally hit the jackpot with this one.

Stevie rolls her eyes dramatically, one side of her mouth lifting in a flirty smile. "If you insist, Simon."

My heart leaps, and my eyes go wide. "Simon?"

"Yeah."

"You must know only the duke's closest family and friends may use his Christian name."

She circles her hand in front of her face and leans forward in a bow. "I do indeed. Might I be so bold as to consider myself among said friends?"

I look at her. Light filling the room. Filling my chest.

"Family," I say. "You're family now."

Her expression softens. "I like the sound of that."

I wanna pull her to her feet and untie that robe and take her back to bed.

But I can't wait. I pull her to her feet and untie her robe and take her right here on the table. Our laptops ping with incoming messages as I pound into her, hard and fast. She sighs, comes, then laughs, and I kiss her chest and wipe my cum off the insides of her thighs with my sweatpants.

Light is everywhere. Stevie's not leaving. Our spontaneity comes not from desperation, but from desire.

"But really," she says when she sits down, breathless after a quick trip to the bathroom, "we're never going to figure this out if we don't stop fondling each other."

I collapse into my chair. "Sorry."

My legs feel like Jell-O, and I'm ravenous. I hope that food I ordered from the main house is on its way.

"Don't be." She puts her laptop on the table and leans in, a crease appearing between her brows as she scans the screen. "Clearly, we need to work things out in advance."

"Right. Yes. Send me your calendar so we can plot out the rest of February and March."

Her fingertips glide over the laptop's mousepad. "On it."

Her calendar pops up in my inbox. We spent the next hour slicing and dicing our schedules. I curse; she starts to cry at one point, but then the food arrives, and we eat our Bananas Foster French Toast, and we both feel better.

Nothing is set in stone. We both have to move some stuff around to accommodate each others' calendars, so we spend the next few hours furiously emailing co-workers, contractors, and committees in an attempt to reschedule calls and meetings.

Stevie makes a dozen calls, her tone firm and professional, and I can't fucking believe it, but I get a half chub again listening to her.

Her competence is just the sexiest fucking thing.

I curse some more and make calls too. I hate doing this—I'm still getting used to making messes. But I gotta practice putting myself first, and there's no better time like the present.

I tentatively book several jets. I also google what the

halfway point is between Nashville and Blue Mountain in case I can't make it through a whole week without her, and I need to meet up for a quickie. Then I make a note to get the Bentley serviced.

Make another note to hire a personal assistant. Not one who works for Blue Mountain, but a person who works for me and only me.

"Would you be interested? In sharing one with me, I mean?" I ask Stevie.

She nods. "Hell yeah, I would. Jesus, I never thought I'd have a big enough life to hire a person whose whole job is to manage that life."

"You mad at it?"

"Nope." Her eyes flick to meet mine. "One of the perks of dating someone who's famous."

"And hot. You forgot the hot part."

"Don't get ahead of yourself."

That crease between her brows stays put as she wrangles the next few months into submission. Or some semblance of it, anyway.

It comes out looking like this: first and foremost, we want to prevent any kind of burnout. So we schedule as much downtime as we can and time for ourselves when we're not traveling or working.

It feels official and . . . lame, if I'm being honest. Scheduling "alone time." But most of adulting is lame, so I might as well accept it and move the fuck on.

I'll be in Nashville next week, pending a few meeting changes. Stevie will be here the following weekend and the week after that. Then I block off a nice two-week chunk for me to go back and forth as my schedule permits.

By noon, my calendar looks like a legit bloodbath. Lots of red and lots of question marks.

"Yikes," I say.

Stevie shuts her laptop and sighs. "I know. But the beginning will be the hardest—"

"Jesus Christ."

"Sorry, sorry," she says, laughing. "The beginning will be the most difficult. But let's think of it as our version of 'they split their time between Lake Como and, I don't know, the Lower East Side.'"

"Except ours is the 'ville version. Asheville and Nashville."

"Exactly."

"You okay with this?" I bend my elbows and put my hands on my knees. "Really? I want to make sure you're happy."

"After the hell that was this past week without you?" Her lower lip dips inside her mouth, followed by a flash of her tongue. "Yeah. Yeah, I'm happy. Stressed. But happy. Relieved. You?"

I stand up and lean over the table to kiss her. "You're here. We're making plans for a future together. What do you think?"

She smiles into my kiss.

"I know what you mean by roots and wings," I say, my lips still on hers. "This feeling I have—it's like flying. But I'm also building foundations with you. I'm grounded, but—"

"Light?"

"Yes." I smile.

I commit the moment to memory. It'll give me something to hang on to when shit really hits the fan after we tell my family our dirty little secret.

What if they reject Stevie? What if they never believe another word I say? To be fair, my family's done their fair share of lying too. We're all sinners in our own way. Beau didn't tell Annabel about his CTE until it was almost too late; Samuel and Emma lied about the feelings they had for each other. Milly's withholding information about Kingsley, and

Rhett is . . . well, Rhett, and he sure as hell isn't being a straight shooter about what's going on in his life.

But my lies—there's more of them. And they feel somehow more intentional than my siblings'. A fake relationship isn't a lie of omission. It's a fucking *scheme*. It was strategized—premeditated—in a way theirs weren't.

I don't think Samuel and Emma will reschedule the wedding, but . . . yeah, this is definitely going to leave a bad taste in everyone's mouth.

A bad taste that might linger for a while. I hate the idea of my family never really accepting Stevie or accepting us together. My sister can hold a grudge like nobody's business, especially when she's as ornery as she's been lately. I want everyone to be happy for us the way we're all happy for Bel and Beau, and Samuel and Emma. It's what Stevie deserves.

But is it what I deserve? After all the dumbass lies I've told?

I hope I haven't fucked this up beyond repair.

Chapter Thirty-One

STEVIE

Hank has Mondays off, but with the sudden change in our schedules, he goes to his office at the Main House around lunch to try to nail down all his proposed new meeting and call times.

I decide to go with him and set up my own little workstation in a leather wingback chair by the lobby's massive fireplace. A waiter promptly brings me a beer—a lager from one of my favorite Asheville breweries, Highline—and house-made pimiento cheese with butter crackers. Just what I need to soothe my frayed nerves.

It's the most manic Monday I've had in a while, but it's also one of the best.

Settling into my cushy chair, I get to work. I just threw a gigantic wrench into my plans going forward, and I have about a zillion and a half things to do to make it all work.

Luckily, the lobby remains mostly empty—it is Monday, after all—so I don't feel weird taking calls or muttering curses at Excel documents.

Hank checks in every so often with a text.

How's it going?

I'm thinking about dinner. Are you thinking about dinner? The Barn Door does a great burger.

I look up from my laptop. My stomach does a backflip when I see Rhett approaching. His face lights up with recognition, and he furrows his brow while a confused little smile appears on his lips.

"Stevie? I didn't know you were here."

"Hey! Hi. Hi, Rhett." I set my laptop on the cocktail table beside my chair and leap to my feet, accepting the hug he offers. "Yeah, I, um, came up here on a little last-minute trip."

"Gotcha," he says, and we pull back at the same time.

A beat of uncomfortable silence settles between us. I imagine Rhett is also scrambling to think of what to say.

"So are you—"

"Here to see Hank?" I lower my voice. "For real, I mean? Not as his . . . you know, whatever I was before?"

Rhett scoffs.

"What were you before?"

My stomach downright *plummets* at the sound of a female voice. The sensation goes on for seconds, days, years, making the saliva in my mouth thicken.

Milly steps out from behind her brother's wide shoulders, and my blood turns to ice at her narrowed eyes and pinched mouth.

Rhett tugs a hand across his mouth, muffling the words, "Oh shit."

"Just his girlfriend," I blurt. "I was just Hank's girlfriend before."

Milly turns her head, looking at me from the corner of her bright, curious eye. "So are you engaged now?"

"No," I say miserably. "We've just . . . decided to take things to the next level."

"You're moving in with him, then."

I glance around the lobby. Where the hell is that server? I need another beer, stat.

"Not exactly. But we're trying to work out a schedule where we get to see each other more often."

The furrow in Milly's brow deepens. "I don't get it."

"Milly," Rhett warns.

Crossing her arms, Milly turns her death stare on him. "You in on this?"

"In on what?"

I wince at Rhett's insincere reply.

Milly looks at me again. "The scam."

The urge to tell Milly the truth—all of it—swells inside me, rising like a fist in the back of my throat. I just want that part of our story to be over already. Now that I'm all in, I feel vulnerable in a way I haven't before. There's so much to lose, and I'm suddenly, painfully aware of how thin the ice is Hank and I have been walking on.

"There is no scam," I say, face burning. "I'm just here to visit Hank. I missed him, so I decided to surprise him by just showing up. He has nothing to do with . . . anything."

More badly delivered lines that don't even make sense.

I'm definitely in over my head. Go figure the second I surrender, the second I trust the water to hold me up, is the closest I've ever been to drowning.

I wasn't there when Hank lied the first time to Samuel and Emma. But I've sensed how deep that betrayal cut, and now that the wound is finally scabbing over, Hank and I are about to rip it back open.

Not good.

Not good at all.

I guess I'd hoped, foolishly, that the Beauregards would take the fake relationship thing in stride. That they'd laugh, give Hank and me a little speech about how dumb we were, and move on.

And maybe that could be the case if Hank didn't have a history of deception. Deception that hurt the people he loves.

"I knew it," Milly says. "I knew there was something fishy about y'all."

"Milly," Rhett says again, glancing around the lobby. It's getting close to five, and guests have started to filter in, gathering at the bar in the far end of the room. "This is not the time nor the place for this conversation."

"So there is a scam."

"I didn't say that."

She spears him with a look. "Well, I did. Y'all have five seconds to tell me what the hell is going on, or I'm making a beeline for Beau's office."

"Please," I blurt. "Don't."

Rhett gives his sister a look right back. "Keep your beak out of this, Milly. I'm warning you. Why do you have to be up in everyone's business?"

"Because I care about my brother, and I want to make sure he's not being taken advantage of. He hasn't exactly been in a great headspace over the past year. He's all mixed up, and that makes him an easy target."

My panic burns to anger. "But he's not mixed up."

"You just said he doesn't have anything to do with your scam."

I want to say there is no scam. I want to say it forcefully, with the weight of truth behind it. Because even though we did lie, the weight of truth is there. The connection we have has always been real. The future we're trying to build is *real*.

The story we told everyone, though? That isn't.

"Have you talked to Hank?" My heart feels like it's going to beat right out of my chest.

"He knows what he wants, Milly," Rhett says.

She looks at him. "You believe that?"

He runs a hand over his mouth again, and I realize how worn out he looks. Bags under his eyes, skin puffy and red.

He is not the steady, capable ally Hank and I need right now.

Oh shit is right.

"I think we all need to sit down and talk before someone says something they'll regret," Rhett replies, casting a meaningful glance at Milly. "I'm talking about you. You're going to say something you'll regret because you're hard-headed, and you have no idea what's going on."

"Fine. We can talk." Milly checks her watch. "I have an insane day. My house, eight o'clock tonight?"

My gut clenches. So much for the cozy evening in Hank and I planned.

Whatever. Cat's out of the bag. Time to face the music. Rip off the Band-Aid.

Using cheesy colloquialisms to explain our predicament makes the whole thing feel slightly less terrifying.

"Works for us," I say. Despite the clusterfuck I'm currently in, I still feel a small fissure of joy at being part of an *us* with Hank. Whatever happens, we have each other.

Another thing I'd forgotten: the comfort that comes with being with someone. The support. For so long, I thought only about the work that came with being part of a pair. Picking up after a partner. Cooking for them. Making space for them.

"I've got, uh, a thing—"

"No, you don't." Milly crisply cuts off her brother. "Be there, or I'll come find you, you hear? The same goes for you." She looks at me.

"I'm not going anywhere."

Milly keeps looking at me, tilting up her chin. "We'll see. Eight o'clock."

She disappears, leaving a cloud of perfume and unease in her wake.

"I'm really sorry," Rhett says. "I don't know whose fault that was, but I'm willing to take the blame. I'm a big fucking idiot, aren't I?"

I put a hand on his shoulder. "I'm the idiot. I shouldn't have brought up what I did three seconds into our conversation. I'm sorry too."

"What can I do to make this right?"

"Honestly?" I shake my head. "I don't know. Hank wanted to have a plan before we told y'all—because we really were planning on telling you guys the truth about what went down—so he's not going to be happy. I guess we'll just have to see how it goes."

He nods, looking distraught. "Okay. Yeah. So you're actually here to see him, right? As his real girlfriend?"

I manage a tight smile. "I am. I missed him so damn much I couldn't stay away. We really are trying to make a relationship work—I'm not lying about that. We spent the whole morning reworking our calendars for the next few months so we can see each other." I swallow. "I love your brother. So much."

"I hope you do."

My heart falls. Rhett wants to trust me. But he doesn't. Not yet.

Doesn't bode well for what's going to go down tonight.

"I should get going," Rhett says, shoving his hands into the front pockets of his jeans. "See you tonight, I guess?"

"Yeah. Yeah, I'll see you in a bit. Thanks for defending me."

"Course. My sister means well. Once she's on your side, she'll go to war for you. She's just stubborn as hell. It wasn't easy for her, being the only girl in a family of boys. I hate to say it, but her weariness around strangers—I think that kinda comes from us."

I nod, a lump forming in my throat.

"Just promise me one thing?" Rhett asks.

"I'll try."

"Don't hurt Hank. He's been through hell and back. He's done some dumb shit, but he's a good man. I was with him for a good chunk of the past year, and yeah, he was lost for a while there. But I don't think he is anymore."

"Thanks for saying that. I appreciate the vote of confidence."

He holds up his hands and smiles. He's got the same dimple Hank does. "Don't get too excited—I'm not the sharpest tool in the shed. But hell, even I can see that has a lot to do with meeting you. You're the real deal, Stevie, and I think in many ways that's what he's always been searching for."

The tightness in my throat becomes painful. I look away, blinking hard, and wonder at the whiplash of the last ten minutes.

The last ten days, really.

Milly isn't my favorite person at the moment. But overall, the Beauregards have proven to be excellent human beings. I get why Hank loves them the way he does. I get why he wants to stay close by, despite what happened with Samuel and Emma.

I hope he'll feel the same after what happens tonight. I won't be the reason he abandons the people he loves again.

I won't be the reason they abandon him.

Chapter Thirty-Two

HANK

"You've gotta be shitting me. She actually said that?"

Rhett purses his lips and pulls them to the side, face screwed up like he smells something bad. "You know how Milly is."

Balling my hands into fists, I plant them on top of my desk. It takes every ounce of self-control not to pick up my laptop and chuck it against the wall.

"That's crossing the line, even for her." I shake my head, clenching my jaw. "How dare she confront Stevie like that? I'mma have *words* with her tonight, man."

"What she did wasn't right, definitely. I defended Stevie as best as I could, but . . ."

"But what?"

"You're gonna make me say it?"

"Quit being a coward and spit it out."

"Hey. I'm not the one who faked a relationship because he was too chickenshit to have a real one."

The arrow lands right where it hurts.

Right where Rhett intended.

Brushing aside the unpleasant sensation in the center of my chest, I say, "I'm in a real one now."

"If you say so."

"What does that mean?"

Agitated, Rhett sits upright in his chair. "Dude, c'mon. I wanna believe you, but you've lied about this shit before. I'm not sure what's true and what isn't."

That's exactly what I'm afraid the rest of my family is going to say.

"Why would I keep faking a relationship with Stevie at this point? Samuel set a date. He's gonna get married."

"But who knows what he'll do once he finds out you weren't dating Stevie, which means maybe you aren't over Emma, which means . . . I don't know what, but it ain't good."

"I am over Emma," I say forcefully. Angrily. "You know I am."

"That, I actually do believe. A bullshit artist like Samuel, though? I dunno. I bet he sniffs around y'all, you and Stevie I mean, looking for cracks in your story."

"I'm going to tell him the story. The whole thing." I glance over my shoulder out the windows. Sun is setting. I wanna get to Stevie ASAP, but I gotta figure this out first.

Goddamn it, I could wring Rhett's neck for letting my secret slip. I could also wring Milly's for, well, being Milly.

"And what if Samuel doesn't buy it?" Rhett asks.

"I'll figure it out."

Rhett makes this face. It's a wince, a grimace, maybe both.

"What?" I growl.

A muscle in his cheek tweaks. "You sure you wanna do this?"

My fingernails dig into the heels of my palms. I wait for him to explain himself.

"I like Stevie. A lot. We all do. She's down to earth, and

she's kind, and she seems to make you happy. But could this be another case of you falling really fast for a girl who's not available? Only this time, you're willing to burn down everything you've built back up over the past year to make something work that, uh, isn't supposed to because you've fucked up once, and you'll be damned if you fuck up again? You forcing it, Hank?"

I see red. He's saying I'm desperate. Desperate enough to make stupid decisions, the way I did a year ago.

I say through gritted teeth, "Stop."

"I'm just saying my piece. I owe it to you as your favorite brother to be honest."

Another arrow. Followed by a tiny pulse of something I do not like at all.

Doubt.

This thing is turning into a fucking nightmare.

I am not the reckless idiot I was back then. I'm certain of that.

Rhett isn't wrong, though. Stevie and I pretty much fell in love over the course of one fucking weekend. Well, two. But that's, what, a hundred hours total together?

I fell for Emma just as quickly. That was different, though. It wasn't lust, exactly. More like I was lonely and burned out and hungry for something I thought I found in her.

I found it in Stevie.

Mama's said shit about love like, "when you know, you know." I buy that. But I also buy Rhett's hesitation.

"You are far from my favorite right now," I say, closing my eyes.

"Wait until Samuel and Beau hear what you've got to say. I'll definitely be your favorite after that."

"I'm not forcing anything with Stevie. What we have is a two-way street. My feelings for Emma only went one way."

"You're an adult. You call the shots. I'm just looking out for you. I'd hate to see you get hurt again."

Hurt. I feel a lot of that right now.

Hurt and anger. The backs of my closed eyelids are still bright red.

"You jealous?" I open them. "Maybe you see the connection Stevie and I have, and you can't stand how great she is. Maybe you want to hurt me because you're hurting. I would know because that's exactly how I felt. Ever since Amelia showed up at the party, you've looked like hell."

Rhett's eyebrows snap together. "Do not fucking go there. Amelia is none of your business."

Ugh, he looks more hurt than angry. I'm doing it again—lashing out at the people I love. I recognize it, and I know how wrong it is. But I'm like a runaway train that can't stop.

"So why is Stevie any of yours?"

"Because!" He pushes to his feet and holds out his arms. "I'm the only witness to y'all's story! The real one, not the bullshit you fed our family. I saw it go down in real time. I was your wingman. Do you not remember telling me not to let you fall in love? I'm part of this story, whether you like it or not."

I straighten and run a hand over my face. I gotta work to make things better, not stir shit up that makes everyone feel worse.

Taking a deep breath, I begin to silently count to a hundred. I wait for my heart rate to slow, which makes the coiling rage in my center loosen ever so slightly.

"You're right," I manage. "I'm sorry."

"You best get your head on straight before tonight, brother. You react this way, and the family's gonna tear you a new one. You and Stevie. Do better."

I blow out a breath, taking another beat. "How do you

think I should go about this?" I say quietly. "Telling everyone."

Rhett takes a minute to think. "Honestly? The truth is best. Just come out with it. Only lead with the truth that's the center of all this—that you love Samuel, and you'd do anything to see him happy. Like pretend to be in love with a smart, gorgeous woman who fucking adores you."

I soften. "We're that obvious?"

"Almost too obvious." He lifts a shoulder. "Could be what made us all suspicious. Love like that—you don't see it all that often."

"What do you mean?"

He makes that face again, the one where he pulls his lips to the side. "I'm talking about real love. Your connection with Stevie—it's kind enough and clear enough to, yeah, maybe make me a little jealous."

Light peeks through the crack that forms in my torso.

"That's how the whole Emma thing started, you know," I say. "Me being jealous of Bel and Beau, and then of Samuel and Emma."

He nods, getting this faraway look in his eyes. "I get that now, yeah."

"Can I give you a little advice about Amelia?"

"That's a joke, right?"

"Number one, no fake dating. Number two, there is life outside of work. And that life is better when you share it with the right person."

He rubs a hand over the back of his neck. "I may have sucked ass last season, but I'm not retiring."

"Whatever you say. Just a little food for thought."

"Who the fuck made you the expert in love?"

"Doing it all wrong. Then doing it right. At least I hope I'm doing it right."

"I hope so too." He turns and heads for the door.

Ideas for my speech tonight float through my head. This conversation with Rhett hasn't been easy, but overall, I feel better having spoken to him. I'm not crazy. He sees what Stevie and I have. *Kind and clear*, he said. It's not the sexiest description of a relationship, but it does feel right.

What else is there to do at this point except to follow what feels right?

"Thank you," I say.

He turns back around at the door. "For what?"

"For telling me the truth. And for falling down on your promise not to let me fall for someone. Was that intentional?"

He grins. "Maybe. Or maybe I was just a lazy fuck who was too busy having his own fun to pay attention to you."

"Right. Cool." I cross my arms. "Did you also just throw wild accusations at me to make me prove how in love I am with Stevie?"

"Also maybe."

"Damn, son, you're smarter than you look."

He nods, giving me a salute. "You're welcome. Don't screw around tonight. Get this shit handled. Then go live out your happy ending."

Chapter Thirty-Three

STEVIE

Hank parks in Milly's gravel driveway and turns off the ignition.

"I'll make this right." He meets my gaze. "I promise."

I grab his hand. "We'll make this right. No more bullshit about fake dating being your idea. We agreed to do that together, and now we'll fix the damage we've done together too. All right?"

Squeezing my hand, he nods. "All right."

His hazel eyes are full, and despite my roiling nervousness, I feel a rush of warmth. I guess I'm still getting over the fact that this sweet, vulnerable, handsome man *is my boyfriend*.

Still, both our hands are clammy as we climb the steps to Milly's front door. Her place is different from her brothers'; a rambling white farmhouse with black shutters, it's much more Southern in flavor, from the tin roof to the wide, wraparound porch.

The door is open. Hank lets us in, my heart pounding at the sound of voices that rise from inside.

I glance at Hank. He glances back. We're wondering the

same thing—not if his family's been talking about us, but what they're saying about our epic, fake relationship fail.

Granted, we failed by falling in love for real. Not exactly a bad thing.

Not gonna lie, though, I wonder if they hate us. Hate *me*. Hank's been through the wringer, so the last thing he needs is another girl who breaks his heart. He told me he wasn't in the best shape the week after I left Blue Mountain. Did his family connect the dots and figure out I left for good after he'd all but begged me to stay? I know I got defensive when my brother's now-wife toyed around with him a little before they got married. It's only natural to want to protect your loved ones.

I hoped we wouldn't be the last to arrive. But when there's trouble brewing, it appears the Beauregard family shows up, and they show up early because everyone is gathered around Milly's kitchen table.

Emma's the first to look up when Hank and I walk in. Her expression is subdued.

Shit.

Milly looks at us too. There is nothing subdued about her. Not the way she stands imperiously at the head of the table, or the way she looks us up and down, or the tone of her voice when she says, "Get y'all's asses in here. Now. You've got some explaining to do."

Hank squeezes my hand.

"Milly," June says. She's sandwiched between Samuel and Beau. "Don't be rude."

"You know what's rude, Mama? Lying about—"

"We know," Beau and Samuel groan together.

"Milly, everyone knows what they've lied about," Beau says. "Rehashing it is pointless."

"So is raking me over the coals when she's pulled shit too," Hank says.

Milly's eyebrows leap to the top of her forehead. "What does that mean?"

"Means you haven't been honest, either. The name Kingsley ring a bell?"

Pink splotches appear on her cheeks. "We're not here to talk about Nate."

"He's got a first name now?" Samuel asks.

"He does," Milly says, looking away. "And he's currently on my shit list, so can we move on already?"

"Who isn't on your shit list?" Hank mutters. "You know, Milly, you've been a jerk ever since I stepped foot back on Blue Mountain."

"Hank." I squeeze his hand. "Not the best way to start this conversation."

"You have anything to say for yourself?" he continues, staring down his sister. "I'm more'n willing to apologize. But what about you?"

Milly crosses her arms. Rhett taps her elbow. "Sit," he says. "You promised you'd give them a chance to explain. Considering you aren't offering to do the same, I'd cool your jets."

For a second, her expression falls and she blinks, hard. "To be honest, I'm not sure what's happening with Nate, so . . . yeah. I don't have anything to say."

"Does he need talking to?" Beau asks, cracking his knuckles.

Milly waves her brother away. "Mama didn't raise you to be a caveman."

"I'm sorry things are, er, complicated with him," Hank says. "That why you've been grumpy?"

"I'm not grumpy." Milly plops into her chair and gives Hank a look. He gives her one right back.

Beau lets out an aggravated sigh as he tears a hand through his hair. "C'mon, Milly."

"Fine, I'm grumpy, and I'm sorry." Milly glances at me. "Now can y'all explain yourselves already?"

"That's one hell of an apology," Hank says sarcastically.

"It's the best you're gonna get, so move on already."

I give Hank's hand another squeeze. Hank's right. Milly's apology is half-hearted at best, but we've got bigger fish to fry at the moment, a thought Hank seems to second when he turns away from his sister.

My thoughts run riot as I sit beside Hank at the opposite end of the table. There's usually music, or a baby, or the clank and clatter of a meal being prepared whenever the Beauregards get together. But tonight, there's just silence.

Awful, heavy silence.

Hank, bless his heart, doesn't cower. Keeping his hand clasped firmly around mine, he inhales, then pulls back his shoulders on the exhale. He looks Milly in the eye and waits a beat, gathering his thoughts.

Pride swells in my chest. Has Hank handled things perfectly? No. Has he always made smart choices? Also no. But he isn't afraid to face the fallout, and he sure as hell isn't afraid to own up to his feelings.

Own up to what he wants. We're alike in that way.

"There's a lot to say," he begins. "But first and foremost, y'all are my family. I love each of you very, very much. I'm proud to be your brother, same as I'm proud to be a Beauregard. Early on, I learned from Mom and Dad the importance of doing anything for your people. Which is how I ended up in this . . . er, pickle."

"I'd say it's your pickle that landed you in this mess," Beau says darkly.

Hank rolls his eyes. "Really? That's the best you can do with pickle?"

"Hank's right. There are"—Rhett blows out a breath—"many, many directions we can go with that—"

"Enough," June says in the most mom-voice ever. "You're just using humor to deflect. I won't see my babies fighting for a second longer than is necessary. The past year has taken a toll on our family. On *me*. Let's get down to business."

Her eyes well with tears, and I watch Hank's Adam's apple bob.

"I'm sorry, Mama."

Across the table, Samuel clears his throat. "I'm sorry too. None of us have been a saint, that's for damn sure."

The urge to add my apology to the pile rises up inside me, the words on the tip of my tongue. But Hank has the mic, and I want to give him the space he needs to say his piece.

"I would do anything for y'all," he continues. "Your happiness means the world to me. For a while there, your happiness actually meant more than my own."

"Doesn't have to be that way," Samuel says. "No one asked that of you."

Hank nods. "That was on me. As great as it sounded in my head, it kinda wreaked havoc on my life. Turns out, putting yourself last is a recipe for disaster."

I find myself nodding along, falling more in love with this man with each passing second.

Maybe that's our glue—the thing that holds us together: the certainty that we'll never allow each other to abandon ourselves again.

"But even after what happened last spring, guess I still hadn't learned my lesson. Samuel, I wanted you and Emma to start planning the wedding of your dreams. I knew how excited y'all were, and how much you wanted to celebrate the fact you found each other with all your friends. I wasn't gonna hold you back. So I cooked up what I thought was a harmless white lie."

The table is quiet as Hank's words sink in.

"My intentions were good. My methods were not. I never

expected to come home and, you know, *bam*, realize I've not only healed from what went down, but I'm also ready to move on to something—some*one*—else. I never expected to fall so hard and so fast for Stevie"—he turns his head to look at me—"but in retrospect, the writing was on the wall from that first night in Vegas."

Annabel arches a brow. "So you guys really did meet in Vegas."

"We did," I say. "The story we told y'all about us pretty much went down exactly like we said."

"That was Stevie's idea, by the way—sticking to the truth," Hank adds.

Beau does not appear pleased by this revelation. "It's not Stevie I'm worried about. No offense."

"None taken," I say.

"It's you." Beau looks Hank directly in the eye. "This worries me. A lot. The brother I knew a couple years back was a man of integrity. He made good choices and did good things. I thought you'd be on your way to becoming that guy again after your year doing, well, whatever the hell you and Rhett did."

Rhett points a finger at Beau. "That is none of your beeswax, okay?"

"Dude, I truly don't want to know." Beau glances around the table. "I think I speak for everyone when I say we had high hopes for your return, Hank."

"He did seem happy," Annabel says, cutting Hank an uncertain glance.

"I am happy," Hank replies. "Because this—me and Stevie—it's real. Y'all really think we could fake *this* much lovey-dovey shit?" He holds up our joined hands.

"You guys are definitely gross," Rhett says.

"We fell for Stevie," June says. "All of us did. Did you not think you'd hurt us all over again by bringing her to Blue

Mountain, saying it was serious, when in reality you had no plans to ever bring her back?"

My face burns. Hank runs a hand over his face. "That's fair. Look, like I said, the pessimist in me was still very much alive and well this time last week. I knew Stevie was great, but I had no idea just how quickly she'd bond with you guys. I honestly thought you'd have some polite chitchat, spend a few hours together, and maybe share some laughs. Did I think my mother would end up twerking with her the first night she arrived?" Hank looks at me. "No, that was definitely something I did not anticipate."

A few chuckles break out, easing the painful silence.

"That was fun," June says. "I'd twerk with you any day of the week, Stevie."

I manage a smile. "Same goes for you, June. I'll never forget that night."

Still looking at me, Hank says, "I think we can all agree that Stevie is exceptional. Maybe my biggest mistake was not realizing it sooner."

Emma, up until now silent, scoffs. "So basically we're all pissed because Stevie is awesome, and Hank fell in love with her without meaning to?"

"Pretty much." Rhett raises his arms and stretches. "Sounds really stupid when you say it like that."

Samuel shakes his head. "But it's not stupid. It's been lies left and right from you lately."

"To be fair, you've lied a lot too, Samuel," Milly says quietly. "I don't want to reopen old wounds, but let's call a spade a spade here."

Hank and I freeze at her unexpected vote of support. A tiny nudge of hope peeks out from behind the panic currently running riot inside my chest.

"She's right." Emma looks at Samuel. "We haven't exactly set the best precedent for honesty in relationships. *About* relationships. We had it bad for each other long before we ever admitted to anything."

Samuel flattens his palms on the table and has the grace to look sheepish. "I know," he grumbles.

"You do know," June says. "And the lying has to stop. Right here—can we all agree to a fresh start?"

Milly shifts in her seat. "I want a do-over. I know I've been a little . . . prickly lately—"

"Cagey too," Hank says.

Her eyes flick to meet his. "I have my reasons."

"I had mine."

"Milly," June warns.

"Why should I trust you again?" Milly says to Hank. "I feel like I've been burned left and right lately by everyone."

"You can't say shit like that about Nate and not explain yourself," Rhett says.

"I told you, I don't *know* what's going on with him. I can't lie to y'all if I don't know the truth myself."

Hank shakes his head. "It's all right, Rhett. I can take it. She isn't wrong to ask why y'all should trust me again."

He squeezes my hand again. His mouth is a tight line. He's choosing his words carefully, but I also get the feeling he's struggling. His siblings' blows have landed hard.

"I want y'all to trust me because I want what you have," he says quietly, glancing around the table. "Some of you are off starting your own families, setting down roots with people you love. I'm happy for y'all. Truly. And I want you to be happy for Stevie and me. I want you to accept her, accept us together, and I know that won't be easy considering the shit I pulled."

"Shit *we* pulled," I say.

Milly looks at me, a funny gleam in her eye.

Respect.

"But I'm asking that of you anyway," Hank says. "Have

faith in me. You won't be disappointed this time because I'm different. I've changed, and you've got Stevie to thank for that."

I meet his eyes. "Give yourself some credit, Simon. You've done a lot of that work yourself too."

"You guys have watched *Bridgerton*, haven't you?" Annabel smiles. "So good."

"So hot," June says.

Samuel groans. "Mama."

"Those who live in glass houses," Rhett sing-songs.

The mood is lightening, but everyone stays in their chairs. They're not one hundred percent convinced. They want more from Hank.

His Adam's apple is bobbing again, though, and his hand is tight around mine.

I give him a beat, then another. Satisfied he's done, and that he might appreciate some help, I take a deep breath and step in.

"You should trust Hank because I do." My voice shakes, but I push forward. "I promised myself I'd never be in a serious relationship again. For years, I stuck to that promise. To be honest, it wasn't all that difficult because there are some pretty terrible people in this world. That's part of the reason I swore off ever falling for someone again, because I learned the hard way I couldn't trust anyone, not even *myself*. Especially not myself. But Hank—he changed my mind in a way no one else could. And even after everything I've been through, even though I'm scared out of my goddamn mind, I'm trusting myself to do the right thing. And the right thing is trusting Hank. He loves me because of who I am, not in spite of it. He supports my dreams and thinks my dedication to my work is sexy. He gets me coffee every morning and has plans for dinner every night. And not only does he play the guitar, but he also writes his own freaking music."

Annabel nods, a knowing smile on her face. "I like the sound of that."

"Because it sounds so much like me?" Beau smiles, resting his arm on the back of her chair.

She elbows him playfully, hair falling over her shoulder. "I love you, but I might like Hank more right now."

Hank holds out his fist for a pound. "Thank you. I have one vote of support. Any others?"

"He's willing to turn his life upside down to have me in it—"

"That explain the fact that his house is an absolute pigsty?" Rhett asks.

"Absolutely, yes," Hank replies.

"Which is inspiring me to do the same," I finish. "In short, Hank is the kind of partner I was too scared to even dream of, much less commit to. But here I am, committing. I'm sorry I lied to you all. I'll regret that for a long time. Believe me, no one is more embarrassed by the whole thing than I am."

"I'd say I'm a close second," Hank replies with a grin.

"I guess I just . . ." Oh shit, here come the tears in earnest now. "I adore him, and I adore y'all, and I sincerely hope you'll forgive us so we can be a part of your big, beautiful family. There are few things I've ever wanted more than that."

It happens like dominoes. First, June bursts into tears, then Annabel. Then Emma and Rhett—yep, snotty nose and all—and even Beau and Samuel share a sniffle or two.

My vision swims, but I'm still able to accept hugs from June and Beau. Hank rubs my back when I sit back down, gratitude written all over his face—bright eyes, small smile.

One notable absence from the love fest: Milly. She stays glued to her chair, her expression unreadable.

"So," Samuel says, crossing his arms as his gaze locks on mine. "Hank is that good, huh?"

I roll my lips between my teeth and nod. "He's that freaking good. So please, for the love of God, stop torturing each other and *forgive* your people."

"I'm game," Hank says. "I'm a changed man, y'all, and if you still don't believe me, I'mma do my best to prove it. You have my word."

Samuel looks at Hank. Hank looks at Samuel. Samuel looks at Beau and then Milly and Rhett.

My heart is liable to beat itself out of my chest. *Breathe*. I have to remember to keep breathing. Hank and I have laid out our argument; we've bared our hearts. Whatever happens next is out of our hands.

I don't know what I'll do if Hank's heart gets broken again. Mine will break right along with it.

Just when I'm about to come out of my skin, all four of Hank's siblings turn their gazes on him. It's a master class in silent communication, and I'm impressed, frankly, by their ability to pull it off without a hitch.

They're close. It's sweet. And downright frightening when you're staring down the barrel of their wrath—or their absolution.

Milly lets out a breath, elbows coming down on the table with a *thump* as though she's finally put down her sword and is surrendering to the exhaustion of wielding it.

"Of course we forgive you." Her eyes move to mine. "Same goes for you, Stevie. We're not thrilled about the shit you two pulled. But we're a family, a family that's been to hell and back." She glances at Beau. "If we didn't give each other second chances, and third chances, and fourth and fifth and eighty-seventh ones, where the hell would we be?"

"In the ground," Beau says definitively.

Hank startles. "Jesus, that's bleak."

"It's true. Y'all know how close I came. But I had my

family to fall back on." He looks meaningfully at Bel. "And my girl."

"I don't know where I'd be," Samuel adds. "It wouldn't be anywhere good, though."

Rhett nods. "I'd be in way more trouble, that's for damn sure."

"Don't call the devil, son," June says.

"I'd probably be just as successful as I am now," Milly says, and immediately everyone boos. Samuel goes so far as to toss a balled-up napkin at her. She catches it, laughing. "I mean it. I love y'all dearly, but I'm really fucking good at what I do. That being said, I'd be way less happy—way less aggravated too, but that's neither here nor there—if I didn't get to see my family every day. Especially now that I have two—no, three—sisters."

She blinks, hard. No tears. But maybe that's Milly's way of showing a softer emotion.

"Wow," Hank breathes.

"Milly, thank you for that," I say. "Thank all y'all. It's an honor to sit at this table."

Hank stands and extends his hand to Samuel. "It's an honor to be your brother."

Samuel studies Hank's hand for a long beat. Then he stands too, and instead of shaking his brother's hand, Samuel walks around the table and wraps Hank in a hug, pounding his back as he murmurs something in Hank's ear.

Suddenly everyone's standing, and everyone's hugging, and the room fills with happy noise—laughter, a curse. The sound of a cork popping, because of course Emma has some undoubtedly delicious bubbly hidden within arm's reach.

Milly, being Milly, is the last to offer me a hug. But when she does, she embraces me fiercely. It's not a threat. It's an admission. As much as I'll probably ever get from her.

It's enough, especially when she whispers in my ear, "If Hank adores you, so do I. Thank you for making him smile."

"Thank *you* for helping raise such a stand-up human being."

Emma pours champagne, and we stand around Milly's kitchen drinking, the tension that permeated the air half an hour ago long gone.

"Wedding is still on, right?" Hank asks, tipping back his flute.

Swallowing, Emma nods, wearing a sly smile on her lips. "That's the real reason we forgave you. Samuel and I already put down a deposit on the band."

"We love you and stuff." Samuel takes his hand out of his pocket to gesture vaguely in Hank's direction. "But yeah, turns out the best Van Halen cover band in the world doesn't offer refunds, so . . ."

Hank gives his brother a shove. "Y'all are the worst."

"And you're damn lucky to have us," Beau says.

Hank raises his glass. "To the worst siblings in the whole fucking world. I love y'all." He turns to me. "I love *you.*"

All the emotions I've felt today finally catch up to me, and I release them on a happy sob as I tilt up my face for a kiss. Hank's lips taste like champagne.

I hope it's the first of a million kisses like this. In kitchens. In the middle of messes we make. In front of family who loves us despite those messes.

Only took a failed marriage and five years of self-discovery, but I finally—literally—know what freedom tastes like.

Chapter Thirty-Four

HANK

"This seat taken?" a woman asks.

I glance up from my phone, stomach dipping as I rake my gaze over the familiar figure. As luck would have it, she's wearing the same outfit she did the first day we met: sneakers, jeans that are painted on, white tee.

Tits for days.

Aw, hell, it's almost like she planned it.

"Goddamn it," I say, lips twitching. "Who told you I was coming? Beau?"

Stevie slides onto the stool beside mine, that supermodel smile lighting up her whole face. "Milly, actually."

"No shit," I reply, genuinely surprised. I shake my head. "Girl can't mind her own business to save her life."

Stevie elbows me. "Believe it or not, she wanted to set up a little surprise of her own."

"Oh?" I lean in close enough to smell the toothpaste on her breath. "Good surprise or bad one?"

Stevie leans in for the kiss. I really want to lay one on her, teenage tonsil hockey style, but this is my first time at Lady Luck's Brewhouse, and I don't want to embarrass Stevie or gross out her patrons or employees. It's early-ish on a Thursday afternoon—just after two—but the brewery is hopping.

I keep the kiss short and sweet, and Stevie's eyes flash appreciatively when I pull back.

"You'll see," she says, and then she turns to the pair of women behind the bar. "Maya, Andi, this is my boyfriend, Hank. Hank, meet the people who pour the good stuff."

One of the bartenders throws a towel over her shoulder and extends her hand, while the other places a menu in front of me.

"Andi," she says by way of introduction. "Pleasure to meet you. We've noticed Stevie's had some extra pep in her step lately. That you?"

"Yes, ma'am," I say, and the three of them laugh at my no-nonsense reply. "I know everything's good here, but what's your favorite?"

"Definitely the Tennessee Brunette," Andi says. "It's an early release of our spring lineup we'll be launching in a few weeks. It's an amber ale with notes of cherry, light on the malt."

"Sounds good to me."

"I'll take the same, please, Andi," Stevie says, her knee touching mine underneath the bar. My body ignites. It's been all of a week since I had my hands on this girl, and I am craving her something fierce.

I put my hand on her thigh. "Hi."

She beams at me, pressing her teeth into her bottom lip. "Hey."

"I'm eager to taste my Tennessee brunette."

"Had to go there right off the bat, huh?" She laughs, a throaty, happy sound, and my chest swells.

"Hey, you went there first by naming a cherry-flavored beer after yourself."

"I named it after Maya, actually." Stevie nods at the bartender, who's busy filling elegant pint glasses with a Hefeweizen. "But I'll take the compliment."

Andi sets our beers on coasters in front of us. The glasses are deliciously frosty, the tiniest amount of foam spilling over the top. Perfect pour. The beer itself is a light reddish-brown color, which, yeah, is pretty much exactly the color of Maya's hair.

"Cheers," I say, holding up my glass. "Thanks for letting me crash your weekend."

Stevie taps her glass to mine. "Thank you for keeping things fresh. This back and forth could get really unfun really fast, but surprises like this—I love it."

I drink my beer and smack my lips. "Damn, that's good. Cherry and malt are very subtle—they don't overpower each other or that nice hit of bitterness."

Stevie pulls back, brow furrowed. "Look at you, throwing around fancy beer words."

"I may have brushed up on my beer vocabulary." I glance around the brewery. "Stevie, this place is incredible. I'm proud of you, honey."

Lady Luck Brewhouse's current space is a cinder block building in Charlotte Pike, one of Nashville's up-and-coming areas. It's not fancy, but it's been lovingly updated with fresh paint, a cool zinc-topped bar, and high ceilings. Large steel windows overlook a sun-drenched patio, where people—lots of people—sip their beers at long farm tables underneath funky tasseled umbrellas.

Acoustic Alanis Morisette plays in the background. The Supremes come on next.

The vibe is a little boho, dash of country, and lots of city from the plush leather barstools to the enormous, brightly colored mural on the far wall. It's a pop-art collage of famous women: I recognize Oprah, Meghan Markle, Dolly Parton, Michelle Obama.

"Thanks," Stevie replies. "It'll be bittersweet moving to a new space. This is where Lady Luck got our start, you know? I painted these walls myself."

"Did you paint the mural?"

She scoffs. "Hell no. That was done by Kelly Zhu, a local artist here in Nashville. Pretty bomb, right?"

"It's awesome. This whole place is . . . Stevie, it's fucking gorgeous. Just like its owner."

Stevie shakes her head, but she's smiling. "You and the cheesy lines."

"I am as God made me. So when are you gonna take me to see the new space?"

"How long ya staying?"

"Milly didn't fill you in on that? I'll be here through Saturday night. Gotta get back to the farm for the Sunday rush."

"Gotcha. Welp, we'll see if we can squeeze a site visit in, then."

"You got big plans?"

Stevie's biting her lip again. She hooks her first finger in the top button of my shirt, raising a brow as she peers at my bare chest. "Maybe."

"How long you gonna make me wait?"

"Not long at all." She grabs her pint glass and holds it up. "Let's finish these. Then we can . . . talk."

We do a lot of actual talking while we drink. Stevie fills me in on the marketing campaign her team is putting together for the launch of the new brewery. I fill her in on my ever-evolving schedule at the farm. It turns out I do better work when I have more freedom in my days, so I'm experimenting with some half-day situations that are going well so far.

We touch, talk, and laugh. I relax into my barstool and enjoy my girl's company. I watch her interact with her employees and the regulars she knows by name. I introduce myself to a dozen people, committing each one to memory. I feel prouder than I probably should when I make Stevie or her customers, or both, laugh.

Stevie plays footsie with me and orders us another beer to split, this time the IPA. Tina Turner comes on, and light slants through the windows and catches on Stevie's hair, and the space between us thrums with possibility. Anticipation.

Stevie Nicks comes on.

I decide I love Nashville.

Stevie takes me home to a pretty bungalow and fucks me in her pretty bed. She wants to have dinner at one of her favorite spots in Germantown, so I whip us up some lattes on her fancy espresso machine—takes a minute to figure out—and she calls an Uber.

We're dropped off in front of a cute restaurant with well-dressed hipsters waiting on the benches outside. I grab Stevie's hand on the walk to the front door. She turns her head and smiles at me, the sex in her eyes softening to something better, and I'm hit square in the chest by something good and deep and real.

The happy ending I wanted so bad for as long as I could remember—I finally got it.

It's finally mine, and it's way fucking better than I could've imagined.

The hostess takes our names, then grabs some menus and leads us into the dining room. It's loud, and I slow my steps when I catch the sound of a familiar voice saying a familiar curse.

"Stevie," I say slowly. "You gonna tell me what you did yet?"

"Please don't hate me," she replies, giving my hand a squeeze.

"That doesn't sound promising."

"Milly and I wanted to do something special for you."

I groan in mock annoyance. "She's rubbing off on you, and I'm not sure I like it."

"Stop. I adore your sister, even if she is a little . . . prickly."

Truth be told, one of my favorite things about Milly is that she's prickly. No fake smiles or simpering "bless your heart"s from that one.

But when I notice a large table filled with familiar faces and the hair on the back of my neck stands on end, I wish for half a second Milly wasn't such a pistol.

Oh Lord, it's everyone. Even Maisie, who's busy shoving goldfish into her mouth.

It's the loudest crew in the restaurant, no question. Mama is laughing at something Bel is saying while Milly and Beau talk over each other as they dig into the loaf of bread on the table. Samuel and Emma are staring into each others' eyes, sipping something red from enormous wine glasses.

Maisie grabs her daddy's knife, which Rhett quickly swipes, making her scream. I flinch. Stevie laughs.

Samuel is the first one to notice us. He looks up at me and smiles—a big, shit-eating smile—and sets down his glass.

"Hello, brother."

"What the hell are you doing here?" I say, bewildered. "I mean that in the most loving way possible."

Milly leaps up from her seat and wraps her arms around my neck. "We're welcoming Stevie into our family the Beauregard way."

"By crashing my first weekend in her hometown?"

"Yes!" Milly holds me at arm's length, hands on my shoulders. "You're welcome."

Beau pulls back his arm and takes my hand in his, our

palms clapping. "But really. To show you we're one hundred percent committed to y'all's relationship—"

"And to show you just how much we adore you both," June says.

"We're going to do a whole weekend in Nashville together."

"Just the nine of us. Isn't it wonderful?" Rhett deadpans.

Mom claps her hands together. "The best. I cannot wait. I do love a Honky-Tonk."

"Of course you do." I tug a hand over the top of my head. "Jesus Christ."

I was really looking forward to spending the majority of this weekend with Stevie. Alone. In bed.

But in true Beauregard form, my family is here to ruin the fun.

I want to be pissed off. I can't imagine this is how Stevie wanted to spend her days off.

My face hurts as I pull out a chair for her. Only when I see her smile do I realize I'm smiling too.

Hard.

Hardest I've smiled in a long ass time.

I put my hand on the back of the chair beside Stevie's. "This seat taken?"

"Actually"—Milly slips between us, settling into the chair like she owns it—"it is. Hi, Stevie. Thanks again for inviting us."

"You and I both know she didn't invite any of y'all," I say, falling into the seat beside Milly.

Stevie puts her hand on top of Milly's. "You guys are always invited. Always. Come visit anytime."

"See?" Milly raises a brow at me. "That's how you treat family."

Samuel elbows me. "Really, I hope it's okay we're here. I

wanted to tell you, but the powers that be decided a surprise would be more 'special.'"

I shake my head, but this smile just won't quit.

Thing is, the surprise does feel special.

This feels special, having everyone I love most in this world gathered around the same table.

"Thank you," I say gruffly. "I'm glad y'all are here."

Samuel claps my shoulder. "We're glad you've found what you were looking for. Congrats."

Stevie's eyes meet mine over Milly's lap. They're wet, dark. Lovely.

"*You're a rock star*," I mouth.

Her shoulders hunch forward, like she's suppressing a giggle. "*What?*" she mouths back.

"*You're a tambourine goddess.*"

Now she really is giggling. "*What?*" she mouths again.

"*I am so glad you took a gamble on us*."

"What?" she finally says out loud.

"Is he being a pervert?" Milly asks. "If he's being a pervert, Stevie, just say the word, and I'll kick his ass."

"Nope. Just reminding Stevie I've got all my cards on the table. It turns out, I got lucky—or maybe I had an ace or two up my sleeve she didn't know about."

"Any eights, though?" Stevie asks, grinning.

"If there are, I know what to do. I learned from the best, after all. As a matter of fact, I look forward to learning much, much more from you."

"He's definitely being a pervert," Beau says, shielding his face with a menu. "And that's definitely a euphemism."

I hold up my hands. "Never said I was a saint."

"Thank God for that," Stevie replies. "Because I really like sinning with you."

Half my siblings erupt in middle schools sounds. An

extended *ew*, a mention of cooties. The other half whistles and claps.

And me? I keep smiling.

If this is what sin feels like—well, I ain't mad at it.

THE END

EPILOGUE

Stevie

Four Months Later

It's a warm summer evening—perfect weather for a wedding.

Emma and Samuel beam at each other as they exchange vows in Blue Mountain's boathouse. Hank stands proudly beside him as one of Samuel's three best men, the others being Beau and Rhett, of course, with Milly as his only best woman.

Tears spring in my eyes as I take in the sight of the Beauregards all together. I grab June's hand—she's sitting beside me in the front row—and give it a squeeze. It's a silent thank you for creating this wonderful family and for welcoming me into it with open arms.

The preacher pronounces Samuel and Emma man and wife, and the three-hundred-plus guests erupt in hoots and hollers when the newlyweds go in for a long, rowdy kiss.

I get a kiss of my own the second I walk into Stag Pavilion for cocktail hour. Hank greets me by wrapping an arm around my waist and covering my mouth with his.

"Hey, honey," he murmurs.

Pulling back, I use the flats of my fingers to wipe his damp cheeks. "Hey, baby. You did great up there. I am digging this suit, by the way." I give his lapel a quick tug.

Hank rolls his eyes, even as his lips twitch. "Gonna have to disagree with you there. I think I look like a douche."

In true Samuel style, he dressed all his groomsmen in blue seersucker. I'm talking head-to-toe Carolina blue-and-white stripe, from the custom Gucci blazer and trousers to the matching horsebit loafers.

It's a look, certainly, but it's one Hank and his brothers somehow pull off. Maybe because they're former athletes? Ridiculously buff? Cocky as all get-out?

Whatever it is, I don't hate it.

Hank, however, clearly feels differently.

"Whatcha drinking?" he asks, turning his head to glance at the massive bar setup on the far side of the pavilion.

"Hmm." I think about it for a minute. "You know, I just might start with a beer. I had some champagne earlier getting ready with the girls, so I should probably take it slow."

Emma's only bridesmaid is her sister, Lindsey. But being the awesome person she is, Emma invited me to get my hair and makeup done with them back at the main house today. We spent the day getting pampered and sipping excellent bubbly.

"Same. Samuel broke out the Appalachian Red before lunch, so . . . yeah. Beer sounds good to me too."

We gawk at Milly's handiwork as we head across the pavilion. She pulled out all the stops: long farm tables are set with fine china, taper candles, and enormous flower arrangements, all done in shades of apricot and green. Candles glow from inside the fireplace (it's too warm for an actual fire), and a string quartet plays in a corner. The ceiling is draped in swaths of apricot chiffon, giving the space the feel of an elegant, if slightly rustic, ballroom.

It's romantic in the extreme. I find myself swaying against Hank in time to the string quartet, our hands clasped between us.

Waiters bearing trays of gorgeous appetizers stop us along the way. I sample a potato-and-bleu-cheese soup "shot," while Hank and I both help ourselves to the mini-fried chicken biscuits.

"Wow," Hank says around a mouthful of biscuit. "Just . . . yeah. That's fucking *good*."

I nod, finishing my own. "Perfect for carb loading too. Can't start a night of drinking on an empty stomach."

Hank looks at me. I look back.

"Should we?" he asks, tilting his head toward the server, who's still holding out his tray to us.

I grin. "We definitely should."

We grab seconds and eat them on the way to the bar. I smile hard when I see a guy sip his beer and hold it out, scanning the label.

"Goddamn," he says. "Best IPA I've had in a long-ass time."

"Let me guess," Hank replies, resting his elbows on the bar. "Hop Girl Summer?"

The guy, one of Samuel's former teammates from his mile-wide shoulders and towering height, nods. "Yes. How'd you know?"

Hank glances at me. "I know the girl who makes it."

"Well, give her my compliments."

"You can do that yourself. She's right here," Hank replies and nods at me.

I hold out my hand to the man. "I'm Stevie, and that's my beer. I'm so glad you're enjoying it."

"It's the most popular beer on Blue Mountain's menu," Hank explains. "Ever since we started stocking it, we can hardly keep up with the demand."

"I see why." The man takes another sip. "IPA hangovers are the worst, but this beer'll make it worth it. Cheers, Stevie."

Hank and I take our beers to our table. We're seated with the rest of his family, and we play footsie under the table while chowing down on filet mignon, fancy mac and cheese made with gouda, and collard greens. The wine is out of this world too, servers supplying us with glass after glass of some of the best stuff I've ever tasted.

It's part country cookout, part fancy pants meal.

It's Samuel and Emma in a nutshell.

The Van Halen cover band starts. Like the food, the décor, and the drinks, the band is incredible. The guitarist nails the riffs while the lead singer absolutely slays David Lee Roth's eighties screech.

"Not sure you can twerk to this," Hank says in my ear. "But I'd love to dance."

"Sure." I let him help me to my feet. "I'll save my twerking for later."

Hank gives my ass a slap, grabs my hand, and leads me to the dance floor. Everyone's going crazy as the band launches into a *very* loud version of "Jump." I'm full and tired and buzzed, and when Hank grabs my hip and pulls me close, I can't help but close my eyes and smile.

Heaven.

This is heaven.

The past four months haven't been all smooth sailing. It turns out long-distance relationships require a constant balancing act that I don't think we'll ever master. But we are making it work, and we're happy—and together—more often than not.

The best part? We're able to enjoy a wedding without wanting one ourselves. Hank radiates genuine joy as he dances his ass off with me, going so far as to pull Samuel onto the dance floor so they can sing "Hot For Teacher" together.

It's hilarious, and I laugh so hard watching them my ribs ache.

I ache all over. A good kind of ache—the one that lets me know I'm exactly where I need to be, with exactly the people I should be with.

Hank is my person. And I'm so damn grateful I found him.

We dance so hard that we sweat bullets. I'm about to suggest we take a beer break when Rhett appears at Hank's elbow.

He's white as a ghost.

Hank and I immediately go still.

"What's the matter?" Hank asks.

Rhett blinks at the words, his gaze snapping into focus when it lands on my face. "Mind if I borrow my brother a second?"

Now Hank is white too.

"Everything okay?" I ask.

He manages a tight smile. "Nope. Not by a long shot."

"Oh, Jesus. What can I do?"

Rhett glances around the pavilion. "Here, y'all both come. I need to talk to someone."

We follow Rhett out of the pavilion onto the smoking patio beside it. Several guests are out here, most smoking the fat Cigars being handed out as favors, so Rhett hustles us to a far corner.

"Rhett," Hank says, voice hushed. "You're really starting to freak me out."

"You're freaked out?" Rhett lets out a bark of mirthless laughter. Tearing a hand through his hair, he paces in front of us. "How do you think I feel?"

I put a hand on his shoulder, stilling him. "Whatever it is, we'll figure it out, all right?"

He swallows audibly. "Swear not to tell a soul?"

"Always. But you and I both know the walls have ears up here. Yes, even these walls." Hank gestures to the night air around us. "You've got about five minutes until Milly finds out, so you might as well just say it."

"True. Okay, so . . . right." Rhett blows out a breath. "Y'all, I have a kid."

My heart trips to a dead stop inside my chest. I meet Hank's eyes, too stunned to speak.

"You have a kid," Hank repeats gently. "Like you got someone pregnant, and they're going to have a kid? Or the kid is already born?"

Rhett falls into a crouch, elbows on his knees, thumbs pressed to his eyelids. "He's two years old, and his name is Liam."

Hank looks at me this time, his eyes wide.

He doesn't know what to say. To be honest, neither do I.

"And you just found out about Liam now?" I manage.

Rhett nods, eyes still closed. "Yes. It's a long story, but . . . fuck, y'all. *Fuck*."

I lean down and run my hand across his back. "It's not the end of the world."

"It is, though," he says miserably. "It's the end of my world."

I want to ask what he means, but he's just received the shock of a lifetime, and it's a miracle he's not emptying his stomach in the grass.

To be fair, he looks to be about four seconds away from doing that. Definitely not the time to ask for what are undoubtedly painful details.

"We'll figure it out," I repeat.

Hank shoves his hands in his pockets and glances up at

the night sky, shaking his head. "Never a dull moment on Blue Mountain Farm, is there?"

Rhett shakes his head. "Nope."

Want more Hank + Stevie? You're in luck - I wrote one hell of a sizzling bonus epilogue for them! Get it by signing up for my newsletter at www.jessicapeterson.com.

Rhett's book is up next! SOUTHERN PLAYBOY is his sexy second chance, nanny/boss, secret baby romance. Keep reading for an exclusive excerpt.

SOUTHERN PLAYBOY EXCERPT

Amelia

What are you doing? What the hell *are you doing?*

Ignoring the chant of my runaway pulse, I let Rhett guide my thumb to his bottom lip. It's soft, hot to the touch, and because I'm wildly, frustratingly turned on, I tug at that lip, pulling it down. The look in his eyes ignites.

The inside of his lip is slick, a deep, gorgeous pink that, if memory serves, matched the crown of his dick.

I should not be thinking about Rhett Beauregard's dick.

But like the man himself said: here we are.

Here I am, about to kiss the man I absolutely, positively *should not touch*, much less make out with.

If only he hadn't confided in me.

If only he hadn't listened to my ideas and responded intelligently and earnestly to them.

If only he hadn't verbalized willingness to change. Not who he is—I'd never ask that of him, nor would I want to—but what he believes. About himself, about the truth.

He's after the truth, and if that isn't the sexiest thing ever, I don't know what is.

Stepping forward, I plaster my body against Rhett's and

urge him backward, so we're hidden from our view of the stairs. There's no way Liam could catch us kissing—he'd have to climb out of his crib, open his door, and walk down the hallway—but it still feels weird to do it out in the open.

"Yeah," Rhett says, reading my mind. His voice husky. "He is a little young for the birds and the bees talk."

"We've talked enough," I say.

"But you said—nip the tension in the bud—"

I look him in the eye. "Maybe I'm changing my mind."

He swallows. "Doesn't change everything we have to lose."

"It's complicated. But I'm not sure that makes it wrong. If you don't want—"

"I do. Christ, A, I don't think it's any secret how bad I want you," he says, eyes searching mine. We're almost exactly the same height, him barefoot, me in my sneakers. Neither of us has to look up or down. We're equals this way.

He's ceding control to me, though. I can tell by the slant of his neck and the heat in his gaze he wants to make a move. But he's waiting for me to decide what happens next.

His consideration makes me ache.

"Fuck you," I whisper. "Fuck you for getting this so right."

And then, before I can chicken out, I tilt my head and kiss Rhett's mouth.

My pulse is drumming a wild, uneven beat, and I close my eyes against the riot of sensation that ripples from the place where our lips meet.

Need.

Tenderness.

Warmth.

I move my mouth, and Rhett responds in kind. It takes a second to find our rhythm, like we're trying to remember the lines of a play we performed a long time ago. They're there, the moves are there, but I have to reach for them. Remind myself it's okay if I don't remember it all perfectly because it's not meant to be the same.

It's *good* that it's different now.

And it is different, if only because neither of us gives up. Our noses bump, and we both pull back for a second to laugh, Rhett's chest barreling out to press more firmly against my breasts.

The pressure is divine.

He finds my mouth again with his, and this time we get it. The seam of his lips opens, allowing the taste of tea and coffee to mingle on my own lips. His are soft and slow, moving like we have all the time in the world.

I put my other hand on his chest, drawing my fingers into a fist around the fabric. He responds with a grunt, putting a hand on the wall beside my head and melting his hips into mine. My eyes roll to the back of my head as he sips me, small caresses that become thirsty pulls. We're breathing hard now. I lick inside his mouth, and he tilts his head, opening his lips to me, and his tongue finds mine, playing, toying. Asking.

The fire I saw in his eyes spreads inside my skin, heaviness gathering low in my core as Rhett kisses me, and *kisses* me. Our heads move in tandem, and he sucks on my bottom lip, just the way I like it. Only this time, he goes back to nip at it, pulling at it with his teeth, something he didn't do before.

My blood jumps. His taste and the way he moves are both familiar and thrillingly new. His stubble chafes my chin, making the throb between my legs grow hotter.

We've had practice since high school, and it shows.

His hand moves to my neck, cupping it, his thumb grazing my jaw. My heart squeezes.

Please. Please don't let this blow up in our faces.

Please don't let me fall for this man just to lose him all over again.

"Lili want We-wa, now!" Liam's little voice plays through the monitor.

Rhett pulls back with a groan, but when I open my eyes, I see that he's smiling, the kind that touches his eyes.

"Sorry."

"Don't be." I glance over my shoulder at the monitor. Liam is standing up in his crib, Pup Pup in hand. "Here, I'll—"

"Dinner. Tonight. Let me take you out for a real date so we can . . . er, connect without being interrupted."

My pulse skips a beat. What if someone sees us out together?

What if we have the best time ever?

The thought of being able to make out with Rhett again—

"Yeah," I say. "But wait, who's gonna watch Liam?"

"I'll have my mom come over. She can meet him, and we can put him to bed together. That way, we won't interrupt his routine."

I flatten my palm against his chest. "Can we go somewhere a little off the beaten path? Just in case—"

"Of course. Actually . . ."

"What?"

He grins, rubbing his hands together. "Nothing. I have an idea. Pick you up at seven thirty?"

"Okay." I blink. "Should I wear anything special?"

"Whatever's comfortable. And cool. We'll be outside."

Of course we will. Because I love any excuse to head outdoors, and Rhett knows it.

"We-wa now!"

My turn to laugh. "Enjoy your workout, all right?"

"Pssshh," Rhett says, rolling his eyes. "But I am gonna enjoy thinking about you without feeling like a scumbag. I really wanna kiss you again, A."

"And your son really wants not to go down for his nap."

"Tonight." His eyes burn. "I can't wait to have you all to myself."

Want to find out just how naked these two get on their date? Grab your copy of SOUTHERN PLAYBOY today! Happy reading.

Thank you so much for reading Hank + Stevie's story! This book was a joy to work on, and I hope that shows. Don't get me wrong, I cried into my keyboard *plenty* during edits, but SOUTHERN SINNER proved to be just the escape I needed during what felt like a very long stretch of quarantine.

Be sure to check out the next book in the North Carolina Highlands Series, SOUTHERN PLAYBOY. It's a nanny/boss, secret baby romance you won't want to miss!

I'd love to hear from you. Here are ways to keep in touch:

- **Check out Jessica Peterson's City Girls, my reader group on Facebook for giveaways, serious discussions of seriously hot guys, and more**
- Check out my website, www.jessicapeterson.com, for a list of my books, my recommended reading order, plus lots of other goodies
- Follow my not-so-glamorous life as a romance author on Instagram @JessicaPAuthor
- Follow me on Goodreads
- Follow me on Bookbub
- Like my Facebook Author Page
- Drop me a line at jessicapauthor@jessicapeterson.com

ALSO BY JESSICA PETERSON

THE SEX & BONDS SERIES

An outrageously sexy series of romcoms set in the high stakes world of Wall Street.

The Dealmaker (Sex & Bonds #1)

The Troublemaker (Sex & Bonds #2)

THE NORTH CAROLINA HIGHLANDS SERIES

Beards. Bonfires. Boning.

Southern Seducer (NC Highlands #1)

Southern Hotshot (NC Highlands #2)

Southern Sinner (NC Highlands #3)

Southern Playboy (NC Highlands #4)

Southern Bombshell (NC Highlands #5)

THE CHARLESTON HEAT SERIES

The Weather's Not the Only Thing Steamy Down South.

Southern Charmer (Charleston Heat #1)

Southern Player (Charleston Heat #2)

Southern Gentleman (Charleston Heat #3)

Southern Heartbreaker (Charleston Heat #4)

THE THORNE MONARCHS SERIES

Royal. Ridiculously Hot. Totally Off Limits...

Royal Ruin (Thorne Monarchs #1)

Royal Rebel (Thorne Monarchs #2)

Royal Rogue (Thorne Monarchs #3)

THE STUDY ABROAD SERIES

Studying Abroad Just Got a Whole Lot Sexier.

A Series of Sexy Interconnected Standalone Romances

Lessons in Love (Study Abroad #1)

Lessons in Gravity (Study Abroad #2)

Lessons in Letting Go (Study Abroad #3)

Lessons in Losing It (Study Abroad #4)

ACKNOWLEDGMENTS

It truly takes a village to bring a book to life. I'm lucky as all get out to work with an incredible team of smart, honest, and hard-working women. It's an honor to work with y'all, and I thank you sincerely for putting up with me.

Thanks to my PA, Jodi, for your thorough work and patience. I feel like I'm constantly falling on my face these days, but you're always there to catch me. Thank you!

Thanks to my publicist, Nina. Girl, you push me hard, and I adore you for it. Can't wait to see where this year takes us.

Thanks to my FB group admins, Emily, Kenysha, Tara, and Ingrid, for holding down the fort while I cry into my keyboard.

Thanks to my awesome, and awesomely detail-oriented, beta readers, Julia, Quinn, Jodi, and Heather.

Thanks to my editing team: Marion, Karen, and Jenny. Y'all made this book shine.

Thanks, as always, to my ARC team, for taking the time to read and review my work. I really appreciate you gals giving me a chance.

And thanks to my readers. I love y'all so much it hurts.

You're the reason I'm able to work my dream job, and your support means the world.

Finally, thanks to my husband and BFF, Ben. Thanks for always supporting my salacious romance novel dreams. I love you. Thanks, too, to my sister Maggie, for all the awesome brewery and beer name ideas!

Printed in Dunstable, United Kingdom

81941261R00201